Praise for

and her b

"With passion, roman and will touch your heart, Emily March takes you on an unhurried journey where past mistakes are redeemed and a more beautiful future is forged—one miracle at a time."
—*USA Today*

"A brilliant writer you'll love creates a world you'll never want to leave."
—Susan Mallery, *New York Times* bestselling author

"A heartfelt story of family, community, second chances, and the power of love . . . Don't miss it!"
—Susan Wiggs, *New York Times* bestselling author

"Emily March's stories are heartwrenching and soul-satisfying. For a wonderful read, don't miss a visit to Eternity Springs."
—Lisa Kleypas, *New York Times* bestselling author

"Characters you adore, a world you want to visit, and stories that tug at your heartstrings. Brava, Emily March. I love Eternity Springs."
—Christina Dodd, *New York Times* bestselling author

"A heartwarming tale of courage and redemption . . . that will have readers cheering."
—*Publishers Weekly*

Also by
EMILY MARCH

Reunion Pass
Heartsong Cottage
Teardrop Lane
Dreamweaver Trail
Miracle Road
Reflection Point
Nightingale Way
Lover's Leap
Mistletoe Mine
Heartache Falls
Hummingbird Lake
Angel's Rest

Christmas in Eternity Springs

EMILY MARCH

St. Martin's Paperbacks

This is a work of fiction. All of the characters, organizations, and events portrayed in this novel are either products of the author's imagination or are used fictitiously.

CHRISTMAS IN ETERNITY SPRINGS

Copyright © 2016 by Emily March.

All rights reserved.

For information address St. Martin's Press, 175 Fifth Avenue, New York, NY 10010.

ISBN: 978-1-250-07298-6

Our books may be purchased in bulk for promotional, educational, or business use. Please contact your local bookseller or the Macmillan Corporate and Premium Sales Department at 1-800-221-7945, ext. 5442, or by e-mail at MacmillanSpecialMarkets@macmillan.com.

Printed in the United States of America

St. Martin's Paperbacks edition / October 2016

St. Martin's Paperbacks are published by St. Martin's Press, 175 Fifth Avenue, New York, NY 10010.

10 9 8 7 6 5 4 3 2 1

Acknowledgments

I want to thank the outstanding team at St. Martin's Press for their enthusiastic support of all things Eternity Springs, in particular my editor, Rose Hilliard. It's a pleasure to work with you. To my agents, Meg Ruley and Christina Hogrebe at the Jane Rotrosen Agency, your professionalism and support are beyond compare. To my personal support team: Mary Dickerson, Christina Dodd, Nicole Burnham, Susan Sizemore, Mary Lou Jarrell, Caitlin Williams and Steve Williams, maybe by book 50 I'll figure out how not to be quite so crazy at deadline time. But probably not. I love you guys dearly.

Christmas in
Eternity Springs

Prologue

The fragrance of Christmas swept into the house along with the tree that the garden center's deliverymen carried inside. As they placed the twelve-foot-tall blue spruce into the stand she'd positioned in front of the living room picture window, Claire Branham allowed herself to reflect on the once-upon-a-time memories triggered by the scent.

Days of Christmas Past. Such happy times—laughter and excitement and family traditions. A home filled with love. All lost, wiped away by the reality of illness and death and broken hearts.

As she watched the workers secure the tree to the stand, she reflected upon what a momentous occasion this was for her. She hadn't put up a Christmas tree in a very long time. For Claire, Black Friday didn't represent the beginning of the holiday shopping season. It signified the day the doctor's office called and changed the lives of everyone she loved.

Fifteen Christmases had passed since that first life-altering year. Some years, she'd gone through the motions of participation, even though her heart wasn't in it. Other years, she did her best to ignore it entirely. Mostly, she'd muddled through, grumpy and unhappy and counting the days until the season was over for another year.

"That should do it," said one of the deliverymen, stepping back from the tree. He handed Claire a little green bottle of preservative. "Mix this with water according to the directions. Add water as needed. Doesn't hurt to check it every day, but it needs to be watered at least every other day."

"Thank you."

"You picked a pretty one, Ms. Branham. You have a perfect spot for a tree in this home. Now . . ." He flipped a page on his clipboard. "Are we decorating the tree, too, or just doing the outdoor lighting and decorations?"

"You're hanging the outdoor lights and helping with the high things inside the house. I'm saving the tree to decorate until my fiancé gets home from a business trip tomorrow."

Claire showed him the outdoor decorations in her garage, then went back inside to begin draping garland on the staircase. Anticipation made her feel like a child on Christmas morning. It had been years since she'd decorated a tree, and she couldn't wait to do it again. This year, Claire wasn't spending her holiday season with her Grinch on. She was going all Elf. Because for the first time in forever, the thought of the holiday season made Claire happy.

It started on Black Friday. Rather than launching her usual month-long depression, Black Friday this year got Claire off to a joyful holiday start. After she and Landon ran the Turkey Trot 10K on Thanksgiving morning, she'd sent him off to the airport with a kiss and a turkey sandwich so he could make his early afternoon flight to the West Coast where he had meetings scheduled with movie executives. Friday morning, rather than lie in bed with her covers over her head as in years past, Claire had bounded out of bed early, joined the shopping hoards, and had a ball doing it.

It set the tone for her days as she anticipated Landon's

return. Claire was happy and excited and joyful. With Landon's help, she had climbed her way out of the valley of loss and loneliness and found her happiness. Now, she was finding her Christmas spirit again.

She had volunteer work to thank for it, since that's how she'd met the love of her life. Volunteer work and a book that was special to her heart. There was a lesson there, one she intended to honor for the rest of her days, because from that relatively simple act of generosity, dreams beyond her wildest imaginings were coming true.

Tomorrow would be yet another milestone. She and Landon would be celebrating their first Christmas in their new home, so the time had come to begin making their own family traditions. She had it all planned. She'd have carols playing softly on the stereo system, a fire in the fireplace, and mulled wine simmering on the stove.

She'd be wearing a little something special from Victoria's Secret.

She simply couldn't wait. She'd had a ridiculous amount of fun shopping for the lights and ornaments and decorations for the tree. She'd even bought and worn a Santa hat while she went about it.

She made their bed with the holiday sheets and comforter, hung holiday towels in the bathroom. She dressed the dining room table with a crimson and gold table runner, and as a centerpiece, used glass ornaments in a crystal bowl. By mid-afternoon, the lights were strung, wreaths hung, and stockings lay draped across the easy chair. Stocking hanging would be one of their traditions, she'd decided. Together, they'd hang the stockings and decorate the tree, ending with the most special Christmas tradition of all—placing her precious Christmas angel named Gardenia atop their tree.

Claire was excited, so excited in fact, that she didn't want to spend the evening home alone and watching a movie like she'd originally planned. She could dive into the holiday baking she intended to do. She'd bought ingredients for her mother's traditional Christmas fudge, three different kinds of her favorite Christmas cookies, and a cake she wanted to try.

She debated the idea for a long moment, then shook her head. Her mother used to say that baking was best done in the mornings.

Maybe she'd do a little more shopping or, even better, a lot of shopping. She could afford it, couldn't she? She'd been meaning to make a run over to Cook Children's Hospital in Fort Worth to check out the waiting rooms and see what was on their wish lists. Why not go today? She could visit the hospitals and maybe have dinner at one of the restaurants on the square downtown. She'd heard the Christmas decorations there were lovely. After dinner, she could stop in at the Texas Ranger baseball shop and pick up another gift for Landon. The man was such a huge Ranger fan. He loved baseball, the law, and her.

Liking the idea, she changed clothes, loaded up her wallet with cash, checks, and cards, and started out the door. At the threshold, she hesitated. She was going to Cook Children's. Maybe she should go prepared. What would be more appropriate than spending a few hours doing the thing that led her to Landon and to all of her happiness today?

Decision made, she grabbed her book tote, checked the contents, then detoured to the family room where Gardenia awaited her big moment the following day. Claire tucked her gently into the bag, then did a slow turn around to soak in the joy of having her home spruced up for Christmas. "It's good. I've missed this. I shouldn't have let it go."

She gave the jingle bells hanging on her door a little shake, then left her north Dallas home. Traffic was light, and the drive to Fort Worth took a little over half an hour.

She made her way to the volunteer office at the children's hospital where she gave the receptionist a little of her history and explained what she wanted to do.

"Oh, that's just wonderful," a middle-aged woman dressed in slacks, a white shirt, and pink vest said. "So generous! My name is Lisa Norris and I'm happy to show you around, but you really need to speak with our coordinator, Stella Hewitt. The Jewel Charity Ball is tonight—Cook's is the beneficiary—and she's meeting with the chairpersons. Stella will know what needs are being met and what wishes are still on our list, but I'm not sure she has time in her schedule to meet with you."

"That's okay. We can do that over the phone another time. I'd like to look at the waiting rooms while I'm here."

"Of course." Smiling, Lisa said, "Follow me. We will start in orthopedics."

Claire stepped out into the hall to wait for her escort. The woman gave a brief history of the hospital while she led Claire to waiting rooms on the first and second floors. Claire took a notebook from her purse and began to sketch ideas. After viewing a waiting room on the third floor, she had her head down looking at her notes when her escort stopped.

"This is handy," Lisa said. She raised her voice. "Stella? Do you have a moment?"

Claire glanced up with a smile on her face. She saw an attractive woman in her early sixties exiting a boardroom followed by a younger couple. Claire's steps slowed. Her smile faltered. Landon? What was he doing here?

And why was that tall, leggy blonde wrapped around him?

Lisa said, "Stella, I know you're frightfully busy, but I'd like to introduce you to Claire Branham. She wants to make a directed donation to outfit our waiting rooms here. Would you have a few moments to visit with her?"

"Of course," the older woman said. She approached Claire, her hand extended. "I'm Stella Hewitt. These are two of the chairpersons for tonight's Jewel Ball, Jennifer Perryman and her husband, Landon."

Her husband, Landon Perryman. Her husband.

My fiancé.

The man wearing a two-thousand-dollar suit and an "oh shit" look on his face.

As the room began to spin, she gazed back at Landon. She could almost see his calculating brain at work. He took a half step toward her, the clingy blonde in tow. "Claire."

She shook her head, lifted her hand palm out to fend off anything he might try to say. She brought her left hand up and placed it over her breaking heart. "Excuse me, I'm going to be sick."

There was a door to the ladies' room ten steps beyond him. Her stomach churning, she started forward. The bile rose and when she was a mere step away, she caught a whiff of his familiar aftershave.

She vomited on his Italian suit and loafers, then giggled a bit hysterically all the way to her car.

Chapter One

In her second-floor apartment above her shop, Forever Christmas, Claire eyed the express delivery envelope lying on her kitchen table as if it were a snake. A six-foot-long rattlesnake. Or, maybe a python. Pythons squeezed the life out of their prey, didn't they? The contents of that envelope were sure to wring the peace right out of her day.

She could see it now. She'd tear open the envelope and a snake with blue eyes and a forked tongue would slither out and wind its way along her arm, climbing up to twine around her neck and—*Clang!*

She jumped at the sound of a wrench hitting a metal pipe.

"Earth to Claire," came a male voice from beneath her sink. "You still there? You zoned out again, didn't you?"

"Sorry." She had a tendency to let her mind wander, especially when she was nervous. "Do you need something?"

"Try the water again."

She leaned over the long jeans-clad legs and twisted on the cold water. A moment later, Brick Callahan said, "That's got it. You're good to go."

Claire switched off the water and stepped backward as the man dressed in worn jeans, a Stardance Ranch T-shirt,

and hiking boots scooted out from beneath the sink.
"Thank you, Brick. I just didn't have the hand strength to
get it tight enough."

"Hey, no problem." A teasing glint entered his forest-
green eyes as he flexed his muscles and grinned. "I'm always happy to show off my guns."

Claire gave an exaggerated huff. "Do you ever *not* flirt?"

Innocence echoed in his voice. "Hey, you're a gorgeous
single woman about my age, and a redhead to boot. I've
always had a thing for redheads. Why *wouldn't* I flirt
with you?"

"I saw you flirt with Elaine Hanks at the Trading Post
last week," Claire challenged. "She's seventy if she's
a day."

He shrugged. "I like women. What can I say?"

"And women like you, too, don't they?"

"It's my cross to bear." He rolled to his feet and studied her. "One of these days when you're ready, I'd like to
hear about the jerk who hurt you."

Claire shook her head at him in bemusement. He'd
asked her on a date after they'd met at the Chamber of
Commerce last spring. She'd thanked him, then explained
that she had no desire to date in the wake of a recent bad
breakup. "Why would you want to listen to my sorry tale
of woe?"

"Because I like you. We're friends. And sometimes you
get a Bambi look going on that makes me want to find the
SOB and knock him on his ass."

"You're a knight in shining armor," she said, her heart
warming. He'd make someone a great catch. Just not her.

Never her. Never again.

Had she not been watching him closely, she'd have
missed the shadow that flitted across his face. "Not always,
sweetheart. Not always."

The note of regret in his voice intrigued Claire. She

wasn't the only one with baggage and regrets, apparently. Brick Callahan was a mystery. Handsome, witty, nice, and a hard worker—why *hadn't* someone snapped him up already?

As it was wont to do, her imagination took flight. There was a woman in Brick's past. Who was she? A driven city girl who didn't like the slow pace of mountain life? Or maybe she was an entertainer, a country music singer. A girl who dreamed of stadiums filled with adoring fans. Perhaps she—

"So," Brick said. "Anything else I need to fix while I'm here?"

Claire crashed back to reality and her gaze shifted to the envelope on the kitchen table. *If only.* "No. That takes care of it. Thanks a million, Brick. I really appreciate the help."

"Not a problem. It's the least I could do after you kept the shop open late so I could get a last-minute birthday present for my aunt Maddie."

She glanced at the clock. "Speaking of last minutes, this took longer than I expected. You'd better get moving or you'll miss the party."

"Not a Callahan party." Brick set the wrench down on her countertop. "We start early and finish late. Sure I can't talk you into going with me?" He held up a hand to ward off her immediate refusal and added, "Friends, Claire. Just friends."

Claire hesitated. She sensed that he meant it. Not all men were liars, cheats, and thieves. Brick Callahan wasn't just saying what he thought she wanted to hear.

Maybe. Probably.

But she couldn't be sure. She'd learned the hard way that she dare not trust her instincts where men were concerned. She wasn't about to trust, period. "Thanks, but not tonight. I'm exhausted. It's been a long week."

He washed his hands in the kitchen sink, and she handed him a dishtowel so he could dry them. "If you change your mind, come on out. You know where our place is on Hummingbird Lake?"

"I do." She handed him the gift box she'd wrapped while he worked on her leaky faucet, then led him downstairs and through the shop. She flipped the lock on the front door. Jingle bells on the wreath chimed as she opened it. "Enjoy your evening, Brick. I hope Maddie likes the tree topper."

"I know she will. Uncle Luke might have been deaf to her hints, but not me."

"Tell her I said happy birthday."

"Will do." Then, because Brick liked to kiss women as much as he liked to flirt, he leaned down and kissed her cheek. "G'night, Claire. I'm glad you moved to Eternity Springs."

She beamed a smile at him. "That's nice of you to say. Thank you. I love it here."

It was true, she thought as she locked the door behind him and gazed around her shop. Her Christmas shop. She would admit that her spur-of-the-moment decision to open a Christmas shop in the middle of Nowhere, Colorado, based on the recommendation of a twinkling-eyed stranger riding a motorcycle could make a decent case study for a psych professor.

However, the town suited her. She was making friends. She was operating her business in the black. Sure, she had issues, but she was working on them, wasn't she? She didn't *want* to hate Christmas. She was tackling one of her biggest demons. And she got points for creating an Angel Room in Forever Christmas, didn't she?

Her gaze drifted toward said Angel Room, where the tree central to the entire display stood with a naked top. A flurry of sales in the past two days had depleted her inventory and she'd been forced to use her sample to fill Brick's request. "Bonus points if you go ahead and put a different angel on top of that tree tonight," she challenged herself.

If she faced the Angel Room and that envelope in the same day, she'd deserve more than just bonus points. She'd deserve ice cream. Two scoops.

Because Claire and Christmas weren't exactly on the best terms. She associated Bad Things with Christmas. Things like illness and death, and more recently, betrayal. She couldn't help it. All of it had happened. Before the Lying Lizard Louse, the holiday season had depressed her. Made her sad. Made her heart ache. Since him, she'd connected Christmas with the molten anger boiling inside her.

And dang it, she was going to change that. Despite the larcenous liar, she was going to learn to love Christmas again. Love the scents and the tastes and the sounds and the colors of Christmas. Love the snowmen and ornaments and peppermints. Love the angels.

The angels. She'd love every freaking sparkling feathery angel. Even if it killed her.

Well, except for Starlina. That was asking too much. Claire still had her pride.

She blew out a breath, mentally reviewed her inventory, and decided on a new angel to crown the centerpiece tree. She carried her ladder from the supply room and positioned it. As she removed a simple white porcelain topper from the box, her gaze stole toward an angel with a tattered dress and a broken wing sitting mostly hidden behind a trio of bright, shiny, beautiful angels. Gardenia.

Emotion roiled within her. With her gaze focused on the bedraggled angel, she thought of the envelope upstairs. Almost against her will, she glanced down at the empty third finger of her left hand. The tears that stung the back of her eyes annoyed her, so she stomped her feet just a little bit as she climbed the ladder.

Claire's petite form came with short arms. Ordinarily when she trimmed a tall tree, she used an extension tool to help her place decorations. She'd already climbed the ladder when she realized she'd forgotten it. Impatient with herself on many levels, she wanted the task over and done with. She climbed another rung of the ladder, extended her arm, and reached for the tip of the tree with the angel topper. And reached. Leaned a little farther. Stretched . . .

"Ow!" Pain sliced through her shoulder as she slid the angel on the treetop. She'd tweaked an old rotator-cuff injury. "This day just keeps getting better and better."

She couldn't even dull the ache with nice glass of cabernet since she still had two days of antibiotics to take after having an emergency root canal on Monday. As she descended the ladder, she grumbled aloud, "A great day in a spectacular week."

Root canal. Flat tire. Shattered phone screen.

Contact from the past she'd run from but could never escape.

Claire exhaled a heavy sigh, put away her ladder, then turned off the shop lights and climbed the stairs to her apartment. Unfortunately, the envelope hadn't slithered off her kitchen table in her absence.

She pulled a bottle of ibuprofen from a cabinet and tossed two into her mouth, chasing the pills with a full glass of water. She set down the empty glass and focused on the delivery envelope. Focused on her name and address. Did her best to ignore the name of the law firm in the upper left-hand corner of the label.

"Do it," she muttered to herself. "Just do it. Get it over with."

Heart pounding, her mouth sandpaper dry, she picked up the envelope, pulled the tab, and looked inside. A black binder clip secured a stack of papers over an inch thick.

She took a deep breath and yanked the paperwork from the envelope.

The check fell onto her table printed side down. Claire flipped it over and read the amount. She stumbled back against the wall. "Sweet baby Jesus in a manger."

Her knees buckled and she melted onto her kitchen floor.

As the sun began to dip below a craggy mountain peak to the west, Jax Lancaster pushed open the gate to the hot springs pools at Angel's Rest Healing Center and Spa. He turned away from a section of the small park where families congregated and chose an isolated pool that offered a great view of the spectacular orange and gold rays framing a purple mountain. Jax appreciated sunrises and sunsets in a way that only a man who'd gone months at a time for years in a row without seeing them could do. He pulled his U.S. Navy T-shirt over his head and tossed it aside before easing his aching body into the steaming waters of the mineral springs.

As welcome warmth seeped into his bones, Jax exhaled a heavy sigh and tried to relax and enjoy the view. Ten days of nonstop travel had taken its toll on his body. Eighteen months of constant worry about his son had worn upon his soul.

The fact that he was dead broke and out of work didn't help matters. Divorce and a custody battle had eaten up his savings, and then ten days ago, he'd walked away from a career he'd loved. He didn't regret the decision. He'd had no choice. Bottom line was Nicholas needed his father.

Whether the boy recognized it or not.

The gate hinges squeaked again and Jax glanced toward the sound. He gave the redheaded woman with a short but sexy pair of legs a quick once-over as she stepped into the pool area. Very nice, he thought. He'd always had a thing for redheads. She wore a black swimsuit cover-up and carried a long beach towel in shades of red and green draped over her left shoulder. In her right hand, she carried a large tote bag with a cartoon character on the side. Rudolph? In July?

When she turned toward the families, he returned his attention to the sunset and his troubles. He'd checked his e-mail after arriving at the resort, but the good news he'd hoped to find waiting for him had not materialized. Jax tried not to brood about the goose egg in his job-offer in-box. He needed to give it some time. Seattle was a big, fast-growing city with a hot economy. Something would come along. Hadn't he been told by more than one potential employer to reach out to them again after his discharge was official? In the meantime, well, he had an offer on the table that would pay the basic bills, didn't he?

Never mind that he'd almost rather panhandle on the streets than work for his ex-father-in-law's chain of independent bookstores.

Jax sank farther into the water and rolled his shoulders. If he had to work for Lara's dad in order to put a roof over Nicholas's head, keep Cheerios in his breakfast bowl, and ensure that the checks to the child psychologist didn't bounce, then that's what he'd do. The boy came first.

An explosion of laughter erupted from the other side of the park. Jax tried to remember the last time he'd laughed like that. Before the accident, certainly.

The accident. What a mild term for such a life-altering event.

Spying movement in his peripheral vision, he turned his head to see the redhead approach. She stepped into a beam of sunshine and the fire in her hair glistened. It was as if the sunset walked right out of the sky and up to the edge of the mineral springs pool where he sat. "Excuse me," she said. "There's a water world war going on in the other pools. Mind if I share your little Switzerland?"

He smiled. "Not at all. *Mi Switzerland es tu Switzerland.*"

"Thanks." She kicked off her sandals, then swiftly unbuttoned her cover-up—no wedding ring on her left hand, he noticed—and pulled it off to reveal a modest black swimsuit. Since her curves were as appealing as her legs, Jax had to force himself to look away.

He heard the splash and then a feminine cough. "Mercy. This is my first time to visit the mineral springs. I hadn't realized exactly how bad they smell."

"You'll get accustomed to it after a couple of minutes. Now, you might not smell anything else for two days afterward, but your sense of smell will return."

"I'll take your word for it. Soaking in a mineral spring is supposed to have health benefits, right? Like soothing sore muscles?"

Jax nodded. "Yes, although I don't know how effective it is. Still, mineral springs have attracted people all across the world throughout history, so on that basis alone, I think there must be something to it. Personally, I like it here because I find this relaxing."

"And I'm interrupting your peace with my chatter. I apologize."

"No need. I'm always happy to . . ." Jax bit back the words "share my tub with a beautiful lady" and settled for something that sounded less like a come-on. "Meet new people. I'm Jax Lancaster."

"Claire Branham. I've recently moved to Eternity Springs and opened a business, which is keeping me busy and is why I haven't visited these pools before tonight. Are you a guest at Angel's Rest, Jax?"

"I am. I'm here for a couple of days to pick up my son from the Rocking L summer camp."

"Oh." The note of sympathy and understanding she managed to insert into the tone of that one short word revealed that she knew the Rocking L wasn't an ordinary camp. "The Rocking L program is fabulous. I know the children who get to attend are thrilled with the experience. How old is your son?"

"Nicholas is eight." Jax hesitated, then because he was curious to get another perspective on the Rocking L program, he added, "He's been having a rough time of it. He was with his mother when she died a year and a half ago, and it damaged him. I'm hoping the weeks he's spent at camp will kick-start his recovery."

"I'm so sorry for your loss."

"His loss, not mine," Jax clarified. Then he winced. "That sounds terrible, doesn't it? That's not what I intended. We were divorced. His mother and I were divorced. Acrimoniously. Ugly custody battle. I've been in the navy and they don't always just let you quit when you want, so Nicholas has been living with her parents and I'm babbling. Sorry. Too much traveling through too many time zones and I'm punch-drunk and nervous about picking him up tomorrow."

"Don't worry about it. I've been known to babble, myself. Frequently. So where did you begin your travels?"

The specific information was classified. Jax picked a point in the middle. "Seventy-two hours ago I was in Dubai."

"Whoa. I'll bet the jet lag is brutal."

His mouth twisted in a rueful grin. "I don't ordinarily spill my guts to strangers. I've embarrassed myself. I'll shut up now."

"Oh, don't be embarrassed. Sometimes sharing a burden makes it easier to carry. And doing so with a stranger instead of a friend protects against potential blowback."

"Blowback?"

"Haven't you ever been a little too honest with friends or family and it comes back to haunt you?"

He thought of the conversation with Lara right before he left on the deployment that doomed his marriage. Oh, yeah. He understood the risk of too much honesty. Been there, done that, got the divorce. However, not even his jet-lagged tongue was loose enough to go there, so he stuck with something lighter. "You mean like telling my ex that those yellow slacks did indeed make her butt look big?"

Claire snorted. "You didn't."

"We started dating our freshman year in college. I was very young and stupid at the time, but I did learn." *Just not fast enough.* Wanting to direct the conversation away from himself, Jax asked, "How about you, Claire? Has honesty come back to haunt you with a significant other?"

"I'm not married. I ended a relationship not long ago, but it wasn't due to too much honesty." Her tone turned bitter as she added, "Just the opposite, in fact."

"Sounds like you have a burden to unload, yourself. Go for it. You won't get any blowback from me."

"Hmm . . ." She shot him a narrow-eyed look. "You said you're only in town for a couple of days?"

"We leave the day after tomorrow for San Diego. I'll pack up my place there, and then it's on to Seattle where Nicholas has been living."

Claire shifted her position in the pool so that she faced the sunset rather than Jax. A full minute of silence ticked by before she spoke again. "I should be celebrating tonight. I should be drinking champagne and having wild sex with a ski instructor named Stamina Sven. Instead I'm soaking an old softball injury in a stinky, steamy pool while drinking sparkling water and spilling my secrets to a stranger."

Jax's brows arched. *Stamina Sven?* "It's obvious you have a shoulder injury when you throw a hanging curve ball like that one."

"Let me guess," she drawled. "Your middle name is Sven."

He waggled his brows. "You can call me Stamina for short. And I understand that room service delivers out here. I'm happy to order a bottle of bubbly."

"Thanks, but no."

"So what are we not celebrating?"

She sighed heavily. "Lawyers."

Jax lifted an imaginary champagne goblet in toast. "I can definitely drink to that."

"And Christmas."

"Christmas? Well, it is July."

"Forever Christmas. My shop. It's doing great. It's on the corner of Cottonwood and Third. I opened it this spring and this month I'm going to finish in the black. By a kitten's whisker, but black is black, right?"

"Right." A Christmas store. Guess that accounted for the Rudolph tote bag.

"I'm trying hard to take pleasure in my shop. I'm giving myself a pass on the angels, although I'm trying very hard to hold on to the rest of my joy, but it's hanging by a strand of tinsel. See, I'd lost it, then I found it, but I discovered it was a lie. Well, he was a lie. What I felt wasn't a lie."

"You loved him."

"Yes, I loved him. I loved the thought of making a life with him, of having Christmas with him. After all those years of missing it, hating it, wishing I could go to a deserted island from Black Friday to January second, I put up a tree in my house and even bought silly holiday towels! He ruined it with his lies, but I'm not letting him ruin anything else. No way. That's what I'm trying to hold on to. I won't let him steal it from me. It's bad enough that I was stupid enough to be fooled by a dirty rotten lying lawyer, that I let him break my heart. I won't allow him to steal my joy."

Jax wondered what sort of problem she had with angels, but he didn't interrupt to ask. She was on a roll.

"I tell everyone that the reason I moved to Eternity Springs was because I saw a business opportunity, but that's not really true. I was running away. From him. From reminders of him. From reality. Eternity Springs was my place to hide and to heal. I thought I was doing a pretty decent job of it. I'm making friends. I'm becoming involved in town life. Forever Christmas is an in-your-face declaration that he's not going to win. It's good. I'm tooling along, getting along, thinking maybe I've got this thing whipped, when today . . . *boom*!" She clapped her hands. "The lousy lawyer and his great big lie followed me home."

Jax sat up straight. Every protective instinct he possessed went into full alert. "This jerk is stalking you?"

Chapter Two

"Stalking me?" she repeated. She lifted her gaze toward the mountains as she considered the question a moment before speaking. "No. Not in person, anyway. I feel as if I'm being hunted, because he did hire a private detective to find me so he's been making constant attempts to contact me, but that can't be termed stalking. He's sending paperwork."

"Paperwork?"

"Paperwork. It's a legal thing I can't sever right now. And whenever I receive communication from him, I can't help but get my Grinch on."

"Ah." Jax relaxed back down into the water.

She gave her head a shake. "But enough talk of lizards. Let's talk about something happier. Tell me about your son. He's eight, you said? What's he like? Is Nicholas adventurous and strong-willed? Talkative and imaginative? Thoughtful and diplomatic?"

Jax tore his gaze away from the glistening sunset of her hair. He didn't want to admit that he didn't know his son well enough to answer her question. "Nicholas has always been detailed and orderly. When he was just a toddler, he spent hours stacking blocks. They had to be color coordinated and positioned exactly so."

The corners of Jax's mouth lifted. *My little engineer,* he remembered thinking. "Before his mother died . . ."—*before our divorce*—"Nicholas was lively and talkative. I'm hopeful his time at this summer camp will put us on the road to finding that happy little boy again."

She encouraged him with a smile. "Well, from everything I hear about the Rocking L, you couldn't ask for a more dedicated staff."

"Do you know any of them personally? Anything you can tell me about the camp from a local point of view?"

"Well, hmm." She considered a few moments, then said, "Like I said, I'm a relative newcomer to town, myself. I don't believe I've met any of the staff. I have met the camp's benefactors, the Davenports, and I like them very much. I also know a couple of the people from town who volunteer up there—the local vet and the owner here at Angel's Rest, Celeste Blessing."

"I met Celeste when I checked in. She told me she leads nature hikes up at the camp."

"I've heard they are fabulous. She seems to have extraordinary luck when it comes to sighting wildlife."

"According to her, my boy has had a great time."

"If Celeste said it, you can believe it. She has her fingers on the pulse of everything that happens in this valley. Plus, she's very . . . well . . . I guess I'd call it intuitive. She has an uncanny ability to say exactly what I need to hear when I need to hear it." She gave a soft, self-deprecating laugh then added, "Unfortunately, she didn't stop by the store today."

"She's quite the ambassador for Eternity Springs," Jax said. "I asked what Nicholas and I should do tomorrow afternoon, and she gave me a list that would take two weeks to complete. Do you have any ideas for me?"

Claire offered her suggestions for afternoon activities in and around Eternity Springs, and after that discussion, conversation naturally paused as they both watched in silent appreciation as a full moon rose over the Rockies.

"It's beautiful here," Jax said.

"Yes, it is. Eternity Springs is a good place. It has good energy. Positive energy."

Jax thought of what lay before him and observed, "I wish there was a way to bottle it up and take it with me."

"You should ask Celeste."

A voice rang out of the shadows behind Jax. "Ask me what?"

Jax glanced over his shoulder to see Celeste Blessing approach, carrying a tray holding a bucket of champagne and two flutes. "I didn't order champagne," he murmured.

"It's for the newlyweds in our honeymoon cottage," Celeste explained. "I noticed Claire headed this way earlier, and I wanted to ask her if she has any news about my special order."

"The Lalique angel? No, I'm afraid not. I called about it this afternoon, and they've promised me a firm ship date tomorrow. If I haven't heard from them by noon, I'll give them another call."

"Lovely. Thank you, dear. Now, Mr. Lancaster, what question may I answer for you?"

Embarrassment turned his smile bashful. "We were just talking about Eternity Springs."

"Jax wished there was a way to bottle up the valley's positive energy to take with him when he leaves," Claire added. "If anyone knows a way to do it, you would, Celeste."

The older woman laughed with delight. "Well, of course I do. That's easy enough."

"I don't think they'll let me on an airplane with bottles of mineral water," Jax observed.

"Oh, it's not the mineral water. It's the basic state of

mind. A positive thought in the morning sets the tone for your entire day."

Jax was fairly certain he'd seen that platitude on a T-shirt.

However, Celeste took it a step further. "Now, the key to having that positive thought each morning starts the night before. I suggest that each night before you go to sleep, you make note of one positive thing that happened in your day. Even the darkest of days will have one moment of light. Make note of it. Write it down. Use it to jump-start your day the following morning. It's like a cup of coffee for your attitude."

"I like it," Claire said.

"Thank you, dear. Now, if you'll excuse me, I need to get this champagne to our honeymooners. Enjoy the rest of your evening and think of something positive that happened today when you go to sleep tonight."

Celeste's words hung in the air long after her departure. Claire twisted her head around to meet Jax's gaze. "See what I mean? She's a wise woman. That's a common-sense idea and it makes so much sense to me."

"It's simplistic," Jax cautioned. "Life seldom is."

"True. Maybe that's the problem. Maybe that's part of what makes Eternity Springs special. I think it's possible to live a somewhat simple life here."

"Because it's a small town?"

"No. More because Eternity Springs had a near-death experience, and it changed the outlook of those who live here."

An easy gust of summer breeze swept petals from the nearby rose garden into the hot springs. Jax idly watched the yellow petals float in lazy circles on the moonlit surface of the pool as Claire told him how the little town had been on the brink of financial failure when Celeste decided to open Angel's Rest, which led to the rebirth of Eternity Springs.

"I studied the stats before I decided to move here," she said. "Since the resort opened, the town has added over three hundred permanent residents and half again as many permanent seasonal residents. The only thing holding back even stronger summer tourism is a shortage of rooms to rent."

"I noticed lots of No Vacancy signs around town."

"We're having a great summer tourist season. I think the change from a bleak economic outlook to a positive one has taken a big burden off the shoulders of people who live here. Life is easier now. People are happier. They have more time and treasure to devote to what matters to them. Here in Eternity Springs, that tends to be friends and family and faith—the recipe for a basic, simple life."

"I dunno, Claire. In my experience, family is the most complicated thing on earth."

Claire smiled ruefully and sadness dimmed her eyes. "I won't argue that, but I think Celeste would say there's a lesson there."

"What lesson is that?"

"Actually . . . I haven't a clue. I'm just certain Celeste would point one out."

The two shared a grin, then Jax said, "I concede you have a point. I've seen how close calls can change an individual's outlook on life. I can imagine that it would work similarly for a community, too. So, if you decided to brew a pot of her attitudinal coffee, what positive thing would you write down about today for tomorrow morning?"

"Hmm . . . that's actually a difficult question. I have a number of positive things that happened today from which to choose."

She stilled and an expression of wonder stole across her face. "Wow. It worked. I was all Grinchy Grouch when I arrived here tonight, but now my mind is filled with good things. That's kinda cool. Your turn, Jax. What was your moment of light today?"

The answer was easy. "You. I met you. You've been my ray of sunshine today."

"Why, thank you." She beamed like the moonlight. "That's the nicest thing someone has said to me in a long time." She glanced toward the west where the glow of sunset faded to night. "I also think it's a good note on which to take my leave."

Claire stood and as she climbed out of the pool and reached for her towel, Jax took advantage of her momentary inattention to ogle her shapely figure. Lots of curves in a compact form. She swiped her towel over her arms and legs before wrapping it around her torso. "I am glad we met, Jax Lancaster. I hope you and Nicholas have a wonderful reunion tomorrow and a fabulous trip home."

"Thank you. I am glad we met, too, Claire Branham." He was sorry to see her go. "I wish you a quick recovery from your shoulder injury, continued success with Forever Christmas, and a life free from lawyers for as long as you'd like."

"Amen to that," she declared. "Good night and safe journey."

"Good night."

As Claire walked off into the shadows, Jax stretched out his legs, laced his fingers behind his head, and tried to recall the last time he'd shared such a pleasant conversation with a woman. Throughout the exchange, an undercurrent of mild flirtation had hummed between them and he'd enjoyed it.

At least, he thought that's what had been going on. He was rusty in that respect. He'd been faithful to his wife, and deployed almost continuously since the divorce, so the opportunities to indulge in flirtation to any degree had been few and far between.

That situation wouldn't be changing anytime soon, either. Nicholas had to be his first, his only, priority for the time being.

Wonder what would have happened if he'd amped things up, if he'd come out and hit on her? Jax didn't pick up women in bars—or mineral pools—as a rule, and she certainly hadn't seemed to be on the prowl herself. And yet, he'd sensed that she was lonely like him. And she *had* mentioned Stamina Sven.

"Jax?"

He lowered his arms at the sound of her voice and sat up straight. His heart began to pound. "Did you forget something?"

"Not really. I had an idea. It's probably really stupid and I can't believe I'm going to suggest it, but what the heck. I think we should do it."

His eyes widened. Sex? She wanted sex? Had he misread her? Had she come back to pick him up?

"See, I think Celeste's suggestion is spot-on," she continued. "I believe in the power of positive thinking, but I also believe in running two miles a day. I'm a pitiful self-motivator. If I have a running buddy, I'm much more successful at dragging myself out of bed and lacing on my shoes. That's where you come in."

Something tells me she's not talking about me dragging myself out of bed with her.

"If I've made a promise to someone, I keep it. So, here's your chance to bottle up the positive energy of Eternity Springs and take it with you to the West Coast, Jax. Want to be my affirmative attitude buddy?"

"Affirmative attitude" isn't the type of "buddy" I'm wanting tonight. Cautiously, he asked, "What would be involved?"

"Well, we could both keep journals, but it needn't be that formal. It can be as simple as promising that each night, you'll make a mental note of something positive that happened that day."

"That's it?"

"Sure. Unless . . . I guess we could pick an amount of time we will commit to doing it. Probably shouldn't leave it open-ended."

"But no accountability between the two of us?"

Claire shrugged. "It's the guilt that works with me. If I say I'll do it, and I think you are doing it too, well, I can't slack off. So, how about it?"

She was so darned cute. So appealing. He felt the urge to tease her. "I don't know, Claire. It has a bit of a girly, 'Dear Diary' feel."

She folded her arms and sniffed with disdain. "Now, that's just wrong. Didn't you tell me you just got out of the navy? I'll bet you made notations in some sort of chart or report every day, didn't you?"

"Well, yes."

"So think of this as a charting. Or, keeping your log-book."

Jax arched an amused brow. "Be captain of my own life?"

"Why not?"

"Why not?" he repeated. "Sure, Claire. I'll play."

"Excellent. Do you want to commit to a time period?"

He rubbed his chin and considered. "How about three months? That's long enough to give it a fair shot and see if it actually works."

"Perfect. And at the end of those three months, if you're so inclined, reach out to me and let me know how it's worked for you. You can always contact me through my Web site. It's www.ForeverChristmasinColorado.com. Or, if you have a chance tomorrow, stop by and I'll give you a card with my info on it. Your son will enjoy the shop. All children do."

No, not my Nicholas. His son would be the exception.

Claire continued, "I'm so glad I came back and asked you to do this with me. Thanks, Jax. This makes me happy. I have a feeling this will be good for both of us."

They exchanged good nights once again, and she departed. Jax listened until the gate squeaked open, and then closed.

"Well, that was an interesting encounter," he murmured. And now rather than relaxing, the hot springs pools felt lonely to him.

He rolled his shoulders, then stood and reached for his towel. He figured he'd head to his room, shower, and go down to dinner. Since a gorgeous redhead didn't appear to be on the menu for tonight, he'd settle for a steak and a nice glass of wine.

Who knows, he might even wander into the Angel's Rest gift shop and buy a notebook.

As he walked back toward the resort, his thoughts shifted to tomorrow. His schedule was packed. He had a phone appointment first thing in the morning with Nicholas's psychologist in Seattle, then a second phone appointment with the woman who'd been his teacher. Also, he'd been invited to a parents' luncheon at Eagle's Way, Jack and Cat Davenport's estate. No way was he missing that. He was glad to have the opportunity to personally thank the Davenports for their generosity toward Nicholas and all the campers.

Pickup time at the Rocking L was one o'clock. Jax intended to be there on the dot. Though he was nervous about what the future held, he couldn't wait to hold his boy once again. He'd missed him terribly.

Tomorrow afternoon, he would like to take his son fishing at Hummingbird Lake. Maybe canoeing, too, if

Nicholas would like that. Anything that might help them get beyond the awkwardness he fully expected to encounter during the first few hours they spent together.

Hours, hell. More likely days. Probably even weeks. Could be months. Who knew what sort of things Lara's parents had been saying about Jax to the boy? Nothing good, based on past experience.

Jax sighed heavily as the tension that he'd soaked away in the mineral springs came flooding back. He very much feared that he and Nicholas had a tall mountain to climb to establish a comfortable father-son relationship. Then he glanced up at the big Victorian house that served as the central building at Angel's Rest Healing Center and Spa, and he heard the echo of Celeste Blessing's advice in his mind. *Even the darkest day has a moment of light. Write it down. Use it to jump-start your day the following morning. It's like a cup of coffee for your attitude.*

He thought about Claire Branham and her challenge, and damned if he didn't feel a little more positive. He could do it. *They* would do it.

Tomorrow was the start of the Lancaster men's fresh beginning. Tomorrow he and Nicholas would begin to forge new bonds in a new version of their family. Shoot, maybe the boy's time at camp in this special little valley might actually help heal some of the wounds upon his poor heart.

How cool would it be if he could take his son shopping at Forever Christmas tomorrow afternoon?

Because ever since his mother's death and the traumatic events surrounding it, Jax's boy—his precious little Nicholas—was afraid of the trappings of Christmas. Deeply, deathly afraid.

The nightmare had started before Thanksgiving last year when his grandmother took him to a mall and continued through the end of the year when the decorations finally came down. He froze at the sight of gift-wrapped packages. The scents of cinnamon and peppermint and fir trees made him sick to his stomach. The sound of Christmas carols sent him into a terrorized stupor.

Unfortunately, Jax's sub had been beneath the Indian Ocean at the time and Lara's parents had taken a "tough love" stance, thinking Nicholas simply needed more exposure to all things holiday in order to get over his fears. It had been a disastrous approach, and by the time Jax learned of it, the damage had been done.

"And you need to manage your expectations, Dad," Jax murmured to himself. Tomorrow, his goal was to get a hug from his son. Beyond that, well, Christmas was still five months away.

Tonight he'd go up to his room and write down his bright moment and do his best to bottle some of this valley's positive mojo.

Too bad they didn't do miracles here in Eternity Springs.

Chapter Three

Hugs are even better than I remembered.
—JAX

Claire deposited a satisfyingly long receipt into the gold shopping bag that bore her store's logo. Wearing a friendly smile, she walked around the end of the antique wood counter and handed two bulging bags to her customer, a lovely sixty-something woman from New Mexico vacationing in Colorado with her husband and two other couples. "Thank you for shopping at Forever Christmas."

"Thank you, Claire!" the customer replied, snapping her wallet closed. "We had so much fun. The display of ornaments and gifts for family members is the most creative thing I've seen in a long time. I can't wait to give my sister the ornament I bought for her. So clever."

"I love the Angel Room," her companion said. "It's easy to imagine that you're being surrounded by love when you walk into that room."

Claire went to work ringing up the second customer's purchases, which were heavy on angels, she noticed. "Are you staying at our local resort, Angel's Rest?"

"No, we're guests of a fellow church member who owns cabins in a little valley not far from here," the first woman said. "It's a fabulous place. There are three cabins—although 'cabin' doesn't quite describe them because they are quite luxurious. And the way each is decorated is just

precious. I've never seen such fabulous tile work as the mosaics in the kitchen and baths and on the fireplaces. They
tell the story of the settling of this part of Colorado. So
creative."

"We love it there," her companion agreed. "Eternity
Springs is just darling. We've heard that Angel's Rest is
wonderful, too. We have reservations for high tea there this
afternoon."

"In that case, be sure to take a peek into the parlor,"
Claire suggested. "The owner has an exquisite collection
of angels on display there."

Once the sale was completed and her visitors departed,
Claire made a quick pass through Forever Christmas. For
the first time since shortly after she'd flipped the CLOSED
sign to OPEN five hours ago, she had a lull in customers.

Good. She could stand to get off her feet for a few minutes. Her choice of footwear this morning had been a
mistake. She knew better than to wear heels at the shop.
Ordinarily she wore sneakers with slacks, a white shirt,
and a Forever Christmas apron. Today for some strange
reason, she'd pulled on a sundress from her closet and
slipped her feet into darling strappy sandals. The same
sandals she wanted to kick off asap.

She detoured into the back room long enough to grab
her tablet, thinking she'd use the time to catch up on
e-mail. She took a seat on the tall wooden stool behind
her checkout counter, which gave her an excellent view of
the street.

All day long she'd watched the front door with more attention than customary. Would Jax Lancaster stop by?
Why did she care? And why in the world had she worn
heels just in case he showed up?

Claire let one shoe dangle from her foot and fall to the
floor. Her gaze stole to the shelf below the cash register
where she'd set the brown leather-bound journal embossed

with the word "Believe" on the front. Simple and masculine, it was perfect for Jax and this particular project. If he stopped by, she planned to give it to him.

Why she cared whether or not he brought his son by the shop, she couldn't say. Seriously, she'd spent a whopping hour with the man. Half of that time, she'd been blabbering on, making a fool of herself. Why in the world did she want to see him again? Yes, he'd been easy on the eyes—very easy—but she'd learned that particular lesson, hadn't she?

Maybe because he'd blabbered on, too?

He'd seemed so genuinely worried about his son. He'd seemed so genuine, period. Maybe she'd needed to be reminded that genuine men do exist after Landon the Louse invaded her world yesterday.

"Genuine men do still exist" had been the message she'd written in the journal she'd chosen for herself last night—a fabric-covered, spiral-bound notebook with a hand-painted star on the cover.

Claire responded to a half-dozen e-mails before both her attention and her gaze wandered. Traffic on Third Street was beginning to pick up.

Jax would have picked his son up by now. Had he said what activity he had settled on for the afternoon? She couldn't recall.

The arrival of a new group of shoppers followed by the UPS truck provided a welcome distraction. She used paint pens to personalize seven ornaments for a grandmother from Denver and sold three Advent calendars, two snow globes, and a beautifully illustrated copy of *'Twas the Night Before Christmas*. When she checked in the delivery items, she discovered that Celeste's special order had arrived.

Jax Lancaster and his son never did.

At five o'clock, she flipped her OPEN sign and locked

the front door. Bookkeeping and housekeeping took her another half an hour, and when she was ready to turn out the lights, she hesitated.

Celeste would be thrilled if Claire delivered the Lalique to Angel's Rest. It would be good business. While she was there, she could drop off the journal for Jax. She wouldn't ask to see him or anything. She didn't want to be a creeper. Thinking that he might use her journal each night gave the project more substance in her imaginings. And the whole thing was about imaginings, right?

She'd do it. She'd wrap it up and leave it for him.

And if part of her was aware that fussing over journals and strangers and gifts was her way to avoid dealing with the paperwork that remained on her kitchen table upstairs, well, okay. Avoidance wasn't a crime.

She wrapped the journal in the gift-wrap paper that was printed in Forever Christmas's logo—Claire was a big believer in branding—and debated a full minute over what to write on the gift tag. Finally, she signed the words "Think positive!" and her name.

Before she could second-guess herself, Claire collected the box for Celeste, deposited it and the journal into a shopping bag, and headed for Angel's Rest.

It was another beautiful midsummer evening and pleasure hummed through Claire's veins as she made her way along Cottonwood toward the footbridge that spanned Angel Creek. She felt energized and upbeat and, amazingly, her feet no longer hurt. Maybe after her errand, she'd treat herself to dinner at the Yellow Kitchen. After a plate of pasta and a couple glasses of nice wine, she might even be up to reading the contract awaiting her signature that was part of yesterday's package.

She waved at Nic Callahan, who was out taking her daily walk, sporting a growing baby bump. Nic waved back, then as she rested a maternal hand atop her belly,

Claire's heart gave a little twist. She adored children and she'd always wanted a big family. Landon had told her too many lies to count, but his oft-stated desire to start a family right after the wedding had been one of the worst.

At thirty-one, Claire's biological clock was ticking and some days it sounded louder than a bass drum. She hadn't given up on her dream of having a family, but as with everything else in her life, she was in the midst of readjusting her expectations. After the debacle with Landon, she couldn't imagine ever getting married, so her dream of having a husband and three or four or even five kids wasn't in the cards.

That didn't mean she couldn't still have a family, Claire knew. A traditional family wasn't the only option available. Hadn't her childhood best friend's mother been a single mom? Mary Elizabeth Sanders had been a great mother to Claire's friend Penny, though her path had not been an easy one. Money always had been tight for the Sanderses, and it was why, when she'd been offered a promotion that required a transfer to Atlanta, Mrs. Sanders had taken the job. Penny and Claire had both been devastated. They'd promised to stay in touch with one another and to visit each other. For a time, they'd followed through.

Then six months after Penny moved, Michelle got sick. Claire had lost touch with Penny as life as she'd known it changed.

Wonder how life might have been different had she had a friend to talk to during those awful months and years? She'd been alone. Too alone, for too long.

Then, she'd picked Landon the Lizard.

"Stop thinking about him," she muttered to herself. It was too beautiful an evening and the goal here was to focus on the positive. Right?

"Absolutely."

So when she caught a whiff of fragrance drifting on the

evening air, she decided to take the long way to her destination and stop and smell the roses. Literally. It would give her something positive to write in her journal, and besides, she was a sucker for flowers.

Angel's Rest boasted an extensive rose garden with one section of Peace roses designated as a memorial garden. A fabulous carved wooden bench provided a place to sit and bask in the beauty and tranquility of the spot, and Claire might have done just that had she not spied Jax Lancaster standing beside the creek, his hands shoved into his pockets. A pair of fishing poles lay at his feet. A young boy—Nicholas, she assumed—stood about ten feet away, his position a copy of his father's. Neither one appeared too comfortable.

Claire hesitated. Maybe she should pretend she hadn't seen them and go on up to the house and drop off her packages. She didn't want him to think she was stalking him.

Even as she prepared to turn and continue along her way, Jax's head swiveled around. He wore sunglasses, so she couldn't see his eyes. Nevertheless, she sensed that his gaze had locked onto hers. He smiled and waved at her to join him. A bit desperately, she thought.

"Claire!" he called. "This is a nice surprise."

The boy looked around. Dressed in jeans and a red Rocking L Summer Camp T-shirt, he wore black-framed glasses with thick lenses and his blond hair could use a trim. The owlish glasses and slight physique gave him a nerdy look that Claire found endearing, but the scuffs on his sneakers and grime on his jeans declared he was all boy.

He glanced from Claire back to his father and narrowed his eyes suspiciously. Jax didn't seem to notice.

"Claire, come meet my son, Nicholas. Son, this is Ms. . . . Branham, wasn't it?"

"Yes." She stepped forward and offered Nicholas her hand. "It's very nice to meet you, Nicholas. Your father told me you've been a camper at the Rocking L. I hear it's a wonderful place. My neighbor is our veterinarian here in town and she volunteers up there. Have you met Dr. Murphy?"

"Dr. Lori?" His expression brightened, chasing away the suspicion. He held out his hand and shook hers politely. "I love Dr. Lori. She's the nicest person. She knows everything about dogs." His little brow wrinkled as a thought occurred to him. "She's your neighbor? You didn't come here with my dad? You're not his girlfriend?"

"Girlfriend?" Claire repeated, confused.

"My mom had a boyfriend and then she married my stepdad. He didn't want me."

Oh. Claire wanted to wrap her arms around the little guy and give him a hard hug.

"I don't have a girlfriend, Nicholas," Jax said, a sharp note to his voice. "I met Ms. Branham after I arrived in Eternity Springs last night."

"Oh. Okay." The boy shuffled in embarrassment as an awkward silence fell.

Claire spoke up brightly. "I live in Eternity Springs, Nicholas. I run a Christmas shop. See?" She help up her bag and gave it a little shake. "Forever Christmas. In fact I'm bringing a gift to . . ."

Claire's voice trailed off when she saw Nicholas's gaze lock on the bag, his eyes going round as ornament balls on one of her trees, his complexion draining of color. "Oh." He took a step backward. "Oh. I . . . I . . ." He took another step back. "I gotta . . . gotta . . . I'm outta worms. Dad, I'm gonna go dig for more worms, okay?"

Without waiting for his father's permission, he turned and ran. Claire stood staring after him, her jaw agape. Jax raked his fingers through his hair as he watched his son flee, his expression stark and a little lost. "What just happened?" Claire asked. "I scared him. How did I scare him?"

"It wasn't you," Jax responded, a heavy sigh in his voice. "It was the bag."

"It's a paper bag. What does he think is in it?" Claire had a vivid imagination, and now it took off, bringing her to an ugly place. Jax had told her his ex-wife had died. That losing her had damaged their son. What if he'd meant it literally? What if Nicholas had been with his mother when it happened? What if the former Mrs. Lancaster had been a victim of violence?

She could see it now.

The beautiful blonde—because a hottie like Jax Lancaster would marry a beautiful blonde—walks through the mall, holding her son's hand. They've just left the food court where she treated Nicholas to a rare soft drink and he slurps from the straw as he attempts to wring every last bit of sweetness from the cup. Then, suddenly, his mother gasps. He looks up to see two men dressed all in black. The first man is pointed away from Nicholas. He's holding a shopping bag that suddenly drops to the floor.

The second man faces mother and son. He pulls something long and dark from his shopping bag. A gun. He points it toward the Lancasters. The beautiful blonde steps in front of her son as shots ring out.

Jax's voice interrupted her imaginings. "It's not the inside of the bag. It's what's on the outside."

Claire studied the shopping bag she carried. It was the store's usual printed bag. Nothing had spilled on it. "I don't understand."

"It's Christmas."

"Forever Christmas," she corrected. "My logo."

"It's a great logo. Great design. I'll bet people use your

shopping bags as gift bags. Great advertising for you, I'm sure."

"I scared Nicholas with a logo?"

"The gift bag. Red and green gift bags are a part of Nicholas's nightmare." Jax kept his gaze trained on his son as he rubbed the back of his neck. "The kid suffered a seriously traumatic experience when his mother died. It's a long story and not a pretty one, but the bottom line is that Nicholas associates his terror with Christmas. All things Christmas. 'Festivalisophobia' is a term sometimes used. The slightest thing can set him off."

"Oh. Oh, no. That's horrible. So the sights and sounds of the holidays . . ."

"Trigger his fears."

The repercussions of such a scenario spun through her head. "December must be miserable for him."

"Not just December. Stores start rolling out the ribbon and wrapping and music earlier every year. Nicholas's grandfather told me he took the boy into a big-box hardware store in September and walked right into an inflatable Santa Claus. He fainted, Claire. Passed out in front of the paint counter."

"Oh, that's heartbreaking. What can you do to help him?"

"I'm willing to try anything and everything. He's working with the best child psychologist in Seattle. He'll be going to private school this fall in a setting where we can control what he's exposed to. The hope is that with another year of counseling, he'll overcome the aversion before it's time to start school in September of next year."

Claire followed the path of Jax's gaze to the spot some fifty feet or so away where Nicholas was down on his knees digging with a garden trowel. Poor little guy. "That must be so hard."

"He breaks my heart. It hasn't helped that my obligation

to the navy kept me from being there for Nicholas when he needed me. I'm hoping that now that I'm able to be a full-time father, he'll feel more secure and that will help. He did make some excellent progress while he was here at summer camp."

"It's Eternity Springs. I'm telling you, it's a magical place."

"Well, you said the magic word when you mentioned your veterinarian's name. She and the swim instructor—a guy named Chase—worked wonders with my son. They helped Nicholas overcome his cynophobia."

"I don't know what that is."

"Fear of dogs. That has been another issue—all arising from the same event." Sighing, he added, "He's been so happy here that I'm afraid he doesn't want to leave. We had a . . . discussion . . . about it shortly before you arrived."

Hence the fists shoved into pants pockets, she deduced. "I think there is another, shorter session of camp coming up. Some of the local kiddos attend it as day camp. If the Rocking L has been that beneficial for Nicholas, perhaps the Davenports would make a spot for him."

Jax's mouth twisted in a wry smile. "I'm afraid Nicholas is thinking longer than a week or two. He wants to move to Eternity Springs."

Claire blinked. Her heart leaped, followed almost immediately by panic. *Wait one minute. Jax Lancaster can't move here. He's my fantasy man. The guy who's honorable and sexy and a good family man. He's supposed to be safe! Safe and far away. So I can fantasize about him.*

Maybe she should discourage him. She could say something bad about the town. What might work?

While Claire's mind was busy drawing a blank, Jax continued, "Celeste didn't help matters any when she mentioned that there's a town ordinance forbidding the public display of Christmas decorations until after Thanksgiving."

"That's true," Claire said. "I had to appeal to the city council for an exception to the no-decorating rule when I decided to open my shop."

"I tried to use Forever Christmas in my arguments with Nicholas. He knows about your shop. He said a person can avoid that part of the street in a town this small."

"He has a point." Claire's gaze stole toward the boy. "Eternity Springs is very traditional. Here, they don't do Black Friday. It's Deck the Halls Friday, and it's an official town festival. This town loves its festivals. Once the decorating begins, they go all out. Nicholas won't be able to avoid it."

Jax's expression went tight with sadness and frustration. "He thinks if he lives in Eternity Springs, he'll be better by then."

She bit her bottom lip. A boy's needs trumped her fantasies. She'd just have to let Jax Lancaster go and return to mooning over fictional characters like Nora Roberts's Roark. "In that case, maybe you should consider it."

"Even if I wanted to move him, I can't. He's in therapy in Seattle and I need a job. My skill set is specialized. I doubt I could find work in Eternity Springs."

"You might be surprised. What did you do in the navy?"

His mouth twisted. "I was a nuclear engineer on a sub."

"Oh. Hmm. That *is* specialized."

"So is the treatment plan for Nicholas, and I won't do anything to put his recovery in jeopardy." He shoved his hands back into his pants pockets. "I just wish he and I hadn't gotten off to such a rocky start today. It's not what I'd hoped for when I got up this morning."

"Which reminds me." Claire reached into her shopping bag and pulled out her gift to him, careful to position herself to block Nicholas's view. "I was going to leave this at the desk for you. Luckily, it's not overtly Christmasy so if you go ahead and open it quickly, I don't think it should pose a problem for Nicholas."

Jax gave her an unreadable look, then stripped away the wrapping paper to reveal the brown leather journal. As his lips lifted in a slow smile, Claire took the crumpled pieces of paper from his hand and shoved them into her bag. He traced the embossed star with the pad of his thumb as his mouth silently formed the word "Believe." "This is really nice, Claire. Really thoughtful. Thank you."

Then in a move as natural as a sunrise, he leaned over and kissed her cheek.

It was as perfect a moment as Claire could have imagined—and she had quite an imagination.

"You're welcome. Good luck to you, Jax. Don't forget to think positive."

"Every morning," he replied, and it sounded almost like a vow.

Claire's smile bloomed like the roses in the garden. She shifted the shopping bag behind her back, shielding it from Nicholas's view, and called out, "I'm glad to have met you, Nicholas. I hope you catch lots of fish."

The boy shot her a cautious glance, and upon judging that it was safe, stood and faced her. "I found sixteen worms."

"A treasure trove," she solemnly replied.

"The trout steal a lot."

"Trout are tricky that way."

The boy took a few steps toward her. "I'm sorry I ran away from you. I'm phobic. Certain triggers cause me irrational fear."

Claire's heart melted as she heard the adult terms coming from an eight-year-old's mouth. She cut a quick glance toward Jax, who silently mouthed, *Damn therapists*.

"Don't fret, Nicholas. Everyone has things that scare him. Personally, I'm a bit creeped out by worms."

He showed her a shy grin, then said, "My friend Dr. Lori told me about you."

Surprised, Claire said, "Oh?"

"She said you're putting Mortimer on a Christmas ornament."

"Mortimer?" Jax repeated. "Isn't that the name of that dog who was up at the camp this morning?"

Nicholas nodded. "The really ugly one."

"You're putting that dog on a Christmas ornament?" Jax asked, his tone incredulous. "The one with the . . ." He waved his hand, searching for words.

"Bug eyes and pronounced underbite?" Claire laughed. "That's Mortimer. He's so ugly that he's quite darling. I think our Mortimer ornaments will sell like crazy. Face it, the dog makes you laugh, and anything that makes the customer laugh is good for sales. I'm doing a limited-edition set: the Twelve Dogs of Christmas. They're all dogs owned by people here in Eternity Springs, and we're selling them as a fund-raiser for . . ." She hesitated. Proceeds were to be used to purchase new Christmas decorations for the town. Instead of providing that detail, Claire kept it general. "The Chamber of Commerce."

"That's a clever idea."

"Thank you. I'm hopeful that it will be successful. People do like their pets, and we will have a good representation of different breeds available. One of our residents is a famous artist, and she's doing the drawings."

Nicholas drew back his sneaker and kicked a stone into the creek. "What about Captain, miss? Will he get an ornament, too? Are you going to use Captain?"

"Yes, I am."

"Which one is Captain?" Jax asked.

"He's Mr. Chase's dog, Dad. He's a golden retriever and he's the best dog ever." Nicholas turned imploring eyes toward Claire. "How much do they cost?"

"The ornaments?" At Nicholas's nod, Claire said, "Twenty dollars. We are selling them for twenty dollars apiece or two hundred twenty-five dollars for the entire set of twelve."

"Okay. Okay, then." Nicholas sucked in a deep, bracing breath, then asked, "Maybe . . . do you think . . . maybe you could save one for me? A Captain ornament?" He glanced at his father and added, "For when I'm better."

Jax opened his mouth to speak, but Claire stilled him by holding up her hand, palm out. "I've been thinking about establishing a layaway program for my shop. This would be the perfect opportunity for me to put that idea into motion. Would you like to put a Captain ornament on layaway?"

The boy narrowed his eyes. "How do I do that?"

"Well, it's a little like a loan, a little like a promise. If you put a Captain ornament on layaway, then you give me a deposit of . . . say . . . a dollar. I take it out of my sales stock, and I keep it in a special section of my shop with your name on it. Every month, you send me another payment and I mark it down in my layaway book. When you have paid the entire twenty dollars, I send the ornament to you."

"Twenty dollars?"

"Yes."

"So if I paid you two dollars a month, I could get it in ten months?"

"Yes. Of course, you can pay it off early. There's no penalty for that. Also, the Twelve Dogs of Christmas ornaments aren't due to arrive until October, so you could delay the start of your payments until then."

"What if I'm not ready for it once I've paid you the whole twenty dollars?"

"I can continue to hold it for you."

"For how long?"

"As long as you need me to hold it."

"Really? What if it takes me a really long time . . . like until I'm a grown-up? What if your store goes out of business or you die?"

"Jeeze, Nicholas," his father said.

"I need to know, Dad!"

"He's right," Claire said. "We are entering into a business agreement, and it's always best to iron out any potential problems at the outset."

Nicholas shot his father a triumphant glare as Claire tapped her index finger against her lip in a show of considering the issue at hand. "I probably shouldn't commit to storing your purchase indefinitely because you're right, the business could fail or something bad could happen to me. Something good could happen, too. I could decide to move to Bora Bora."

"Where's that?"

"The South Pacific."

"Are you thinking about moving to Bora Bora?" Jax asked, his eyes gleaming with amusement.

"Not right now, but like Nicholas, I do like to keep my options open." To the boy, she said, "I have an idea. If you're not ready for me to send you the Captain ornament when you make the final payment, I could always send it to your dad to keep for you until you're ready."

"He's the one who goes away all the time."

Jax closed his eyes and sighed. Then he ruffled his son's hair. "Not anymore, son. You're stuck with me. And one more thing. Based on what I saw earlier today up at the Rocking L, I'm convinced you're not going to need to leave your dog ornament in layaway for a long time."

Nicholas looked up at his father with hope beaming in his eyes. "Really? Do you really think so? Are we going to move to Eternity Springs?"

"Yes, I really think so, Nicholas. And no, we're not

going to move to Eternity Springs. I don't think you need to move. I think you're doing great now, and you'll continue to do great once you're back in Seattle. I have every confidence that you're going to want to hang your Captain ornament on our very own tree this coming holiday season."

Behind the thick lenses of his black-rimmed glasses, Nicholas's owl eyes blinked back tears. Solemnly, he said, "Maybe I can. Miss Celeste says that if you want something bad enough to tell the angel inside you. She says 'From your mouth to an angel's ears.'"

"An angel's ears?" his father repeated.

Claire thought of Celeste and of her own angel room where precious little Gardenia sat upon a shelf. Reaching out, she touched Nicholas's shoulder. "This is Eternity Springs. Angels are our specialty."

Chapter Four

Autumn colors in the mountains make my heart sing.
—CLAIRE

SEPTEMBER
SEATTLE, WASHINGTON

Jax opened the box of books and grimaced. If he had to look at one more bare-chested cowboy, he swore he might just hurl. He couldn't believe the way those paperback books flew off the shelves. To hear Nicholas's grandfather talk, nobody was reading anymore and those who were downloaded their books from pirate sites on the Internet.

After six weeks at this suburban strip-mall store "training from the bottom up" per his ex-father-in-law's requirements, Jax was just about ready to call bull on that. This store was as busy as a brothel during Fleet Week. If even half of the twenty-seven locations of Hardcastle Books had this sort of traffic, this amount of sales, then the old family business was doing just fine—despite Brian's dour proclamations.

Jax acknowledged that Brian Hardcastle was a brilliant businessman. He had successfully guided his privately held company through the contraction in the industry and the digital revolution, and now the stores were thriving. By all outward appearances, he was a decent man, too. He loved his wife and had all but worshiped his only child. Now he focused all that adoration on Nicholas.

His interference was giving Jax fits.

Brian didn't hesitate to show the passive-aggressive side of his nature to Jax. He'd always been outwardly friendly, but from the moment Lara had introduced them, Jax had never doubted that Brian believed the navy man wasn't good enough for his little girl. While Jax certainly didn't lay blame for the failure of his marriage at his in-laws' feet, he knew in his bones that they—his father-in-law, in particular—hadn't helped the situation, either.

How it galled him to be dependent on the man. He'd like nothing better than to tell Brian Hardcastle to take a flying leap, but he couldn't do it. Not because he wanted this job, certainly. (Seriously, what did women see in kilts, anyway?) No, he had to play nice with Brian and Linda because of Nicholas.

The psychologist told him so.

Nicholas's schoolteacher told him so.

Hell, even his old shipmate and friend to whom he'd poured out his troubles along with half a bottle of good Kentucky malt during the man's twenty-hour layover on his way home for a two-week R & R had agreed. For Nicholas's sake, for the time being, Jax had to put up and shut up with Brian Hardass Hardcastle.

"Young man? Excuse me, young man?"

Jax turned to see a woman who was the stereotypical little old lady. "Yes, ma'am. May I help you?"

"I'm looking for the new Mallory Hart. The one that has the handcuffs and pearls on the cover? Today is its release day and I don't see it anywhere."

Jax blinked hard. Mallory Hart, he'd recently learned, wrote erotica. Seriously down-and-dirty stuff. Granny and handcuffs? He did not want to think about it. "Um . . . it's over here."

He led the customer to the end cap where he'd stocked the shelves after closing last night and stopped abruptly.

The shelves were totally bare. Huh. "Looks like we sold out. Let me check stock in the back."

"Thank you, dear. I preordered my digital copy and read it first thing this morning, but I want a hard copy, too. It's a wonderful story. Have you read it?"

Wonderful story? Damn, he thought, as his cheeks grew warm. Was he blushing? Was he a submariner or a schoolgirl? He'd been to the flesh pits of the Orient. Hell, he'd *sampled* the flesh pits of the Orient. Now a little old lady was making him blush in the aisle of his father-in-law's suburban Washington bookstore? *Dorothy, you're not in Kansas anymore.*

"Um, no, ma'am."

"Well, you should. I imagine even a big, good-looking fella like yourself can learn a few new tricks."

"Uh. Yes. Well. Excuse me, I'll go check for your book." Jax beat a hasty retreat to the stockroom. By noon, Hardcastle's had burned through its entire stock of Mallory Hart's newest novel and he'd fielded seven . . . *seven!* . . . come-ons from strangers of both sexes. It even outsold *The Christmas Angel Waiting Room,* which was flying out the door due to the promo blitz for the upcoming animated movie based on the story.

Fighting the traffic home at the end of a very long day, he muttered, "If one more person asks me if I'm a cover model, I swear I'll kick a kitten."

As uncomfortable as the situation made him, it at least served as a temporary distraction from his worries, and he didn't have an opportunity to brood further until the drive home.

Nicholas wasn't improving. If anything, since Jax's return he seemed to be regressing.

Their trip from Eternity Springs to San Diego and on to Seattle had gone well, and Jax had high hopes as they settled into their new reality. In hindsight, his first mistake had been agreeing to spend even one night in the Hard-castle home. Once Linda Hardcastle saw her grandson returned to the bedroom where he'd lived ever since his mother's death, she'd wanted him to stay put. Jax had had a helluva time prying him away, but in that at least he'd stood his ground and moved the boy to an apartment. He might be the world's most insecure dad, but he knew in his bones how important it was for him and his son to begin to forge a family. They'd never do that as long as they were both living beneath Brian and Linda's roof.

Not that Jax didn't appreciate the help the Hardcastles continued to give him with Nicholas. He owed them big-time. If they hadn't stepped up when the navy had refused Jax's discharge request, Jax didn't know what he would have done. They truly loved the boy and, heaven knows, that was important.

But Jax was Nicholas's father. He needed to *be* his father—a decision-maker, an authority figure, a disciplinarian. Wresting that job away from Brian was proving to be a challenge. It'd be so much easier to manage if Jax didn't second-guess everything where Nicholas was concerned.

The fact that he was so dependent on Brian didn't help matters at all. With any luck, he'd get good news about the job with Boeing soon. They'd led him to believe he'd hear by the end of the month, and the salary they floated would go a long way toward allowing him to snip some of the more uncomfortable strings.

Who knows? If the job panned out, maybe he'd be able to buy a house.

Jax had that dream for Nicholas. Not a big, fourteen-room mansion filled with leather and crystal and brocade draperies. He wanted a basketball goal on the garage. He wanted a house that a kid could run through. He wanted a sidewalk where Nicholas could ride his bike.

And maybe someday in the not too distant future, a backyard for a dog.

"Hey, nothing wrong with positive thinking," he murmured aloud as he accelerated onto the interstate.

Then, upon realizing what he'd said, Jax lifted his lips in a wry smile. The image of pretty little Claire Branham drifted through his mind—and not for the first time. He found he liked fantasizing about his chance encounter with the shopkeeper from Eternity Springs.

Wonder what she thought about cover models?

His cell phone rang, distracting him from his musings. He checked the number. "Hello, Brian. What's up?"

He expected to hear something about the day's record sales—Brian loved talking about business winners—but something about the pause before his son's grandfather spoke made the hackles rise on the back of Jax's neck.

"It's Nicholas. He's at Seattle Children's."

The hospital? Nicholas was at the hospital? Everything inside Jax went cold.

"He'll be fine, but we'll be here overnight."

"Why?" Jax's gaze flicked to the rearview mirror, and then he engaged the blinker and cut across two lanes of traffic in order to make the next exit and turn around.

"There was an incident at the therapist's today. He's been sedated."

"Today? His appointment is for tomorrow."

"We moved it."

Jax ground his teeth. He had arranged his work schedule so he could take Nicholas to his therapy appointment.

He bit back a caustic comment—he'd address the high-handed move later. "So what happened?"

"She tried hypnosis and—"

"Without my permission?" Jax shot his words like bullets.

Brian drew in an audible breath, then spoke calmly. "Technically, his grandmother and I are his guardians of record at Dr. Meacham's practice. You signed a power of attorney."

Well, that sure as hell is gonna change.

"Linda and I discussed it with Dr. Meacham at length, and we agreed it was time. Nicholas hasn't been progressing, and the Christmas season soon will be upon us."

Jax gripped the steering wheel so hard that his knuckles went white.

Brian continued, "Actually, there wouldn't have been a problem had Nicholas not hit his head upon coming out of it. The cut only needed five stitches, but you know head wounds bleed. The blood set off his panic attack."

Jax's lips formed a silent curse fitting of his navy background before firing off a round of questions. "When did this happen? How long has he been out?"

"The appointment was at one-thirty this afternoon. We arrived at the hospital around two-fifteen or two-thirty. They tell us he's not 'out' at this point, but sleeping."

"Two-fifteen." Jax held on to his temper by the thinnest of threads. It was after five. In a measured tone, he said, "You're just now calling me?"

"I knew your work schedule. Linda and I had it handled."

If Brian Hardcastle had been within arm's reach, Jax would have decked him. "What room is Nicholas in?"

"Seven twenty-one."

"If he wakes up before I get there, please tell him I'm on my way." Jax disconnected the call without waiting for a response from Brian. He stewed and broke the speed limit the rest of the way to the hospital. He parked illegally and didn't give a damn.

Getting to room 721 meant navigating a rabbit warren of hallways, and he took two frustratingly wrong turns before he found his way to his son's room. The door was open. Jax stepped inside. His gaze zeroed in on the boy in the bed, and his heart broke. It split right in two.

His little boy lay still and sleeping in the hospital bed, a big white bandage on his head and an IV hooked up to his arm. His complexion was pasty and pale. Vulnerable and younger than eight years old.

A whale-sized lump lodged in Jax's throat. When he finally looked up at Brian and Linda, it took every ounce of discipline he possessed to refrain from lashing out. The former naval officer managed a calm, even voice as he asked, "Did he wake up?"

"No," Linda said, her gaze soft with love as she watched her grandson. "He's been sleeping peacefully."

"I want to speak to his doctors."

"Dr. Meachum has already visited tonight. She said she'll be back in the morning."

"She's a psychologist. Who is treating the head injury?"

"I wouldn't call it a head injury," Brian began. His voice trailed off when the flutter of Nicholas's eyelids attracted everyone's attention. The boy started to sit up, but when he moved his head a grimace contorted his face. He croaked out an "Ow! It hurts!"

Linda and Brian both moved toward Nicholas. A week ago, Jax would have let them direct this little tableau. Hell, an hour ago he'd have held back and waited to greet his son. Now he stepped right in front of his boss. He brushed his boy's bangs away from his eyes and asked, "Hey, buddy. How ya doin'?"

"Where am I?"

"You're in the hospital, son."

"Am I gonna die?"

Jax said a definitive, "No!"

Brian said, "Don't be silly."

Because Jax believed that information was power, he added, "You have a cut on your head, and you needed rest so that your body could recover from the effects of the hypnosis."

Nicholas brought his hand up to his forehead and tears filled his eyes. "Daddy, it hurts!"

"I imagine so. I hear you got five whole stitches. The guys at school are gonna be impressed."

"Is five a lot?"

"Darn sure is. Want to sit up taller? You can raise the bed without moving your head too much by pressing the up arrow on this." He handed his son the hospital bed's remote control and guided his thumb to the up button.

As Nicholas and Jax searched for the sweet spot on the mattress incline, Brian and Linda both moved around to the other side of the bed. Linda took the boy's hand in hers. Brian set his manicured hand on his grandson's shoulder. "Nicholas," he said, his tone gruff with emotion. "I know that your Mimi sure would like to see one of your smiles. Think you could manage one for her?"

Nicholas's gaze shifted to his grandparents. He gave half a nod, froze, winced, then bravely showed a smile.

"Oh, baby." Linda's eyes filled with tears. "Look at you. Aren't you the sweetest little boy in the whole wide world? You had us so worried."

The smile fell off Nicholas's face, and his eyes grew round. Fear added a squeak to his voice as he asked, "Why? I am gonna die, aren't I?"

"No, sweetheart," his grandmother said. "You know me. I always get worried."

Nicholas must have accepted that as fact, because he turned his gaze back toward his father. "So I can go home to Granddad's house, then?"

"Tomorrow," Jax said. "You and I are bunking here at the hospital tonight."

"We'll stay," Linda began.

Firmly, Jax said, "No. Thank you. You've done more than enough today. I have this covered."

Linda got that mulish look on her face that always reminded Jax of Lara. He'd learned shortly after joining the family that despite Brian's commanding personality, the women of the family usually got their way. Linda said, "Jax, I don't think that's a good idea. Women do better with this type of thing. You go home and—"

"No. Thank you, but no."

"I'm his grandmother."

With that, Jax had had enough. He threw down the gauntlet. "And I'm. His. Father."

Chapter Five

*A warm blanket in the middle of the night makes
a hospital stay bearable.*

—JAX

His declaration hung in the air and, based on the expressions on Brian's and Linda's faces, totally shocked them. When was the last time that someone had stood up to them?

I damn sure haven't done it before.

Frustration seasoned with a dash of self-disgust rolled through him as he waited for their response. How had they gotten to this place? That was pretty easy to figure. He'd let these people run right over him ever since he'd set foot in Seattle.

No more. Certainly no more tonight.

He realized he'd won the skirmish when Linda lifted her chin with regal disdain. He recognized that snippy, I'm-seriously-not-happy expression, too. Lara had given him that look often.

Linda dismissed him by turning her attention back to Nicholas. "I guess Granddad and I will go home, sweetheart, but we'll be back first thing in the morning."

Jax shot a look toward Brian. "Isn't the plan for Nicholas to go home tomorrow?"

"What about school? Am I going to miss school tomorrow?"

"I expect so," Linda replied, leaning over to kiss her

grandson's cheek. "Hospital discharge often takes longer than one would think."

"Oh." Nicholas exhaled loudly and appeared to wilt with relief.

Jax frowned. What was up with that? Nicholas loved school. At least, he used to. Jax realized he hadn't been chattering about school as much the last week or so. Not like he'd done the first week of the school year. *I should have noticed.*

He needed to bring up the subject once they were alone. His teacher had assured Jax that the boy was settling in just fine with the new school year, but maybe he should probe a little bit.

It took the Hardcastles another five minutes to clear out, and when Jax and Nicholas were finally alone, it was Jax's turn to sigh in relief. He took the smaller chair in which Linda had been sitting and moved it closer to Nicholas, flipped it around, and straddled it. "Can I get you anything, buddy? You hungry?"

"Where are my glasses? I need my glasses. And yeah, I'm hungry . . ."

Following a short debate and consultation with a nurse about available options, Jax called out for a pizza. He decided questions could wait until after his son had his supper, so he showed Nicholas how to work the TV. They found an old black-and-white episode of *The Andy Griffith Show,* which for some weird reason was one of Nicholas's favorites.

The pizza arrived just as the closing credits began to roll. Nicholas sighed and said, "I like Mayberry. Maybe we should move there."

Jax explained that Mayberry was a fictional place.

"People seem nice there. It makes me think of camp. Camp was the best thing ever."

Ah. Now I understand. Jax paid the pizza guy, requested

extra napkins, then set the box on Nicholas's tray. He was pleased to see his son sitting up straight. Looked like the smell of pizza had made him forget about his headache. As they both helped themselves to slices, he suggested, "Maybe we can find a camp for you to attend next summer."

"Nah," Nicholas said, his mouth full. "It wouldn't be the same." He chewed, swallowed, then looked up at his dad. "Unless . . . is there another summer camp in Eternity Springs?"

"I don't know. But Nicholas, why would it matter where the camp was located as long as it had horseback riding and canoeing and mountain climbing?"

"Swimming, too."

Jax grinned at that. When Nicholas first went to the Rocking L summer camp, he couldn't swim. "Swimming, too. So tell me why it would matter?"

"It makes me feel better."

"What makes you feel better?" Jax took a bite of pizza and the spicy taste of pepperoni exploded in his mouth.

"Eternity Springs."

"Hmm. Well, then . . . let's see." He pulled out his phone and connected to the Internet. He couldn't fork out the money for camp today, but if he hadn't found a job that paid well enough to send Nicholas by next summer, well . . . hell . . . he'd swallow his pride and ask Brian to fund it.

"Okay," he said a few minutes later. "I see one camp. Stardance Ranch, but I don't think it's the right kind. What the heck is a glam camp, anyway?"

"That's Mr. Brick's camp. Dr. Lori said his camp is for adults only."

Adults only! "What do they do—never mind. Who's Mr. Brick?"

"He's Dr. Lori's friend. Not her boyfriend. Mr. Chase

is her boyfriend. Maybe her husband. Trevor told me they're getting married, but I don't know when."

Trevor was Nicholas's friend from camp. He lived in Florida, and every so often, Trevor's parents and Jax allowed the boys to talk on the phone. Listening to them was a hoot. Trevor was a little wild man. Jax knew he should be glad that the kid lived on the other side of the country, but the look of happy anticipation Nicholas displayed prior to every phone call made him wish the boys lived closer. The loneliness in his son's expression when the boys hung up hurt Jax's heart.

"I see. Well, buddy, I'm afraid that except for the Rocking L, I'm not finding any kid camps in that area. I think I should point out that we didn't know Eternity Springs was special until we visited. Maybe we should give other places a try. We might find another camp, another town just as good, if we looked."

Nicholas shook his head and spoke in a doleful tone. "There's only one Eternity Springs."

Jax didn't have a response for that, so he took another piece of pizza and polished it off. When Nicholas reached for his fourth piece of pizza, Jax quirked a grin. "Better watch out, kiddo. You eat that and you're liable to have to stay here another day because of a bellyache."

Nicholas froze with the pizza halfway to his mouth. His big blue eyes filled with fright as he stared up at his father. "Will I die?"

Three times? Jeeze. "No, buddy. No! I was kidding you. I'm glad to see you eat so much."

"Pizza is bad for you. Mimi says so."

The Lancaster boys had pizza once a week. Leave it to Mimi to always find a way to get in her digs. "Sure tastes good, though, doesn't it?"

"It's my favorite."

"I know, bud." They might just start having it for supper twice a week. "If you want that piece of pizza, have at it." Deliberately, he added, "A bellyache won't kill you."

Nicholas flicked a measuring gaze up at Jax, then took another huge bite. He ate all but the crust of his fourth piece of pizza, and when he settled back against his pillow, Jax decided his questions could keep no longer.

However, he wanted to work his way up to the tough ones slowly. Keeping a close eye on his son, he said, "So, Nicholas. You looked really happy when your grandmother said you wouldn't be going to school tomorrow. What's up with that? I thought you loved school."

His son's head dipped, and he shrugged. "I dunno."

Well, hell. Obviously, something was going on. How had he missed it? "So what's going on? You having a problem I need to know about?"

A second shrug. An added pout. "I dunno."

"Please tell me."

Silence dragged. Nicholas bit at a hangnail. He picked at the blanket on his bed. Although Jax felt the urge to speak and fill the void, he refrained. Recent experience had taught him that Nicholas would eventually respond. He was a boy who rather desperately wanted to please—something else that destroyed Jax.

Finally, Nicholas's eyes began to blink rapidly and Jax felt his desire for answers wane. He didn't want to make his son cry. It would kill him to make his son cry. At the end of his last R & R when he'd had to return to his assignment, the boy had stood at the Hardcastles' front door with big fat silent tears rolling down his face, and it had ripped Jax's heart in two. Climbing into the waiting cab, he'd promised himself never again. At least, not until his son had defeated the demons that his mother's death had brought into his world.

Even as the words "never mind" formed on Jax's lips,

Nicholas swiped his hand across his eyes and declared, "I don't like school."

Well, this is new. "Why not? What happened?"

"If I miss school tomorrow it'll only make it worse."

"Are you behind, Nicholas?"

"Behind what?"

"I mean, are you not doing well with your schoolwork?"

"I'm smart."

"I know you're smart. 'Smart' doesn't always matter where grades are concerned."

Nicholas plopped back against his pillow. "I did make a ninety-eight on a math paper last week. Miss Kelly took off two points because my eight looked too much like a three. But all my other papers are one hundreds."

The way he flung himself around his bed demonstrated to Jax that at least Nicholas's head felt better. "So it's not your grades. What has happened to make you not like school, son?"

The tears returned to his eyes. He folded his arms and accused, "They're mean!"

Okay. Now we're getting somewhere. "Who's mean?"

"Aiden. Jackson and Brayden, too, but mostly Aiden."

"What did they do?"

Jax expected to hear that they made fun of his glasses or his small stature or that they called him Brainiac. What Nicholas said floored him.

"They found out about me and Christmas. They bring stuff to school and surprise me with it."

The little bastards. "They're jerks. Bullies. Don't worry, Nicholas. I'll put a stop to that."

"No! Don't! You can't!" Nicholas said with a screech in his tone. "That will just make things worse. Promise me, Dad. Please! You can't say anything to anybody. Please!"

Jax panicked a little bit himself. If he were responsible

for bringing on another panic attack, he'd never forgive himself. "Okay. Okay. I won't say anything."

"You promise?"

"I promise."

"Good." Nicholas visibly relaxed.

Jax reached up and rubbed the back of his neck. Great. Just great. Now what did he do? He couldn't let this kind of bs continue. But he'd made a promise to his kid. One hard-and-fast rule he'd made for himself during the debacle of the divorce was that he would never, under any circumstances, break a promise he made to his son.

So what the hell did he do now?

He went with his instincts. "So, I guess if I don't stop this nonsense from happening, we need to figure out a way for you to do it."

"Me?"

"Yep. We need a plan. Those guys are being bullies, Nicholas. Everyone has to deal with a bully at some point in their lives—"

"Even you?"

"Even me," Jax replied as the image of Brian Hardcastle flashed in his mind. "Learning how to deal with a bully is part of growing up. Let me think on it a bit, and we'll make it happen."

"Think fast, Dad."

Jax reached out and ruffled Nicholas's hair. "We'll have it in place before you go back to Northwest Academy."

The hope in Nicholas's eyes all but did Jax in. He wanted a distraction before the kid asked him any more questions about this imaginary plan. Things were different in schools now than when he was growing up. His own father's advice to Jax about dealing with a bully simply wouldn't do.

Tackling kids and throwing punches on the playground led to expulsion in this day and age.

"I'm going to duck out real quick and see if the nurse can score me some sheets for my bed. Why don't you see what's on TV?" No way was he going to ask Nicholas about today's doctor's visit after seeing his reaction to Jax's "easy" question.

"Okay."

When he returned a few minutes later with sheets and a pillow for the foldout bed, Nicholas was watching cartoons. Jax bit back a sigh. Wonder how much this episode of *Paw Patrol* was going to cost him? Wonder how good the employee insurance at Hardcastle Books was?

Fatigue suddenly hit him like an eighteen-wheeler. He kicked off his shoes, stripped down to his T-shirt and slacks, then took a seat in the room's recliner with his feet up, ready to watch Rubble and Tracer and Rocky while yearning for some good old Donald Duck.

Immediately, his thoughts turned to his in-laws. He had two plans to concoct before morning. He simply could not allow their actions today to go unchallenged. Everything from changing the day of the appointment to making a decision about the treatment to trying to oust Jax from his son's hospital room—they'd not only crossed the line, they'd obliterated it. They'd refused to recognize Jax's authority and, frankly, his rights. This couldn't go on. It simply couldn't. Otherwise, things were bound to get ugly between Jax and the Hardcastles, and that wouldn't be good for Nicholas.

Anger that had simmered inside him all evening flared to a raging flame. No one could make him crazy like a Hardcastle. This was the second angriest he'd been in his life.

Lara still held the number one position, and he hoped like hell that nothing ever knocked her out of her spot. If anything ever happened that made him angrier than learning that his wife had run off with then six-year-old

Nicholas rather than let Jax have him for Christmas—per their bank-breaking custody agreement—then he feared he was likely to stroke out.

So what are you going to do about it?

Bottom line? Whatever was best for Nicholas.

He needed a job—one independent of Brian Hardcastle. He needed to assert himself when dealing with the Hardcastles. He needed to—

"Dad?"

"Yeah, buddy?"

"I don't think I'm getting any better."

Jax sat up. He leaned forward, his elbows resting on his thighs, as he studied his son. Nicholas stared straight at the cartoon, but Jax sensed he wasn't seeing the TV at all. "Because of what happened today?"

"I liked Dr. McDermott a lot better."

Dr. McDermott. Jax mentally ran his finger down the long list of doctors his son had seen during the past two years. "Your doctor at summer camp?"

"Yeah."

Dr. McDermott. What did Jax recall about him? Wasn't he the guy Jack Davenport had brought in who'd worked at Walter Reed with veterans suffering from PTSD? "He's older than Dr. Meacham."

"He's old. He's retired."

The seed of an idea that had just begun to form blew away in the wind of Nicholas's words.

"He told me he liked Eternity Springs so much he was going to move there."

"He did, did he?"

The seed blew back and planted itself in the once barren soil of Jax's wishes and desires, now fertilized by the manure supplied by Nicholas's grandparents.

By the time he made up his bed, kissed Nicholas good night, and turned off the light, Jax knew how to handle the bully situation. He knew how to deal with Brian and Linda. He just needed a few things to fall together. He'd start making calls first thing in the morning. By the time he drifted off to sleep, the seed had sprouted into a fully formed plan.

He dreamed of a field of red and green lollipops planted like corn. A puffy white cloud floated in a heavenly blue sky. From it rained sparkling, nourishing, healing . . . angel dust.

Chapter Six

Fantasies enrich your life.
—CLAIRE

Claire awoke in a full Grinch mood. Probably because she'd dreamed about lawyers last night. A lawyer. The lawyer.

She was lonely.

She didn't want to get out of the bed. She wanted to lie there with the covers pulled over her head and indulge in a pity party. Even as she contemplated doing just that—at least for a few minutes—her gaze fell upon the journal on the nightstand beside her bed. "Positive thoughts," she murmured. "Think positive thoughts and positive things will happen."

Maybe.

Probably not.

Life wasn't fiction. Grinches stay Grinched and Scrooges don't change.

Lawyers live.

"Now how's that for positive thinking. Not." She threw back the covers and climbed out of bed. She needed to do something to shake off her blue mood. Today was Tuesday. Nothing much was going on in town right now. The next conference booked into Angel's Rest didn't begin until Thursday. Traffic in the store would be light today. Maybe she'd close down for a few hours and go for a walk around the lake. Autumn leaves were glorious right now. The golden leaves on the white-barked aspen made the hills literally glow. Snow had yet to make it to the valley, but Murphy Mountain now wore a top hat of white. The Deck the Halls Festival would be here before she knew it.

Thinking of the festival made her think about little Nicholas Lancaster. She wondered how he was doing. She'd received another two dollars in the mail for his lay-away last week. She wished he'd said something more than "For my Captain ornament" in the note he'd sent along with it. Maybe when she sent his receipt back she'd include a little note of her own for Jax. That wouldn't hurt anything, would it? Just being friendly. Friendly was the Eternity Springs way.

She wouldn't have to tell him that he was the star of her fantasy life. Her very active fantasy life. After all, Claire was a girl with a vivid imagination.

She could see it now. *She'd be dressed in something filmy and flowing. Emerald green. Seated at a Queen Anne writing desk, a fountain pen in hand. In front of her, the same stationery that the Duchess of Something uses, a cream color with her name in robin's-egg blue. Dear Jax, she'd write in beautiful, flowing handwriting . . . poof!*

That was too much fantasy for even her imagination. Claire had never had pretty handwriting, much to her despair.

Amused at herself, she threw back the covers and climbed out of bed, feeling somewhat more positive about the day. She made coffee, then showered, dressed, and walked downstairs to open Forever Christmas.

The delivery driver arrived a few minutes after nine. Will Brodsky greeted her and added, "I have a truckload for you, Claire. Literally."

"Oh." Concern washed through her. "My market orders must have arrived."

"You obviously made lots of salespeople happy."

Claire recalled her spending spree at Market Hall in Dallas in March when she'd returned to town to deal with the sale of her house. She'd made a lot of salespeople delirious during her frenzied, emotionally fueled shopping spree.

The delivery driver went to work hauling in boxes and Claire tackled making room in her stockroom. It quickly became obvious that no matter how hard she tried, she couldn't find a place for everything.

Will pulled the plate of the dolly from beneath a stack of boxes taller than he was and surveyed the stockroom. "Sorry, Claire. That's about all that's going to fit back here. Is there somewhere else you want me to drop stuff off?"

She didn't have anywhere else. She bit at her bottom lip as she shook her head in dismay at the mountain of boxes yet to find a home. What in the world had she been thinking?

She hadn't been thinking. She'd been fury shopping.

What was she going to do with all of this stuff?

"I don't have anywhere else, Will," she told the deliveryman. "Just stick boxes wherever you can find a spot. I'll figure something out."

"I'll do what I can, Claire. Maybe if we stack them to the ceiling, you'll at least have clear aisles."

"Thanks, Will. I have faith you can make them all fit. You did a masterful job fitting as much into the storeroom as you did. You're a geometrical genius."

"Thanks." The twenty-something deliveryman shot her a grin. "I'm gonna tell my wife you said that. Just this morning she called me an idiot."

He spoke in a tone that combined offense and sheepishness. Claire took his measure and asked, "What did you do?"

"Accidentally left the milk out after my middle-of-the-night kitchen raid. I tried to tell her it was her fault for baking such a delicious cake that lured me out of our bed."

"Good try."

"It's true. Now I can't wait to get home and tell her I'm a genius. Of course, I darn well better not forget to stop and buy a gallon of milk on my way." He handed her his signature pad to sign, then wheeled his dolly toward the door, saying, "See you soon, I imagine."

"Yes, I'm afraid this is only part of my order." Claire sighed as her gaze returned to the boxes. She braced her hands on her hips and tried to figure out what to do with them. She'd bought enough stock to fill a store twice this size. *Real bright, Branham.*

Her first mistake had been going by the house. She could have—she should have—hired somebody to empty the house in preparation for the sale, but she'd had a few mementoes she'd wanted to be sure didn't get lost. If she ever found out just which of her busybody neighbors had ratted her out to Landon in time for him to show up as she loaded the last box into her rental car, she'd take up voo-doo and name a doll after them.

The scene still haunted her.

"Claire, honey. Where have you been? I've been so worried. We have to talk. I know it looked bad but—"

"No! Don't go there. Do *not* go there."

She would need to read her positive-thoughts journal for two days straight to shake off the funk of that particular memory.

She turned around intending to head to her checkout counter and tripped over a stack of boxes, catching one just before it crashed onto the floor.

"Stupid. Stupid. Stupid, Claire."

She'd have to rent a warehouse for all this stuff. Did Eternity Springs even have a warehouse?

She started to laugh, a small giggle that rose in volume and pitch that bordered on hysteria. Seriously, was there anything in Market Hall that day that she hadn't purchased for Forever Christmas?

Um, yes. You didn't spend a penny on Starlina, now did you?

Claire had enough self-awareness to recognize that her run-in with Landon wasn't the only reason she'd over-bought. Oh, no. She'd gone more than a little crazy at Dallas Market Hall because every time she'd turned around, angels had accosted her.

Live, costumed "angels." Angels in every shape, size, and style imaginable.

Claire had learned firsthand that it was one thing to tell herself she was taking back her Christmas joy and another thing to actually confront the angels and do it.

One certain pink-cheeked, blond-haired, sparkling and courageous and faithful angel, in particular.

She'd responded by whipping out her credit card and buying anything and everything that appealed to her. Now her sins had come home to roost in the aisles of Forever Christmas. Heaven knows it would take forever to sell all this stuff.

She turned at the sound of her door chime. Sneakers squeaked against the wood floor, and Claire heard Celeste Blessing laugh. "Oh, my."

"I sure hope nobody cancels Christmas anytime soon," Claire said glumly. "Not in the next three years, at least."

"Three years? More like five."

"It's pitiful. I knew I went a little crazy at market, but this . . ."

"In my experience, show specials are irresistible," Celeste said. "Sometimes I just lose control."

"Oh, I do know that feeling. What am I going to do with all of this stuff, Celeste?"

"Well, that's easy. You should convert your apartment to retail space and find somewhere else to live."

Claire shot her an intent look. Now, there was an idea. Considering the battle she'd been fighting with her Grinch lately, it might do her good to get away from Christmas 24/7. She couldn't deny that her determination to hold on to her Christmas joy was flagging. She'd just about had her fill of the holiday—and that's before she tackled any of today's arrivals.

"I recently did something similar at Angel's Rest," Celeste continued. "We built the little cottage where I live now last year after demand for rooms in the main house grew so fierce. I must say I do enjoy having a nest that is completely separate from my work space."

"I don't know," Claire said, despite the immediate appeal of the idea. Wouldn't decamping from her apartment be running away? Hadn't she sworn she was done with letting the Lying Lizard Louse send her scurrying? Wouldn't moving away from the shop be letting him win again?

No, stupid. He wins if you let him steal your joy.

Celeste took a seat on one of the boxes and crossed her legs. Claire noted that her canvas shoes were decorated with angel wings. "Correct me if I'm wrong, but last summer when we were discussing the Twelve Dogs of Christmas, didn't you mention that you'd like to have a dog, but that having one while you lived in an apartment wasn't your cuppa? If you lived in a house, you'd have a yard. You could get that dog you want."

Yearning washed through Claire. She had lost her beloved collie, Buttercup, the week before she'd discovered the truth about the Lying Lizard Louse. She did miss

having a pet, but they were a commitment. Did she feel
settled enough now to adopt a dog?

Maybe. And if she moved in order to have a yard for a
dog, that took care of the whole running argument, didn't it?

You're arguing with yourself, Claire. Get over it.

Yet, she felt compelled to make one final argument.
"Buying a house and getting a dog are big steps. I don't
know if I'm ready for that."

"Actually, I know of a place you could rent short-term
that would be perfect for you—plus, having you there
would do my friend a big favor. Bob Hamilton owns three
wonderful cabins in a fabulous little private valley a short
drive from Eternity Springs. He's named them the Three
Bears, and the valley is meant to be a family retreat. Bob
lives in New Mexico and his family is spread all over.

"He called me just yesterday to ask if I knew of anyone
looking for a place to live until spring break. Apparently
babies due to be born and a family wedding mean the
cabins won't get any use from now until then. He'd like to
have a caretaker there over the winter. I suspect he won't
even charge you rent."

"I can pay rent," Claire murmured. It sounded wonderful. It sounded like a perfect solution. "Maybe Lori Murphy can help me find a dog."

Celeste's blue eyes twinkled. "What do you think about
a collie? I believe that the Mellingers still have one puppy
available from the litter their Primrose gave birth to nine
weeks ago."

A collie? "You are unbelievable, Celeste."

Celeste put her hand on her chest and drawled, "Me?
But I try so hard to be believable."

Believe. That comment triggered the memory of the
journal she'd given to Jax with its embossed "Believe." She
wondered if he ever used it. She wondered what his handwriting looked like.

And why in the world was he on her mind so much today?

Because he's the fantasy and you don't feel quite so Scrooged when you're fantasizing, that's why.

Celeste patted her arm. "Tell you what. Why don't you humor an old woman and drive out to Three Bears with me this afternoon and take a look. I have a set of keys in case of emergency. No sense fretting over your delivery today if it's not necessary. If the Three Bears appeals to you, we can stop by the Mellingers' house and look at the puppy."

The temptation of a puppy sold her. "That sounds like an excellent idea."

"It's a nice, sunny day today. Would you like to ride out on my Gold Wing or should we take my Jeep?"

Claire had never ridden a motorcycle. Well, when in Rome . . . or Eternity Springs . . . "Sure. Let's take the Gold Wing."

"Fabulous!" Celeste's sunbeam smile lit up the morning. "Shall we make it two o'clock?"

"Sounds great."

So shortly after two P.M., Claire pulled on the helmet the older woman handed to her and climbed on the back of the Gold Wing. Fifteen minutes into the trip at the apex of a hill, Celeste turned onto a road marked PRIVATE and drove around a curve. Claire caught her breath.

Wearing a crown of autumn color, the valley was right off the page of a tourist brochure. It was not much bigger than a football field and a frothy, sparkling creek ran through its center. Three log cabins nestled up against the mountain. All they lacked was welcoming light in the windows and smoke rising from the chimneys. "It's gorgeous here," Claire said when Celeste switched off the motorcycle engine. "Beautiful . . . but cozy."

"I know. I adore this valley. I have to tell you I was

anything but happy when I discovered that it had been for sale and Bob Hamilton beat me to it. Wait until you see the insides of the cabins. Shannon Garrett did tile mosaics. They're works of art."

That jogged a memory. "I think I had customers who were guests out here. They talked about the mosaics."

"Let's start with Papa Bear, shall we?"

They oohed their way through Papa Bear, then aahed as they toured Mama Bear. When Claire began dithering between which kitchen she could most easily picture herself in, she knew she was on the verge of becoming a commuter. If one could call a twenty-minute drive a commute.

Then they walked into Baby Bear. It was a dollhouse, a dream cottage with a luxurious bathroom and a bed fit for a princess. "Oh, wow," Claire said with a sigh.

"You love it, don't you?"

"To quote Goldilocks, it's just right."

"So you'll do it?"

"I can't say no."

Celeste bent her fingers, blew on her knuckles, then rubbed them against her shoulder. "Am I good or what?"

The two women shared a look and laughed.

"I'll call Bob this evening. He'll be so pleased. Shall I tell him you'll move in right away? You can take care of the lease through e-mail. Bob uses the same one that I use for my rental properties. I can assure you that you won't find any surprises."

Claire thought of the boxes stacked in Forever Christmas and her mind began to spin. "Yes. The sooner the better, I guess. It'll take me a while to decide on a display plan for expanding the shop, but at least I can get the boxes out of way. What will I do with my furniture? I don't have all that much, but what I do have I want to keep."

"You're welcome to store your things in the Angel's Rest storage room. We have lots of space."

"Thank you. It won't be much. I imagine I'll use some of it as display space." As ideas started flowing through her mind, excitement began to hum in her blood. The smile that spread across her face was as bright as one of Celeste's. Impulsively, she reached over and hugged her friend. "Thank you, Celeste. This was a great idea. I'm really excited."

"Excellent. So, shall we stop by the Mellingers on our way back?"

A dog. A puppy. A collie.

A commitment.

Was she ready?

Claire nibbled at her lower lip. "Do you know if the puppy is a boy or a girl? Is it healthy? Are its parents well behaved?"

"I don't know the answer to any of those questions, but I know someone who does." She pulled her cell phone from her wallet and scrolled through her contacts list. When the call connected, she said, "Hello, Lori dear. I know you're a busy beaver with the wedding in just a few weeks, but would you have a few minutes to meet us at the Mellingers'? I think Claire is considering adopting their last pup, and she has a few questions." She paused and listened for a few moments. "Wonderful. Just wonderful. See you shortly."

When Celeste hung up, Claire spoke with a touch of panic in her tone. "Wait! I didn't say I wanted the dog."

"You haven't committed to anything. We'll just stop by to visit."

"The Mellingers might not be home."

"Barbara Mellinger will be there. Today is her laundry day. Her husband changes shirts twice a day and she still irons. She'll be glad to have an excuse to take a break. Trust me."

Claire thought that Celeste Blessing might be just about

the one person in the world whom she could trust without hesitation.

"However, I'll give her a quick call just to make sure."

Second thoughts began to plague Claire as they made the ride into town. Not about moving to Three Bears Valley. That, she knew was right for her. Her hesitation had to do with a dog.

She barely could manage her own life. How could she possibly give a dog all the love and attention that it would need? Yes, she would plan to take her puppy to Forever Christmas with her, but there were times when she'd be busy. Times when the dog would have to be crated. Especially a puppy! And frankly, was Baby Bear any better than an apartment for a dog? Long runs through a mountain meadow were six or maybe even eight months away. Winter was right around the corner.

Buttercup had loved the snow.

But think about all that fur. *You've been furless for a while. Do you really want to go back to dog-hair hell?*

So get her groomed. Daily. You can afford it.

At that thought, she snickered a little darkly.

She spent the rest of the ride testing the feel of possible puppy names on her tongue.

They arrived at the Mellingers' house at the same time that Lori Murphy pulled up in her fiancé's Jeep. The town's veterinarian, Lori was the descendant of two of Eternity Spring's founding fathers. Since her fiancé, Chase Timberlake, was a descendant of the third, their marriage would be a uniting of the royal houses, so to speak.

As Lori bounded out of the Jeep, happiness enveloped her like Pigpen's cloud. Her smile beamed, her eyes sparkled. A unflattering wave of jealousy rolled through Claire. She liked Lori very much. They were close in age and well on their way to becoming friends. But oh, how she envied Lori her relationship home run.

Not that Lori and Chase hadn't faced their share of serious obstacles. They'd overcome great odds—and a former fiancée—on the way to their happy ending, set to occur on the fifteenth of October.

Today the bride-to-be sauntered toward Celeste and Claire wearing jeans, a flannel shirt, and a smirk. "Okay, Branham. What's the deal here? When I tried to talk you into adopting a puppy from our shelter you weren't hearing anything about it. What does Celeste have that I don't?"

"Bears."

At Lori's blank look, Celeste laughed and explained about the new living arrangement. Unbelievably, Lori's eyes brightened even more. "You get to live in Baby Bear? Color me green. Baby Bear even beats Heartsong Cottage for cuteness. I guess the trade-off is we get double the Christmas cheer. This is going to make my mother very happy. She's a decorating fool. And then there's . . ." Lori tilted her head in Celeste's direction. "Is there an angel made that she doesn't own?"

"I'll have you know that just this morning I saw one that I simply must have in a new catalogue," Celeste said. "But enough chitchat. Let's get down to business before Barbara begins to wonder if we got lost. Claire, do you have questions for Lori before we go inside?"

She did. She asked Lori what she knew about the pup's sire and dam, their health history, and any behavior issues they might have.

"They are both good dogs, both AKC registered," Lori told her. "This is Primrose's first litter and it will be her last. The Mellinger children wanted to raise one of Primrose's babies so they waited to have her spayed. And they put a lot of thought and research into their choice of sire. I honestly think that if you want purebred collie, you won't do better than this little girl."

"Why is she still available?"

"I know this answer," Celeste said. "Barbara promised her to the Coleman family, but then Crystal learned she was expecting. Surprise, surprise. You'd think after four she'd know the signs, but this time, she thought it was menopause. Anyway, they decided they don't need a puppy and a baby."

"Isn't her oldest daughter pregnant, too?"

"Yes. It's their own real-life movie—*Father of the Bride II*."

"Loved that movie," Lori observed. She flashed a wicked grin and added, "I wonder if Mom knows about Crystal? Chase and I want to start a family right away, and I know Dad thinks Michael needs a sibling close to his own age."

"Nic would love that. I know she's been bugging her friends to give little John Gabriel a playmate or two."

Puppies and babies, Claire thought. This conversation was so Eternity Springs—and she loved it.

She opened her mouth to ask how the new mother was doing when the squeak of door hinges distracted her. She glanced around toward the Mellingers' front porch—and fell in love.

Barbara Mellinger walked out of her front door carrying the cutest little bundle of fur Claire had ever seen. "I'm toast."

"I expected you would be," Celeste said.

Barbara approached and said, "Hello, dears. Claire, I was so excited when Celeste told me you are a collie person, too. We are picky about who we'll let have our dogs. I know you'll give this precious little girl a wonderful home."

Claire started to open her mouth to say she hadn't committed to taking the pup yet, but she knew that would be a lie. She'd committed her heart the moment she saw those big brown eyes.

"She's meant to be yours," Celeste told her, the look in her sky-blue eyes warm, her tone filled with certainty.

"I think you may be right." When she took the little bundle of cuteness in her arms and stared down into big, soulful eyes, certainty filled her.

This was right. The whole thing. She finally felt as if she were ready to put Landon and his lies behind her and move forward. It was time to kick her Grinch to the curb for good and dive headlong into a fresh start—a new dog, a new place to live, a new . . . everything. Who knows, maybe someday she might be ready for a new man, too? The real, flesh-and-blood kind.

It could happen. Wasn't Eternity Springs the place where broken hearts came to heal? Maybe it was working its mojo on her! "I'd love to have her."

"Then she's yours." Barbara gave the pup a scratch behind the ears. "Would you ladies like to come inside? I have a fresh pot of coffee brewing and a coffee cake still warm from the oven. Not as good as your mom's, Lori, but not half bad, either."

"I'll have coffee, but don't tempt me with cake, Barbara. I'm on a diet until W-day."

"I can be tempted," Celeste said.

"Claire?" Barbara asked.

"Why not? It seems to be my day for indulgences."

Lori's wedding was the thoroughly enjoyable main topic of discussion during the twenty-minute coffee break.

Claire couldn't stop smiling as she departed the Mellinger house with a puppy in her arms. What a day this had been! When she climbed out of bed this morning, little did she think that she'd end the day with both a new place to live and a bundle of four-legged love to mother. Shoot. Today she was the poster child for the power of positive thinking!

"And . . ." she said dramatically to the precious bundle

in her arms, "the day's not over yet. Who knows? Maybe I'll run into Mr. Flesh-and-Blood before dinner."

The puppy—who needed a name—stared up at her with chastising eyes. At least, Claire decided to interpret them as chastising. "I get to do that because I'm your mommy now."

Her focus on the puppy, she turned a corner without looking where she was going and barreled right into another pedestrian.

Muscular, flesh-and-blood arms came around her and her gaze flickered up to meet hauntingly familiar eyes.

Her fantasy just got real.

Chapter Seven

I am my own boss.
—JAX

As Jax approached the intersection of Third and Pinion, he had his hands full. He had a stack full of files in his arms, a ringing cell phone—Brian, oh shock of shocks—and Nicholas was dragging his feet. They had an appointment at the medical clinic in twenty minutes to get Nicholas set up with a new GP, and after the events of last week, his son had decided he'd had enough of doctors. Jax couldn't blame the boy, but he wanted to get all these arrangements made before Nicholas started his new school tomorrow.

After all, it wouldn't do for anyone to be able to say he wasn't properly caring for his son.

Along those lines, his next priority needed to be finding a job that would give him enough jingle in his pocket to provide an upgrade in lodging from the Elkhorn Lodge.

"Dad, I don't wanna go to the doctor. I don't need to go to the doctor."

"Buddy, I told you Dr. Cicero won't do an exam today. This is just a get-to-know-you meeting and to get you signed up as a patient in case you stick a marble up your nose."

"Why would I stick a marble up my nose?"

"Why do kids do anything?"

He looked down at his son just as they reached the intersection, so he didn't notice the woman rounding the corner until she slammed right into him. Reacting instinctively, he dropped the files and caught her in his arms.

"Oh. I'm so sorry," she said.

He held her just a little longer than he absolutely needed to, and only released her when the puppy in her arms began to squirm. Her name rolled off his tongue like a song. "Claire Branham."

"Jax," she said, her luminous, cinnamon-colored eyes becoming round. "Jax Lancaster? You're here? Seriously? Today of all days I run into you on a street corner in Eternity Springs?"

Today of all days? What did that mean? Did she want to run into him? More importantly, did he care if she had? "Why 'today of all days'?" he asked.

"Oh. Never mind." Color stained her cheeks. "I'm babbling. Why do I always babble around you? Honestly, I'm not a babbling sort of woman! I haven't babbled since the last time you visited Eternity Springs."

She made him smile. Something about this woman simply lifted his spirits. "Well, that could be a problem for you," he teased. "Nicholas and I have moved to town."

A look he couldn't quite define entered her lovely eyes before she took another step away.

"Wow. That is big news." She shifted her gaze toward his son. "Hello, Nicholas. People around here are going to be so excited to hear you're back. You made a lot of friends around town when you were here at camp."

"Grown-up friends," he said with a shrug. "I wish Trevor lived here instead of in Florida. Is that your dog?"

"Yes. She is."

"What's her name?"

"Well, she doesn't have one yet. I didn't know I was

going to adopt her until just a little while ago. I haven't had time to come up with the perfect name for her yet." She paused, tilted her head, and studied the boy for a moment before she asked, "Names are very important. Want to help me decide on one for her?"

Nicholas pushed his glasses up on his nose and stared up at Claire, his expression deadly serious as he asked, "How?"

"Well, I think a name should appropriately reflect a dog's personality. For example, I know you met Mortimer last summer. It wouldn't fit him at all to be named 'Serenity.'"

Jax remembered Mortimer very well. What had to be the ugliest Boston terrier on the planet held a special place in his heart because he'd been the star of a presentation Nicholas had made to demonstrate to Jax that for the most part, he'd overcome his cynophobia.

"Dr. Lori said he'd eat anything. She said that one time he ate a whole plastic picture frame."

"Mortimer does have a reputation around town," Claire agreed.

"He shouldn't be Beauty, either. More like Beast . . . You know, from the movie?"

Her laugh rose on the crisp autumn air, and when Nicholas joined in, Jax thought it the sweetest sound he'd heard in months. "So true."

"What kind of personality does your puppy have?"

"Well, I don't know yet. We'll have to spend some time with her."

"Me, too?" The boy's eyes bugged out a little like Mortimer's.

Claire studied him closely to judge whether it was fear or excitement that she saw in his expression. Excitement, she decided. "If you want to help pick her name, then yes, you, too."

Nicholas shot a hopeful glance toward his father. "Can I, Dad?"

"Sure." Jax took it as a good sign. During the past week they'd discovered that Nicholas's progress had done some backsliding since the hypnosis debacle. Not so much that he feared dogs like he had before Chase Timberlake and Lori Murphy worked with him at the Rocking L summer camp, but he was cautious now.

"When?" Nicholas asked. "When can I play with her? Can I play with her today? She needs a name. A dog shouldn't go without a name."

Claire glanced up at Jax, the question in her eyes. As happy as he was to see a spark in Nicholas's eyes because of a puppy, he still had to be a parent. "We have a doctor's appointment we need to be getting to."

"And I have a full afternoon myself."

"How about dinner?" Jax suggested. "Nicholas and I have had our hearts set on one of the burgers they sell at Murphy's. I recall that their patio is dog friendly. Would you and the little one like to join us?"

"That's a great idea. Thank you, I'd love that."

"What time works for you?"

Following a moment's consideration, she said, "Sevenish is probably best for me, but I'm flexible."

"Seven it is." Jax smiled at her, then checked his watch. "Whoa. We'd better get moving or we'll be late for our appointment. Ready, buddy?"

"Just a second." Tentatively, Nicholas lifted his hand, reaching for the dog. He scratched the puppy behind her little ears and actually giggled when she licked him and nipped at his fingers.

The last doubt that Jax had harbored since making the decision to move to Eternity Springs disappeared.

"I'm glad you ran into us, Miss Claire," Nicholas said.

"Me, too!" she declared.

"We really need to go," Jax reluctantly said to both woman and boy.

Nicholas rolled his eyes. "Dad hates to be late ever."

"I do, too. I'll tell you a shortcut to the clinic from here." She pointed toward an alley halfway up the street. "Cut through that alley to Cottonwood. The clinic will be there on your right."

"Thanks," Jax said. "See you tonight, Claire."

"We'll be there with bells on."

"Bells?" Nicholas asked, worry clouding his tone. "Like 'Jingle Bells'?"

Claire's expression went soft. In a gentle voice, she explained. "No, we won't be wearing bells. That's just an expression. It means we will be happy to be there."

"Oh. Okay. That's good. I thought . . . well . . . you're the Christmas lady."

She lifted her hand, and for a moment, Jax thought she might tousle Nicholas's hair—something he hated strangers to do. Instead, she rested it briefly on his shoulder. "Nope. I'm not the jingle-bell-wearing type."

"Come on, Nicholas," Jax said, giving the boy's shirt a tug, then Claire one more wave. As they entered the alley, Nicholas began to chatter, as animated as he'd been about anything in a very long time.

Jax understood the boy's enthusiasm. He was plenty excited, himself. He had a dinner date with a beautiful woman.

Except, it wasn't a date. Not a "date" date. He'd have his kid along and she would have her dog and there wouldn't be a good-night kiss involved, much less sex. It was not a date.

Wonder if I'll have time to wash a shirt?

"It's not a date," Claire told the pup, who lay plopped in the middle of her bedroom floor, chewing on the dog toy

that was part of the welcome-to-pet-ownership kit that
Lori had dropped off earlier. "That's a good thing, too.
Dreaming about Mr. Flesh-and-Blood is one thing, but acting on it is something else entirely. I don't need to bite
off more than I can chew. I'm better off approaching this
fresh start with puppy steps. Romance is the very last thing
I need in my life right now!!!"

If she said it with enough exclamation points, maybe
she'd actually mean it.

She couldn't believe the star of her fantasy life had
moved to town. Claire was dying to know why. Surely
she'd find out at least part of the story tonight.

Celeste probably knew. Celeste seemed to know everything that happened around town. Curious, though, that
she hadn't mentioned new residents to Claire this morning.
That's the sort of news that interested everyone in town.

Bet the reason he's back had something to do with
Nicholas. That poor little guy. She'd thought about him
often, too. She'd even snooped around a bit, trying to
learn more details about his situation. The last time Cat
Davenport had shopped at Forever Christmas, Claire had
brought up Nicholas Lancaster.

"I can't disclose anything from his file," Cat had told
her. "However, much of it is public information. A re-
porter interviewed Nicholas's grandmother shortly after
the tragedy. If you're curious, Google 'Hardcastle Books
heiress.'"

Claire had heard of Hardcastle Books, of course.
That night after closing up the shop, she'd indulged her
curiosity. The news articles written about the tragedy had
been plentiful and heartbreaking. What Claire learned
was enough to give *her* nightmares—much less a six-
year-old boy.

None of them did more than mention in passing that the
woman's ex-husband served in the navy.

The puppy gave out a little yelp, and Claire looked away from her closet to check into what her new pet was doing. "Hey, little girl," she said as she scooped the puppy up and set her on the floor away from the bed. Handing her a different chew toy, she scolded, "Don't chew on the furniture!"

She turned her attention back to her closet. What should she wear? Something casual, certainly. She didn't want to dress as if this were a date. Because it wasn't a date. She'd let him buy dinner, but she'd spring for a welcome-to-town brew. She was being neighborly. That's what people did here in Eternity Springs.

She'd wear a sweater and jeans. "That says after-work casual, right?"

The puppy didn't pause in her mauling of the rubber toy. Grinning, Claire realized that when she wrote in her positive-thoughts journal tonight, she needed to include the fact that she'd no longer need to feel bad about her habit of talking to herself. From here on out, she'd be talking to the dog. "It's the little things in life that can make your day brighter, right? And talking to you will be even easier once you have a name."

She'd surprised herself with her offer to Nicholas, but the moment she'd asked the question, she'd known it was the right thing to do. He was such a sad little boy, full of yearning and fear. She sensed he might have suffered a setback of some sort in the weeks since he'd left Eternity Springs.

Maybe that's why the Lancasters had returned. Maybe they were looking for some more of that Eternity Springs magic.

"If so, then we need to do our best to give it to them," she informed the dog.

Claire believed in the magic of her adopted town. Of course, she'd believed in Santa Claus until she was eight, too, so go figure. Still, hadn't she come a long way herself since moving to Eternity Springs? Tonight was a prime example. A year ago, she'd no sooner have accepted a not-a-date with a drop-dead-gorgeous fantasy man than she would have gone out and bought a copy of that damned book. She might not be ready to trot herself into the cineplex in Gunnison, throw down money for buttered popcorn, and settle down to watch the most popular children's movie in America, but she darn well was ready to manage a nondate with Jax Lancaster!

Except, she wasn't ready. She was standing in front of her closet in her bra and panties. "Better get moving. You know the man will be punctual."

She debated between two V-necked cashmere sweaters, one red, one brown. The red one flattered her skin tone and hair color—she was one of those redheads who could wear red. The brown sweater matched her eyes and fit a little looser. "What do you think?"

The puppy just looked at her. Wonder if she could train the little dear to bark when she asked a question?

"The brown is probably a better choice. Not as datey."

Ten minutes later, she went downstairs carrying her new pup and wearing the red sweater, jeans, and her favorite red leather cowboy boots. She arrived precisely at seven and found Jax and Nicholas already there, hanging up their jackets on the coat pegs on the wall beside the door. Both males turned when she opened the door. Both smiled identical smiles when they identified her as the new arrival.

It did Claire's heart good.

Of course, Nicholas wasn't really grinning at her. He was grinning at the puppy. That made Claire's heart happy, too. "Hello, you two."

"Hi, Claire."

"Hi, Miss Claire. How is she doing?"

"She's great. We had a fun afternoon."

Nicholas frowned. "She's wearing a pink collar."

Unfortunately, that was true. Claire stocked dog collars at Forever Christmas, but they were all Christmas themed. Under the circumstances, she wouldn't have put one of those on her dog. She'd had to pick one up at Lori's, and sadly, her choice had been pink or pink. "It's temporary. I'm going to order one that suits her better once we've figured out her name."

Nicholas nodded sagely.

It took them a good five minutes to make their way out to the patio because the patrons of Murphy's Pub all wanted to see the puppy. In keeping with her plan, Claire declared the first round on her as a welcome to Eternity Springs. Jax carried the beers outside when they finally made it to their picnic bench.

Claire put down the dog and offered Nicholas the leash. "Would you like to be in charge of this?"

"Yes, please."

She ceremoniously handed over the leash and a bag of toys to a tentative Nicholas. The two adults didn't speak as they watched the boy and puppy grow accustomed to one another. When within just a few minutes, Nicholas got down on the floor to play with the puppy, Claire and Jax shared a happy smile. He lifted his pint in toast. "Thank you, Claire."

She clinked glasses with him. "You are very welcome, Jax."

"Pretty risky thing for you to do, you know. What if he chooses a name you hate?"

"I don't think that will be a problem. I'm pretty open-minded, and Nicholas doesn't strike me as someone who'd set his heart on something unfortunate. Besides, I'm an excellent negotiator. I feel certain that if necessary, I'll be able to talk him around to my way of thinking."

Jax snorted. "Don't have much experience with eight-year-olds, do you?"

"Is that a warning?"

"Let's just say you'd better bring your A game."

A giggle from the floor caught their attention, and Claire turned toward the sound. Nicholas sat cross-legged on the ground, his glasses askew, and his arms full of puppy. She was up on her haunches, licking his face.

"I cannot tell you how happy it makes me to see this. It's as if a thousand-pound burden has been lifted from my shoulders."

"Something happened since July?"

He hesitated, giving her the impression that he was deciding just how much to say.

Finally, in a tone low enough that the boy couldn't overhear, he confided, "Nicholas's therapist tried a new direction in his treatment that backfired. His grandparents and I disagree about his care, and the power struggle between us wasn't helpful for my son." His mouth flattened in a grim smile and he added, "At all."

"But you're his father. You get to make decisions about your son."

"Absolutely. But in their defense, they took care of him and made those decisions for more than a year while I was trying to get out of the navy. I understand how they found it difficult to let go, but it reached a point where I had to say 'enough.'"

She studied him over the top of her beer. "Let me guess. They didn't take your decision well."

He snorted. "Not by a long shot. Remaining in Seattle became untenable, and Nicholas thought Eternity Springs would be a great place to go to third grade, so we decided we are going to take a bit of a breather here and figure out what is the best thing for our little family of two."

So it wasn't a permanent move. Okay. That was even better for her. She didn't have to wrestle with the question of whether or not her own heart had healed enough to venture out into relationship waters again. Knowing that Jax's stay in town was temporary made it possible for her to dip her toes back into the water, so to speak, should he ask her on a date.

Because this was not a date.

Never mind the fact that she'd spent nearly half an hour deciding what to wear. And it did appear that he had shaved since their collision earlier that afternoon.

"Enough of my woes. Let's order dinner, shall we? Then you can tell me what's been happening in your world since July."

They all ordered the Murphy's special burger. Claire subbed a side salad for fries, and Jax requested another beer. "So, Claire, beyond a new puppy, what's new?"

Just then Nicholas let out another laugh. She shared another grin with Jax, then said, "The biggest news is that I'm expanding Forever Christmas."

She told him about her storage problem and the solution Celeste had suggested. That led to discussion about Celeste's angel collection and other general town gossip. Jax mentioned he had a meeting with the owner of the lumberyard the following morning.

"I need work while we're living here," Jax said. "Since I doubt there's much of a market for nuclear engineers in Eternity Springs, I'm going to try to get on with a construction crew."

"Oh? Have you done that type of work in the past?"

"Yes. My father was a contractor, and I grew up working in construction. I can do a little of everything. I like working with my hands." He shrugged. "Frankly, the idea of doing this type of work for the next ten months appeals to me. I'm hoping Larry will give me the inside scoop on who to approach."

Just then the door between the pub and the patio swung open and the Callahan twins ran outside. Eight-year-old Meg and Cari had their strawberry-blond hair pulled up into ponytails, and they carried big fat sticks of sidewalk chalk in their hands, their focus on the section of concrete floor set aside for outdoor games. Upon seeing Nicholas with the puppy, they came to an abrupt halt.

"Puppy!" Meg squealed.

Cari pivoted toward Nicholas. "Can I hold her?"

"She's not my dog," Nicholas replied, holding the pup protectively.

Claire knew a prime opportunity when she saw one. Tomorrow, these three children would be in the same class. The Callahan girls were live wires, but they had kind hearts. Nicholas's introduction to a new school would go just a little bit easier if he made friends with them today. Standing, she said, "It's okay, Nicholas. I know these girls. Their mother is a veterinarian like Miss Lori. They are always kind to animals."

"Is this your puppy, Miss Claire?"

"She is."

"What's her name?"

"Nicholas and I are working on that. He's going to help me name the puppy. Girls, I want you to meet Nicholas. He'll be joining your class at school tomorrow. Nicholas, this is Meg and Cari."

"You look just alike," he said, his gaze shifting from one girl to the other. "Except your freckles are different."

Cari nodded twice. "We're identical. You're the first kid who noticed our freckles. Our daddy says that's how he tells us apart."

"My mom called freckles 'angel kisses,'" Nicholas said.

Cari grinned at him. "Miss Celeste says that, too. Can I hold the puppy?"

Nicholas hesitated only a moment before handing the dog over.

"Whew," Jax said in a near whisper. "I was worried about that for a minute. Eight-year-olds aren't always great about sharing."

Claire opened her mouth to reply, then gave up when the girls' squeals went to fire alarm level.

"Whoa, there." Brick Callahan sauntered onto the patio carrying a beer and two soft drinks. "Put a lid on it, squirts. Our eardrums are about to blow." Then, catching sight of the puppy, he added, "Whoa. If that picture's not too full of cute. Whatcha got there, Little Bit?"

"My new puppy," Claire offered.

Brick turned to her with a grin. "Well, well, well. A new puppy. A fluffy one at that. Cool. You won't have to use fake snow anymore in your displays at the shop. You can repurpose dog hair."

She rolled her eyes and gestured for him to join her and Jax. "Jax Lancaster, meet Brick Callahan. He owns Stardance Ranch, which isn't really a ranch, but a combination campground and resort."

"Glamping. I read your Web site. It's an interesting concept."

"It fills a void in the market," Brick replied.

Claire added, "Stardance isn't far from the Rocking L. Brick, you met Nicholas last summer, didn't you? Jax is his dad, and they're the newest residents of Eternity Springs."

"Oh, yeah? In that case, welcome."

"Thanks," Jax said, as the two men shook hands.

"Sunday night is your usual date night with the twins. Is something happening on the baby front?" Addressing

Jax, she explained her question. "The twins' parents are expecting a baby any time now. Gabe Callahan is Brick's uncle."

Brick shook his head. "Nope, no baby news, but Nic is as cranky as Mortimer on bath day. Being the spectacular family member that I am, I sent them over to the Yellow Kitchen for a really nice dinner, and told them I'd have the girls to my place for a sleepover."

"We're having pizza and Coke for supper!" Meg called.

"And chocolate cake for dessert!" Cari added.

Claire scolded Brick with a look. He replied, "Am I a great cousin or what?"

"Can I have chocolate cake and Coke, too, Dad?" Nicholas asked.

"Sure. Why not?" When Claire included him in her scolding look, Jax shrugged. "Peer pressure gets me every time."

"Are we talking about them"—Claire nodded toward the twins—"or him," she finished, jerking her thumb toward Brick.

Jax grinned mischievously, and Claire's heart went pit-a-pat.

She cleared her throat and changed the subject. "Brick has done some building up at Stardance, Jax. He might know something about contractors in the area."

Jax's interest perked up. "You know of any crews that can use help?"

"What do you do?"

"A little of everything. I grew up in the business."

"Right now, all the contractors who work the area are based out of Gunnison, but I don't think you need to sign onto a crew. Eternity Springs needs a general handyman. Ask people to spread the word that you're available. If you're good and dependable, you'll find all the work you want, and you'll earn more doing it, too."

"That's good news. Thanks for the tip."

"Glad to help." Brick rose and picked up his drink. "Since the urchins are occupied, and I don't want to horn in on your date any longer, I'll take my beer inside and see if I can't hustle up a game of eight ball."

"It's not a date!" Claire and Jax said simultaneously with similar alarm in their voices.

"Uh-huh." Brick rolled his tongue around his mouth, then said, "Nice sweater, Claire."

She sensed the warmth of a flush on her cheeks and decided she'd find a way to pay Brick back another time.

Jax picked up his glass and met and held her gaze with a steamy one of his own as he took a long sip. "It *is* a very nice sweater, Claire, and I want you to know something. When I take you out on our first date, it'll be for something better than burgers, and I won't bring my kid along."

Oh, my. The pitter-patter of her heart turned into a *thump, thump, thump.* Thankfully, Nicholas threw her a lifeline when he stood up and approached their table. "Miss Claire?"

She wanted to hug him for the interruption. "I have an idea."

"I like ideas. What is yours?"

"About her name. What it should be."

"Oh? Well, let's hear it."

"My new friends Meg and Cari call you Miss Christmas."

"Yes, they do." She darted a glance toward Jax. Would this be a problem for Nicholas?

"I think you should name her something Christmasy."

"You do?" The suggestion both surprised and delighted her. It had to be a good sign for the boy that he would suggest such a thing, didn't it? "Do you have something in mind?"

He nodded and his glasses slipped down the bridge of

his nose. He pushed them back up. "She's bright and shiny and soft and she makes people happy. You could call her Tinsel."

"Hmm . . ." Claire folded her arms and considered.

In an obvious effort to buy her time, Jax repeated, "Tinsel makes people happy? Does it make you happy, Nicholas?"

"I remember when it did."

"Oh, yeah? When?"

"That one time the navy let you come home for Christmas. Remember? We decorated a tree and you bought boxes of tinsel and Mom called them icicles and you said it was tinsel and she said icicles and she threw a piece at you and you threw some back and we had a tinsel war?"

Jax slowly grinned. "I do remember that."

"Everybody laughed. It was fun, Dad."

"Yes, it was. We were all happy that day."

Listening to the Lancasters share a memory of a happy Christmas past, Claire's heart melted. When Nicholas turned back toward her, she said, "I happen to know that tinsel comes from the French word *étincelle,* which means 'spark' or 'glitter.' I think you're right, Nicholas. Tinsel is a perfect name for her."

The boy's face lit up like a Christmas tree. "You really think so?"

"I really think so. Meg, may I borrow the puppy for a minute?"

The little girl rose gracefully to her feet and carried the pup over to Claire. Claire snuggled the dog against her for a moment, lifted her to her face for a little nuzzle, then stared into those liquid brown eyes and said, "Puppy mine, I hereby christen you Tinsel."

Claire thought she would probably remember the look

of delight on Nicholas's face forever. The look on Jax's face was more difficult to interpret. Approval, yes. Gratitude, certainly. But also, something more. Something that sparkled like tinsel on a Christmas tree.

It warmed her clear down to her toes.

Chapter Eight

A puppy's kiss is sweeter than honey.
—CLAIRE

Jax's heart gave a little twist when he delivered Nicholas to Eternity Springs Community School for his second first day of third grade. Unlike the first day of school in Seattle, his son didn't drag his feet. Meeting Cari and Meg last night had made a world of difference to the boy, especially after they told him he could be friends with the Cicero family boys, Keenan and Galen. "They'll be so happy a boy close to their age moved to town," Cari had assured Nicholas. "Third grade has tons of girls."

So now, today, he hopped out of the car and ran toward the front door with barely a "See you later, Dad."

As happy as it made Jax to see the boy so excited about school, a little part of him did miss the "us against the world" closeness they'd shared since Jax had told the Hardcastles they were moving to Eternity Springs.

Watching his boy disappear through the school's front doors, it occurred to him that maybe he'd been depending on Nicholas as much as his son depended on him.

Jax continued to feel rudderless in this new world of his. Being career military, he'd had a clear picture of his course for a very long time. Now, he drifted at the mercy of the wind and unfamiliar currents.

Keep in mind that it's temporary, he told himself. These

months were his breather, his time to reset. His time to figure out how he wanted to best use his education, training, and experience. His time to forge a bond with Nicholas that would last for the rest of his life.

There's your rudder for the next nine or ten months. Remember that.

He walked into his meeting with Larry Wilson with his self-confidence restored, and when he left the lumberyard an hour later, he had a course ready to chart.

And a reward waiting because of it.

He strolled up Aspen to Third and headed for Forever Christmas. He'd been curious about Claire Branham's shop since July, and he finally had the opportunity—and excuse—to take a tour.

He knew the address. He'd looked it up so he could avoid the block when he had Nicholas with him.

He spied Claire's store easily. Other merchants had pots of red geraniums and purple petunias and yellow daisies hanging on to summer lining the sidewalk in front of their stores. The pots in front of Forever Christmas sported Christmas trees complete with lights. The awning above the shop's red door was striped like a candy cane.

Drawing closer, he spied bows and wreaths and window displays worthy of Macy's in New York. Strings of lights lit the place up like . . . well, like Christmas. Jax wasn't much of a shopper, but Forever Christmas even beckoned to him.

"She has a talent for this," he murmured as he reached for the doorknob.

Hmm. His gaze flicked to the store hours posted on the door. The door chimes played the opening notes of "Frosty the Snowman" as Jax stepped inside. His gaze found her immediately.

She wore a Christmas-green apron embroidered with the Forever Christmas logo over a Christmas-red blouse and black slacks. The combs in her glorious hair were made of silver and matched her star-shaped earrings. She stood surrounded by boxes. "Good morning, Miss Christmas."

The smile she turned his way warmed him like hot apple cider on a snowy day. "Hello, Jax. How are you this morning?"

"I'm doing just great, thanks. Nicholas couldn't wait to go to school this morning and my business with Larry went well. He agreed with Callahan that I can keep as busy as I want to be working as a handyman."

"That's excellent news."

"Yeah." He shook his head and repeated, "Yeah. It's a good solution. Not something I figured to do again after college." Dinged his pride a bit, to be honest. "But sometimes it can be good to go back to your roots, right?"

"Absolutely. Falling back to your roots can give you time to figure out which direction to grow next."

"I like that. So, care to show me around your shop, Miss Christmas?"

"I'd love to. But I have to warn you to be careful of the boxes. They're stacked everywhere. I've decided to close down for a couple of days while I knock this project out."

"That's probably a good idea."

"So, Nicholas wasn't nervous about meeting new classmates?"

"Apparently not." Jax shoved his hands in the back pockets of his jeans. "He wouldn't let me walk him inside today. Just ran off and left me behind like an afterthought."

"Good for him."

"I figure the big test will be tomorrow. If he drags his feet in the morning I'll know today didn't go as well as we both have hoped. Enough about us. Show me your place."

Claire made a flourishing gesture with her arm and

said, "Welcome to Forever Christmas. Honestly, the best way to see it is to explore at your own pace. My customers tell me that wandering through the shop is like a treasure hunt. I do have items grouped by subject, but right now I only have one dedicated room, though that's going to change. I sell lots of Baby's First Christmas ornaments and decorations. When I expand upstairs, I'm going to make one of the bedrooms into a nursery. I have plenty of merchandise to keep it stocked."

Jax listened to her words, but what captivated him was her enthusiasm. This was a woman who loved her work. She sparkled with it. He looked at her and thought of champagne. A champagne toast after midnight mass on Christmas Eve.

Beneath a ball of mistletoe. Mistletoe adorned with glittering tinsel.

When he realized that she now looked at him expectantly, he cleared his throat. "That's a great idea."

She beamed. "Thank you. I thought so, too. Why don't you look around a little bit. You'll see that I have merchandise stuffed—I mean displayed—in every nook and cranny in the place. I need to make two phone calls to let customers know that their orders have arrived, but then I'm flipping my sign to CLOSED and going into move mode."

"Need some help? I don't have anything else on my docket until it's time to pick Nicholas up from school."

"Only a fool would refuse moving muscle. Thank you. I don't have all that much. No heavy furniture. Just boxes. Though I should warn you there are stairs involved."

"Stairs don't scare me. Pianos scare me."

"No pianos," she promised with a laugh.

Jax tore his gaze away from her smiling lips and turned his attention toward her shop. He honestly enjoyed exploring Forever Christmas. She had created a homey world with evocative scents and sounds that tugged memories of

Christmases past from the recesses of his mind. She stocked everything from high-dollar collectibles to low-priced impulse items. Christmas china and linens set a sparkling holiday dining table. She'd arranged soft goods—towels and bedding—in visually pleasing blocks of color along one wall.

The woman had some money invested in this place.

With that realization came a faint niggle of unease. The last thing he needed was to get involved with another wealthy woman. He'd learned that lesson the hard way.

Not that he planned on getting involved with Claire Branham or any other woman, for that matter, while he was here in Eternity Springs. Nicholas needed to be Jax's only focus for a while. He'd have time enough to dip his toes into the relationship department once they settled somewhere permanently. Besides, it wouldn't be fair to anyone to start something that could never move beyond casual.

Unless all she wants is casual.

A uniquely lit display of glass ornaments caught his notice and he paused and read the sign. "HANDMADE IN ETERNITY SPRINGS. Visit Whimsies to see a larger selection of beautiful art glass." Jax tugged a four-color brochure from an acrylic holder and flipped through it. He wasn't much of an art connoisseur overall and he knew nothing about glass art or artists, but being married to Lara Hardcastle had educated him to some extent. He liked this Cicero guy's work. The pieces in this brochure were cool.

Hearing Claire come up behind him, he glanced over his shoulder. "It's nice that you advertise for other businesses in town."

"It's the Eternity Springs way. They advertise for me, too."

"I like your shop, Claire. It's festive."

"Thank you. I'm proud of it."

"It shows." Not just in the shop, but in her countenance. The woman glowed.

"Just wait until I've thinned it out a bit down here and have the upstairs the way I want it. It's going to be fabulous."

"Speaking of upstairs, want to show me what we'll be moving? Larry Wilson has a trailer we can use if we need it."

"That's nice of him," Claire said as she walked toward the stairs. "I can't begin to tell you how much I appreciate your help, Jax."

"Glad to . . ." His voice trailed off as they walked past the Angel Room. *It's a cross between Christmas and heaven,* Jax thought. Without making a conscious decision, he veered inside.

Angels, angels everywhere. The colors in the room were predominantly gold, silver, and a celestial blue. "It's like the parlor at Angel's Rest, only . . . more."

"Celeste is my best customer. I swear if I didn't have another customer until the end of the year, she'd do enough business to keep me afloat."

"It's magical."

"Thanks."

He folded his arms and studied her. "Do you believe in angels? Believe that they're real?"

For a long moment, she didn't respond. Her gaze drifted around the Angel Room. Finally, she nodded. "I do. Everyone should believe in angels because no one can deny that they walk among us. They're the people who nurse the sick and feed the poor and offer that kind word when it's needed. They're people like Celeste Blessing whose unbounded generosity is motivated by love. They are the people who bring light into the dark places."

"That's a broad definition of angels, but I get your

point." He waited a beat, then asked, "So what about the spiritual angels. Do you believe in them?"

"I do." She gave him a curious look. "You don't?"

"I did. I was raised in a religious family. When I was a kid I used to make quick glances into mirrors thinking I might be fast enough to catch a glimpse of my guardian angel."

"What made you stop believing?"

Jax thought of that god-awful day and that terrifying phone call. "If guardian angels exist, where the hell was Nicholas's when he needed one?"

Claire reached out and touched Jax on the arm. "I'm so sorry. I don't know all the details, but what I know of the accident is heartbreaking."

"I need to be drinking to tell that story. Suffice to say I've lost my faith in angels."

"Don't let Celeste hear you say that," Claire warned. "She'll make you her next project."

Jax's lips twitched. "I dunno. That might not be a bad thing." As Claire laughed, he gave the Angel Room one final scan, until his gaze snagged on something almost totally hidden behind an elaborate tree topper on a shelf.

"What's this?" he asked. He stepped into the room in order to see it better. Though she was hidden, one angel stood apart from every other angel in the room. She was a tree topper . . . and not a new one. Both the burlap overskirt and glittery silver underskirt sported a tear. Her silver pipe-cleaner halo was bent. One dingy white-feathered wing was broken in half. She was one bedraggled Christmas-tree angel—and the sight of her made Jax smile.

"I see what you've done here." When she returned a blank look, Jax nodded toward the angel. "You've created your very own *Christmas Angel Waiting Room*. She's Starlina. I worked in a bookstore for the past few weeks so I am up-to-date on my movie tie-ins. Clever marketing, though. Consumers are bombarded with Starlina everywhere they go. Your approach is subtle. You bring people right into the pages of the storybook. Bet you sell a truckload of those little angels."

"No!" Claire snapped. "She's not for sale and her name is not Starlina. She's Gardenia."

Jax could tell he'd touched a nerve, but he didn't know how. He lifted his hands in surrender. "Oh. Okay. Sorry."

She grimaced and gave her own head a little slap. "No. I'm sorry. My bad. I have this . . . thing . . . about that book."

"Apparently," he drawled.

She blushed, closed her eyes, and gave her head a little shake before attempting to explain further. "Gardenia is a family heirloom. I keep her there as a reminder to myself of the reasons I chose to move to Eternity Springs and open Forever Christmas."

Jax sensed some complexity in those reasons.

Claire continued, "Also, the commercialization of the book rubs me the wrong way."

"You don't stock it at all? I noticed you have a section of the shop dedicated to books."

"People can buy that book everywhere so, no, I don't stock it. I offer my customers the unusual and the unique, items that stand the test of time. The vast majority of my inventory is made in America, Germany, or Italy. A little in England and Ireland. I want to be the source for my customers' next family heirloom. Stuffed Starlina dolls are manufactured in the sweatshops of China and aren't future heirlooms!"

Jax thought it advisable not to mention the manufacturing origins of the Pez candy containers by her checkout counter, though even if he'd wanted to, she didn't give him a chance. Claire Branham was on a roll.

"And Starlina. What they've done to that character. The

way she's drawn with those exaggerated eyes . . . you'd think she was a sci-fi character instead of an angel. And the clothes they put her in for her adventures aren't right at all. Something different every page. You know why they did that? Not because the story required it. Because it enhanced the merchandizing opportunities. Now they can sell tutus and leotards and ballet shoes *and* cowboy boots and hats and flannel shirts. Flannel shirts! Who ever heard of an angel wearing a flannel shirt?"

Her snit amused Jax. Obviously, Claire Branham felt passionate about angels. He couldn't help but tease. "Well, what about those earthly angels you spoke of earlier? I'll bet Celeste has worn a flannel shirt a time or two."

Claire waved it away. "I'm talking about Christmas angels. Two different things."

"Ah."

"As a small-business owner, I have the freedom to sell what I choose, and I choose not to support that book. I will encourage my customers to try other Christmas classics that haven't been ruined by commercialization. *The Polar Express* is a perfect example. It hit big. It had a movie. It's still a charming story, unlike the Starlina show."

Another time, Jax might have argued with her. *The Christmas Angel Waiting Room was* charming. The message about the key to Christmas was subtle and sweet and appealing to both children and adults. That's what had made it so successful. Well, that and a kick-ass title.

Instead of challenging her, he tried to calm the waters. "I think a lot of people dream of owning their own business due in part to reasons like that. It's basic nature to resist giving up control, but when you work for someone else, that's exactly what you do. There's power in being the decision-maker."

"Yes, there is. Of course, along with the power comes

the burden of responsibility. And I'm not the only decision-maker where Forever Christmas is concerned." She ticked off names on fingers. "There's the banker, the tax man, the landlord, the city and its restrictions . . . I can go on and on."

"But you love it, don't you?"

Claire's gaze stole to the bedraggled Christmas angel hidden on the shelf. "Not always, no. Sometimes I can be a real Grooge."

"Grooge?"

"A combination of Scrooge and the Grinch."

"Ah."

"But I'm trying," she hastened to say. "I really am. And you're right, more often than not, I do love it." Then she gave a little laugh and added, "I'll love it even more once I get this move behind me."

"Then let's get to it, shall we?"

He followed her upstairs, enjoying how her slacks pulled tight against her shapely ass as she climbed the steps. He didn't feel a speck of guilt about his licentiousness. Helping her move should have some perks, shouldn't it?

In her apartment, he discovered she'd been busy since making the decision to move to Three Bears Valley. "That's a lot of boxes."

"I know. I'm not quite sure how I've accumulated so much stuff. My closets aren't that big. Of course, most of the boxes are filled with books."

"That sound is my back groaning."

She glanced at him in alarm. "You don't have to help, Jax. I planned to hire some—"

He cut off her protest by placing his index finger against her lips. Her full, soft, cherry-red lips. His voice rough, he said, "I was teasing."

She'd gone still. The pulse at her neck visibly fluttered.

Jax recognized that he'd made a mistake by touching her. However, now that he'd done it, he couldn't seem to stop.

He allowed his finger to slide, stroking her bottom lip back and forth. Her mouth fell open. Back and forth. "Do you like to be teased, Miss Christmas?"

"No. Yes. It depends," she replied, her voice low and breathy.

Jax chuckled softly. "You're quite a tease yourself."

"Why do you say that?"

Had she swayed toward him as she spoke? Maybe so. "You have mistletoe hung from every doorway in the building."

"That's not t-t-teasing. It's marketing." Her gaze was locked on his mouth. "Customers who shop with their significant others tend to love it. They linger."

He lifted his free hand to her waist. "I like to linger."

"You do?"

"Oh, yeah." He pulled her closer. "I've been thinking about lingering since last July."

"You have?"

"You ask a lot of questions, Miss Christmas."

"I'm curious."

"You're delicious."

"How do you know?" she challenged. "You haven't kissed me."

"Now, you have a point right there. But like I said, I like to linger."

He tilted her face up to him and finally . . . finally . . . lowered his mouth to hers.

Jax hadn't kissed a woman in a very long time, and he wanted to savor the experience, so he lingered as promised. He nipped and nibbled and leisurely explored, banking the rising heat her response triggered and keeping the moment within the bounds of a totally appropriate first kiss.

So when it suddenly caught fire, it caught him by surprise.

He wasn't aware of backing her against the wall. He didn't consciously tug the tie of her apron and free the knot, then slip his hand beneath her blouse to skim across the downy softness of her skin. She tasted of peppermint—*of course she does, she's Miss Christmas*—and smelled of cinnamon and made him ache. For sex, oh, yeah, definitely for sex, but also for something more.

For home.

For hearth.

For love.

Whoa. That last was just what he needed to shock himself out of the sensual haze into which he'd fallen. He shifted his hands back to safer territory and broke the kiss, lifting his head and gazing down into her upturned face.

The vision of her lips pink and wet and swollen from his kiss proved irresistible. He needed one more taste, so he dove in again.

The one more taste became a second taste and then a third. Only when it threatened to flare out of control completely was he able to release her and take a step back. For a long minute, they gazed at one another in a bit of a daze. When Jax finally found his voice, he said, "Wow. You pack a punch, Miss Christmas."

The slow smile that spread across her face was as sweet as a candy cane. "That's the nicest thing anyone has said to me in a very long time."

"That kiss is the nicest thing I've shared with anyone in a very long time," he responded honestly.

She opened her mouth to speak, but hesitated. A shadow crossed her face and her teeth nibbled at that sweet lower lip. "What's wrong?" Jax asked.

"I just . . . well . . . this is probably the absolutely wrong thing to say. Way too presumptive. But . . . after my last romantic disaster, I promised myself . . . you see . . . expectations are a dangerous thing. I don't ever want anyone to think . . . I don't want you to think . . ."

"Spit it out, Claire."

"I like you, Jax. I really, really like you. And Nicholas, too. Like I said, I know this is presumptive, but I'd like to spend time with you. I'd like to share more . . ." She waved her hand about, obviously searching for a word. "More. But I'm not in the market for a relationship, and I want to be up-front about that."

"A point of clarification. Define 'relationship.' And maybe 'more,' too."

An embarrassed flush crossed her face. She looked so adorable that he wanted to kiss her again.

"This is so not me," she muttered. "My definition of relationship is the kind that leads to a ring. I don't want a ring. Been there, done that, had my heart broken."

"We are on the same page there. Nicholas and I will be moving on next summer."

"I know. That's what makes you perfect."

"For . . . more?"

"Yes!"

"I think you're definitely going to need to tell me what 'more' means to you." If she was about to tell him that "more" didn't include sex like he feared, he might just break down and cry.

"An affair! Sex!"

God bless Eternity Springs. "You want to have a fling?"

Her flush deepened and she nervously twisted her hands. "Well, if the idea appeals to you, then it's probably something . . . okay, it's definitely something . . . I'd be interested in."

"Okay, then."

She held up her hand, the universal signal for stop, and quickly clarified. "Not today or anything. We'd have to work up to it. But if it doesn't appeal to you, that's perfectly fine and I still want to be your friend and I don't want it to be weird between—"

For the second time that day, Jax stopped her by placing his finger against her mouth. He followed that with a quick hard kiss. "No wonder they call you Miss Christmas. You've just given me the best gift I can imagine. I'm definitely on board with the idea and to make it official . . ."

He took two steps toward the nearest doorway, reached up, and snagged a sprig of mistletoe. Then he laid it in the palm of her hand and folded her fingers around it. He brought her hand to his lips, kissed it, and asked, "Claire Branham, will you do me the honor of being my mistletoe fling?"

Chapter Nine

*A positive thought? I'll give you
a positive thought. Sex!*
—JAX

Claire's pulse raced like a mountain biker's descending Sinner's Prayer Pass. She couldn't believe that she was doing this. Never had she been so precipitous and presumptive. Never in her life had she been so bold. The only explanation had to be that the man's kiss had short-circuited both her modesty and her sense of caution.

Yet, she had hung on to at least a thread of the latter because she managed to ask, "What is a mistletoe fling?"

"Whatever we want to make it." He nibbled her finger and sent a shiver racing up her spine. "Though, since it is mistletoe, I think we should include kissing."

"Okay." Her cheeks grew warm.

His blue eyes glittered. "Lots of kissing."

Heat flushed her entire body. "Okay."

"I really like the way you kiss, Miss Christmas."

Claire was foundering. She'd didn't have experience with this sort of . . . frankness . . . and it seemed that her brazenness had evaporated. Landon had been her first serious relationship since college, and he'd been Mr. Smooth Seduction, not Mr. Circling-Like-a-Shark while flashing a grin that telegraphed the message that he was waiting for the perfect moment to take a bite.

"You're a flirt, Mr. Lancaster."

"Not usually, no. You bring it out in me. You're fun to tease. You get the prettiest embarrassed flush on your face. Lovely color against that alabaster skin of yours. Makes me wonder if you flush like that all over. I can't wait to see."

She closed her eyes and swallowed a groan, then ducked out from beneath him and said, "I think maybe that's enough for now. It's work hours, not playtime."

Her thundering heartbeat pounded out the seconds as she waited to see how he'd react. She couldn't have said whether she was relieved or disappointed when he nodded and took a step back. "I respect a taskmaster. Where do you want me to start?"

She opened her mouth to say "the bedroom" but better sense prevailed. "The kitchen, please."

It was the easiest, most enjoyable move she'd ever made. They debated playlists for the worst music of the nineties and argued the merits or lack thereof of television sitcoms. Jax carried the larger, heavier boxes, and asserted his masculinity by fussing at her when she lifted something he judged to be too heavy. She tried not to ogle his muscles after he stripped off the flannel shirt he wore to reveal a plain white T-shirt, but doing so proved difficult. The man was built. Some of his time on the submarine must have been spent in a weight room.

She rode with Jax on the short trip out to Three Bears Valley. They exchanged casual conversation that helped her relax. The occasional steamy glance kept a nice little buzz running through her blood.

At his first look at the valley, Jax gave an appreciative whistle. "Now that's something right out of a tourist brochure."

"That was my first thought, too. I'm so excited to have the opportunity to live here for a little while. Wait until you see the inside. Shannon Garrett created these fabulous mosaics in the kitchen and bath and on the fireplace facade."

"Shannon from Murphy's Pub?"

"Yes."

"That baby of hers is a beauty. How old is she? Six months?"

"Five, I think. Brianna is a doll and Daniel—Shannon's husband—is so cute with her. Have you heard how he ended up in Eternity Springs?"

Jax shook his head. "I don't believe I've met him."

"He's a great guy and what happened to him is horribly sad." She gave him a brief rundown of the tragedies Daniel Garrett had suffered and his role in Hope Romano's happy ending. "He's a real hero to the Romano family. Everyone is thrilled that his heart finally mended, and he's found his second chance at love."

"You know, Claire," Jax observed. "For a woman who isn't looking for a relationship, you sure sound like a romantic."

"Oh, I'm a believer in relationships, and I love romance. Romance novels are my secret vice. It's just that relationships and forever-after are just not for me."

They drove the next two miles in silence until Jax observed, "The lawyer really did a number on you, didn't he?"

She reached for nonchalance and studied the damage moving boxes had done to her manicure. "The contemptible Lying Lizard Louse? Yes."

Jax took his gaze away from the road long enough to shoot her a steamy look. "His loss is my gain. If I ever meet him, I'll shake his hand." He waited a few beats and added, "After I've knocked him on his ass."

"My hero," Claire said with a smile. Jax Lancaster was good for her psyche.

After they moved her boxes into Baby Bear with Jax

toted the majority of her books up to the cabin's attic, God bless him, they returned to Forever Christmas where he insisted on helping tote the boxes that she needed upstairs up to her former apartment.

He trapped her twice beneath the mistletoe and kissed her senseless. Claire was happily anticipating a third time when he got a cell phone call and his first official job as Eternity Springs's new handyman.

"Gotta go," he told her, catching her hand in his. "Larry has hooked me up with somebody who needs a faucet installed."

"I can't thank you enough for your help, Jax."

"I enjoyed it." He skimmed his finger down her nose. "I discovered my newest favorite plant."

"Mistletoe can kill its host, you know."

"Yeah, but what a way to go."

He gave her a thorough good-bye kiss and grabbed his flannel shirt and headed for the front door. Once she recovered enough to think again, she hurried after him. "Jax? Let me thank you for your help today. How about I cook dinner for you and Nicholas?"

"We would never turn down a home-cooked meal. When?"

She considered the question. "Give me today and tomorrow to get settled. Friday?"

"It's a date," he said. Then with amusement glimmering in his eyes he added, "Although, that was a poor choice of words. This meal won't be a date, either, since I'll have Nicholas with me. And, you invited me rather than vice versa."

"I can invite you on a date," she protested.

"Absolutely. And I hope you will. Just not for our first date. I'd have to turn in my man card."

"Now that's being chauvinistic, Jax Lancaster."

"I'm a traditionalist about some things, Miss Christmas.

Fair warning." He gave a wave, and then the door chime sounded as he exited the shop.

Claire returned to her boxes and floated along in a happy daze for hours. If a soft little voice whispered in her ear to be careful, that she wasn't cut out for mistletoe flings and she was setting herself up for heartache, well, she did her best to ignore it. By mid-afternoon, she had three-fourths of the apartment converted to showroom, and she decided she'd shift her attention to settling into Baby Bear.

She set up her kitchen, made up her bed, and unboxed about half of her books before declaring that she'd done enough work for the day. Then she poured herself a glass of wine and took Tinsel out to play.

For supper, she decided to grill a steak. "I want to test out the gas grill before we have our first dinner guests," she told Tinsel. "Although I might actually cook something. Maybe Tuscan chicken. Nothing smells better than rosemary and garlic sautéing in olive oil."

And she wouldn't need to worry about garlic breath and . . . mistletoe . . . since Nicholas would be there.

Happy with her decision, her dinner, her life, Claire switched on the gas fireplace, chose a book from her to-be-read stack, cuddled Tinsel in her lap, and settled down to lose herself in a swashbuckling pirate historical romance. She hadn't enjoyed a day so much in a very long time.

It established a pattern for the next week. Claire had fun rearranging Forever Christmas, and she fell more in love daily with Tinsel. Chewing proved to be a bit of a problem, but house training was going better than she'd expected, so all was good.

After much debate, she stuck with steaks the night Jax and Nicholas came to dinner. Good thing, too, since Jax didn't let the lack of mistletoe stop him from taking advantage of his son's rapt attention on the puppy to steal a kiss.

That Saturday, despite the fact that for a rare weekend, Angel's Rest wasn't hosting a conference or wedding or other event that brought tourists to town, Forever Christmas had its biggest sales day ever. Maybe her buying craze at the summer market wouldn't turn out to have been such a disaster after all.

The excitement didn't stop there. On Wednesday, she was on a ladder in her Angel Room dusting the ornaments in preparation for the day when someone pounded on the front door of her shop. "What in the world?" She glanced at her Christmas cuckoo clock. Nine-fifty. She didn't open until ten.

Knock. Knock. Knock.

"Just a moment," she called, more than a little annoyed as she descended the ladder. Who was in such a hurry today?

Walking toward the front of the shop, she spied a familiar figure through the glass. She stepped up her pace, threw the lock, and opened the door. Brick Callahan looked tired and disheveled, and he had a red stain on the front of his shirt. "Oh, Brick. What happened? Sit down, let me get the first-aid kit."

"I don't need first aid."

"But you're bleeding!"

"Bleeding?" he repeated, frowning in confusion. When she gestured toward his shirt, he glanced down. "Oh. No. That's not blood. Strawberry Kool-Aid. I've been babysitting the monsters while Nic and Gabe were busy bringing another one into the world."

Relief washed over her. "Oh! Nic had her baby?"

Though his eyes remained tired, his smile flashed bright as lightning. "Yep. John Gabriel Callahan, Jr., arrived safe and sound twenty minutes ago, weighing in at a hefty eight pounds, twelve ounces." He picked Claire up, spun her around, and kissed her hard on the mouth. "We have another Callahan man to unleash upon the world!"

Her friend's joy was infectious, and Claire laughed and returned his hug. It wasn't until he set her back on her feet that she saw someone had been watching the exchange.

With arms folded. And wearing a scowl.

She wiggled her fingers. "Hi, Jax."

Jax knew he had no right to be so pissed at the sight of Claire with her mouth on another man. Nevertheless, he wanted to march forward and demand that the cowboy get his hands off Jax's mistletoe. Instead, he drawled, "Am I interrupting?"

Callahan turned toward him with a wide smile and not a glimmer of guilt. "Lancaster! Here, I have something for you."

He reached into his pocket and pulled out a cigar and handed it to Jax. "I have a new cousin to celebrate. I know that handing out cigars is usually the father's job, but Gabe asked me to help spread the word, and my grandfather sent about a million of the things to pass out. You want one, Claire? I know some women are into cigars these days."

"Not me. No, thank you."

The baby news mollified Jax. He wouldn't begrudge a friend a celebratory kiss—even if it was a shade too . . . enthusiastic. "Congratulations, Callahan."

Claire asked, "Speaking of your grandfather, I thought Gabe and Nic were going to name the baby after him?"

"They originally intended to do that, but once Branch got word of it, he put the kibosh on the idea. Said it felt like a memorial, and he wasn't on the wrong side of the grass yet."

Claire laughed and explained to Jax. "Branch Callahan is a rancher and oilman from Texas, and the best example of a lovable old curmudgeon I've ever met."

"That reminds me," Brick said. "Word around town is that you might be interested in doing some finish work we need done out at the North Forty, Lancaster. If you've got time in the next few days, I'd like to get your bid."

Another job. *Yes.* With that he felt a little more generous toward the man. "The North Forty?"

"It's the family's summer retreat out at Hummingbird Lake. My uncles work together to build something every summer. This year's project was a dance hall, and as usual, the scope of the thing grew while they were building it. They didn't get it finished. I have my hands full with Stardance, so I don't have time to mess with it."

"I'd be happy to take a look at it. How about tomorrow morning after I drop my son off at school?"

"That'd be great." As Callahan gave him directions to the property, he spied someone else with whom he wanted to share news about the baby. He handed Jax a second cigar and moved on.

Jax arched an eyebrow toward Claire. "So, Miss Christmas. You share your mistletoe often?"

She scolded him with a look. "Actually, at least once a day. Mr. Pritchett stops by for his kiss every afternoon."

The look in her eyes challenged him to ask, so he obliged her by guessing, "How old is Mr. Pritchett?"

She wrinkled her nose, obviously unhappy that he'd guessed her ploy. "Ninety-two this month."

"You vixen, you."

Now she rolled her eyes and headed back inside, calling over her shoulder, "What brings you by this crisp autumn morning, Mr. Lancaster?"

"Two things." He caught up with her, snagged her hand, then pulled her beneath the nearest doorway. "This." He kissed her thoroughly, and his tone was husky as he added, "And this. Nicholas has been invited to a birthday party on Friday the fourteenth. I won't have to pick him up until ten. So, Claire, would you like to go to dinner with me that evening?"

"A date."

"Yeah. A real, honest-to-goodness, official date. Our first. I know it's still a couple weeks away, but I worried your social calendar might fill up."

Her smile bloomed like a daffodil in spring. "I'm free on the fourteenth, and I'd love to go to dinner with you then."

"Excellent." He kissed her once more, then said, "I've gotta run. I have a job at Vistas Art Gallery today, and if I'm not mistaken, you have an angel waiting at your door."

Claire twisted her head around to see Celeste with her hands cupped against the glass, peering inside Forever Christmas. She rapped firmly on the door.

"Now I'm embarrassed," she said. "She'll tease me mercilessly, you know."

"Maybe I'll stick around and watch for a minute." Jax stuck his hands in his pockets. "I do love to see you blush."

She made a strangled sound, then opened the door. "Good morning, Celeste. Sorry I'm a few minutes late opening but—"

"Claire, dear. I have troubling news. I was having coffee with Savannah and Zach this morning when Zach got a call. Do you have Tinsel with you today?"

"No. Why?"

"Oh, dear. I hate to be the bearer of bad news, but there's a fire out at the Three Bears."

Chapter Ten

*I never realized that positive thoughts
could offer a lifeline.*
—CLAIRE

"Wildfire season is over!" Claire exclaimed, certain there had to be a mistake. Before the sentence left her mouth, Jax was out the door.

Celeste said, "I know. I'm not sure it's a wildfire. Honey, could you have left something on in Baby Bear that might have malfunctioned? The gas fireplace?"

"No." Claire hurried toward her checkout counter where she kept her purse and keys. "I haven't used it in days. I didn't even make coffee this morning. I have to get out there. I have to get to Tinsel."

"Yes, but first we should stop by the sheriff's office and tell the dispatcher to radio Zach and let him know that Tinsel is inside Baby Bear."

"Do you know his number? I'll call him."

"Better to use the radio," Celeste advised, her bright blue eyes dimmed with concern. "His phone is sure to be tied up. With a volunteer fire department, that tends to happen—no matter how much training our people receive."

Claire was startled to hear the wail of a fire engine as she hurried out to her parking spot in the back of the building. The sheriff's office was only a short walk away, but she'd take her car so that she could head up to the valley right after delivering her news.

She was scared to death for her puppy. Fires were horrible things. She'd never forget the time a house burned across the street from the home where she'd grown up in a north Dallas neighborhood. It had happened fast, the result of a lightning strike during a springtime thunderstorm. No one had died in the fire, thank God. The owner's dog had alerted the family to smoke that had begun to pour from the second-story attic while they ate their supper down in the first-floor kitchen. Everyone made it safely out of the house—though with seconds to spare.

Claire and her parents and her younger sister, Michelle, had stood on their front lawn and watched flames envelop the house as firefighters fought a losing battle to save it.

Within half an hour, it was over. Claire would never forget the devastation on the neighbors' faces as they viewed the smoldering ruins.

It was a twenty-minute drive to Three Bears. What would she find upon her arrival? Fear wrapped a noose around her throat. *I never should have left Tinsel crated. I don't care what the experts say. I'm not doing it again. I'll keep a crate at the shop.*

Celeste followed on her heels and climbed into the passenger seat of Claire's SUV. They delivered the message to the dispatcher in less than five minutes.

Five minutes seemed to take five hours when a fire was burning. The twenty minutes up to Three Bears took a lifetime.

"Who discovered the fire?" she asked Celeste as they took the first hairpin turn on the road to Three Bears.

"Cole Hoelscher's wife gave him a drone for their anniversary, and he was taking it up to Lover's Leap to fly. He spotted smoke, checked it out, and called it in."

"Was he sure that it was Baby Bear that's on fire?"

"No. He said the big house, so I'm assuming it's Papa Bear. Hopefully, that's all that is involved."

"Okay. Good. That's good." Claire found that bit of news reassuring. "I'll bet Tinsel is scared to death."

Celeste didn't speak, but reached over and gave Claire's leg a comforting pat.

Claire's car was one of a line of vehicles heading up to Three Bears Valley as members of the volunteer fire department responded to the call. She was glad to see them, but she really wished that she were in the front of the pack instead of the middle. She'd have driven a lot faster if she were leading the way.

She held her breath as they finally approached the curve in the road that provided the first look down into the valley. *Please, God. Let Tinsel be okay.*

The car rounded the curve. Claire's gaze went straight to Baby Bear. "Oh, dear God. No."

The roof was on fire.

"It's arson," Jax said to Sheriff Zach Turner. He'd arrived at the scene moments after the sheriff and before the fire truck.

"Yep. Has to be. All three places are on fire."

"How far out is the pump engine?"

"Four minutes, they say."

Jax looked at the flames climbing across the roof of Baby Bear. "Claire's dog is in the small one. I don't think we can wait on gear."

The blanket Nicholas had used to cuddle beneath on their trip from Washington was still in the backseat of Jax's truck. He grabbed it and a hammer and headed for the creek.

"Wait a minute, Lancaster," Zach called. "I'll go. I've had training."

Running toward Baby Bear with a soaked blanket in his arms, Jax called, "Me, too! I lived on a nuclear submarine. We had fire training all the damned time!"

That rescuing a puppy from a burning building hadn't been part of that training wasn't something he wanted to dwell on at the moment.

He hoped like hell that whoever had built these cabins had used fire-retardant shingles. Smoke figured to be the biggest problem at this stage of the game. He also hoped like hell that she hadn't moved the spot where she kept Tinsel's crate since his previous visit. Jax needed to get in and get out without any delays.

"At least the place is small," he muttered to himself as he covered the last few yards to Baby Bear, dread slithering through him at the possibility of what he'd find. He prayed he wouldn't be forced to make a terrible choice, but as Nicholas's only living parent, he couldn't be reckless.

A glance through the window reassured him. A little hazy, but no visible flames. Draping the wet blanket around him, Jax decided to try the door before he broke the window. He gave it two sharp kicks and sprung the lock.

He heard Tinsel's whimpers the moment he stepped inside, and he breathed an inward sigh of relief. He wouldn't have wanted to face either Claire or Nicholas if the pup had suffocated in her crate.

Keeping low, he made his way to the crate and in less than a minute and without incident emerged safely from Baby Bear with a shaking puppy in his arms.

"Damn, man," Zach Turner said. "That scared the crap out of me. I hate fire."

"Me, too." Jax's response was heartfelt. But even as he stood in the safe morning sunshine scratching Tinsel behind her ears, his gaze strayed back to the cabin where flames continued to spread across the roof.

Zach said, "We're gonna work this from the least engaged property to the most. Tackle Mama Bear first, then come here."

Jax thought of all those boxes of books he'd hauled up

to the attic. She hadn't brought much else. The books must be a treasure of hers. *She's going to lose them.*

Well, better books than her puppy.

He remembered the one box marked "Favorites" that she'd asked him to carry to her bedroom. Dare he try?

Make up your mind. Every second counts.

He shoved the dog toward the sheriff. "Hold her a moment, please."

As he headed back toward Baby Bear, he heard Zach exclaim, "What the hell!"

Jax scooped up the wet blanket on his way and darted back inside the cabin. The smoke was heavier, but still not too bad. He'd give himself no more than a minute and a half. Entering her bedroom, he surveyed the area and cursed. It had been too much to hope that she'd have been slow to unpack the box.

She'd brought in a five-shelf bookcase. He scanned the titles. Mostly children's books. Christmas-themed children's books. *Grooge, my ass.* Tattered and taped spines suggested oft-read stories. He glanced around, spied her laundry basket—it contained only a pair of red thong panties.

Miss Christmas!

Making an instant decision on what to save, Jax went to work. He emptied three and a half shelves, and when the basket was full and instinct told him to get the hell out, only paperbacks remained. He picked up the basket and dashed for the door.

Outside, Zach identified what he carried and slowly shook his head. "You are one crazy guy. If you even think about going back in there again, I'm going to arrest you."

"I'm done. What can I do to help?"

The sheriff pointed toward the fire truck. "See the guy on the radio at the front of the ladder engine? He's our chief. Go ask him."

By now cars and trucks and SUVs were spilling into the

small valley, and soon what appeared to be the majority of the residents in town pitched in to help. With the fire at Mama Bear out and a full crew working at Baby Bear, Jax went to work battling the blaze at Papa Bear.

What had everyone nervous was the not insubstantial risk that the increasing breeze would kick up the flames and spread the fire. Locals told Jax that although it was late in the season for wildfires, the beetle kill had been especially bad just over the hill from Three Bears Valley, so there was plenty of dead wood to burn.

When the fire chief finally declared the fire out, the collective population heaved a sigh of relief. Then talk turned to the cause and the probability of arson raised the threat level all over again.

"Jax?"

He turned away from his discussion with Lucca Romano and Cicero to see Claire standing with Tinsel clutched against her chest. Her gaze was round, her gorgeous brown eyes luminous with the remnant of tears. "Hey."

"Can I speak with you a moment?"

"Sure." He excused himself from the conversation and placed his hand on the small of her back, guiding her away from the crowd. When they'd walked far enough to have some privacy, Claire turned to him. "They told me what you did. Jax . . . I don't know what to say. That's the most stupidly heroic thing anyone has ever done for me, and I feel like I should scold you for taking such a risk, but I can't. I'm so grateful."

"I couldn't let Tinsel get hurt. She's a sweetheart, and besides, Nicholas would have killed me."

"He'd have killed you if you'd died in that fire!"

"Now, that's silly. He can't kill me if I'm already dead."

"You obviously don't watch zombie TV." She poked his chest with her finger. "Enough of that sort of talk. Jax, going in after Tinsel was above and beyond the call. Going back after my books . . ." She shook her head. "What in the world were you thinking?"

"They are your treasures. I didn't want you to lose them."

"They *are* treasures, and I'm glad they didn't burn up but they are only things, and no *thing* is worth risking your life!" Frustration flashed in her eyes as she added, "You are Nicholas's only parent!"

I even like the way she scolds. Jax reached out and scratched Tinsel behind the ears, then smiled down into Claire's reproachful gaze. "Believe me, I considered that. If I had judged it to be too risky, I wouldn't have gone into Baby Bear at all."

"Okay. Good." She nodded decisively. "That's good. It makes me feel better."

He gave Tinsel another good scratch. "My judgment is pretty good, Claire. You can trust me."

Her lips twisted and he heard a bitter note in her voice when she spoke again. "Trust isn't my strong suit."

"Oh, honey." Jax shook his head, then gave in to his desire to touch her and trailed the pad of his thumb down her cheek. "I've decided it's going to be a goal of mine to make you forget all about that lawyer. What's his name?"

"Landon. Landon the Lying Lizard Louse."

Pursing his lips didn't keep them from twitching. "Quadruple L."

She smiled, shrugged, and when her eyes filled with tears, dipped her head and rested it against his chest. Softly, she said, "I was so scared."

"I know. I know you were. But it's over. Nothing has been destroyed that can't be fixed or replaced. Smoke is your biggest problem. You might have some trouble getting it out of your bedding and clothes."

"That's not a big deal. Clothes and bedding are easy to replace."

Expensive, too, Jax thought. Those silk shirts she liked to wear to work couldn't be cheap. He thought back to his married days. If Lara had lost her entire wardrobe, not only would the world have come to an end, but she would have bankrupted him replacing what she'd lost.

"They say it's arson," she said, her gaze sweeping over the valley's three cabins, one of which had burned to the ground. "Who would do such a thing? Why?"

"I don't know. Some people are just crazy. Whoever it was, I have a feeling that your sheriff won't stop until he finds the guy. Zach Turner strikes me as a badass, and he's seriously pissed."

As he said it, Jax turned his head to look at Turner and realized that at some point during the past few minutes, he and Claire had become the center of attention for a number of people in the crowd. Mostly the women. Females must be born with some sort of romance radar, he thought. And Celeste . . . well . . . that woman was simply scary.

The puppy began to squirm. Claire stepped away from Jax and set Tinsel down on the ground as Jax heard Lori Murphy call his name. She and Chase Timberlake walked toward them. "I need to give you a hug," Lori said to Jax. "You are this veterinarian's hero of the day! That puppy wouldn't have tolerated much smoke."

"Look, it wasn't a big deal. I got in and out before the smoke got bad."

"You're wasting your breath, Navy," Chase said. "This is a dog-loving town. You went into a burning building to save a puppy. You're a bona fide hero from here on out."

"He's right," Lori agreed. "You might as well—"

She broke off abruptly at the sound of a gunning engine and screeching tires. They all looked around to see the sheriff's truck race toward the road.

Within moments, news of the reason why Zach had

sped off filtered through the crowd, and the worried expressions that had dissipated with the extinguishing of the fire returned.

Brick Callahan was the one who clued them in. "Looks like we have a motive for arson at Three Bears Valley. Someone wanted to get people out of town so he could rob the bank."

Chapter Eleven

*It feels good to do something for someone
you care about.*
—JAX

"Rob the bank? You're kidding," Claire said in a disbelieving tone. "People don't rob banks in this day and age. Not in Eternity Springs."

"Apparently they do," Brick responded.

"What about the school?" Jax demanded, his lips flattening into a grim line. "Do I need to worry?"

"It's on lockdown. The sheriff's department is telling everyone to stay inside and keep their doors locked."

"Good."

Lori shook her head. "I can't believe this. I don't know that our school has ever been on lockdown before. Our bank hasn't been robbed since the 1880s, and if we've ever had a case of arson, it didn't make the history book. I would have remembered studying that in school."

"Today has certainly been a day for the history books," Chase observed. "A new Callahan, a fire, a bank robbery. And it's not even noon. I'm almost afraid to see what's going to happen after lunch."

"I probably should get back to town," Lori observed. "I want to check my clinic, make sure we haven't had a vermin invasion."

"You're not going anywhere without me. Not until Zach catches this jackwagon."

The news of the bank robbery cleared out Three Bears Valley quickly as people rushed back to town to protect their property. Indecision kept Claire rooted to her spot. She didn't know whether to remain here and get to work assessing the damage to her things, or return to town to make sure that Forever Christmas didn't have any bank robbers hiding in the Angel Room or stockroom.

"What do you want to do?" Jax asked her.

"I don't know. It's a bit overwhelming."

"I think you should stay here and go through Baby Bear. For one thing, traffic back to town is going to be nasty for the next little while. Give it a chance to clear out and you'll save yourself the headache of a traffic jam."

"An Eternity Springs traffic jam," she mused. "Now that is a rare animal. Happens only a few times a year, I understand. Mostly when we pack the town for one of our tourist festivals. You make a good point, Jax. I think I'll stay."

"*We* will stay," he corrected. "I'm not leaving you out here by yourself. Not until the arsonist is caught, anyway."

She wasn't going to argue with him. She'd probably be more than a little creeped out if she were out here by herself today. Except . . . "What about Nicholas?"

"The school sent a text saying they'll give parents a thirty-minute warning once the decision is made to release the kids. That's plenty of time to—" He broke off abruptly when Celeste approached at a brisk walk.

"Claire, honey. I'm going to ride back into town with Lori and Chase. Before I leave I wanted to let you know that I've spoken with Bob Hamilton. He said to tell you to make a list of everything you own that's been damaged in any way, and he'll see that it's replaced. He has excellent insurance. You won't be out a dime. Also, he suggested you move into Mama Bear until whatever necessary repairs are done to Baby Bear. He'll ask the contractor he hires to begin work there."

"That's good," Jax said. "Sounds like you've lucked out with your landlord, Claire."

"He's a wonderful man," Celeste commented. "Jax, you might be interested to know that his father was a navy man during World War II. A submariner."

"Really," Jax said. "Now those men had it tough. Today's boats are like a luxury yacht compared to what they put to sea in during the Second World War."

"Yes, I imagine so. Bob had a message for you, too, Jax. I told him about your new business, and he wants to know if you'd like the contract to restore the buildings. I can assure you he pays top wages, and as soon as Baby Bear is livable again and Claire can return to it, Mama Bear will be available for you and Nicholas. Rent free, of course. It will be good, steady work for months. "

Jax's chin dropped. "Seriously? Why would he do that? He doesn't know me."

"I vouched for you. The work you did for me was excellent."

"Celeste, I fixed a loose step on your back porch!"

"And you did a fine job of it. You showed up when you said you would, you did the work, and you charged me a fair price. You also have the authority to work with some of our more . . . independent, shall I say . . . subs."

"Independent?" Claire said. "What they are is impossible. We have one electrician in town and one plumber. You can't count on either one of them to do what they say."

"And Jax was a naval officer. I have no doubt he'll manage them. So, dear, shall I give you Bob's number so you can call and discuss the particulars?"

"Absolutely. I'll call him this afternoon."

Celeste gave one of those brilliant grins that seemed to light up the entire sky. "Wonderful. Now, Lori and Chase are waiting, so I'd best hurry along. I want to be there when

Zach captures that horrible person who's responsible for today's trauma. I'm quite unhappy that he chose today of all days to cause his mischief. Although no one will ever forget John Gabriel's birthday."

"True," Claire agreed. "I'm thankful this didn't happen on Lori's wedding day."

"Oh, Claire." Celeste covered her mouth with her hand. "Perish the thought."

Both women took a moment to imagine the turmoil that would have caused and shuddered. Celeste took her leave and Claire turned her attention back to Jax. He appeared stunned. "I hate to feel grateful for your misfortune, Claire, but this job is a godsend. I'll be able to get Nicholas out of that awful motel we're in!"

The smile he aimed her way rivaled Celeste's in brightness and proved just as infectious. Claire laughed aloud as he picked her up and twirled her around, then kissed her hard.

"I do like exuberant men," she observed when he set her down. "But you cheated."

"Cheated?"

She pointed toward the sky above. "No mistletoe."

Now his smile slid into a sexy grin that she felt clear to her toes. He made a show of looking up. "You're wrong, Miss Christmas. Look at those clouds. If that's not a ball of mistletoe above us, then I'm Frosty the Snowman. Believe me when I tell you, I'm not the least bit cold."

"Yeah, well, neither will the gossip be once the subject of babies, arson, and bank robberies dies down," Claire pointed out. "Residents will return their attention to the usual fare of who's romancing who, who is no longer romancing who, and what in the world is so-and-so thinking by going out with that you-know-what? After that display you just put on, you and I will be hot topic number one."

Jax shrugged those broad shoulders of his. "I don't care. Actually, I'm glad to make my claim public if it'll help discourage other guys from making a run at you."

"Your claim?" she repeated, arching a challenging brow. "Did you really say that? Your *claim*? Not very PC, are you, Lancaster?"

"Nah. I'm a Neanderthal. Fair warning." Proving his words, he slapped her butt. "Ready to tackle Baby Bear? I'd like to get a sense of how long it'll take to get it livable again. I suspect Nicholas's grandparents are going to swoop in for a surprise visit any day now, and it would be better for everyone if we're not still residents of the Elkhorn Lodge."

Claire took a minute to consider her next words. He had no way of knowing it, but his lack of concern about gossip warmed a place in her heart that had been cold for over a year. The Lying Lizard Louse always had been careful to keep their relationship low-key. At the time, it had hurt her feelings. When she'd finally discovered the reason why he'd placed so much emphasis on privacy, she'd felt totally stupid for having missed the clues.

Jax wasn't a liar. He wasn't a louse or a lizard, either. He was a hardworking, honest, straightforward man who was trying hard to be a great father. In other words, he wasn't anything like Landon.

And he'd gone into a burning building to save her puppy.

"You don't have to wait, Jax," she said. "Mama Bear has three bedrooms. As far as I'm concerned, you're welcome to move in today."

He jerked his gaze around to stare at her. "Seriously?"

"Sure. Why not?"

"Aren't you worried about what people will think?"

"No. I find I don't really care."

He repeated the pick-her-up, swing-her-around, plant-a-hot-kiss-on-her move. She was still reeling from it when he said, "Am I good or what? Sleeping together even before our first date!"

She elbowed him in the side, then walked on toward Baby Bear, a smile on her face.

Jax did a walk-through of each of the cabins and compiled a list of the extent of the damage. Mama Bear's roof needed only a bit of patching. Baby Bear needed a whole new roof, new attic insulation, some wiring repair, and a complete interior paint job. Unfortunately, after viewing the extent of the damage at Papa Bear, he concluded the best solution there would be to clear it to the slab and start over.

He made the call to the property owner, and in the forty-minute conversation that followed, secured the job that offered a stress-relieving salary and arrived at a rebuilding plan. Bob Hamilton wanted Papa Bear restored exactly as the original but for the minor change of a different style of front door. Luckily, he'd kept a detailed file of everything Jax needed to know to complete the job.

"I'll overnight it to you, Jax," he said. "The only real concern I have is that Shannon won't be willing to re-create the mosaics. Since little Brianna was born, she's cut way back on her work schedule. We might have to sweet-talk her into doing it."

Jax had met Shannon Garrett in July, and he was pretty sure he'd won the exhausted new parent's eternal gratitude when he'd passed along a trick that had worked when Nicholas was teething. "I don't think it'll be a problem, Bob. I have a marker with her I can call in if necessary."

"Excellent."

Before ending the call, Jax thanked him again for both the opportunity and the housing. "Don't thank me. Thank Celeste. She gave you a glowing recommendation, and I've learned I can rely on her judgment."

"I won't let either of you down," Jax replied, his promise solemn. "You have my word on it."

As Jax thumbed the red circle on his phone to end the call, a wry smile lifted his lips. He wondered if Celeste ever did anything that wasn't "glowing." That seemed to be her modus operandi.

Returning to Baby Bear to check on Claire, he found her in her kitchen unloading the contents of a refrigerator into a cooler. Seeing him, she asked, "How did it go?"

"Great. He seems like he'll be easy to work with."

"I'm so glad."

"Any word from town?"

"I talked to Lori a few minutes ago. She said tensions are high. Zach doubts that the guy hung around Eternity Springs, but until he picks up a trail, no one can be certain. She also said you need not worry about Nicholas. In addition to the school being on lockdown, Zach has stationed a couple of deputies on the grounds as added precaution.

"Good."

Claire shut the refrigerator door and lowered the lid on the cooler. When she went to pick it up, Jax said, "Let me carry that."

"It's not heavy, Jax. I can get it."

He ignored her and headed for the door and short walk to Mama Bear. He didn't miss her muttered, "Neanderthal," and he grinned in response.

It didn't take long for them to get Claire settled into Mama Bear. He attempted to insist that she take the master suite, but she flat-out refused to do it, showing a stubborn side of her personality Jax hadn't seen before.

It only attracted him more.

At two P.M., they received word of an official announcement from the sheriff's department that an arrest had been made. The man in custody had a Denver address and a trunk full of money and empty cans of gasoline. The townspeople breathed a collective sigh of relief and life returned to normal, with the dismissal of schoolchildren to occur at the usual time.

Jax followed Claire back to town, then honked goodbye when she turned toward Forever Christmas while he drove on to the school. He worried how his son might take the news of evil having touched Eternity Springs, but his concerns disappeared when Nicholas climbed into their truck bubbling with excitement.

"Did you hear what happened, Dad? We had a bank robber! They locked up all the doors and wouldn't let us go out to recess. We got to play dodge ball in the gym!"

They still played dodge ball in the school here? It had been forbidden at the boy's last school. Labeled too dangerous. "I know about the bank robber, yes. Did you hear about the fire at Miss Claire's house?"

Nicholas's eyes went wide and round. "No! Is Tinsel all right?"

"Yes, Tinsel is fine. But don't you think you should have asked about Claire first?"

Nicholas's gaze grew stricken. "Is *she* hurt?"

Jax inwardly cursed. *Ham-handed there, Lancaster.* "No. She's okay."

Quickly, he told his son the news that he figured would distract him. "Distracted" wasn't close to being the right word for Nicholas's response at the news that he'd be sharing a house with Tinsel for a little while. He bubbled, he giggled, he clapped his hands and asked about a million questions. Why did the house have such a superstupid name? Where would the puppy sleep? Could he feed her? Take her on walks? Maybe she'd be lonely during the day. Wouldn't she be lonely? They didn't want her to be lonely. "We should get a dog, Daddy."

We should get a dog, Daddy. Jax recalled the little boy who'd screamed in terror when unexpectedly coming upon some woman's leashed purse pet at a sidewalk café during Jax's last visit home prior to his discharge. Nicholas had been scared clear to the marrow by a Maltipoo. A Maltipoo!

"What kind of dog?"

"A golden retriever like Captain."

Captain was Chase Timberlake's dog, that magical mutt who, with the help of the Rocking L summer camp and Chase and Lori in particular, had healed the part of Nicholas's damaged psyche that had sent him into tremors at even near proximity to a seven-pound dog.

Now, the boy was asking for a dog of his own. Damned if Jax's eyes didn't tear up at the thought. "Tell you what, hot rod. Let's see how we like living with a dog, and if everything's cool, we'll talk to Dr. Lori."

"Really? I can have a puppy of my own? Really?"

"We might want to get one who's out of the puppy stage. They're a lot easier to care for."

"That's okay. I'd like any dog. He doesn't have to be a golden or a collie. I'd rather have a boy dog, but a girl would be okay, too."

"If we decide to get a dog, I'm sure we can find a boy dog."

"I've decided, Daddy."

"And I said we are going to wait and see. Now, enough about a dog. Since we've been a bachelor household, we haven't worried too much about niceties. That's gonna change. We'll be living with a lady for a few weeks, and they're particular about such things. So, there's gonna be a few rules. I expect you to follow them, matey, or I'll make you walk the plank."

"Aye, aye, Captain."

They discussed important matters like hanging up towels, raising and lowering the toilet seat, putting dirty dishes in the dishwasher, and managing a belch and fart in polite company.

"James didn't put the toilet seat down," Nicholas confided. "I remember Mom yelling at him about it."

Jax glanced at his son. He rarely spoke about his mother or his stepfather. The fact he did today in such a matter-of-fact manner served to bolster Jax's confidence that bringing the boy to Eternity Springs had been a good decision.

"It was one of her pet peeves. Most women feel the same way. Do yourself a favor and get in the habit now and save yourself a world of grief when you grow up."

They returned to the Elkhorn Lodge and packed up their gear, then made a quick stop at the lumberyard to pick up a few supplies for their new digs. "Wow!" Nicholas exclaimed upon catching his first look at Three Bears Valley. "That house is all burned up!"

"Yep."

"That robber was a bad man."

"Yes, he certainly was."

Flatly, Nicholas announced, "He didn't belong in Eternity Springs."

"You are exactly right about that, son."

Jax pulled his truck to a stop in front of Mama Bear and Nicholas scrambled out of his seat and was halfway up the front porch steps before Jax managed to follow. The boy burst inside calling, "Miss Claire? Miss Claire? Can I play with Tinsel?"

Upon entering the house, Jax followed his nose and a delicious aroma to the kitchen. Claire had chocolate chip cookies still warm from the oven and glasses of milk waiting for them. Cookies and milk. *I'll be damned.*

Jax decided he liked playing Santa Claus to her Miss Christmas.

As the days passed, they settled into a routine. Claire drove Nicholas to school in the mornings on her way to Forever Christmas. Jax worked at Three Bears Valley until mid-afternoon when he went to town to do errands before picking Nicholas up at the end of the school day. He stopped in at Forever Christmas most days to lure her beneath the mistletoe for a few minutes, since he seldom found the opportunity to do so at Mama Bear—despite the fact that he'd tacked up numerous sprigs of the stuff at appropriate spaces around the house. He and Claire traded nights cooking dinner and cleaning up afterward, then for Jax it was homework supervision, bath, and bedtime. Some nights stretched out longer than others because he was reading the last book of the Harry Potter series to Nicholas, and he often got caught up in the story and read longer than he'd intended.

Only twice during that first week did they find time at the end of the day to share a glass of wine, a little conversation, and some mistletoe time. To his surprise, Jax discovered that he enjoyed the slow pace of the seduction.

Because that's what it had been. A slow, sensual seduction the likes of which he hadn't enjoyed in a very long time.

Then on Wednesday of their second week at Three Bears, an excited Nicholas climbed into the truck after school and presented Jax with an interesting opportunity. "Guess what, Dad? Galen invited me for a sleepover at his house after the birthday party on Friday. Can I go? Please?"

A sleepover at the Cicero house on date night! Yes! "That might be doable. I need to speak with Dr. Rose or Cicero first and make sure it's okay."

"Can you call them right now, please?"

"When we get home."

Home. For the first time since leaving the navy, he felt like he actually had one. Complete with waiting woman. Emphasis on the waiting.

Friday night. If Nicholas wasn't teasing him, if the stars finally aligned and nobody got a stomach bug or had a

Christmas crisis or accidentally cut off his leg while using a Skilsaw, Friday night just might see the end of his drought and the dance that up to this point had been his mistletoe fling.

Back at the Three Bears, he'd just hung up the phone from speaking to Rose Cicero when a Jeep entered the valley and drove toward the cabins. Outside playing with Tinsel, Nicholas turned toward the sound. "It's Mr. Chase. Look, Dad, it's Mr. Chase! I wonder if he has Captain with him? Maybe Captain and Tinsel would like to play. What do you think, Dad? Would that be all right? Would Miss Claire let Tinsel play with Captain?"

"I imagine it's fine as long as the puppy doesn't appear to be afraid of Captain."

"She won't be. I know it. She's a great dog."

When Chase opened his door and a golden retriever hopped out, Nicholas cheered in delight. "Captain! Look, Dad. It's Captain. He likes her. See? Mr. Chase, is it okay if Tinsel plays with Captain?"

"Sure." Chase strode over to where Nicholas wrestled with the two dogs. He ruffled Nicholas's hair and said, "Howya doin', Tadpole?"

"Great! Tinsel is staying at my new house until my dad gets Baby Bear fixed and I get to play with her every day. I'll get to play with her even when Miss Claire goes back to Baby Bear. Isn't that awesome?"

"Totally awesome." He hunkered down beside Nicholas and petted the puppy. "So, this is the famous Tinsel. She is cute, isn't she?"

"She's famous?" Nicholas asked, his eyes going round with wonder.

"In Eternity Springs, she is. After all, your dad went into a—" Chase caught sight of the slicing motion Jax made across his throat and finished. "Long story about how cute she is when I saw him at the lumberyard the other day. Dr. Lori sent some puppy treats with me for her. They're in the backseat of my Jeep. Want to go get them?"

"Sure."

Chase rose and sauntered on toward Jax, who checked his watch. Ten to five. Close enough. "Want a beer, Timberlake?"

"With every fiber of my being, thank you."

Jax made a quick trip inside to the refrigerator, then rejoined Chase, who said, "Today was final tuxedo-fitting day and Cam and Devin had an issue with theirs. I thought my veterinarian bride might take a gun and shoot a dog."

"Let me guess. The infamous Mortimer was up to his old tricks? What'd he do? Eat a bow tie?"

"No. Cummerbund. I am grateful for the wonderful women I have in my life, but I have to tell you, weddings are not for the faint of heart."

Neither were divorces. Under the circumstances, with Chase's wedding a little over a week away, Jax kept that reality to himself. He tossed a beer toward Chase. "Truer words. So, what brings you out our way?"

Chase caught the can, popped the top, and took a long sip before answering Jax's question. "My blushing bride and I were talking about Tadpole today, and she made a suggestion." He glanced over to make certain that Nicholas couldn't hear him when he said, "No pressure here, because we have other arrangements made already, but Lori thought that if you and Claire were amenable, we'd ask Nicholas if he'd like to dog-sit for us while we're on our honeymoon."

Jax glanced toward his son, who stood throwing a stick for Captain to fetch. Nicholas's expression was lit up like a tree in Forever Christmas. "I'll have to speak with Claire—"

"Lori already did. She thinks it's a great idea."

"In that case, I think it's a great idea, too. He'll be

thrilled." Plus, it would give Jax a chance to evaluate how the boy would manage the responsibility of having a dog were Jax to decide to give the go-ahead to get one for the boy. Since Claire acted as caretaker for Tinsel, Nicholas had all the fun without the responsibility. With a dog of his own, that would need to change. "Why don't you go ask him?"

Jax sat on the front porch steps and sipped his beer as he watched Chase Timberlake's long-legged saunter toward his son. While the two played together with the two dogs for a few minutes, Jax reflected on the blessing the former jet-setter had been in the Lancasters' lives. Last summer when Nicholas arrived at the Rocking L summer camp, he'd been a fearful shell of the boy he was today. Much of that transformation was due to the man playing with the boy now. Chase had not only taught the boy to swim, he'd accomplished the first breakthrough in Nicholas's recovery from the traumatic events of his mother's death.

I owe him more than I'll ever be able to repay.

Jax's gaze slid down his son's figure and focused on his ankle where vicious scars served as evidence of his son's horror.

Nicholas's excited cheer diverted Jax from the dark direction of his thoughts, and he watched with a glad heart as the boy's joy exploded like a skyrocket on the Fourth of July. If the Hardcastles could see him now, they couldn't deny that Jax's decision to bring his son to Eternity Springs had been the right one.

"Dad! Dad! Guess what? You gotta say yes, Dad. Please say yes!"

He gave his lecture about responsibility and care and then said yes. Much happiness abounded in Three Bears Valley.

He relayed the details of the moment with Claire later that evening when they shared a glass of excellent wine after he put Nicholas to bed. "Chase and Lori are good people. I didn't know everything Chase had been through when I met him last summer, but I heard the story from Shannon when I grabbed a burger for lunch at Murphy's one day last week. It's no wonder Nicholas bonded with him. They both lived through a really horrific experience."

Claire swirled the wine in her glass. "I know that Nicholas survived a car accident that killed his mother. Yesterday when he stripped off his soccer cleats and socks after showing me his new peewee uniform, I noticed the scars on his legs. Is that from the accident? Or did something else happen to him?"

Jax rubbed the back of his neck. He rarely spoke of the event that had caused such grief for so many people, and even when he did, he only relayed the basic facts. Facts couldn't convey the horror, and he'd never told anyone the entire story.

To his surprise, he found he wanted to tell Claire.

He swallowed hard, licked his lips, and began. "For me, it all started on Christmas Eve. According to our custody agreement, I had Nicholas every other Christmas. My ex had him for Christmas the first year following our divorce. It was my turn."

Excitement hummed through Jax's blood as he pulled his car to a stop at the curb in front of Lara's home in Seattle on the twenty-third of December. He'd been on a boat for the past ten months, and as a result, hadn't seen his son since Valentine's Day. Ten months was a significant chunk of the life of a six-year-old, especially when the boy's mother didn't send the pictures and updates Jax had requested. His need to see his son was a living, breathing being inside him.

He bounded up the front steps and rang the doorbell precisely at ten A.M., the time he'd told Lara to expect him

*in the e-mail they'd exchanged a week ago about the ar-
rangements. He was prepared for Lara to be difficult
about this. She hadn't responded to any of the e-mails he'd
sent over the past two days that asked questions about
supplies he would need during the eight days Nicholas
would be with him. More than likely, he'd be winging this
visit, but that was okay. He was a submariner. He'd been
trained to handle a nuclear accident on a sub. He could
deal with any surprises a six-year-old boy threw his way.*

*Then Nicholas's stepfather opened his front door and
threw out a surprise that Jax never anticipated.*

"What do you mean, they're not here?" Jax demanded.

*"I thought you were Mr. Brilliant." James Karston
sneered. "What's so difficult to understand? They're gone.
Outta here. Vamoosed. Lara took the kid and left me. She
left me three effing days before Christmas!"*

*She's trying to keep Nicholas from me, he thought. Fury
ignited in Jax's gut. Grimly, he asked, "Is she with her
parents?"*

*"Hell if I know. She probably did go home to Daddy. She
could have climbed on a rocket ship to the moon. The
woman is batshit crazy."*

*The first wave of unease rippled through Jax. "Why do
you say that?"*

*"Because she is! She's been this way ever since she lost
the baby in August."*

*She'd lost a child? Jax hadn't known that. The fact gave
his heart a little twist. Before their marriage fell apart,
he'd wanted more children. She'd refused to consider it.*

*Karston started to slam the door in Jax's face, but Jax
stuck his foot inside to prevent it. "Have you called her
parents' house?"*

*"Hell, no. Let her run to Mommy and Daddy. I don't
care anymore."*

The Hardcastle home would be Jax's first stop. He fully expected to find her and Nicholas there, but just in case . . . "What's she driving?"

"If I tell you will you go the hell away and leave me alone?"

"I'll leave." Though he might come back if she wasn't at her parents' and he needed more information—like access to her credit cards—in order to track her.

"She's in a sweet little BMW hybrid. I gave it to her for our anniversary. How stupid am I?"

"Tags?"

Jax committed the license tag number to memory and turned away as the door slammed. Back in his car, he took a few minutes to rein in his temper before he began the fifteen-minute drive to the Hardcastles'. He wasted those few minutes because by the time he arrived at his former in-laws' home, he was loaded for bear.

No one answered the doorbell. He walked around the house peeking in the windows and saw no signs of life.

Nor did he see a Christmas tree.

The sound of a shotgun being racked behind him was unmistakable.

"What in sam blazes do you think you're doing, young fellow?"

Jax pinpointed the voice. The neighbor. The widowed rancher from Montana who'd moved in with his daughter's family after his wife died. He raised his hands away from his body and slowly turned to face him. "Mr. Waggoner? I'm Nicholas's father."

"Navy man. Submariner."

"Yessir."

The Montanan lowered the shotgun. "What you doin' snoopin' around the Hardcastle place, son?"

"I'm looking for Lara. I was supposed to pick up Nich-

olas from her house this morning, and they're not there. Have you seen them?"

"Miss Lara? No. No. Not for quite some time. She and her folks have had a falling-out. Brian and Linda are heartbroken about it. They haven't seen the boy since Halloween. They've gone to Hawaii for Christmas to get away. Left yesterday afternoon."

That bit of news left Jax speechless. "Perhaps they reconciled. Maybe Lara went with them to Hawaii."

"Well, if she did, her mother didn't know anything about it when she came over yesterday and had a cup of coffee with my Cecilia. She was right upset about not seeing her girl on Christmas."

What the hell, Lara? Was this the same woman who had refused to meet him in Tahiti—Tahiti!—for his R & R because it meant she'd miss Christmas with her parents?

Jax needed to get in touch with Brian Hardcastle, but the only number he had for the man was their landline. "Did they leave an emergency number with you, by any chance?"

"I don't know. Come on inside and ask Cecilia."

Ten minutes later he left the Hardcastles' neighbor's house with Brian Hardcastle's cell number, a sackful of homemade chocolate chip cookies, and a heightened sense of anxiety.

He climbed into his car, took a moment to compose his question, then placed the call.

He awakened Lara's father from a sound sleep. "Lancaster. How the hell did you get my number?" Before Jax could respond, Brian added, "Oh, no. Is it Nicholas? Did something bad happen to Nicholas?"

"No." Jax damned sure hoped the answer was no. "That's not why I'm calling. I'm trying to locate Lara."

"Why? You sure nothing's wrong with Nicholas?"

"I haven't seen Nicholas," Jax snapped. *In crisp, concise sentences, he relayed the events of the morning, ending with, "I expected they would be with you."*

"No." Brian's tone was clipped. *"She left James? This is worse than we realized."*

Jax's unease spiked at the admission.

"We invited Lara and James to join us in Hawaii, but she didn't want to come with us."

There was no love lost between Jax and Brian Hardcastle, but the worry Jax heard in Brian's voice convinced him that his former father-in-law was telling the truth. Jax verbalized his one hope. "Maybe she plans to surprise you."

"I don't see how. We never told her where we are staying."

Jax dragged a hand down his face. What the hell have you done, Lara?

It was a question he repeated often over the next twenty-four hours. Then, forty-eight. Then, seventy-two. Christmas came and went without any sign, anywhere, of his ex-wife and son.

Now two years later, he still asked the same question. Sharing the story with Claire, his voice went rough as he relived the torment of those dark days.

"We reported her missing to the police, but that was mostly a waste of time. She was an adult who'd left her spouse. Besides, it was Christmas. Everyone was too busy spiking their eggnog to worry about a woman who'd had a fight with her husband."

"I can't imagine how horrible that must have been for you, Jax. I hate when policies prevent people from listening. There was a child involved!"

"I tried to play the kidnapping card, but it went nowhere. I hired a private investigator and the Hardcastles flew home from Hawaii. Brian had social ties with the police chief, so he was able to light a fire under the authorities and get the search taken seriously. They were the longest four and a half days of my life."

"How were they found?" Claire asked.

"By the grace of God. Honestly, Claire. I had begun to despair. She wasn't using her credit cards. We got no response when we pinged her phone. It was as if they'd disappeared off the face of the map. Then at nine-seventeen on the morning of the twenty-seventh, a call came in from Idaho."

His throat tightened up, and he paused a moment until he figured he could speak without his voice wobbling. "Snowmobilers had discovered the wreck. She'd gone off a mountain road. The car slid thirty feet down the side of a mountain and slammed into a tree. She died of blunt force trauma. The doctors told us that she probably didn't live through the crash."

Claire placed a comforting hand on his knee. "Nicholas?"

"He must have been in his booster seat. Physically, he suffered a few scrapes and bruises—mostly from when the rear side airbags deployed."

"The airbags caused those scars on his ankle?"

Jax closed his eyes and sucked in a deep breath. He recalled his first glimpse of the damage done to his son's ankle and leg when a nurse changed his bandages following his surgery. "No. The snowmobilers saw animal tracks in the snow. They couldn't identify them, and by the time the rescue crew got finished, the tracks had been obliterated. Best we could figure was that at some point, Nicholas got out of the car and was attacked. Wolves or wild dogs."

Claire covered her mouth with her hands. "Oh, Jax. My heart just breaks for him. For you both."

"An analysis of the time and distance they traveled and, frankly, the decomposition of Lara's corpse, proved that he'd been trapped in that car with his mother's body for days. He didn't utter a word for weeks afterward."

Jax rose and paced the room, lost in the memory of that horrific time. The Hardcastles' collapse. The funeral. Nicholas's pallor and his pain and silent suffering.

Jax's own despair after opening that first hospital bill.

His fury when the navy deemed him mission critical and refused his request for early discharge.

"I could have used your positive-thoughts journal during those months, Claire."

She made a little whimper, drawing his glance. A pair of tears trailed slowly down her cheeks.

Jax's heart warmed. He couldn't resist a woman who would cry over his little boy's pain. Not that he wanted to resist her.

I want to win her. Keep her. Marry her.

The truth of the thought rocked him. What the hell? Marriage! What in the world was he thinking? This was a fling, not a relationship. That had been clear from the very beginning. They hadn't even been on a date yet. He hadn't slept with her. How could his mind possibly go to marriage?

Because your mind follows your heart, Lancaster. It always has. Always will.

Damn, he was in trouble.

"I can't imagine. I think I would have melted into a messy blubbering puddle. How afraid you must have been."

"Terrified."

That part hadn't really changed.

The breakup with Lara had nearly destroyed him, both financially and emotionally. He didn't have it in him to go down that road again, not even with someone who did it for him as much as Claire Branham did.

Oh, get your head out, Lancaster. Talk about borrowing trouble. He had them married and divorced before their first date!

Jax was almost glad when Claire asked another question. "It's obvious why Nicholas developed a fear of dogs. I guess he associates the accident with Christmas?"

"Yes. After he got out of the hospital in Idaho, he went to live with his grandparents in Seattle." Jax told her a little about his futile battle to secure an early discharge and the panicked phone call he'd received the day after his sub arrived in port in Hawaii. Speaking of the events catapulted him into the past.

"What do you mean he's catatonic?" Jax demanded of Brian Hardcastle.

"Linda took him to a charity event this afternoon and when they walked into the building, he froze and went stiff and . . . away. He just checked out, Lancaster. No reason. No warning."

Jax rubbed his temples between his thumb and forefingers and tried to make sense of what he was hearing. "What sort of building was it? What type of charity event?"

"It's an exhibit hall in the convention center. Nothing special about it. The event was her sorority's Christmas in August Craft Fair."

"Christmas," Jax repeated. Sonofabitch! What the hell had Linda been thinking? "He must have had a flashback."

"Whatever is going on, it's lasted six hours."

And I'm just NOW getting a phone call? "What's the prognosis?"

"The damned doctors can't tell us a blessed thing. I'm headed back up to the hospital now. Came home to change clothes and found your message on the landline. Thought I should call since you're on land. I'll e-mail you updates as we get them."

Jax went straight to his commanding officer and begged

leave. Six hours later, he went wheels up on a military transport headed to Southern California. From there he caught a commercial flight to Seattle and arrived at the hospital just in time for evening rounds the following day.

Nicholas had opened his eyes, but he had yet to interact with anyone. The doctors had concluded he should be transferred to a psychiatric hospital, and Brian jumped in and began making arrangements. Jax let him. He took a seat beside Nicholas's bed and held his hand. Throughout an interminable night, he didn't let go.

At 4:22, Nicholas made his first sound, a little soulful moan. Jax rose from his chair and stepped toward the bed. "Hey, buddy."

"Daddy?"

"I'm here, buddy."

"No. No. No. No. No." Nicholas kept his eyes scrunched closed, grabbed the blanket, and pulled it over his head. "You're not real. You're one of the monsters. My daddy's far, far away."

"I am real, little guy, and I'm right here." Jax rested his hand on the lump that was Nicholas's shoulder. "I heard you were sick and I came home."

A full twenty seconds passed before his little hands tentatively lowered the covers. "Daddy?"

"Hello, Nicholas."

"Are we in heaven?"

"No. We're at a hospital in Seattle. Your grandparents brought you here after . . . well . . . I'm not really sure what happened. The doctors are going to find out, though."

"I just want to go home, Daddy. Can we go home?"

"Not right now, but soon, I hope. We need to find out what happened so we can make sure it doesn't happen again."

The little boy's big blue eyes flooded with tears. "I know what happened. I heard the music again. I don't like that music. It scares me. I got scared, Daddy."

Christmas carols. Bet they'd been playing Christmas carols at the charity fair. Bet Lara had been playing Christmas carols when she wrecked the car.

Nicholas's next words confirmed the suspicion.

"I was so cold and Mommy wouldn't answer and the songs played and played and played and I couldn't make them stop but then they stopped and the animals howled and I was so scared, Daddy. I was so scared!"

Jax sat on the side of his son's bed, took the boy in his arms, and rocked him while he cried.

As he remembered that exchange, Jax's heart broke all over again. He cleared his throat and responded to Claire's question. "The car was packed full of wrapped Christmas gifts. Lots of red and green and ribbon and bows. And we're pretty sure that the radio continued to play long after the accident. He hasn't opened a Christmas present since."

Claire pushed to her feet and crossed the room to grab a tissue from the box on a table. "I think this might be the saddest story I've heard in a very long time," she said, wiping her eyes. "Now I better understand what a victory it was for him to conquer his fear of dogs."

"It was huge. Chase and Lori and Eternity Springs worked a miracle with my son."

"Well . . . here's what I think." Claire picked up the wine bottle and topped off their glasses. "I think Eternity Springs needs to go for a two-fer."

"You're talking about working on his fear of Christmas?"

"I am."

"I appreciate the thought, Claire. Truly, I do. I'm just not sure that either Nicholas or I is ready to tackle that beast. He's getting along so well right now, and after the hypnosis debacle, I'm hesitant to upset the applecart."

"Isn't healing his Christmas phobia a big part of the reason why you moved here?"

"Yes, but—"

"You have to think positive, Jax. You have to believe. Don't forget, this is Eternity Springs."

"I know. The longer I'm here, the easier it is for me to believe in its mojo. My fear is doing something that backfires. I don't want another situation like the one we went through in September. Nicholas's grandparents had good intentions and look what happened."

"Well, we're not his grandparents, and this isn't Seattle. Chase and Lori found the right combination to deal with his fear of dogs. I'll bet we can come up with a plan to tackle his issues with Christmas in a nonthreatening way. Let me put a little thought into it, Jax. They don't call me Miss Christmas for nothing."

Hearing that bit of positive thinking and seeing the confident determination on Claire Branham's face, Jax Lancaster took a tumble toward love.

Chapter Twelve

*Winston Churchill said we make a life by
what we give. Smart man.*
—CLAIRE

The following morning as she got dressed for work,
Claire's mind buzzed with ideas for her newest project.
After Jax gave her his blessing to launch a well-considered
Christmas campaign on Nicholas's behalf, she'd focused
her thoughts on creating a plan that incorporated the successful exposure-therapy strategy Chase had employed in
order to overcome the boy's fear of dogs. She had an idea
she thought might work, but only if Nicholas would buy
into it.

Claire and Jax agreed that springing something unexpected on Nicholas would be the worst thing they could
do. But if Nicholas was ready and willing to dip his toe in
the holiday pool, so to speak, then she was ready to assist.
How terrible for this to happen to a child, to lose Christmas. She knew from personal experience. However, as
complex as her own Christmas-related issues were they
paled in comparison to Nicholas's.

Maybe helping Nicholas would do something for her,
too. That's how the volunteer work she used to do had
worked. She'd always felt best about herself when she
brought a little joy into the lives of others. Maybe this project would help them both.

The boy who skipped downstairs that morning and

chattered nonstop about Captain and Tinsel through breakfast showed no sign of emotional stress. If the right moment presented itself during their drive to school, she
planned to broach her idea. From her perspective, they had
little time to waste. Eternity Springs might start the official Christmas season later than other towns in America
these days, but Thanksgiving and Deck the Halls Friday
were right around the corner.

Claire knew that helping Nicholas find his Christmas
spirit would be rewarding. This undertaking might well be
exactly what she needed to finally kick her own Grinch to
the curb.

The boy's excited chatter continued during the drive to
school. They were halfway to town when he let out a joyful sigh and said how happy Chase's request had made
him. Claire concluded that she wouldn't get a better opportunity.

"So, Dr. Lori told me about how Chase worked with you
during summer camp to conquer your fear of dogs. She
said you were one brave little boy."

His smile didn't dim. "Dr. Lori helped, too. We worked
on it a little bit each day."

"Your father said you thought if you came to Eternity
Springs you might be able to do the same thing where
Christmas is concerned."

At that he went still for a long moment, then sent a cautious gaze her way. "Yeah."

"You know, Nicholas, I wouldn't mind helping you with
the project. Sort of like Chase and Dr. Lori did. I think I'd
be good at it. I am Miss Christmas, after all."

"I don't know . . ."

"That's okay, Nicholas. No pressure. You just think
about it and let me know."

He remained silent the rest of the way into town. If
Claire felt just a little bit of disappointment, well, she knew

she had to temper her expectations. If Nicholas's troubles were easily solved, his father wouldn't have moved him from Washington to Colorado.

Approaching the intersection where one of the town's two stoplights switched to yellow and then red, she braked to a stop. She told herself she shouldn't be discouraged. Considering everything the boy had been through, they all should probably look at this journey as a marathon rather than a sprint. And every long-distance runner began by taking baby steps, right?

Can you mutilate a metaphor any more, Branham?

Probably. Nicholas tickled her imagination. Didn't he remind her of another bedraggled angel with a broken wing? If she hadn't sworn off creating any more adventures for Gardenia, she could easily see her making a new friend.

He'd have blue eyes and wear big glasses that wouldn't stay up on his nose. He'd wear a T-shirt with paw prints all over it and . . . No, wait. He'd be a dog. A talking dog. His T-shirt would say DOGS ARE PEOPLE, TOO.

Gardenia sits on her mantel blowing dust off her wings. The new cleaning service people are afraid to dust her at night and Holly Sugarplum hasn't looked twice at Gardenia in weeks.

"So what else is new?" Gardenia said, rustling her wings, sweeping dust off her shelf to settle on the beautiful china doll angel with golden hair and a satin gown.

Achoo. Achoo. Achoo. Achoo. Gardenia's eyes rounded at the unexpected sound.

She peered over the edge of the shelf. A white dog with honey-brown spots and droopy ears stood on his hind legs, his front paws folded over his chest. He wore round black glasses and growled up at her. "Stop that. It's rude to blow your dust around. Some of us are allergic to dust, you know."

"You are talking to me!"

"Yes. You're the one blowing dust, aren't you?"

"Nobody but Holly Sugarplum ever talks to me."

"Why? Are you mean?"

Gardenia shook her head. "I'm a good angel."

"No you're not. Good angels blow golden angel dust. Your dust is gray and makes me sneeze."

"You're a mean dog! Why are you in the Angel Room?"

"I'm not mean. I'm lost. My name is Nicholas, and I'm looking for the Christmas Key."

"Miss Claire? Miss Claire?"

She turned her head toward the voice, expecting to see a droopy-eared dog wearing black-rimmed glasses. Nicholas Lancaster said, "The light is green, Miss Claire."

"Oh. Oh!" Embarrassed, she felt her cheeks flush with heat as she flicked her gaze up to the rearview mirror before pressing the gas pedal. Three cars were lined up behind her. She stuck her arm out the window and gave a little "I'm sorry" wave as she drove on through the intersection.

"I'll hear about that later," she murmured. "I've been caught daydreaming too many times lately. People like to tease."

"I get teased, too, Miss Claire. Dad says when it happens, to put on your cool look."

"My cool look? What's a cool look?"

"Well, it works better when you're standing up. You have to put your hands in your pockets and get all loosey-goosey. Loosey-goosey. Isn't that a stupid word? Anyway, you roll back on your heels and bounce a little. That doesn't matter. But you gotta keep your shoulders squared and your chin up. That's important."

"I see."

"That's not all, though. This next part is *really* important. You smile at 'em and say, 'Thank you for sharing that with me.' "

Claire gave him a sidelong look. "Oh, yeah?"

"Yeah. Dad says it really works. I was going to try it with the bullies in Seattle, but we moved to Eternity Springs instead."

"Awesome. I'll be sure to remember to try it. Maybe I'll practice my loosey-goosey to get ready." Claire pulled her SUV into the circular drive in front of the school and said, "Thank you for the tip, Nicholas."

"You're welcome." The boy unfastened his seat belt, but rather than hop out like he usually did, he remained seated, staring straight ahead. "How would you do it? The . . . um . . . other thing."

Claire's pulse picked up. "You mean Christmas?"

Still not looking at her, he nodded.

Yes! Claire managed—just barely—not to pump her fist. She strove for a casual tone. "I'm certainly open to suggestions, Nicholas, but I thought that a good place to start might be books. Your dad told me y'all are about to finish reading Harry Potter. What would you think about me reading a little bit to you at night from my collection of Christmas stories? For the most part, they are very short."

He pursed his lips. "One of them has ghosts. I don't want any ghosts."

"That's Dickens's *A Christmas Carol*. We'll mark that off the list. Actually, I thought we'd start with the story where it all began—the Gospel of Luke from the Bible. That seems appropriate, don't you think? We can give it a try and if it's a problem for you in any way, then we'll just forget it."

Nicholas sat for another fifteen seconds, staring straight ahead. Then he licked his lips and opened the car door. "I'll think about it, Miss Claire."

"Fair enough. You have a good day at school today, Nicholas."

"I will. Bye."

He slammed the door and ran off toward the school's front door.

"Yes!" she exclaimed, giving in to the fist-pump urge. Claire grinned all the way to Forever Christmas.

She spent every free moment during her workday in her book section choosing stories to share with Nicholas. By the time she closed her shop and headed home, she had three tote bags stuffed with books.

Over supper that evening, she asked Jax how many nights of Harry Potter they had left. "Three chapters. One tonight. I figure we'll do two tomorrow night and finish it up."

"Saturday night is movie night. We don't read on Saturdays. Want to watch movies with us, Miss Claire?"

"Well . . ." She glanced at Jax for a signal, and he nodded enthusiastically. "I like movies—as long as they're not tearjerkers. What are you watching on Saturday night?"

"Submarine movies," Nicholas said. "It's fun because Dad talks all the way through them, and he gets grumpy when they get things wrong, and they always get things wrong. You should watch with us."

"Submarine movies, hmm? Okay. Thanks for the invitation, Nicholas. It's a date. I'll bring the popcorn and hot chocolate."

"Cool! Then maybe Sunday night you could read to me."

In the midst of spooning a second helping of green beans onto her plate, Claire froze. Her eyes widened and she darted a look at Jax before she responded. "If it's okay with your dad, I'd like that very much, Nicholas."

"Good." The boy shoveled another bite of spaghetti into his mouth, sucked in an errant strand, then added, "Dad,

Miss Claire is going to read to me about Christmas. From the Bible."

"And Dr. Seuss. Clement C. Moore. O. Henry," Claire added as clarification.

"She said they're short. Is it okay with you, Dad? You'll still read Percy Jackson to me, right?"

"Absolutely." Jax stabbed a meatball off his son's plate and brought it toward his own mouth. "Sounds like an excellent idea to me."

"Hey, Dad! I was saving that!"

"Snooze you lose, boyo." Jax's eyes twinkled with pleasure as he looked at his son, and when he shifted his gaze toward Claire, they softened with a combination of gratitude and hope and approval that warmed her to her toes. "Miss Christmas's meatballs are spectacular."

Claire schooled her expression into one of disapproval. "Don't worry, Nicholas. I believe there are two meatballs left in the sauce on the stove. You may have them both."

"Score!" Nicholas chortled.

The rest of the evening passed in an easy, upbeat atmosphere that reminded Claire of the happy family of her childhood before Michelle got sick. When Jax went upstairs to read a chapter of *Harry Potter and the Deathly Hallows,* Claire knew a yearning that all but took her breath away.

She wanted this. She wanted a family.

She wanted to be part of *this* family.

Whoa. Whoa. Whoa. Hold your jingle bells right there, Miss Christmas.

Family wasn't on the table. They'd made that clear from the beginning. She'd been the one to take relationship *off* the table! Tables weren't even involved here. Just a bed. This was a mistletoe fling.

Although, come to think of it, there was no reason a table couldn't be involved. Jax seemed like the type who once he'd begun flinging, wouldn't care too much just where the mistletoe lay. So to speak.

Needing a distraction from her thoughts, Claire considered skipping the nightcap with Jax that had quickly become their habit and going up to bed herself. But that struck her as cowardly, so instead she fell back on another crutch. She took a box of brownie mix from the pantry and set about mixing them up.

She'd just slid the pan in the preheated oven when Jax entered the kitchen. "Brownies? You're making brownies? Better be careful, Claire. I'll sabotage the repairs to Baby Bear to keep you here."

Because words that were totally unacceptable hovered on her tongue, Claire diverted by asking, "How are the repairs coming along?"

"I'm afraid we've ground to a halt until the electrician manages to find his way out to Three Bears. Every day I call and every day he gives me another excuse for why he can't make it out. I've done all I can do without a license. It's frustrating."

"It's hunting season," Claire explained. "Unfortunately, our plumber and our electrician are serious hunters, and as a result, jobs back up."

"Oh . . . that explains a lot." Jax lifted the bottle of Chianti they'd opened to have with their dinner and topped off Claire's glass and then his own. "I should have picked up on it. I'll work at Papa Bear in the meantime, but if Nicholas and I are wearing out our welcome . . ."

"Not at all," she hastened to say. "I enjoy the company."

It was true. She hadn't realized just how lonely she'd been until now.

He handed her the wine. "Claire . . . about the Christmas bedtime stories . . ."

"If you don't think we should—"

He interrupted. "No. It's brilliant. Especially beginning with the Bible story."

"He's the reason for the Season."

"And your plan is nonthreatening, and most important of all, it's something Nicholas wants to try. But if it doesn't work . . . if he's not ready . . . I don't want you to be disappointed."

She sipped her wine and smiled. "Like I told Nicholas, no pressure."

She had to repeat those words to herself Sunday evening as she waited for Nicholas to get ready for bed. She was surprisingly nervous. She wanted to help him so badly. And, she very badly didn't want to frighten him or cause him any grief.

When the mantel clock chimed eight P.M., Jax set down the thriller he'd been reading since Nicholas went up to take his bath half an hour ago and stood. "That's our cue. Are you ready, Miss Christmas?"

No! "I am."

She picked up her Bible—her mother's worn and tattered one—and took the hand that Jax extended to her. Her mouth was dry as straw in a manger.

"I'm nervous," Jax told her.

"I'm not," she fibbed. "No pressure."

Nicholas wore Seattle Seahawks pajamas, and he held the first volume of the Percy Jackson series in his lap. His blond hair was damp from his shower. He'd obviously neglected to comb it after toweling it dry since it stuck up all over his head. He sat a little stiffly in his bed, and behind the thick lenses of his glasses, his blue eyes were round and big as an owl's.

"Did you brush your teeth?" Jax asked.

"Yep."

"Prove it."

Nicholas opened his mouth, stuck out his tongue, and made an "ah" sound.

Jax nodded, then sauntered over to the dresser, where he picked up a small black comb and tossed it to his son. "Use it. Claire, you want to sit in the rocking chair?"

"Okay."

As she took a seat in the chair at the foot of the bed, Jax nonchalantly slid onto the mattress beside his son and slung his arm around the boy's shoulder. "I'm ready. You ready, Hot Rod?"

The boy's knuckles went white as he tightened his grip on the book. "I'm ready."

Claire cleared her throat and said, "Dr. Lori shared something Celeste shared with Mr. Chase not long ago. She said that courage is a muscle that is strengthened by use. You're getting to be a very strong young man, Nicholas."

Then she opened her mother's Bible to the second chapter of Luke and read. " 'And it came to pass in those days there went out a decree from Caesar Augustus that all the world should be taxed.' "

When she closed the book a few minutes later, she was almost afraid to look at the troubled eight-year-old. Then he asked, "I thought there were camels in the story?"

Relief rolled over Claire in a wave. "That's Epiphany. It's in the Gospel of Matthew." She hesitated a beat, then added, "We can read it tomorrow if you'd like."

"Okay." Nicholas handed the Percy Jackson book to his dad. "Your turn."

Jax's smile was Star of Bethlehem bright.

Chapter Thirteen

It's nice to work in the sunshine.
—JAX

A week of good weather, available subcontractors, supply orders that arrived in a timely manner, and three not insignificant checks for progress on projects he'd been hired to complete had put a spring in Jax's steps on Friday morning. The fact that Claire and Nicholas had plowed through *How the Grinch Stole Christmas!, The Polar Express,* "'Twas the Night Before Christmas," and "The Gift of the Magi" so far this week didn't hurt his mood any.

Neither did the fact that he had a date tonight.

While varnish dried on the wood floor at Baby Bear and the framing crew tackled Papa Bear, Jax drove over to the Callahan compound on Hummingbird Lake. He went to work installing reclaimed wood on the walls of the dance hall to the notes of Texas country music loaded into the portable sound system that sat on what would be the stage once the building was finished. The physical work was just what he needed, and he was whistling along to Pat Green's "Carry On" when the music abruptly switched off. "Buy you a beer, Lancaster?"

Jax turned toward the speaker. Brick Callahan looked like hell. "You okay, man?"

"Yeah."

His expression said otherwise. Jax arched a brow and waited.

Brick scowled at him and said, "Okay, actually, my day has sucked. Seriously sucked. It's Friday afternoon. You're not on any hard deadline here. Clock out early. Come have a beer with me."

Jax checked his watch. "I have an hour and ten minutes before I need to pick up Nicholas from school. You want to go to Murphy's?"

"Nah. I'll raid my dad's refrigerator. Meet me down at the pier."

"Okay."

Jax pulled the tools from his tool belt, returned them to his toolbox, and stowed it in the bed of his truck. Then he strolled down to the pier that stretched out into Hummingbird Lake. He heard the bang of a screen door, and he glanced behind him to see Brick Callahan carrying a small cooler on a strap over one shoulder and a tackle box. In his opposite hand, he carried two fishing poles.

He didn't say anything when he joined Jax at the end of the pier, simply handed him one of the poles, then set down the cooler and fished out a couple of microbrews.

Jax understood the peace that could be found in silence, so he didn't press the issue. The men fished and drank their beer for a good ten minutes before Brick said, "Women."

Aha. So that's what this is about.

"I hear you, brother."

"Scuttlebutt in town says you got divorced before your boy's mother died. Is that true?"

"Yep."

"Wasn't it hard to do that with your kid?"

"It wasn't my preference." Jax grimaced as he recalled those soul-crushing days and his despair when he realized his efforts to retain shared custody were sunk. "Not my choice."

"Funny how often it's not our choice, isn't it?" The bitterness in Brick's voice said as much as his words did.

Jax rarely discussed his marriage, but something told him Brick needed to know he wasn't alone. "She left me for another guy."

"Well, that sucks rocks."

"My ego certainly took a hit." He waited a beat, then asked, "You have a kid, Callahan?"

"Me? No." He shook his head. "My ex does."

"You're divorced, too?"

"Nah. I was engaged, but we never made it to the altar. Money got in the way."

"Now, that's something I understand."

"Oh, yeah?"

Jax nodded. "Money caused a lot of our problems. My wife's family was loaded. I didn't realize going into the marriage how much I would resent her going to her daddy for everything she wanted." For her part, Lara hadn't realized how much she'd hate being a navy wife.

"See . . . what is it about women and money? My ex wanted me to take anything and everything my grandfather offered. The man's favorite pastime is giving stuff to his grandkids. But I didn't grow up wealthy. I was adopted as a baby, and my mom and pop are salt-of-the-earth, middle-class folks. Hell, I didn't meet my dad until I was ready to go off to college. He and my uncles are all hardworking men who've built their businesses and earned everything they have with their own two hands. That's what I wanted. She couldn't see it. We had a big fight about it and she decided the grass—not to mention the cash—was greener with a banker. Damned if she didn't marry him. Have a baby with him."

"You still love her." Despite the fact that the woman sounded like a gold digger.

Brick finished his beer and tossed the empty into the cooler. "Want another?"

"I'm good."

He reached for another beer, twisted off the cap, then took a long sip. Then he set down his beer and picked his fishing pole back up. Reeling in the line, he said, "I loved her for a long time. Maybe a part of me does still love her, but I don't like her very much. She calls me. Called me again just this morning. She says she's leaving her husband. The old 'marry in haste, repent at leisure' thing. She wants me to take her back."

This time Jax was the one who took a long sip of his beer, more to fill his mouth with something other than advice than because he was thirsty. The man hadn't asked. He wouldn't offer. Guys didn't do that. "What did you tell her?"

"No. I told her no." Brick gave his fishing pole a hard yank, and cranked the reel with excess enthusiasm. "It just about killed me, but I told her no."

Good.

Brick changed his bait and cast his line once again. "Sure would like to catch some fish. My mouth has a hankering for trout tonight for dinner."

"It does sound good," Jax agreed.

After a few moments of silent fishing, Brick declared, "I'm not going to be her crutch. I'm not going to be her excuse. Even if her marriage really is over and it has nothing to do with me, the things that got in our way are still there. Some things can't be fixed. Some things don't change. My attitude toward money hasn't changed. Did yours? Did the breakup with your ex change how you felt about money?"

"No. Not at all. If anything, I think it solidified my position. I don't care how gorgeous she is, I'm not ever getting involved with a wealthy woman again. Money makes life easier, but it doesn't necessarily make life happier. My boy is happier now than he ever was in Seattle. I screwed up when I didn't listen to my instincts. I'm not doing that again."

"You're telling me I should listen to my instincts."

"I'm not offering any advice here, Callahan. You asked a question and I answered it."

"Yeah . . . yeah . . . yeah. The thing is . . . I know that telling her no was the right thing to do. I haven't changed. My grandfather is my business partner. We're in it fifty-fifty. He provided the stake, but I'm building sweat equity. I'm not going back to the Bank of Branch anytime things get a little tight. I'm scraping by with Stardance right now, but that's okay. I'm pouring almost everything I make back into the business. I think it will succeed. I think I'm building something I'll be proud of someday. Hell, I'm already proud of it. You're a guy. You can understand that, right?"

"You don't have to be a guy to understand that, Callahan. The right woman will understand."

Claire understands why I've strapped on a tool belt rather than send out my resume to corporations who have a use for nuclear engineers.

"The right woman," Brick repeated. "I'm afraid that in order to make room for her, I gotta get the wrong woman out of my head first. My ex has really messed with my mind."

"Looks to me that by telling her no, you've taken the first step towards fixing that."

"Yeah. Well. I guess." Brick gave his head a shake, shrugged his shoulders, and then a sly look come over his face. "Maybe you're right. Maybe I do have room now, and I should start looking for her. Maybe I should start with a certain shopkeeper with an affinity for red and green."

Jax knew that Callahan said it as a friendly dig. Nevertheless, that didn't stop his hackles from rising. He snapped, "Claire is taken."

Callahan smirked. "Is she now?"

"Yes." Honesty made Jax add, "I think so. I hope so. We have a date tonight."

"Oh, yeah? Where are you taking her?"

"The Yellow Kitchen."

"Points for that." Brick's pole bent and he yanked and set the hook. Reeling in his catch, he added, "Best place in town."

"So I understand. I haven't been there yet."

"How did you get a table for tonight? Town is bursting at the seams with all the visitors for the big event tomorrow."

"I guess I'm living right."

"I guess you are. Treat her good, Lancaster. Miss Christmas is special."

"I will. I know. She's . . . right."

Brick pulled his catch out of the water. Not a trout, but somebody's lost sneaker. "Story of my life, Lancaster," Brick lamented, staring at the dirty, dripping shoe. "Story of my life.

Friday at five after three, Claire rang up a sale for an Advent calendar purchased by a former crew member of Chase's TV show who was in town for the wedding. She slipped the calendar into a bag, thanked him for his business, and told him not to miss the Italian cream cake at the wedding reception the following day. Once the customer left, she flipped her OPEN sign to CLOSED.

Yes, she was closing two hours early. Yes, she'd likely miss some sales because the streets were busy with visitors, but that's okay. She had bigger fish to fry today.

She needed to go back to Mama Bear and prepare for her date.

Her date.

She couldn't believe she had a date tonight. A first date. The last first date she'd gone on had been with Landon.

She'd worn a little black dress and stiletto heels and carried the Jimmy Choo evening clutch bag she'd bought at a resale shop for the occasion. He'd taken her to a five-star restaurant and ordered five-star wine and entertained her with tales of the sports stars his firm's entertainment division worked with.

"Need a new train of thought," she scolded herself. She refused to spoil the excitement of her mistletoe fling by dwelling on the past.

She *was* excited. Jax had a dinner reservation at the Yellow Kitchen. She'd been surprised by that bit of news when Jax shared it this morning, since she'd assumed the restaurant would be closed for Chase and Lori's rehearsal dinner. According to Jax, the Timberlakes were hosting that event in their home at Heartache Falls. With so many people in town for the wedding, they wanted the restaurant available to accommodate the visitors.

"Ali took my reservation when I called," he'd told Claire. "When I told her I was taking you out on our first date, she said she'd give us her best table."

"That was nice of her."

"That's what I told her. She said she's always happy to further the cause of romance."

Claire had almost challenged him on the word "romance." After all, a fling did not a romance make. The opportunity passed when Nicholas came running downstairs in a panic because he'd forgotten to study his spelling words and the test was that morning. Jax had calmed him down and quizzed him, and Nicholas had sailed through the list, stumbling only on one of the words. "Remember, '*i* before *e*, except after *c*,' big guy."

Nicholas had hit his head with the palm of his hand and said, "D'oh!"

Then the pair traded lines from *The Simpsons* TV show until Claire and Nicholas left for school.

She smiled at the memory of the exchange throughout the day. The more time she spent with Jax, the more she liked him. He was such a good dad, and his doubts about that only made him more endearing. He was smart and witty and hardworking. Sexy. My oh my, the man was sexy.

Which was why after her shower, she spent a ridiculous amount of time choosing which body lotion to smooth onto her skin.

She had plenty from which to choose. Claire liked fragrances. Luxurious body lotions were one of her personal indulgences. Ordinarily, she chose her scents by what mood she was in. Tonight, she had Jax on her mind as she surveyed her selection. Would he like spicy? Floral? Exotic? Something heavy? Light? Which would make her feel good? Pretty? Sexy?

For her mistletoe fling.

Her teeth nibbled at her lower lip. Was she really going to do this? She'd never had a fling before, never gone to bed with a man unless they were in a committed relationship.

As far as you knew at the time, anyway.

Yeah, well, she wasn't going to think about the Lying Lizard Louse tonight now, was she?

She chose a fragrance that made her think of summer nights in Hong Kong and slathered her skin with lotion and pulled on a robe before facing her closet. Deciding what to wear proved to be a significant challenge. Only a couple pieces of the limited wardrobe she'd brought with her to Eternity Springs had survived smoke damage in the fire, and when she'd sat down and ordered an entire new wardrobe from her favorite retailer, she'd gone a little overboard with "date night" clothes. This was Eternity Springs, after all. With winter just around the corner. She didn't have much use for little black dresses and four-inch heels when there were four inches of snow on the ground.

So why did she have three of them hanging in her closet?

"Too much mistletoe," she murmured as she debated between an off-the-shoulder gold blouse that brought out the streaks of summer sunshine in her hair or a green V-neck with an after-five plunge. She finally settled on the green blouse and her black silk bolero pants and chose filmy, emerald-green silk lingerie to wear beneath them.

She finished dressing, touched up her lipstick, then turned toward Tinsel. "Well, sweetheart. How do I look?"

Tinsel's ears perked up and she abandoned her chew toy to come stand at Claire's feet. "I'll take that as a positive response."

Claire took the puppy outside for one more potty break, then tucked her into her crate with a rubber chew toy stuffed with peanut butter and settled down to wait for Jax. She'd heard him leave with Nicholas half an hour ago. He should be back soon.

The ringing of the doorbell a few minutes later initially surprised her, but then she smiled. *He's treating this like we aren't living together.* The gesture made her feel special.

Excitement hummed through her as she took one last glance in the mirror. She wiped her suddenly damp palms on her slacks, reminded herself that flings were meant to be enjoyed, and opened the door saying, "Good evening . . . oh."

Two strangers stood on the front porch of Mama Bear. Both were in their sixties, she'd guess. Both were handsome people, both expensively dressed. The expression on their faces was as confused as hers. "Can I help you?"

The man spoke first. "I'm afraid we've taken a wrong turn. We were looking for Three Bears Valley?"

"This is Three Bears."

"Oh. Well." They shared an unreadable look, then the man said, "We were told our grandson is living here?"

"You're Nicholas's grandparents?"

"Yes. I'm Brian Hardcastle. This is my wife, Linda."

"I'm Claire Branham." She stepped back, opening the door wide. "Please, come in."

They stepped inside Mama Bear and both made a quick scan of the room. Linda's voice held a note of censure in her tone as she asked, "Our grandson is living with you?"

"Yes, he is." Claire recognized that the optics here weren't good, but she didn't figure it was her place to explain it. So she said, "Jax will be here in a few minutes. May I take your coats?"

"Thank you," Brian said.

He helped his wife off with hers, and when he handed both coats over to Claire, she added, "May I get you something to drink? Something to warm you up, perhaps? It's chilly out this evening."

"No, thank you," Linda said.

At the same time, Brian said, "I'd love a cup of coffee."

Claire could have kissed him, so grateful was she for his having provided an excuse to flee the room. Thank goodness Mama Bear's floor plan wasn't "open" with the kitchen part of the great room like Papa Bear's and Baby Bear's. "Please make yourselves at home, and I'll be right back with your coffee."

She hung up their coats and retreated to the kitchen where she instantly regretted not detouring by the mantel where she'd left her phone. Jax should have a heads-up that he had company.

It was obviously a surprise visit. A surprise visit with impeccably poor timing from her point of view. Nothing like having former in-laws pop in for a first date.

She delayed her return to the living room as long as she could manage by putting together a plate of cookies. She placed it, along with Brian Hardcastle's coffee and paper napkins, on a serving tray and carried it into her guests.

She almost dropped it when Brian demanded, "So, what's going on here? You're shacked up with our grandson's father? That's a damned poor example for the boy. How long has this been going on? Did he bring you with him from Seattle?"

Claire was saved from answering because halfway through the man's diatribe, the door opened and Jax stepped into the room. Claire had never been so happy to see someone in her life.

He wore a dress coat and a suit, and he looked so handsome that under other circumstances, he'd have set her heart aflutter. The thunderous scowl on his face distracted her from everything else, even the bright bouquet of flowers he set down on the entry table.

"That's enough, Brian," he snapped, his voice as cold as a snowdrift. "You've stepped way over the line."

"Oh, have I? Have I really? Nice flowers, Lancaster. Where's my grandson?"

His arms at his sides, Jax fisted his hands. "Claire," he began.

"Excuse me," Claire said. "I hear my dog crying. I should run up to my room and check on her."

"A dog?" Linda asked, aghast. "You've forced Nicholas to live with a dog?"

Oh, for heaven's sake.

Claire heard the echo of her mother's voice. *If you can't say something nice, don't say anything at all.* She continued upstairs without responding to Nicholas's grandmother.

There, she sat on the edge of her bed and waited. She heard raised voices downstairs, but she didn't try to eavesdrop. She was too busy brooding. She was so disappointed. She'd been looking forward to their date so much, and now it was ruined. The fact that she was thinking about herself right now made her feel small and petty and mean.

This was one night. Her date. Her fling. It was Jax and Nicholas's life.

"Pity parties are so unattractive," she muttered aloud.

Finally, she heard the front door open and close, and moments later, car doors slammed and an engine started. She waited a few minutes before opening her bedroom door in case Jax needed time to settle himself.

She was surprised to find the great room empty. *He's probably in the kitchen raiding the above-the-refrigerator liquor cabinet and pouring himself an extra-tall bourbon on the rocks.*

She'd taken two steps toward the kitchen when the doorbell rang for the second time that night. "What now?" she murmured. Had the Hardcastles forgotten their coats?

She considered darting back upstairs to hide, but sympathy for Jax stopped her. She noticed that the flowers were missing just as she reached for the doorknob.

Jax stood on porch, the flowers in his hand, an easy smile on his face and a determined glint in his eyes. "Hello, gorgeous. Sorry I'm a little late. I was temporarily held up by a little unimportant family business."

So he thought to pretend that she hadn't been party to the drama of the past twenty minutes? "I appreciate the effort, but that didn't sound like unimportant family business to me, Jax."

"I have a first date with a fascinating woman tonight. I'm not going to let uninvited visitors spoil it. Tomorrow is soon enough for that drama."

He sounded so certain that Claire's heart soared. He wasn't going to allow their date to be ruined. *Works for me.*

Playing along, she said, "Not a problem. I was running a little late myself. Would you like to come in and have a drink before we go?"

"Absolutely."

He stepped inside and handed her the bouquet. "For you."

"Thank you. They're beautiful. I love peonies. Would you like to fix the drinks while I put these in a vase?"

"Happy to. What's your preference?"

"Whatever you're having is fine."

She all but floated into the kitchen. When she returned a few minutes later with a vase filled with flowers, he was pouring drinks into a pair of crystal martini glasses. "How many olives?"

Might as well go wild. "Three, please."

He handed her a vodka martini with three olives and lifted his in a toast. "To mistletoe."

Her pulse went thud-a-thump and her mouth went dry.

He held her gaze over the top of his glass as they sipped their drinks. "Mmmm . . ." Claire said. "I haven't had one of these in a long time. I'd forgotten how delicious they are."

She licked her lips, and he abruptly set down his drink. "Okay, that's all I can take. I tried, Claire. I really tried."

Then he dragged her beneath the mistletoe and kissed her senseless.

Jax had intended to treat this evening like a real first date, which to him meant holding off for a good-night kiss. He'd been prepared to resist the pull of her beauty, but that sensuous slide of her tongue across her full, moist lips defeated resolutions already weakened by his confrontation with Brian.

Right this moment, he needed something positive to offset the negative looming tomorrow and, as usual, Claire Branham supplied it. In spades.

"I feel so lucky to have met you," he told her when the kiss finally ended.

"That's an incredibly nice thing to say, Jax."

"You make me feel pretty incredible." He released her and took a step backward. "Shall we go to dinner?"

He left the words "while we still can" unspoken.

"Sure."

They chatted about inconsequential things during the drive into town. Upon their arrival at the restaurant, they visited a few minutes with Brick, who introduced Jax to his father, Mark Callahan, and Mark's wife, Annabelle, before being seated at their table.

After their waiter took their orders, conversation turned to tomorrow's big event—Chase and Lori's wedding. "I'm looking forward to it," Jax said. "I've been hearing about this special wedding cake ever since we moved to town."

"Maggie Romano's Italian cream cake. It's become quite a tradition for weddings, not to mention the adult-only cakewalk that's part of the school fund-raising festival. I think this year they're talking about selling tickets to watch the competition. It's become quite the brawl."

Jax smiled. "This is the first time I've lived in a small town. I wonder, are all these traditions common in small towns everywhere or is Eternity Springs special?"

Claire sipped her wine. "Eternity Springs is definitely special, but I don't know about other small towns. This is my first, too."

Over their entrées, they talked about places where they'd lived and then places they'd visited. He'd grown up in Arizona, gone to college in California, and traveled the world in the navy. She'd been born and raised in Dallas, attended college in Austin, and her foreign travel was limited to one European trip during high school. It was an appropriate get-to-know-you-better first-date conversation that gave Jax new insight into Miss Christmas. "Dallas, hmm? How did a city girl come to choose Eternity Springs for her new home and business?"

Claire hesitated. She lifted her napkin and wiped her mouth and Jax thought she might deflect the question. She surprised him.

"After I discovered the truth about a certain Lying Lizard Louse, I basically ran away from home. I ended up in this little town about two hours west of Fort Worth, and I needed a potty break and gas for my car. In the bathroom at the minimart, I had a bit of a meltdown." She paused and searched and found a smile. "It was my good luck that a biker gang had pulled in right behind me."

Jax did a double take. "A biker gang?"

She nodded, and a sparkle entered her eyes. "I was sobbing my heart out in the ladies' room, and one of the riders walked inside and took me in her arms and rocked me like a baby."

"Wait a minute." Jax held up his index finger, making a point. "I think I know where this is going. Did this particular biker woman dress in white and gold leathers and drive a Honda Gold Wing?"

"Got it in one. Celeste was riding with a group of friends she'd made while visiting the Callahan ranch in Brazos Bend. She asked me what was wrong, and I started blabbering—surprise, surprise. Seems to be a habit of mine. I still don't know how she managed to get me to tag along to lunch with the group, but before I knew it I was sitting in a little country diner having chicken-fried steak."

"Cream gravy? Fried okra and mashed potatoes, too?"

"Yes."

"Wait a minute, Claire. We should have a moment of reverential silence."

"Seriously, Lancaster? You just plowed away enough pasta to feed a high school cross-country team."

"Yes, and it was delicious. The Yellow Kitchen has more than lived up to its reputation. However, I haven't had chicken-fried steak and cream gravy since I was in college. It was a religious experience."

Claire gave a little laugh. "Well, my meal at Mary's Café was delicious, but I'd classify it as therapeutic rather than religious. Celeste somehow managed to pry the low points of my woebegone love life from me, and show me a path forward if I were brave enough to take it. That woman has an uncanny way of saying just what you need to hear when you need to hear it."

"She convinced you to move to Eternity Springs?"

"Nothing that direct. She talked up the town, though. She mentioned that she thought a Christmas shop would do well here, and that planted the seed. She said something else that resonated in me."

"Oh, yeah? What was that?"

"It sounds a little woo-woo, but remember, we're talking about Celeste. She told me that the way out of the darkness was to discover my own inner light and let it shine. I took that to heart. It took me a little while to get my light lit, and frankly, it still flickers from time to time, but I'm making progress."

"Well, if it's any consolation, from my perspective your light is high-voltage."

"That's a lovely thing to say, Jax," Claire said, beaming.

"It's true." He wanted to ask her for more details about her relationship with old quadruple L and the "truth" that had sent her running away from home, but he reminded himself that this was a first date, and the conversation had taken a serious turn. Better to lighten it back up.

So he asked her what kind of music she liked, then after their server brought dessert—chocolate cake to share— she asked him what exotic foods he'd sampled during his travels. That conversation lasted until the plates had been cleared, and as they sipped one final cup of decaf, talk turned to Forever Christmas and her plans for her upcoming reception unveiling the Twelve Dogs of Christmas ornaments. "By the way, Nicholas made his final layaway payment for his Captain ornament last week."

"He told me. He says you're holding it for him until we put up a Christmas tree."

She lifted the coffee cup in toast. "Thinking positive."

So was Jax. He was positively rethinking his decision about his approach to the end of this first date.

On the drive back to Three Bears Valley, she asked him about life aboard a submarine, and he shared a couple of the more amusing stories. Her laughter was a welcome sound that Jax couldn't help but compare to the tight-lipped, angry response that any mention of the navy invariably elicited from Lara.

When he pulled the car to a stop in front of Mama Bear, the easy mood evaporated. Tension hummed between them. Claire reached for her door release and Jax said, "Wait. Let me come around."

She grinned up at him when he extended his hand to help her out of the car. "Opening the door for a lady, Jax? A little old-fashioned, aren't you?"

"I'm Navy."

"An officer and a gentleman?"

"I'm trying, Claire," he told her honestly. He didn't release her hand. "You make it difficult."

That shut her up. They didn't speak as they climbed the steps toward the front door.

The porch light cast a soft yellow glow across the portal. Claire's shoulders lifted as she sucked in an audible breath, then exhaled a little giggle. "Okay, this is a little weird. I'm not sure of the rules here. Do I ask you in, even though you live here? This is my first mistletoe fling."

Her obvious nervousness was just the push he'd needed. "Don't be nervous, Miss Christmas." He drew her into his arms. "The nice thing about having a mistletoe fling is that we get to make up the rules as we go along. As much as I'd like to dive into Christmas morning, I think it's only fair to us both to have a bit of an Advent, don't you?"

She blinked. "You don't want . . . ?"

"Oh, I want, Claire. I want very, very much. But this was our first date. As much as it pains me to say this, I think first dates should end with a kiss. Don't you?"

Her smile dawned slowly, but its brilliance lit up the night. "I do."

Jax set about to give her a first-date kiss to remember. He figured he must have succeeded because when he finally lifted his head, she stood stupefied until he reached past her and opened the door. "Good night, Claire."

"Oh. Um, good night, Jax. I had a lovely time."

"I did, too."

"Okay, well. I guess I'll . . . um . . . see you in the morning?"

"Yes. I'll see you in the morning, though I expect I'll dream of you tonight."

It was as good an exit line as he'd managed in a very long time, so he turned and left. He was halfway to his destination when she called out. "Jax? Where are you going?"

"To jump in the ice-cold creek."

Her laughter rang out upon the night like a song.

Chapter Fourteen

Mistletoe, mistletoe, and more mistletoe.
—CLAIRE

Saturday morning dawned clear and crisp and gorgeous. As Jax drove into town to pick up Nicholas after his sleepover, he noticed the heavier-than-normal bustling of both vehicle and pedestrian traffic. Lots of visitors in town for the big wedding, he guessed. Wonder if Brian and Linda had had trouble finding a place to stay.

The argument yesterday had been intense. Jax had seen red when he'd heard Brian attacking Claire, and for a few minutes there, he'd come close to throwing a punch. He might have done it, too, if not for dinner reservations for the date. He'd wanted the Hardcastles out of the way fast, and he'd known that decking Brian wasn't the way to accomplish that. Making an appointment to meet them first thing Saturday morning with Nicholas was, so that's what he'd done.

He rang the doorbell at the Cicero home and visited with Rose and her husband for a few moments before hustling Nicholas toward the car. Ordinarily, coaxing his son away from his friends would have taken effort, but Nicholas knew they'd be picking up Captain for his visit to Three Bears, so he was ready to go.

"Did you call Mr. Chase, Dad?" the boy asked as he

climbed into Jax's truck and fastened his seat belt. "Does he know we are on our way?"

"I talked to him. We've had a bit of a change of plans. Instead of you and me driving up to the Timberlakes' house to get him, Chase's dad is bringing Captain to us in town. I have another surprise for you. Guess who has come to visit you?"

"Who?"

"Your grandparents."

"Really?"

"Really. We're meeting them for breakfast at Angel's Rest."

"Cool. Except I already ate breakfast. Miss Rose made us pancakes."

"Your grandfather said something about cinnamon rolls."

"I can always eat cinnamon rolls."

"That's what I figured."

They arrived at Angel's Rest five minutes early for their eight-thirty appointment, and as Jax parked his truck, he spied the Hardcastles already waiting on the front porch of the resort's main structure, Cavanaugh House.

"There they are," Nicholas said. He scrambled down from the truck and took off running toward his grandparents.

Jax watched the reunion with mixed emotions. Obviously, Lara's parents loved his son, and Nicholas returned that emotion. It was in the boy's best interests for Jax and the Hardcastles to reach some sort of peace between them.

Upon spying Nicholas, the Hardcastles rose from their seats and descended the porch steps.

Nicholas ran into his grandparents' arms. "Mimi! Pops! I didn't know you were coming."

"We wanted it to be a surprise," Linda said to the boy.

Brian extended his hand toward Jax. "Good morning, Lancaster."

"Brian."

"Thanks for coming," Brian added as the two men exchanged a handshake.

"I said I'd be here."

"Guess what?" Nicholas broke in. "I'm taking care of Captain while Mr. Chase is on his wedding vacation. Remember Captain? He's Mr. Chase's dog who I made friends with during camp. I get him today because Mr. Chase and Dr. Lori are getting married later. Dad and I are going to the wedding. I got new clothes to wear because I've outgrown my other dress-up clothes. Captain isn't going to be at the wedding. He's going to stay at Three Bears with Tinsel. Tinsel is Miss Claire's dog. She let me pick out her name. I help take care of her, but I'm not in charge of Tinsel. I'm gonna be in charge of Captain. I have to feed him and make sure he has water. Dad says he can sleep in my room, but he's not allowed to sleep in my bed."

When the boy finally stopped to catch a breath, his grandmother laughed. Brian said, "Sounds like you're happy here, Nicholas."

"I love it here. I have three new best friends and a bunch of regular friends. Guess what? I scored a goal at soccer practice yesterday! Can I have a cinnamon roll now? Daddy said we're having cinnamon rolls."

"I'm sorry, Nicholas, but the bakery is closed today, and I wasn't able to get any cinnamon rolls. However, Ms. Blessing has coffee cake for us. I sneaked a bite. It's very good."

"Cake for breakfast? Cool!"

Brian met Jax's gaze. "The dining room is full, but we have a table reserved on the upper verandah, if that's all right with you."

"That's fine."

"Is Mr. Timberlake on his way with Captain now, Dad? I don't think Miss Celeste allows dogs upstairs."

"You have time to eat coffee cake with your grandparents before Captain arrives. You'll be able to watch for him from the verandah."

Linda and Nicholas led the way, and when Jax started to follow, Brian stopped him with a hand on his arm. "If I could have a minute, Lancaster?"

Expecting another attack, Jax braced himself. "Sure."

"I owe you an apology."

If he'd declared he was a Martian, Jax wouldn't have been more surprised. In his experience, Brian Hardcastle didn't apologize for anything.

"I was out of line last night. I'm sorry I gave Ms. Branham a hard time."

"You owe her the apology."

"I know," Brian said with a wince. "I intend to see to that before we leave town."

"Good."

Brian stuck his hands into his pants pockets and rocked back on his heels, his expression earnest. "I want this to be a good visit, Jax. Can we start over?"

Brian Hardcastle was treating Jax with a deference he'd never shown before, and Jax didn't quite know what to make of it. "Sure. We'd better catch up with Nicholas and Linda or the kid will eat our share of coffee cake. He's been a bottomless pit lately."

Up on the verandah, Nicholas chattered on like a magpie while downing two and a half pieces of coffee cake. Jax didn't miss the fact that the Hardcastles asked probing questions of the boy, but he honestly didn't mind. If they'd traveled to Colorado thinking they'd find their grandson unhappy and more emotionally troubled than before, the best way to prove them wrong was to let Nicholas ramble.

Nicholas was telling them about the haunted house

Brick Callahan was putting together out at Hummingbird Lake for Halloween. "It's gonna be a haunted pirate ship. My friends Meg and Cari say it's going to be really, really cool. I can't wait."

"A haunted house?" Linda repeated. To Jax, she asked, "Do you think that's something he should be doing?"

Annoyance rolled through Jax's gut. "I think I'm going to take my cues from Nicholas."

"But—"

"There's Captain!" Nicholas said, his voice filled with gleeful excitement. "I've gotta go."

He waited long enough to shovel one last bite of coffee cake into his mouth, then he scrambled from his chair and darted toward the staircase.

"Don't run in the house," Jax called after him.

"Well," Linda said, a bittersweet smile on her face. "He certainly seems to have settled in well here. It also appears he's conquered his cynophobia."

"I think we can pretty much call him cured in that respect," Jax agreed. "He's trying to convince me that he should have a dog of his own."

"That's amazing," Brian said.

Jax met his gaze directly and said, "Eternity Springs is amazing. He's made some progress with regard to Christmas, too."

"Is it the psychologist he's seeing? The one from the camp?"

"Dr. McDermott. Actually, Nicholas hasn't been able to meet with him yet because Dr. McDermott has been on an extended vacation with his wife. He's due back around Thanksgiving. Nicholas has an appointment then."

"So who is he seeing in the meantime?" Brian asked.

"No one," Jax responded, his chin lifted and a defiant gleam in his eyes.

Brian and Linda shared a look, but to Jax's surprise,

they didn't attack. So he told them about Claire's reading program and Nicholas's positive response to it. "She owns a Christmas shop in town, and she's having a big event there next week. Nicholas wants to go."

Linda brought her hand to her chest. "To a Christmas shop? Is that advisable, Jax?"

"Nicholas is the one steering the boat here. I take all my cues from him. So far, it seems to be working."

"The change is amazing," Brian said. "And after all the things we tried to do to improve the situation in Seattle. To think that all it took was a small town."

"It took *this* small town," Jax corrected. "And these people."

"Hey, Mimi and Pops!" Nicholas called from below. "Look. This is Captain! Come down and meet him."

Brian signed the tab and the adults went down to join Nicholas. Outside, Jax spied Mac Timberlake speaking to Celeste, and he veered toward them while the Hardcastles joined his son.

"I loaded Captain's bed and some food in the back of your truck, Lancaster."

"Thanks. How's everything going at your place?"

"So far, so good. Chase is Mr. Cool today."

"Good for him."

Jax heard Nicholas call his name. "We're going for a walk, Dad. I'm gonna show Mimi and Pops my school and the park where I play soccer. Want to come?"

"Sure."

Nicholas answered his grandmother's questions about his teacher and his classmates as they strolled toward the footbridge that crossed Angel Creek. They continued down Sixth Street to the school and then on to Davenport Park. After that, Nicholas wanted to show his grandparents the library and Galen's dad's glass studio. "It's really cool, Pops. Mr. Cicero has these ovens and they're superhot and the glass is all melted and he puts it on a stick and shapes it. He's working on a big project right now, but when he's finished he's going to let me and Galen make something."

"I've heard of Cicero," Linda said. "He's a very talented artist."

"He has long hair like a girl. But I like him. I like Galen's mom, Dr. Rose, too. She made really good pancakes."

Jax tagged along, not really offering much of anything to the conversation, giving Nicholas free rein to wander where he liked. It was a perfect day for a stroll. Eternity Springs buzzed with energy, the streets and shops bustling with visitors in town for the wedding. "Based on the notices in the shop windows, this place is shutting down at noon," Brian observed.

"The wedding is at two," Jax said. "I think they've invited every local resident."

"Miss Claire is closing at noon." Nicholas looked at his father. "I think we should go there now. Mimi and Pops need to meet Miss Claire."

Jax couldn't hide his surprise. "You want to take your grandparents to Forever Christmas?"

Nicholas nodded. "Captain and I can wait outside."

Jax placed his hand on his son's shoulder. "Hot Rod, you might not know this because we never go down that block of Cottonwood. Miss Claire has Christmas trees in pots outside on the sidewalk."

Nicholas sucked in a breath, and for the first time that morning, his tone sounded subdued as he said, "Oh. I didn't know that."

"We can visit your Miss Claire another time," Linda suggested.

"No." Nicholas lifted his chin and he courageously met Jax's gaze. "I can walk down the street."

Jax had a flashback of the last time he'd seen the boy

lying in a hospital bed, and he had to bite back a ferocious
"No!"

Instead, he reminded himself to take his cues from his
son. "All right. We can give it a try. If you change your
mind, no harm, no foul."

Brian Hardcastle opened his mouth, but at a sharp look
from Jax, shut it without comment. Linda didn't take the
hint. "Jax, I don't think—"

"Linda!" Brian interrupted. "Remember . . ."

She listened to her husband, zipped her lips, and followed Nicholas.

The closer they drew to the intersection of Third and
Cottonwood, the slower Nicholas walked and the quieter
he became. When he fell back to walk beside his father,
Jax rested his hand on the boy's shoulder.

The big pots with lighted evergreens that sat on either
side of Forever Christmas's front door came into view on
the opposite side of the street. Nicholas saw them and
stopped. Linda Hardcastle reached for her husband's hand.
Jax gave Nicholas's shoulder a reassuring squeeze. "No
harm, no foul, buddy."

Nicholas shoved his glasses up on the bridge of his nose,
took a deep breath, and said, "It's okay, Dad. I can do this.
They are just trees. I can do it."

And darned if he didn't do exactly that.

Nicholas and Captain walked right up to the street lamp
across from the Christmas shop, and while Captain sniffed
around the base of it, Nicholas's gaze darted toward the
big glass display windows where lights twinkled and angels flew and a snowman bowed his top hat. The kid didn't
flinch. "Take Mimi and Pops inside, Dad. Captain and I
will hang here. I doubt Miss Claire would want Captain
running around her shop. He's pretty big."

Grinning, Jax nodded. "I think you're right. Want me
to tell Miss Claire you said hi?"

"That'd be good."

"Stay out of the street." Jax motioned toward the Hardcastles. "Shall we?"

As the three adults crossed the street, Brian said, "He's a different boy."

Jax held the door for Linda and as the chimes rang "Jingle Bells," he said, "He's healing. He's getting back to being the boy he used to be."

Claire's welcoming smile upon seeing Jax faded somewhat when she spied who arrived with him. Brian kept his word by rolling out an apology that sounded sincere, and graciously, Claire accepted it before excusing herself to answer another shopper's question. While Jax positioned himself in the book section near a window where he could keep an eye on Nicholas, Linda said, "If we have a few more minutes, I think I'll look around a bit. It truly is a fabulous store."

Brian nodded. "Go ahead. I'll take this opportunity to speak with Jax."

What now? Jax wondered as Brian perused the shelves. "This is quite an excellent selection of books. I'm impressed. Looks like she needs to restock *The Christmas Angel Waiting Room,* though."

Jax shook his head. "Do me a favor and don't bring that up. What is it you want to talk to me about, Brian?"

The older man sighed and rubbed the back of his neck. "Well, first thing I'll say is that it's obvious that this trip to Colorado has been good for the boy. In all honesty, it's not what we expected. You were right and I was wrong."

"Wow," Jax drawled. "I feel like we need a plaque or something to mark this moment."

"I deserve that." Brian exhaled loudly, then added, "I might as well eat the whole crow. Linda and I were wrong to try to take the parenting decisions out of your hands."

At that, Jax's suspicions went on high alert. "What's your game, here, Brian? What do you want from me?"

Hardcastle's gaze shifted toward the window, and Jax watched him watch Nicholas. The older man cleared his throat and said, "We miss him. We came out here hoping to convince you to come home to Seattle."

"Seattle is not my home."

"It can be. I come bearing a job offer."

As Brian reached into the inner pocket of his jacket, Jax shook his head. "I'm not a bookseller, in any way, shape, or form."

"It's not from Hardcastle Books."

He handed over a sealed envelope. Jax recognized the logo in the upper left-hand corner. Boeing.

His breath whooshed from his lungs. He pulled out his pocketknife and slit the envelope open. Removing the three-page offer, he scanned the contents and his heart began to thud. A dream job—in his field. A dream salary. Hell. It was three steps higher than the job he'd originally applied for.

"How did you manage this?"

"I play golf with the CEO."

Jax's mind spun. His pride would prefer that he got a job as a result of his own efforts, but there was truth in the old saying that it wasn't what you knew, but who you knew. The man couldn't have pulled this particular string back in July? Nevertheless, it didn't matter. "I promised Nicholas we would stay here through the end of the school year. I'm not going back on my word."

"Fair enough. It's obvious he's happy here. Believe it or not, Linda and I wouldn't want to do anything to change that. Coming here . . . seeing him . . . seeing the progress he's made . . . we don't want to upset that applecart. Check the offer dates, Jax. You have some time."

He scanned the letter once again and located the date on the third page. "July Fourth? It's good to July Fourth?"

"My golf buddy is a patriot. He supports the military. Supports veterans. And, he knew Lara when she was a little girl. He cares about her son."

Wow. As Jax rubbed his hand across his stubbled jaw, his gaze sought and found Claire. Beautiful, sexy, and sweet Miss Christmas.

Miss Eternity Springs.

Damn. He couldn't be a handyman the rest of his life. "I don't know what to say, Brian."

"You don't have to say anything. It's something to have in your back pocket."

"And in return?"

"Nothing. No strings attached. Linda and I recognize that we could have . . . we should have . . . handled the situation better. Like I said, we miss Nicholas. We hope you'll allow us to be part of our grandson's life."

"It's not my intention to keep him from you. I think—"

He broke off when Claire and Linda approached. "Mrs. Hardcastle said you have a surprise for me?"

"I do. Actually, though, it's Nicholas who has the surprise. Take a look." Jax motioned toward the window and Claire's face lit up. Seeing that Nicholas was looking their way, she waved. The boy waved back. "He wanted his grandparents to meet you."

"He's looking into the shop, Jax."

"I know. Isn't it great? I think I've figured out what this is about. He's working up to attend the big event next week. I'll bet you money."

"The Dog Room," Claire said. "That does make sense. He's asked a lot of questions about it."

At Linda's quizzical look, Claire explained about the Twelve Dogs of Christmas ornaments and described the special display of all things pet-and-Christmas-related that she planned to unveil during a reception the following week. "I want to go out and say hi to him. Jax, would you watch the shop for a few minutes for me?"

"Sure."

The Hardcastles accompanied Claire, and Jax watched through the window as his son began speaking animatedly to his grandparents and Claire. Idly, he reached out and ran his finger along the wing made of feathers on an angel ornament hanging on the Christmas tree decorating the window. He recognized that he needed to readjust his thinking where his former in-laws were concerned.

They'd done him a solid when they stepped up and cared for Nicholas when Jax couldn't get free of his contract to the navy. He didn't often think about it from their point of view. It couldn't have been easy for them. Healthy six-year-olds were a lot of work. A child like Nicholas who suffered nightmares and panic attacks and instances of inconsolable crying had been exponentially more work. But Brian and Linda never hesitated. They'd stepped up and given him a home and loved him—even in the depths of their grief over the loss of their beloved only daughter.

Nicholas was all they had left of Lara. Since Jax's parents were deceased, the Hardcastles were the only grandparents his son had. They didn't threaten the boy's health or safety or security. They no longer threatened Jax's relationship with his son. He needed to let go of the anger that he'd nursed since the hypnosis debacle and welcome them back into his son's life.

Claire returned to the shop with her eyes sparkling. "Your son is spectacular."

"I know. I'm so proud of him."

"Looks like he's soothed the grandparent waters, too. The last thing I expected was for Mr. Hardcastle to walk in here and apologize."

Jax smirked. "Must be that Eternity Springs mojo at work."

"Must be."

"So, you're closing at noon? We'll see you at home shortly afterward?"

"That's my plan, but if you need to spend more time with Nicholas's grandparents, I'll certainly understand. I can find my way to the church by myself."

"Nope. We're not missing the wedding. I suffered through the trauma of buying the boy new dress clothes, new shoes, and getting him a haircut in preparation for Chase and Dr. Lori's wedding. We're not missing it." He leaned down and kissed her cheek. "I'll see you in a couple of hours."

Jax rejoined Nicholas and the Hardcastles, and they continued their walking tour of Eternity Springs, ending back at Angel's Rest. There, Nicholas grabbed a tennis ball from Captain's box of toys, removed the retriever from his leash, and he and his grandfather began taking turns throwing the ball.

Linda took a seat on a park bench to watch the action. Jax sat atop a four-foot rock wall that divided Celeste's contemplation garden from the open area where the boy and dog played. The silence between them was comfortable enough, so when Linda finally spoke, he wasn't expecting an attack. "You and Lara never suited."

Jax almost groaned out loud. It was always one step forward, two steps back with the Hardcastles.

"Her father always put her up on a pedestal, and right or wrong, she needed the same from the man in her life. You expected more from her, and she couldn't make that jump."

Jax couldn't argue with that, so he kept his mouth shut.

"I think she could have been happy with James," Linda continued, "but the miscarriage damaged her. I don't know if it was hormonal or emotional or a combination of the two, but she wasn't thinking right. I told her to seek help, but I blame myself for not following through, not making sure it happened. As a result, I overcompensated where Nicholas is concerned."

"It's not your fault, Linda. Or Brian's. In the end, it wasn't even Lara's fault. In her right mind, she never would have done anything to put Nicholas at risk."

"She was a good mother."

"She was a fabulous mother. I remember how great she was with Nicholas when he was a colicky infant. I would be tired and frustrated and at my wit's end, and she always stayed calm and collected. That is the Lara I'm going to try to remember from now on. That's the Lara I plan to share with Nicholas as he grows up."

"You are a good man, Jax. I know that Brian apologized, but I need to do so, too. I'm so sorry, Jax. You and Lara might not have been right for each other long-term, but I think you must have been meant-to-be for a time in order to give this world Nicholas. You and my daughter created a fabulous, special child. Seeing him today so happy and engaged has been so reassuring. You're a good father, Jax."

"Thank you, Linda. I appreciate your saying that." He focused on the rush and bubble of Angel Creek and thought of his ex-wife without resentment for the first time in a very long time. "Nicholas is lucky to have you and Brian. I've been lucky that Nicholas has you. Claire told me recently that Eternity Springs is a great place for making fresh starts. What do you say we give it a try?"

"I think that's a fabulous idea."

"In that case, do you and Brian have plans for Thanksgiving? Claire and I have already made plans to cook for a few friends. If you and Brian would like to join us, we'd love to have you."

Tears flooded her eyes and she gave him a tremulous smile. "We'd like that very much. Your Claire wouldn't mind?"

He didn't correct her "your" reference. He certainly thought of Claire as his at this point. "I'll check with her, but I'm sure she'd want Nicholas to share the holiday with his grandparents."

"She's a lovely woman, Jax. I can tell that she cares about both you and Nicholas."

"She is. She does. We like her very much."

"I'm glad, Jax. I want you both to be happy."

"We're getting there." His gaze shifted in the general direction of Forever Christmas. If Nicholas managed to conquer his fear to the point where he could enter the store, Jax would change that from "getting" to "almost" there.

"One other thing I might mention," Linda said. "Brian and I recognize how difficult it is to be a single parent. If you ever want a break, if you ever need a babysitter, I hope you'll consider us. We'd be happy to fly in for a long weekend, or even bring Nicholas out to Seattle, if you think that would be good for him. I promise we'd be careful with him, and we'd follow all your wishes."

Jax considered her. At this point, he wouldn't have any reservations about allowing Nicholas to spend some time with his grandparents and without him. Fresh starts, and all. "That's quite an offer, Linda. Quite a timely offer. Nicholas has a Friday and Monday off from school the first week in November. Teacher in-service days. Shall we ask him if he'd like to visit Seattle?"

"Nothing would make me happier."

The prospect of four days alone with Claire made Jax pretty darn happy, too.

Chapter Fifteen

*Whoever invented teacher in-service
days needs a raise.*
—JAX

Claire attended Lori and Chase's wedding and reception with Jax and Nicholas. The ceremony was lovely, the party fun.

Before the father-daughter dance, Cam Murphy made a speech about love and the power of perseverance that brought everyone to tears. Chase gave a public tribute to his mother that made every woman in the room a little wistful. Later in the evening, Claire discovered that Jax was quite the dancer, and following a discussion about Texas red dirt music with Brick and Devin Murphy, Jax had joined in with Daniel Garrett to sing a few old Willie Nelson tunes. She discovered he had quite a voice, too. Celebration, laughter, and joy proved to be quite the mood lifter, and by the time the bride and groom departed Angel's Rest to begin their honeymoon in Tibet, she had a whole chapter's worth of positive thoughts to record in her journal.

The Hardcastles departed Eternity Springs for their return trip to Seattle following a Sunday-afternoon picnic at Hummingbird Lake. That night, after Nicholas's bedtime stories, Claire and Jax shared their first time alone since their Friday-night date.

He caught her beneath a sprig of mistletoe that hadn't

been hanging from the kitchen doorway threshold when she'd gone upstairs to read "'Twas the Night Before Christmas."

After kissing her senseless, Jax said, "Claire, have you ever been to Silver Eden Resort?"

"No, I haven't. I've heard it's fabulous, though."

"I happen to have a voucher for a two-night stay at Silver Eden, part of a swag bag that was given to parents of Rocking L campers. Nicholas is going to Seattle for a long weekend the first weekend in November. It's a perfect opportunity to put the fling in our mistletoe. How about it, Claire? Would you go away with me for the weekend? I thought I'd make a reservation in the name of Stamina Sven."

Claire's heart began to thud. A long weekend at a romantic resort? Heck yes! "I'd love that, Jax."

"You can get someone to cover for you at the shop?"

"I'll just close it for the weekend." She could do that. She was the boss. "I'll look forward to the trip, Sven. Thanks for the invite."

They exchanged another long kiss beneath the mistletoe, and she had a difficult time going to sleep that night. Luckily, prep work for the Chamber of Commerce event scheduled the following week kept her busy during the days, so she didn't waste too much time in daydreams. The evenings were a long, slow sexual-tension build, held in check by the presence of a third-grade chaperone.

Each evening, she continued to read to Nicholas, and with every day that passed, he seemed a little more comfortable with the subject matter. He walked by the shop on two separate occasions. A third time, he actually crossed the street and walked right past her Christmas tree pots just as a customer opened the door to exit the shop.

He went a little pale at the sound of the jingle-bell chimes, but he didn't run away. Claire was so proud of him.

On Thursday night, he asked about the upcoming chamber event. "Are you really going to have a whole room in your shop for dog stuff, Miss Claire? A room like your Angel Room?"

"Yes. I'm calling it the Christmas Doghouse."

Nicholas giggled. "That's funny. Isn't that funny, Dad?"

"I think I've been there before," Jax drawled, a teasing glint in his eyes. "So which of the rooms are you using for your Doghouse?"

"One of the ones upstairs. I've noticed that some of my customers hesitate to go up there, and I think the Doghouse will draw them up."

"Good thinking. You have a knack for retail, Claire. Which room are you using? The living room?"

"No." She hesitated a moment before confessing, "My bedroom."

Jax grinned. "Is there some symbolism in that choice, Miss Christmas?"

"Only square-footage concerns, Mr. Lancaster," she replied. "It's the largest room upstairs, and I have lots of merchandise to display."

"Is it all set up already?" Nicholas asked.

"It's about half done. I hope to finish up on Sunday afternoon while the shop is closed."

"I sure would like to see it," Nicholas said, a wistful look on his face.

Claire patted his hand. "When I get it all set up, I'll take pictures. I'll show them to you if you'd like."

"Maybe." He picked up one of the Christmas books she'd left lying on the foot of his bed and flipped through it. "All the kids at school are going to the party. Galen says Mrs. Murphy is baking cookies for you shaped like dog paws."

"Yes, she is." Claire shared a quick look with Jax. "You know, Nicholas, you're welcome to visit the shop any time you'd like, but things are going to be pretty crazy around there Tuesday night. I could give you a sneak peek once it's all set up if you want to try it."

He shrugged. "Is there really going to be a dog parade? Galen said so. He said all the dogs who are on ornaments are going to be in a parade wearing costumes. I said I don't think that's true because I'm in charge of Captain and Captain's on an ornament and I haven't heard anything about a parade. And what about Mortimer? I don't think it's a good idea to let him go inside Forever Christmas."

"Twelve dogs in Forever Christmas? The very idea makes me shudder. No, Nicholas. Galen is mistaken about that. We're not having a parade. The dogs will be there in ornaments, only. Well, except for Tinsel, of course."

"Is *she* going to wear a costume?"

Claire tilted her head and considered the answer. "I don't know. I've considered it, but honestly, I have too many too cute costumes to pick from." Casually, she said, "Would you like to help me choose? I could bring the possibilities home tomorrow night."

"Sure. We could try that."

Later when Jax came downstairs after his part of storytime, Claire handed him his glass of wine and lifted hers in toast. "Here's to progress."

They clinked glasses. "He wants it. That's a big part of the battle, I think."

"I have a large selection of Tinsel-sized dog costumes from which to choose. They run the gamut from innocuous to five-alarm Christmas. What do you think I should bring?"

"Bring 'em all. I have a sneaking feeling that he's going to show up at your reception on Tuesday night."

"From your mouth to an angel's ears," Claire said.

After closing the shop the following day, Claire filled a bag with a variety of costumes for Tinsel. Had she really purchased twelve different costumes for dogs ten pounds and below? "Ridiculous, Branham."

Although she'd bet that Sage Rafferty would buy seven or eight of them for her Snowdrop.

She arrived back at Three Bears Valley to find Jax on a ladder at Baby Bear, adjusting the downspout of a gutter. She took a moment to appreciate the view of worn jeans stretched tight across a firm butt. "Tinsel, the first week in November can't get here soon enough."

As she and Tinsel exited the car, Captain rounded the corner of Mama Bear, a big rawhide bone in his mouth. Jax waved and descended the ladder. He met her with a toe-curling kiss. "You're home early."

"I wanted to get home before Nicholas. He's still at soccer practice, isn't he?"

Jax checked his watch. "It ends about now. Cicero is driving him home."

"Good. I'd like you to look at these costumes. Weed any out that you think might be too much for him."

"Okay."

He asked her about her day as he and both dogs followed her up the steps into Mama Bear and on into the kitchen. While he washed his hands, she spread the costumes out on the kitchen table. Jax dried his hands on a dishtowel and surveyed the stack. He checked the Forever Christmas price tag on the reindeer costume at the top of pile and shook his head. "Seventeen dollars? Seriously? People will pay that for a dog costume?"

"It's cute. It has matching reindeer antlers."

"People have more money than sense, I swear."

"How do you think Nicholas will react to them?"

Jax flipped through the stack. "Honestly, I don't have a clue. I don't know what to expect from him at this point. The only thing that gives me pause is the jingle bell necklace."

"I know." Claire bit at her bottom lip. "I debated even bringing that one home."

"Still, I hate to underestimate him. The door chimes didn't faze him. I say keep the bells in there and see how it goes. The 'take our cues from Nicholas' approach seems to be working all right."

"Okay."

She returned the costumes to the bag and then suddenly found herself backed up against the kitchen cabinets. His hands on her hips, Jax stared down into her face, a now-familiar wicked glint in his eyes. "Fifteen days, Miss Christmas."

She smoothed her hands across his chest, the soft, well-worn flannel of his shirt a sharp contrast to the hard, unyielding muscles of his chest. She wanted to purr. "I know."

"It seems like forever."

"I know. I looked at their Web site today during lunch. They have a spa that makes the one at Angel's Rest look spartan."

"Oh, yeah?" He was staring at her mouth. "We'll have to check it out."

"The massages looked interesting."

He arched a brow. "I think you're already booked for massages with Sven."

"Oh? He does massage, too?"

"Honey, Sven will massage anything you want, for however long you want. As many times as you want."

She blinked. Twice. And blushed red as Santa's suit.

Jax laughed then closed his mouth over hers in a steamy kiss that ended only when the bark of the dogs alerted them to an approaching vehicle. "The anticipation may be the death of me."

"I know . . ." Claire moaned. "You know, Jax, I do close the shop for lunch breaks. While the children are in school."

"Miss Christmas, I'm shocked, I say. Are you proposing a nooner?"

"I . . . uh . . . that's not the term I'd use."

"Oh? Do tell."

"Well . . . how about . . ." She licked her lips slowly. "Rendezvous?"

"French. Brings to mind French maids. Claire, you have all those costumes . . . what do you have in adult sizes?"

She trailed a finger down the center of his chest. He sucked in his gut reflexively when she reached his navel. "I do have a closet you might want to peruse sometime during the next two weeks. It's in the second bedroom of the old apartment. I keep it locked. You can ask for the key."

As Nicholas's footsteps pounded on the porch, Jax grabbed her finger and nipped it. "You play to win, Miss Christmas."

"Always," she said lightly, though it took effort to maintain the tone. As much as she enjoyed this long seduction, it was killing her, too.

Especially since this fling had taken on the sense of being something more serious.

Jax released Claire's hand and took a step backward as Nicholas burst into the kitchen. "I'm home. I'm starving! Do we have cake? I want cake."

"I want to win the lottery, too," Jax replied. "Guess we will both have to settle for fruit."

"Fruit! Ah, Dad. We ran laps today. I should get something better than fruit."

"It's pizza night. You know the rules."

"Pizza!" Without further argument, Nicholas ran to the fruit bowl and grabbed a banana and an apple. He sat in his usual chair and eyed the bag sitting in the middle of the kitchen table. "What's that?"

Mindful of his previous reaction to her red-and-green

logo bags, she'd used an unmarked trash bag for her booty. "I brought home costumes for Tinsel."

"Oh." He contemplated the bag as he ate his banana.

"Want to talk about school, Hot Rod? How did you do on your math test?"

"Good. I'm sure I aced it. I suck at soccer, though."

"Language, boyo," his father cautioned.

"Sorry. I don't like bouncing the ball off my head and I keep forgetting I'm not supposed to use my hands. I'll be glad when soccer is over. I want to do basketball."

"Didn't you score a goal recently?" Claire asked. "I think you're probably better than you give yourself credit for."

Nicholas shrugged. "I'm still ready for basketball to start."

"It won't be long now," Jax said.

"November tenth. Right when I come back from visiting Mimi and Pops. I saw Coach Lucca at school and he told me." He shot them a wicked grin and added, "I caught him smooching on Mrs. Lucca when I delivered a note for the principal to the kindergarten room."

"Oops," Claire said.

"Mrs. Lucca had a message for you, Dad. She said that Holly would finish her CPR class this weekend, so she'll be ready to start babysitting. What's CPR, Daddy?"

"It's an emergency first-aid technique."

"Oh. Are you going to let Holly Montgomery babysit me? I like her. She's good at basketball."

"We might give that a try," Jax said, with a glance toward Claire.

Nicholas polished off his banana, licked his fingers, and said, "In the picture Miss Celeste showed me of Three Bears before the fire, Papa Bear had a basketball goal. Are you going to build it back, Dad?"

"I am."

"You should do it next."

"That could probably be arranged."

"Awesome. Miss Claire? Would you show the costumes to me?"

"I will. How should we do it? One at a time or should I lay them out for you to see all together?"

"All together, I think. So what sort of costumes do you have?"

She ticked them off on her fingers. "I have three or four different Santa suits, a reindeer, a snowman, one that's made to look like a gift box. An elf. An angel. A Christmas tree. Hmm . . . what else?"

"Those all sound sorta lame. Of course, Tinsel is a girl so she can wear something embarrassing. Captain wouldn't wear a costume."

"I'm not sure, but I think I should be annoyed about that," Claire teased. "I'll set them out on the sofa in the family room, and you come out when you're ready."

Nicholas bit into his apple as Claire exited the kitchen. Her nerves were strung tight. She sent up a quick little prayer that they were doing the right thing, then she set out the dog costumes. Nicholas and Jax exited the kitchen a few minutes later, both looking tense.

Nicholas took small steps toward her. His gaze zipped over the items she'd left out on the sofa, right to left. He looked a second time, and then relaxed.

He stepped forward, studied the costumes one by one, and slowly shook his head. He picked up a Santa beard and held it out toward her. "Miss Claire. Do you really want to embarrass Tinsel this way?"

"Too much, you think?"

"Yeah."

She motioned toward an elastic band covered in green

velvet and sporting a dozen jingle bells. "What about the necklace?"

Claire held her breath as Nicholas picked it up. Bells jingled. Tinsel tilted her head toward the sound.

Nicholas went down on his knees and snapped his fingers for Tinsel. Both she and Captain moved toward him. He slipped the jingle bells around Tinsel's neck. The collie shook. Bells pealed. Claire gripped her hands so hard that her knuckles turned white.

Nicholas shrugged. "I guess that's okay. Just don't put a hat on her. Hats on dogs are just embarrassing."

Then he looked up at his father. "Can we go out and play, Dad?"

"How much homework do you have?"

"None!"

Jax hooked a thumb over his shoulder. "Hit the grass, Jack."

Claire grabbed the jingle bell off Tinsel right before she darted outdoors after the boy and the other dog. Laughing, she turned a triumphant gaze toward Jax. "How about that!"

He picked her up, spun her around, and said, "You are a miracle, Claire Branham. I want you to know one thing. Hats . . . you know, those little French-maid lace blob things? Hats are okay with me."

At noon on the day of the Chamber of Commerce fundraiser, Jax sauntered into Fresh bakery and waved a hello to Sarah Murphy, who was speaking on the phone. She held up a finger signaling just a minute. Jax made himself at home by pouring a cup of the complimentary coffee Sarah kept available for customers whenever the bakery was open. He sat sipping the strong brew and waited for Sarah to finish her conversation with her son Devin. After his sister's wedding, the young man had returned to the

Caribbean, where he ran a charter fishing service out of Bella Vita Isle.

Sarah had tears in her eyes when she hung up the phone. "Everything okay?" Jax asked.

"Yes. I'm just missing my kids. I've decided I don't like having an ocean or two between us."

"Any word from the honeymooners?"

"We heard from them yesterday. They're having a blast. Chase is over the moon with excitement over the rafting trip Lori arranged as a surprise. He asked about Captain. I told him that Nicholas brought him by to visit over the weekend. Your son is just so darned cute about being the dog-sitter for Lori and Chase."

"He's taking his responsibilities very seriously," Jax said.

"He seems to be doing well. Eternity Springs agrees with him?"

"It does. He says he's going to Claire's reception tonight."

"Oh, that would be fabulous, Jax."

"I'm hopeful. And I'm here to pick up dog paw cookies for Claire."

Sarah laughed. "They're ready. I'll bet she's a busy little beaver today. Our chamber meetings aren't always well attended, but I haven't heard of anyone who is planning to skip tonight's reception." Slyly, she added, "So, you're an insider. Have you seen what she's doing with this Christmas Doghouse?"

"Not yet. She's putting the finishing touches on it today. That's why she's closed this afternoon."

"She's such a clever girl. People around here do love their pets. I'll be curious to see just how much money she raises for the chamber with the ornaments. Celeste is president of the organization this year, and she has big plans for the money."

"Claire mentioned to me that the chamber has earmarked the funds the ornament sales raise for new Christmas decorations for the town."

"The stuff we have now is tired and tattered and a mishmash of styles. I know Celeste has been poring over catalogues for months and she has a wish list a mile long. The past couple of years we've had a decent bump in the winter tourist season, and we need to put a good foot forward year round." She reached beneath her counter for a stack of cookie boxes marked "Claire" and added, "Besides, the whole dog ornament thing is just fun. Sage and Claire kept the drawings secret, so we don't quite know what to expect—especially when it comes to Mortimer. Have you seen them?"

"Nope. One thing I'm learning about Claire, when she wants to keep a secret, she keeps a secret."

He didn't mention that she'd offered to give him and Nicholas a sneak peek. Claire thought the boy might do better facing his demons in a setting that wasn't filled with other people, but Nicholas had disagreed, telling them he was tired of being "special." He wanted to be a normal kid and go to the party just like everyone else.

"I can do it," he'd said this morning at breakfast. "I'm not afraid anymore."

Jax prayed the boy was right. He'd have preferred Claire's approach, but since he'd committed to taking his cues from Nicholas, he couldn't argue with his son.

He finished his coffee, loaded the cookies into his truck, and called Claire to tell her that he was on his way.

"The back door is unlocked," she told him. "Will you come in that way, please? Leave the cookies in the storeroom."

"Is there anything else you need me to bring?"

"Not right now. The champagne's being delivered, and Ali won't have the hors d'oeuvres ready to pick up until four."

Jax parked next to Claire's car in the alley behind the store, and he carried the boxes of cookies inside. Deciding his efforts had earned him a treat, he stole a cookie and headed for the stairs. The life-sized display of Sage Rafferty's Snowdrop dressed in an elf suit complete with ears brought him up short.

A similar display staring Mortimer in a Scrooge hat made Jax laugh out loud. Claire's voice greeted him from the second-floor landing. "Cute, aren't they?"

He lifted his gaze, and his heart grew like the Grinch's. "You sparkle, Miss Christmas."

"I'm excited. I'm so pleased with how this whole project has turned out. Eternity Springs has given me so much since I moved here. It's a great feeling to give something back in return."

"Do I get a tour?"

"I should make you wait, but I could use your long arms. Come on up."

He took advantage of the mistletoe hanging in the doorway to what had been her apartment before the upstairs remodel.

"Ten days," he murmured when they ended the kiss. "You gonna let me have a peek at the costume closet while I'm here?"

She rolled her eyes. "I swear, Lancaster, the dog room is a perfect fit for you."

Then she took his hand and led him into the "Doghouse."

An artificial tree stood in the center of the room, and it showcased the Twelve Dogs of Christmas ornaments. The glass balls had a white background and the sketches of the dogs were done in red, green, gold, and silver. He recognized Gabe Callahan's Clarence, Zach Turner's Ace, and the Cicero family's wheaten terrier. He didn't know who the little terrier belonged to, and a couple of the dogs depicted didn't fit any breed he recognized. Mutts, he imagined.

In addition to the ornaments, Claire had trimmed the tree with dog-themed ribbon, garland shaped like dog bones, twinkling lights and bubbling lights shaped like doghouses. "So what do you think?" she asked.

"If it starts barking, I'm outta here." Then he shot her a grin. "You've hung Captain front and center. Nicholas will love this. It's all wonderful, Claire. The ornaments are great."

"I think so, too. They turned out even nicer than I envisioned."

"To be honest, I expected something cutesy and cheesy. More along the lines of the dog costumes. These ornaments are traditional and classic—they'll fit into a lot of different décors. I'm impressed."

"Thank you. Sage deserves most of the credit. She did a fabulous job with the drawings. They're individual enough that those of us who know the dogs will recognize them, but she kept enough of the different breeds' particular qualities to appeal to owners of a variety of dogs."

"I don't know, Claire. I can't imagine there being another Mortimer in the world."

She laughed. "He is unique. Sage drew a more generic Boston terrier for me. I've had them produced, but I'm not featuring them tonight. Could I get you to put the topper on the tree for me? Do you want the ladder?"

Jax shook his head and gestured toward the stepstool that leaned against a wall. "That'll be fine."

She handed him a theme-appropriate angel for the top of the tree. Jax took in the floppy-eared, plush dog with a goofy grin, wings made of feathers, and a gold halo that was tilted at an angle that suggested the dog wasn't always angelic.

With the tree trimming finished, Jax took a few minutes

to study the other merchandise displayed in the room. In addition to the costumes, she had holiday sweaters, Christmas-themed treat jars, food bowls, and chew toys. Collars, leads, stockings, photo frames, wrapping paper, and more. He picked up a bag of bacon-flavored treats shaped like little elves and asked, "What more could a dog want?"

"Tinsel loves them," Claire said. "Captain does, too."

"I'm sure." An old memory flashed through his mind and, without thinking about it, he shared it with her. "Lara had a dog when we got married. A little terrier. She kept treats for her in a cookie jar in the kitchen. We had a party one weekend, and some of my navy buddies came to it. One guy drank too much and bunked on our sofa. Raided the cookie jar in the middle of the night. The next morning, he asked Lara for the recipe for cookies. Said he'd never had bacon-flavored cookies before, but he loved them."

Claire smiled and waited a couple of beats before observing, "That's the first time I've heard you mention your ex-wife with a smile on your face."

Jax tossed the dog treats back into their basket. "I think it's Eternity Springs. My boy wasn't the only Lancaster who needed healing. So, what else can I do to help you?"

He thought of that moment later that evening as he showered before returning to town for the reception. It was nice to be able to think of Lara without all the rage and pain. Someday, Nicholas would want to talk about his mother. Jax needed to be able to remember and share memories of the good times in his marriage.

Knock, knock, knock. "Hurry up, Dad. We don't want to be late!"

"Hold your horses," Jax called out as he towel-dried his hair. His phone lay beside his razor on the countertop beside the bathroom sink and he checked the time. "The doors don't open for forty minutes yet."

"But we have to find a place to park. That might be hard. Everyone is going to Forever Christmas tonight. Hurry up, Dad."

Jax switched on his electric razor and grinned at his reflection in the mirror. Nicholas wouldn't be this excited if he was still afraid. *Everything is going to be okay.*

With a towel wrapped around his hips, he exited the master bath and walked into his bedroom. Nicholas sat in the middle of his bed with Captain in his lap. "On my bed? Really?"

"Sorry." Nicholas pushed the dog off the bed. "Guess what, Dad? Miss Claire left a present in my closet. It wasn't in a box or a gift bag. It was just hanging there. See?"

He scrambled to his feet, standing in the middle of the mattress. "It's a new shirt. Look what's on the pocket. It's a paw print and it says 'The Twelve Dogs of Christmas.' She pinned a note to it and said I didn't have to wear it, but I wanted to. It's soft. And, it's red and green and I'm wearing it. I'm wearing it! And guess what? I looked in your closet and she left one for you, too. Will you wear it? It's not the same color so we won't match and be lame."

"We wouldn't want to be lame."

"Hurry up, Dad. Cari Callahan says that Mr. Chase's mom is sending meatballs, and they're really good. And Coach Lucca's mom is sending cake. We don't want them to all be gone before we get there."

Jax pulled on jeans and then the brown flannel shirt with the dog logo embroidered in tan thread on the pocket. "All right. All right. Take Captain out to pee and then we'll go."

"Hurray!" Nicholas scrambled off the bed calling, "Come on, Captain. Gotta go do your business."

He chattered all the way to town, and his excitement was infectious. Jax's mood was upbeat as he parked his truck on Third Street, a block and a half away. Nicholas ran ahead of him, and Jax had to lengthen his stride to keep up. Maybe it was the power of positive thinking at work, but he honestly believed that Nicholas had his issue beat as they made their way toward Forever Christmas.

So it was especially crushing when the boy came to an abrupt halt ten feet from Claire's front door.

Jax detected the aroma of mulled cider in the air at the same moment he saw color drain from Nicholas's complexion. The boy weaved on his feet and brought his hands up to cover his ears. He let out a scream.

The shrill sound drowned out the sweet voices of Meg and Cari Callahan, approaching the shop from the opposite direction and singing the chorus of "Angels We Have Heard on High."

Chapter Sixteen

Positive thoughts are difficult to come by some days.
—CLAIRE

When Jax heard his son scream, his heart dropped to his feet. He sprinted toward Nicholas and scooped him up into his arms even before the boy drew another breath.

"It's okay, buddy. It's okay. I'm here. Daddy's here."

Heedless of the attention they'd received from others on the street, Jax turned around and started walking, not sure where he was going to take the boy, just knowing they needed to get away from Forever Christmas.

Nicholas buried his head against Jax's chest and sobbed. "I'm so scared, Daddy. I don't want to be scared."

Jax's heart broke right along with his son's. "I'm here, Nicholas. I've got you. It's okay."

They were one block away from the health center. He should go there. Nicholas might need a doctor. Hell, Jax needed a doctor. He needed somebody who knew what the hell they were doing. He damned sure didn't know what to do. He sucked at this. At parenting. What had he been thinking? Whatever made him think that reading a few books and wearing a shirt meant the boy had overcome a traumatic experience almost beyond imagining?

The idea that a place can heal a damaged psyche? What a crock.

In his arms, Nicholas cried his heart out. "Daddy. Daddy. I hate that music. I hate it. It scared me so bad . . ."

"I'm here, buddy. I know. I'm sorry."

"She was singing, Daddy. Mommy was singing that song and playing the music loud."

Jax's steps slowed. Was he talking about the accident? Nicholas never talked about the accident. *Oh, hell. What do I do?*

"She was singing and she was crying and then she started laughing. I was so scared."

Six years old. He'd been six years old. Could he remember details like this about what had happened? Were these real memories or his nightmares? And did that even matter? This was what was in his mind.

And he's talking about it. He's talking about his mother. He never talks. Never.

Talking was good, wasn't it? Keeping everything inside was poison. He needed to talk. Hadn't the psychologists told Jax that?

Yes. Back before you stopped taking him to psychologists.

I suck at this.

Jax needed to keep him talking. He needed to vomit out the poison like when you drank too much. Vomiting kept you from getting alcohol poisoning. Jax wished he had alcohol right now.

Ahead of them half a block, Jax spied a couple of boys on Nicholas's soccer team. Crap. Not what they needed now. Not at all.

Thinking fast, Jax crossed the street to where the gate to the prayer garden beside St. Luke's Episcopal church stood open and welcoming. He entered and carried his son toward a wrought-iron bench that sat across from a concrete birdbath and a metal plaque inscribed with a Bible verse that read: "*Your word is a lamp to my feet and a light for my path.* Psalms 119:105"

Nicholas continued to cry, though his sobs had quieted somewhat. Gently, Jax rocked his son back and forth, murmuring soothing sounds, whispering calming words.

Nicholas shuddered. "I put my fingers in my ears because I didn't want to hear her sing anymore. Then the car was going sideways and there was a big boom and we crashed. I bumped my head and it hurt. I cried for Mommy but she didn't answer. She didn't talk to me at all. I said, 'Mommy, Mommy, Mommy,' and she wouldn't answer."

"I'm so sorry." Jax was horrified. Poor Nicholas. Poor Lara. Knowing that she'd broken her neck in the accident had been bad enough, but hearing this account of the event from his son . . . dear Lord. His heart squeezed in pain. No child should see something like this. Ever.

"It's awful. She died. She wrecked the car and she died and I was all alone. I even yelled 'Help!' but nobody came. Nobody."

"It was a terrible thing, Nicholas. It was a horrible, terrible thing that happened to you. But you aren't alone anymore."

"Why am I still scared? I don't want to be scared anymore. I'm a baby. The kids at my old school said that, and now everyone here will say it, too, because I couldn't go into Miss Claire's shop."

"No. You're the bravest boy I've ever met."

"No I'm not, Daddy. I'm not brave at all. I'm not better. I thought I was better."

"You *are* better, Nicholas. It's true. I'm not a doctor, and I could be wrong about this, but I think you have some really scary memories hiding in your brain. Something happened a few minutes ago, something touched those memories and they came out of hiding."

The song the Callahan girls had been singing, he'd bet. "I smelled it," Nicholas said.

He smelled it? "What did you smell? Christmas trees?"

"No. Not that." Nicholas shrugged. "I don't know what it is."

What had the boy smelled a moment ago? The cider? Could Lara have had a thermos of cider with her? Jax tried to recall what had been found in the car with Nicholas, but beyond the wrapped Christmas gifts, he came up empty.

He brushed Nicholas's bangs off his forehead. "Smells are a powerful memory trigger, son."

"How do I make it stop?"

"That's something we can ask Dr. McDermott when you see him in a few weeks. In the meantime, I'm not a doctor, but I'll tell you what my gut tells me. I think maybe that something like what happened today needs to happen. I think those memories need to come out."

Nicholas stirred and sat up. He gave Jax an incredulous look.

Jax attempted to explain. "Remember when we were moving that lumber at Papa Bear last week, and you got a splinter in your hand?"

"Yeah."

"You tried to ignore it. Tried to pretend it wasn't there. But it didn't go away, did it? Every time you bumped it, it hurt."

"It hurt when you dug in my finger with a needle."

"Yep. But I opened a path to the splinter and got hold of it with the tweezers and pulled it out. It hurt coming out, but once it was out, the hurting stopped."

"You're saying my memories of what happened with Mommy are splinters?"

"Big sharp thorny ones. But I'm thinking that maybe talking about them works like a needle and tweezers."

"Huh." Nicholas considered the idea, then his eyes filled

with fresh tears. "I don't think you're right. If the splinter was gone, I could go look at the Christmas Doghouse, but I don't want to. I mean . . . I *want* to . . . but I can't."

"Here's the thing about splinters, big guy. Sometimes you can't get hold of them and pull 'em out whole. Sometimes you've got to make a couple runs at getting them. Sometimes they break and little pieces get left behind. But if you've opened a path to them, lots of times they'll work themselves up toward the surface so that you can get 'em."

"I don't remember Mommy very good," Nicholas said in a small, hesitant voice. "Except for the bad time. I remember that. She made me sad and scared. Mimi says Mommy loved me a whole lot."

"She did."

"I want to remember good things about Mommy."

"You will, buddy. I'll help you."

"You will?" Nicholas swiped the back of his hand across eyes now filled with hope, then wiped his nose on his sleeve.

"Absolutely, I will." Jax shifted his son out of his lap and onto the bench beside him. He fished his handkerchief from his pocket and handed it to his son. "Blow."

Nicholas did, then handed it back. Jax continued, "It'll do me good to remember the good times with your mother. Let's start right now, shall we?"

"Okay."

Jax pursed his lips and made a show of thinking hard. "Hmm . . . let me see."

He snapped his fingers. "Here you go. I remember that your mommy liked the color purple a lot. And she loved for the three of us to play the game Twister together. Remember that?"

"Maybe . . ."

"She also loved to make peanut butter cookies and put a big Hershey's Kiss in the middle of them."

Nicholas's eyes rounded. "I remember that! I used to help her take the foil off the Kisses."

"That you did." Hoping that this was a good direction to take, Jax ventured, "What else did Mommy like?"

Nicholas thought for a moment, playing with an imaginary spot on Jax's sleeve. Then he smiled. "She liked to go to the zoo! We'd take a cooler that rolled and go to the zoo and have a picnic. I'd eat pimento-cheese sandwiches."

Jax nodded, recalling the photos of the zoo trips that she'd e-mail to him when he was at sea. "Did she have a favorite animal?"

"Giraffes. Mommy liked giraffes."

"Good job, Nicholas. Those were some really good memories."

The boy exhaled a heavy breath. "I wasn't so scared. Usually, I'm too scared to remember because instead of good things I always remember that bad time."

"Whenever you try to think of Mommy and get scared, come and find me and we'll talk about her just like we did now. Anytime you want to talk about Mommy or about being scared or about anything at all, you just let me know. Okay?"

"Okay."

"All right, then. You ready to go home, buddy?"

"Yeah. What about Miss Claire? She'll worry when we don't show up."

"I'll send her a text."

"Meg and Cari saw me cry. Everyone is going to know I'm a scaredy-cat. They'll make fun of me at school."

"I don't think so. This is Eternity Springs. Everyone I know is rooting for you, Nicholas."

"Maybe. Galen said his mom died, too. In a hospital, though. She was sick for a long time, he said. I told him I was sorry. People say that to me sometimes."

"I didn't know that about Galen. I'm glad you guys are friends. Did you tell him about Mommy?"

"No. He already knew she died so I didn't have to talk about it."

"See? People are different here in Eternity Springs."

"Yeah, I like it here, Daddy."

Jax stood and extended his hand to his son. The boy took it, and they walked back to Jax's truck in silence, both of them lost in their own thoughts. On the drive back to Three Bears, Jax replayed the incident in his mind. Had he handled it okay? Should he have taken the boy to the clinic, after all? Should he call Rose and ask her advice? Maybe she'd advise him not to wait for Dr. McDermott's return from vacation.

Maybe she'd tell him not to send Nicholas to Seattle.

Well, hell. He needed to consider that possibility. Maybe sending his son away for a long weekend would be the absolute worst thing he could do.

When it comes to parenting, I am so in over my head.

"Dad?"

"Hmmm?"

"Would you think Miss Claire has pictures of the Doghouse on her phone?"

Jax shot Nicholas a sidelong look. "Actually, I know she does. I watched her take a few when I dropped off cookies."

"Maybe I'll ask her to show them to me. Maybe."

"If you want to see what it looks like, I think that's a fine plan."

Since they'd planned to make a meal on Yellow Kitchen appetizers, Jax had to scrounge for his and Nicholas's supper upon their arrival back at Mama Bear. He decided to keep it easy and do breakfast for supper, and he'd just pulled bacon out of the refrigerator when he heard a car approach.

Sitting on the kitchen floor wrestling with Captain, Nicholas scrambled to his feet and ran to the window. "It's Miss Claire. Why is Miss Claire home so early? The party isn't over yet."

"I don't know."

Moments later, she hurried inside carrying two bags with the Yellow Kitchen logo on the side, Tinsel trailing at her feet. Jax saw the worry on her face as she studied Nicholas. Nevertheless, she kept her voice casual as she said, "Hey, guys."

"Why are you home early, Miss Claire? Did something bad happen at the party?"

"No. Everything is going fine. Since Celeste is president of the Chamber of Commerce, I turned the evening over to her." Claire set the bags on the kitchen table. "I brought food."

"Good. I'm hungry." Nicholas pulled a kitchen chair away from the table, climbed up on his knees, and peered into the bag. "What's in the box?"

Claire reached into the bag and pulled out a large square gift box adorned with red glitter hearts against a silver background. She set it on the table. "Well, I visited Shannon Garrett at Heartsong Cottage the other day, and her house put me in the mood for Valentine's Day. I'll tell you a secret, Nicholas, if you promise not to tell anybody else."

Interest lit the boy's eyes. "I promise."

"My favorite holiday isn't Christmas. It's Valentine's Day."

Nicholas gave her a "you're crazy" look. Claire laughed.

"It's true. I've been known to put up a Valentine's Day tree and decorate it. So, I thought I'd better bring home a few Valentine's tree ornaments before they were all gone."

Nicholas narrowed his eyes. "I'm not dumb, Miss Claire. I know what's in that box. You brought home the

Twelve Dogs of Christmas. You brought them so I can see them."

"Okay. You caught me. I know how badly you wanted to see the ornaments and I thought this might be a way to do it. You keep this box and open it when you're ready. And it's not too much of a stretch to think of them as Valentine's-themed things. After all, what's the main message of Christmas?"

"Presents?"

She ruffled his hair, then leaned over and kissed the top of his head. "Love, Nicholas. The key to Christmas is love."

Three days later, Claire's thoughts were on the Lancasters as she restocked the shelves in Forever Christmas shortly before closing time. Despite Nicholas's setback the evening of the reception, Claire was encouraged by his progress. He'd asked to see pictures of the Christmas Doghouse. He'd requested she continue to read to him each night. Last night, he'd opened her Valentine's box.

And Jax was at the boy's side offering support every step of the way.

He was such a good father. She wished he could see that. Ever since Nicholas's setback, Jax had second-guessed each of his parenting decisions. He'd had a conference with Nicholas's doctor and his teacher. He'd called the Hardcastles and updated them about their grandson's situation, and they'd gone back and forth about whether or not to go forward with Nicholas's trip to Seattle. The fact that the boy wanted badly to go had weighed heavily in the decision not to change their plans.

Selfishly, Claire had wanted to cheer.

She also believed that Jax was doing everything right with Nicholas. True, she wasn't a health-care professional, but she lived with the boy. She witnessed the progress he made on a daily basis. Jax was too hard on himself.

Her door chimes sounded, and she exited her stockroom to see the man himself rush in with a panicked look on his face. "Help!"

"Jax, what's wrong?"

"I need your ideas. I'm not asking you to do it. I want to be clear about that. But I'm coming up with a great big goose egg, and I need some fresh ideas."

"About what?"

"Halloween. Tomorrow is Halloween. I didn't know it was such a big deal. Have you seen the costumes kids do these days? Talk about elaborate. The kid showed me some on the Internet. Whatever happened to throwing a sheet over your head and cutting out eyes and going as a ghost? And Nicholas tells me parents dress up now, too! I'm not dressing up to take my eight-year-old trick-or-treating. That's crazy."

The affronted expression on his face made her laugh. "What does Nicholas want to be for Halloween?"

"He doesn't know, but it has to be cool. What the heck am I supposed to do with that? Why do I have to come up with an idea, anyway? It's not like he's five and needs help. Shouldn't he be doing this himself?"

"I think Halloween has changed in recent years, Jax. It's not just for kids anymore. Adults are really into it. Parents do dress up."

"Yeah. Well. Not me. I'm drawing the line there. He said the Ciceros have been working on their costumes for weeks. We have a little more than twenty-four hours to come up with something for Nicholas. And never mind that I'm trying to fit four days of work into two out at Papa Bear because I actually have a firm commitment from the electrician for next week, and I can't miss that window. I'm not dragging out the sewing machine that's in the storage closet in Mama Bear, so if Nicholas and I can't put a costume together with safety pins, Super Glue, or staples, it's not happening."

"You can use a sewing machine? I'm impressed."

That distracted him from his rant. He shot her a quick grin and said, "I'm extraordinarily talented with my hands. I'm looking forward to showing you. In fact . . ."—he gave her a slow once-over—"if you haven't had any luck finding that French maid outfit, I could be persuaded to fire up the sewing machine."

Claire's cheeks heated. "You are such a flirt."

The teasing glint in his eyes changed to something hotter and more intense. "One week, Miss Christmas. Seven days."

She wanted to fan her face. Instead, she decided to give him a taste of his own medicine. She slowly skimmed her gaze down his body, licked her lips, and dragged her gaze back up to his face. "One hundred sixty-eight hours."

He fell back a step. Thumped his hand over his heart.

Claire couldn't stifle a grin. "First, though, we have Halloween to deal with."

Jax grimaced. "From the sublime to the ridiculous. Any suggestions for me?"

"Let me think about it. We'll come up with something Nicholas will like."

"Thanks, darlin'." He picked her up, whirled her around, and kissed her hard. "I knew I could count on you."

She mulled over possibilities as she finished stocking her shelves. Something "cool" that didn't involve needlework and could be thrown together in one evening. That was the stumbling block. Internet shopping made life in Eternity Springs easier, but experience had taught her that you couldn't count on overnight delivery. The last thing they needed was to be waiting for UPS to show when the sun went down on Halloween.

She had a pretty good idea of the clothes they had to

work with currently in Nicholas's wardrobe. Bet she could scrounge up other supplies by calling around to friends. They needed a theme.

"Hmm . . ." she murmured aloud. She took a look around her Angel Room, but nothing there gave her any ideas. Though she did wonder how many Starlinas she'd see tomorrow night. "Now there's a thought guaranteed to put me in a witchy mood."

At least Nicholas won't want to dress up as that commercialized fake.

She shook her head, chased away the annoying thoughts, and finished prepping the shop for closing, cleaning the restrooms, adjusting the heat, turning on some lights, turning others off. Upstairs in the Christmas Doghouse, she hesitated. An idea flitted through her mind.

She had an entire line of items embroidered or embossed or printed with "Believe." She thought of Jax every time she sold one of those items, every time she stocked one. *Wonder if he ever used his journal?* She'd never had the nerve to ask him. Probably not. He probably considered the whole thing silly, and if that were the case, she didn't want to know it. She wanted to keep that particular fantasy alive.

Fantasy. Jax Lancaster was a living, breathing fantasy. Was he just teasing her about the whole French-maid thing, or did he really want to go into role-playing during their first . . . fling? Wasn't that a little bit much for the first time out? This whole situation was simply beyond her experience. She was living with the man, but not sleeping with him. Playing house. Playing mother to his son.

And my, oh my, was she having the time of her life.

Seven days. Seven days of waiting, then three days of wicked. She'd bought the little costume complete with fishnet hose and the little blob of a cap. She'd probably pack it. If she'd be brave enough to wear it . . . well . . . who knows?

"And first you have another costume to concern you," she murmured.

The more she thought about it, the more she could see it. She could be wrong, but she thought her idea might appeal to Nicholas. And, it could be managed with scissors, staples, and Super Glue—though a needle and thread would make it nicer.

Claire gathered up the supplies they'd need if the boy liked her idea, locked up her shop, and went home to Three Bears Valley.

Chapter Seventeen

Best. Halloween. Ever.
—JAX

"I can't believe you got me to dress up for Halloween," Jax groused as he parked his truck at the Callahan compound on Hummingbird Lake.

Claire rolled her eyes. "You are wearing your suit, Jax."

"And an armband."

Claire shared a look of disapproval with Nicholas, who sat between them in the front seat of the truck. "You should bite him, King Komondor."

Nicholas rolled his head around and the long strands of coiled cotton glued to his old baseball cap went flying. Then he bared his teeth and growled.

Jax narrowed his eyes. "Careful there, you'll lose your Best in Show ribbon."

The boy panted and pawed at Jax's suit jacket. "Mutt," he declared, but belied his gruff tone by reaching into his pocket and producing a vanilla wafer "treat." Nicholas freed himself from the seat belt, nipped the cookie from Jax's hand, then went up on his knees and kissed his father's cheek.

Jax grinned. The kid was really getting into this.

Frankly, so was he.

Exiting the truck, they joined the crowd of Eternity Springs trick-or-treaters making their way toward the bank of Hummingbird Lake where Brick Callahan had docked his haunted pirate ship, which on other days was his uncle Luke's houseboat, the *Miss Behavin' VI*.

Halloween in Eternity Springs was one big party for both children and adults. They'd been blessed with good weather, so the door-to-door part of the evening had been a convivial stroll through the residential streets. Word quickly passed among the crowd of kids about not-to-be-missed houses. The Murphys were giving away Sarah's cookies. The Rafferty house had caramel apples. Maggie Romano at Aspenglow B and B was giving popcorn balls.

"Dr. Davis is handing out toothbrushes and toothpaste again," a boy on Nicholas's soccer team had warned.

"We have to go there," Galen had told an alarmed Nicholas. "It'll hurt his feelings if everyone skips. Besides, the Davis home is next door to the Turners'. Sheriff Turner usually gives full-sized candy bars to make up for the toothbrushes."

Overhearing the exchange, Jax had made sure they didn't miss the town dentist's home.

With the trick-or-treating part of the evening over, the revelers had moved on to the climax of the evening—Brick's pirate ship. According to Claire, a number of the Callahan family members had gathered in Colorado for the event. They met Brick's aunt Maddie at the spot where the line formed. The redhead introduced herself then turned her attention to Nicholas.

"Now whoever designed your costume was thinking," she said in a slow, sexy voice full of the South. "I can recall plenty of Halloweens where my life would have been easier if I'd had a leash on my kids. I take it you're a show dog?"

"Dad and I are going as the Westminster Dog Show. I'm a komondor and I'm Best in Show."

"You certainly are." She grinned at Jax and Claire, then

handed Nicholas a child-sized life jacket. "And now, me matey, in order to set sail aboard the *Black Shadow* with Captain Callahan, you'll need to don your pirate's vest. Jax, if you and Claire want to wait for him at the dance hall, we have a selection of grog from which to choose."

"Thank you," Claire said. "That sounds—"

Maniacal laughter boomed across the night, and Claire turned toward the sound. Brick Callahan stood decked out in full pirate regalia—tall boots, skintight black pants, a low-cut flowing white shirt, a pirate's eye patch, and a tricorn hat. He held a sword up in the air as he threatened to make Cari Callahan walk the plank.

In line behind them, Rose Cicero observed, "Now that's a sight to make a damsel's heart go pit-a-pat."

Her tone nonchalant, Claire said, "I certainly enjoy a good costume as well as the next damsel."

Jax twisted his head and stared at her. Claire arched a saucy brow. *"Oui, Monsieur Lancaster?"*

Keeping his voice low and for her ears only, he said, "You're trying to kill me, aren't you?"

She laughed and led him toward the dance hall, where Gabe Callahan introduced Jax to more members of the Callahan clan. Claire glanced around the crowded hall. "Celeste mentioned that your father made the trip this time. I'd like to say hi to him."

"Branch is working the boat with Brick," Mark Callahan said. "Playing a curmudgeonly old pirate is right up his alley."

Nic Callahan scolded her brother-in-law with a look. "Your father is a sweetheart. Have you seen how wonderful he is with the baby?"

"He's great with all his grandchildren," Mark's wife, Annabelle, observed.

Gabe Callahan laughed. "Have you talked to Brick

lately? I suspect he'd weigh in on our side of the argument. Branch has decided your son needs a woman."

Mark winced. Luke and Matt laughed out loud. Luke clapped Mark on the back. "Might as well start planning the wedding now."

"What do you want to bet he has another . . ."—Mark made quote signs with his fingers—heart attack?"

Gabe shook his head. "Nobody's dumb enough to take that bet. So, who needs another beer?"

About half an hour after they'd left Nicholas to board the *Black Shadow* with his friends, a gaggle of boisterous children invaded the dance hall looking for their parents. "He made us touch eyeballs in a bowl, Mom," said one girl.

"And brains, too!" called another.

They chattered about ghosts and sea monsters and chain saws. "Chain saws?" Clair asked. "On a pirate ship?"

Jax spied his son, his face alight with happy excitement, and he waved Claire's protest away. "Creative license. Hey, you can't have a decent haunted house without a chain-saw massacre."

Nicholas obviously agreed. Ten minutes later, loaded back into the truck and headed toward town, he talked nonstop about his "perilous journey."

". . . and some parts were really stupid. Everyone knows that the eyeballs were peeled grapes and the brains were spaghetti. But the girls screamed and Mr. Brick's grandpa was kinda scary. I don't know what he meant by 'Davy Jones' locker' but it didn't sound good."

"I'm glad you had fun, son," Jax said.

"I didn't get scared at all. And some of it was pretty scary. Mr. Brick's aunt Maddie can really sound like a witch."

The boy fell silent then, and Jax thought he might have

finally run out of steam. But after a few minutes of quiet, Nicholas surprised him. "I'm not a wussy. I'm very brave."

"Yes, you are."

"You are the bravest boy I've ever met," Claire added.

"I knew those things weren't real. I let myself get scared, because I knew they weren't real, and they couldn't hurt me." He turned his head and looked at Claire. "Nothing in your shop can hurt me. It's just a store. The things inside it aren't eyeballs."

Jax met Claire's startled gaze. She was looking to him for guidance, but he had none to give.

"That's true enough. I don't have any peeled grapes, either."

They drove another mile in silence, then Nicholas said. "I want to go there. Now. I went through the *Black Shadow,* and I didn't scream once. I can go inside Forever Christmas. Will you take me, please, Dad? Now?"

Jax gripped his steering wheel hard. Hell. What should he do? Today had been a great day. He didn't want to ruin it by exposing Nicholas to his terrors. And yet, wasn't the plan to take his cues from Nicholas? If he turned the boy down, what sort of signal was that sending? It might make matters worse.

He glanced down at his son and noticed the leash and dog collar that had been part of his costume tonight. Believe.

Well, hell. What else could he do?

"If that's what you want, Nicholas. Of course, I'll take you to the shop. As long as it's okay with you, Miss Christmas?"

"Of course."

A few minutes later, Jax parked his truck on the deserted street in front of the store. Claire suggested, "Why don't you let me go in first and turn on a few lights. I expect you want to see the Christmas Doghouse?"

"Yes."

"Okay. I'll wave to you from the door when I'm ready."

Claire slipped out of the truck. Jax watched her remove her keys from her purse and unlock the door. Moments later, lights switched on inside. Not twinkling tree lights, but overhead lights. *Smart girl.*

"You sure about this, Nicholas?" Jax asked as the second floor lit up.

Nicholas unbuckled his seat belt. "Yeah."

"If you have any second thoughts, just say the word."

"Okay."

Claire appeared in the doorway and gave them both a little wave. Nicholas said, "Nothing in that store is going to hurt me. Let's go, Dad."

Jax sent up a quick, silent prayer and took his son's hand. Together, they approached Forever Christmas to face Nicholas's demons on Halloween night. The irony of the moment wasn't lost on Jax.

Nicholas kept a tight grip on Jax as he paused at the front of the shop and drew a deep breath. Claire offered an encouraging smile. "Welcome to Forever Christmas, Nicholas. The Doghouse is upstairs."

After that moment's hesitation, the boy forged right ahead.

The lights Claire had turned on cast a soft glow throughout the shop, chasing away the shadows but not highlighting any of the displays. Nicholas darted glances right and left, but he didn't dawdle as he followed Claire toward the staircase.

"Doing all right, buddy?" Jax asked, bringing up the rear as he climbed the staircase. Tension gripped him.

Nicholas responded with a nod.

Claire glanced back at them and began to patter. "I ordered twice as many of the Twelve Dogs of Christmas ornaments as I thought I'd need. Based on the first few days of sales, I should have ordered four times more. The chamber has sold enough to get everything on Celeste's wish list. I hope we have plenty of volunteers for Deck the Halls Friday because we're going to need them. Time is flying. It'll be here sooner than we know it."

"Maybe we can volunteer to help, Dad."

Jax briefly closed his eyes. "That would be great."

Claire led the way to her Doghouse. There, she'd turned on a few more lights—including those on the room's centerpiece Christmas tree. Jax held his breath and waited for his son's reaction. To his shock, the boy did something completely unexpected.

Nicholas laughed out loud. "Are those real dog biscuits on the tree? How do you keep Tinsel away from them?"

Jax took his first easy breath since Nicholas expressed the desire to visit Claire's shop.

Nicholas took his time exploring the Christmas Doghouse. He picked things up. Turned them on and off. He shook the snow globes and jingled the bells. When he twisted the key on a music box, Jax opened his mouth to caution him, but Claire stilled him with a slight shake of her head. The music box played the theme song from *Paw Patrol*.

Throughout it all, Nicholas chattered excitedly. The only reason they heard the sound of something crashing downstairs was because it happened while he was taking a breath. Jax looked at Claire. "What was that?"

"I don't know," she said, starting toward the stairs. "It sounds like something fell off one of the shelves."

Jax frowned. They hadn't locked the door behind them. Crime wasn't a problem in Eternity Springs as a rule, but . . . "Hold on, Claire. Let me go check."

She dismissed him with a wave. "No, you wouldn't know what to look for."

Jax listened to the sound of her footsteps as she descended the staircase. He heard a few clicks as she switched on more lights. Then . . . nothing. He didn't like this one bit. "Wait here, Nicholas."

Jax followed Claire downstairs, his gaze scanning the area for signs of an intruder. The front door remained shut, the store felt empty. He found Claire standing in her books section, a perplexed look on her face. He asked, "Everything okay?"

"Yes. Everything's fine. I found four books on the floor. Someone must have looked at one of them today and didn't shelve it properly. Law of physics at work."

Jax figured she probably was right, but it wouldn't hurt to take one quick turn through the shop. He proceeded to do that and had just exited the stockroom where he'd double-checked that the back door was locked when he heard Nicholas say, "Wow, Miss Claire. That's really pretty."

The boy stood at the threshold of Claire's Angel Room. Shocked to see his calm and collected son downstairs in the middle of Christmas central, Jax pulled up short.

Nicholas said, "Look, Miss Claire. Something has fallen."

The boy disappeared into the room followed by Claire. Jax hurried to join them and arrived in time to see Nicholas pick up a tattered angel off the floor, the same angel that had set Claire off the day he'd compared it to the children's book character. Nicholas handed the angel to Claire.

"Gardenia," she said softly. "How did she wind up on the floor?"

"Maybe she fell from the sky," Nicholas said. "Look. Her wing got broke."

"Her wing has been broken for a very long time," Claire said. She brushed off the angel's bedraggled skirt and gently straightened its halo. "Of all the angels in the Angel

Room, she is my favorite. She didn't fall from the sky, Nicholas. My mother and my sister and I made her for our family's Christmas tree. She was born out of the love in our hearts."

"You must have used her for a long time for her to be so beat up."

"Actually . . . no. Gardenia never made it to the top of our tree. My sister got sick, and we didn't have Christmas anymore."

"Did she die like my mom?"

"Yes. Yes, she did."

"So she's an angel, too. I'm sorry, Miss Claire."

"Thank you, Nicholas. Me, too."

"Why didn't you have Christmas?"

Claire set the angel on a shelf half hidden by new and sparkly angels. As he watched her, a hazy thought drifted at the edge of Jax's mind, but before he could grasp hold of it, Claire distracted him with the answer to Nicholas's question.

"My sister was sick a long time. She was in the hospital the first year we didn't have Christmas. And the second. After she died, my mom just didn't have the heart to celebrate the holiday."

"What about your dad?"

"I'm afraid his heart really broke. He passed away not long after my sister did."

"That's terrible, Miss Claire. I'm really sorry."

A lump formed in Jax's throat as he watched his son wrap his arms around Claire's waist and give her a hug. "You and I are alike. You lost Christmas, too."

"Yes, Nicholas. You're right. For a long time, I did lose Christmas."

"But you got it back. You have Christmas every day now, don't you?"

"Forever Christmas," Claire said, returning his son's hug.

Nicholas stepped away and gazed up at her solemnly. "You know what, Miss Christmas?"

She pulled one of the cotton strands hanging on the hat he still wore. "What, Mr. Best in Show?"

"After tonight, I'm pretty sure that I got Christmas back, too."

It was all Jax could do not to break out into the chorus of "Joy to the World."

After she read Nicholas his Christmas story, Claire considered going straight to bed rather than wait downstairs for Jax for their customary shared nightcap. Talking about Michelle tonight had left her emotions raw. At the same time, she wanted to celebrate Nicholas's big step forward with Jax. It didn't seem right to bail on him just because his son's questions had stirred up old hurts.

Nicholas. What a tough little trouper he was. She was so proud of him and, frankly, pleased that she'd played even a small part in his recovery. Because it was a recovery. Yes, he might well have more setbacks. Yes, he would likely fight this particular fight for years to come. But tonight, on this special Halloween, he'd won.

"Forget the wine," she murmured to herself. She reached into the refrigerator for the bottle of champagne she kept on hand. If any occasion called for champagne, this did.

She was up on her tiptoes reaching for the champagne glasses on the top shelf of the wet bar cabinet when Jax joined her. "Wait. Let me help."

"I thought champagne was in order," she said, as he snagged the glasses.

Emotion hitched in Jax's chest. None of this would have happened had he not come to Eternity Springs and met Claire Branham. In a voice husky with feeling, he said, "I wholeheartedly agree. I like the way you think, Miss Christmas."

He popped the cork, poured the champagne, then lifted his glass in toast. "To you, Claire."

"Not me. To Nicholas."

"To you and Nicholas, then." He clinked his glass against hers, then sipped his champagne. "He might have eventually taken this step on his own, but you made it happen a whole helluva lot faster. I can't thank you enough for all you've done."

"I'm glad I could help."

He leaned in and took her lips in a long, steamy kiss that left her weak in the knees. "I'm not ready for this evening to end. How about I make a fire? Will you sit with me, Claire? Talk with me? Make plans with me?"

"What sort of plans?"

"We haven't discussed your wishes for our trip. Silver Eden has all sorts of amenities we can choose from. I don't know if you're the tennis type or if you'd want to go horseback riding. You should take a look at the spa brochure on the Web site because we should probably book that before we go."

She put the champagne bottle in an ice bucket and carried it and their glasses to the coffee table near the fireplace. While he started the fire, they discussed the upcoming trip and decided they both preferred a visit to the resort without a set agenda. With logs crackling and flames flickering in the hearth, he took her hand and led her over to the sofa, where he pulled her down to sit beside him, keeping his fingers threaded with hers. He dropped his head back against the cushion and released a heartfelt sigh. "What a day. An exhausting day, but a great day."

"I'll second that."

"Something tells me that the kid is going to keep me on my toes for the next ten years."

"Ten?" Claire laughed. "Try twenty. Maybe thirty."

"True, that. However, I'm going to remember this day for a long time. A very long time." He brought her hand up to his mouth and kissed it. "I'm happy that you shared it with us."

"I am, too," she said softly.

They sat in comfortable silence for a few moments, watching the fire. The scent of burning pine swirled through the room. Claire sipped her champagne, relaxing and reflecting on the evening's events at Forever Christmas.

Jax's thoughts must have gone that in direction, too, because he said, "I feel like a heel. I've been so focused on Nicholas and our problems that I never asked you about your family. Tell me about your sister, Claire. Was she your only sibling?"

"Yes." The image of a pale young body wasted away by illness flashed in her memory. "Her name was Kelley Michelle, and she was my baby sister. She was two years younger than me. She fought leukemia for four years."

"That's tough. Hard on your whole family."

"Yes, it was a horrible time. A roller coaster of hope and despair. My parents tried to stay positive, but I could tell they were scared to death. Michelle was so frightened, so sick. Some of the treatments were worse than the disease. I was . . ." Her voice trailed off.

"You were what? Frightened? Sad? Confused?"

"All of the above." She stared into the fire, remembering. She never talked about Michelle or her parents. Never talked about that life-changing time.

She knew so much about Jax. He'd shared his struggles, his failures, and now, this great success. She'd told him very little about herself, and after tonight, that didn't seem right. Jax shared so much, but she'd kept all her secrets.

Maybe it's time you opened up. Not about everything. But about some of it.

"I had a great family, a great childhood. I was ten, not much older than Nicholas, when my sister got sick and my whole life changed. My parents did their best, but they focused all their energy and attention on the child who was ill. I was scared and I felt . . ."

"Neglected," Jax suggested.

"Yes. I felt neglected and angry and oh, so guilty because I felt neglected and angry. I mean, my sister was dying. What sort of evil person was I because I was upset that we skipped Christmas a few times?"

"How long did she fight it?"

"Four years. We lost her the year I turned fourteen. At Christmas."

"Oh, Claire." Jax brought her hand up to his mouth and kissed it. "And then you lost your father. That's devastating. What of your mother? Is she . . . ?"

"She's gone now, too. She lived fourteen years after we lost Dad and Michelle, though I would say it was more existing than living. Her light died with them. Three years ago, she caught the flu and developed pneumonia. I don't think she had the heart to fight."

"Nicholas got it right, didn't he? You lost Christmas, too. It's no wonder you relate to him so well."

"He's a special little boy, Jax. He's lucky to have you as his father."

"Not always," he said. "I can't go back and change the past, but I am determined to be a good father from this day forward." He trailed his thumb gently down her cheek and studied her intently. "To that end, tell me something, Miss Christmas. What made you so strong?"

That startled her. "Strong?"

"Like Nicholas, you had Christmas stolen from you.

How did a girl with every reason to be Ms. Grinch find her way to becoming Miss Christmas?"

"Oh, believe me," Claire replied with an uneasy laugh. "I can still get my Grinch on. I think I learned . . . I am learning . . . just what is truly important in life."

"Christmas?"

"What Christmas represents. It's personal and it's different for everyone. For some people who come into my shop, Christmas is all about family. For others, it's about tradition. I'm encouraged that the religious nature of the holiday remains strong and important to the majority of people with whom I deal, despite claims to the contrary. Of course, there are some who don't look beyond the gifts stacked at the bottom of the tree, but they definitely are not the majority."

"What does Christmas represent to you?"

She stared into the fire. "It's a mountain I'm trying to climb. I'm making progress, but I still have a ways to go to reach the summit."

Admiration gleamed in his eyes. "You and my son make quite a pair."

"He inspires me."

"You fascinate me."

His voice was a caress and made her shiver. He kissed her as the hall clock began to chime, his lips gentle and sweet and almost worshipful. Jax Lancaster had kissed Claire many times, in many ways, but never quite like this before.

This kiss paid her tribute and for some strange reason made her want to cry.

The clock chimes had long faded by the time he lifted his head. "Claire . . . I . . ."

Suddenly nervous, she stood and stepped away. "Oh, wow. Eleven o'clock. I have a breakfast meeting at six A.M.

I'd better go upstairs before I turn into a pumpkin." She
made a general wave toward the hearth. "Will you . . . ?"

"Yes. I'll tend the fire and lock up. Good night, Claire."

"Good night."

He waited until she was halfway up the stairs to say,
"Claire, you are farther up the mountain trail than you
think. I want you to know that I'm damn glad to walk beside you."

Chapter Eighteen

I've always liked the name Sven.
—CLAIRE

Five.

"Hello. I want to book the spa romance package, please, on Saturday afternoon. Yes. For two. It's under Lancaster." *Aka Stamina Sven.* "Yes. Yes. On my credit card. Excuse me? You said it's how much, again?" *Sheesh.* "Yes. That's fine."

Four.

"Did I hear you cough, Nicholas? Are you getting sick? C'mere. Let me check your temperature. You're not getting sick, are you? If you feel the least bit sick I want you to tell me so we can get you to the doctor and on some medicine. It'd break your grandparents' hearts if you couldn't go to Seattle this weekend."

Three.

"Hello. Jax Lancaster here. Wondering if I could stop by and pick up a check for that work I did two weeks ago? Yes, I invoiced you. Sure. I'd be glad to make another copy." *Deadbeat.*

Two.

"We don't have a dry cleaners? How can a town not have dry cleaners? I have Racer Rafferty's caramel apple handprints on my suit coat, and I need to wear it Saturday night."

The resort restaurant had a dress code. Why hadn't he thought to check that before today? He'd have to get his suit cleaned at the hotel. Guess he could switch around their reservations, and they could do the casual restaurant the first night instead of the fancy one.

Or maybe room service. Room service would be good.
One.

"Hello. Jax Lancaster again. Yes, tomorrow. For the dinner in the suite tomorrow night, go ahead and change it to the premium menu selection, please."

This weekend was going to cost him a fortune. Not that he cared. He didn't. Claire was worth every penny. It's just that he got sticker shock every time he contacted the hotel.

Besides, deadbeats aside, he was doing just fine, wasn't he? He was turning away work. Barring some unforeseen disaster, he wouldn't have any trouble paying his bills, not even this weekend's already humongous tab at Silver Eden.

This weekend. Tomorrow.
Today!
"Mistletoe!"

Five.

"This is Claire Branham. I'm sorry to bother you again, but I'm hoping you can add a few more things to my order? The off-the-shoulder two-piece swimsuit that's on page four of the current catalogue. Style number seven seven five. In red, please. In fact, why don't you go ahead and send me everything the model is wearing on that page. Yes, the cover-up, shoes, and jewelry, too. The sunglasses? Hmm . . . yes, why not? Overnight, please."

Four.

"This is Claire Branham. Yes, it arrived, thank you. I love it. That shade of red is spectacular. I think I've changed my mind about the dress. Why don't you go ahead and send the one on page ten. Everything. Suitable lingerie, too."

Three.

"Hello, Susie. Yes, it's me. I know, I know. How did I ever manage without a personal shopper? The dress is fabulous, but I'm not certain about the evening bag. And I love, love, love the silk teddy! The emerald green is spectacular."

Two.

"Luggage! I can't believe I never thought about luggage!"

One.

"Forever Christmas. How may I assist you today? Oh, hello, Susie. Yes, I'm all packed. Thank you so much. You've been a godsend."

Today!

"Fling!"

Silver Eden Resort took luxury to a new level. Perched halfway up the side of a mountain, the resort blended into its surroundings with clean, modern lines and plenty of glass. "Look at that infinity pool," Claire said as they approached the hotel's entrance. "Is it indoors or outdoors? I can't quite tell."

"Both," Jax said. "It has a retractable roof."

"Cool."

Their personal concierge greeted them upon arrival. Amy Gilbert was an attractive, efficient woman in her mid-forties who vowed to see to their every need. Based upon his interaction with her during their numerous phone conversations, Jax could attest to her attentiveness.

She took them on a tour of the facilities before showing them to a two-bedroom, three-bath suite with three fireplaces, and a private outdoor hot tub. Because he hadn't wanted to appear presumptuous—despite his presumptions—Jax had requested that his and Claire's bags be placed in separate bedrooms. When Amy left them alone in the suite, he spent a moment arguing with himself. He wanted to pick Claire up and carry her straight to bed. Instead, recognizing her nervousness by the way she kept playing with the shoulder strap on her purse, he asked if she'd like a little time to herself in order to freshen up after the drive.

"Thank you," she said with evident relief. "That would be perfect."

She turned toward her room, but he reached for her hand and stopped her. "Hold on a minute, honey. I'd be remiss if I ignored this."

"Ignored what?"

He pulled her into his arms and nipped at her earlobe. "Look up."

She looked up at the light fixture above them and laughed. Laughter that Jax cut off abruptly when he captured her mouth in a hot erotic kiss—beneath the mistletoe.

When the kiss finally ended, Jax pointed Claire toward her bedroom and gave her fanny a gentle swat. "Go on while you still can."

She floated into her room, and once the sensual haze created by his kiss dissipated, she went into her bathroom, stripped off her clothes, and took a quick shower. When she reached for a towel to dry herself, she noted the trembling in her hands.

She was nervous. She wanted . . . she *needed* . . . to get this first time behind her. When she realized she'd squeezed antibacterial ointment onto her toothbrush instead of toothpaste, she'd admitted that this fling needed to be flung before she lost what little sense she had left.

She didn't know exactly why her nerves were strung tighter than a fiddle string. Yes, she hadn't been with a man in a long time, but she wasn't a rookie. She was a modern, experienced woman who knew what she was doing in the bedroom. One thing she'd say about Landon, he'd taught her to be adventurous. So what if that adventurousness had gone rusty?

Or had it? Heaven knows, a fling was adventuresome. At least, it felt that way to her.

She rifled through the basket of toiletries the hotel provided and found a new toothbrush. As she brushed her teeth, she concluded that her problem was the fling aspect of the fling. She was a rookie in the fling department. Every other time she'd gone to bed with a man she'd been in a committed relationship.

Correction. She'd *thought* she was in a committed relationship at the time.

This was the first time she'd ever planned to have sex for the sake of sex alone. Casual sex. A fling.

It doesn't feel like a fling.

It felt more serious than that. It felt important. It felt like commitment.

It feels like love.

"Whoa. Hold it. Wait one blessed minute." Watching herself in the mirror, Claire saw the color drain from her face.

No. She wasn't in love with Jax. No. No. No. No. No. This was sex. Just sex. Casual sex. They'd agreed to that from the beginning. Fun and games and mistletoe flings.

Yeah, but . . . this guy seems different.

"No!" Claire took a deep breath. *Eyes wide open, woman. Can't go there. Can't get hurt like that again. Can't. Won't. Ever.*

"You'd better remember that," she told her reflection. "You'd better make darn sure you don't forget it. This weekend is a short-term adventure, not a lasting relationship. Treat it that way."

Determined to heed her own warnings, Claire decided to act. She plucked another item from the basket and announced, "Let the flinging commence."

After kissing Claire senseless, Jax went into his room and called to check on Nicholas. His son had arrived in Seattle safe and sound and seemed happy as a clam. After the call, he took a shower. A cold shower, since it appeared that this ongoing seduction would continue at least a little while longer.

They'd left Three Bears Valley at nine o'clock this morning, arriving at the Gunnison airport half an hour before the charter carrying Brian and Linda arrived from Seattle to pick up Nicholas. Jax had felt a little guilty about being so happy to see him off, and he'd confessed as much to Claire during the four-hour drive to Silver Eden.

"That's understandable, but silly, considering how excited he was about seeing his grandparents," she'd replied.

"True. He was one happy little boy, especially after he learned that the Hardcastles invited his friend from camp to join them for the weekend. Brian and Linda may live to regret that. Trevor is a live wire."

The trip had passed quickly. They'd argued about sitcoms from the nineties, discussed their favorite curries, and talked about novels they'd read so far this year. Claire had seemed comfortable with him right up until their arrival at Silver Eden. "Nerves," he said to his reflection in the mirror as he towel-dried his hair.

She hadn't even seen his bedroom yet.

Jax had requested the room be staged for romance, and wow, had the folks at Silver Eden gotten it right. Candles, flowers, soft music, sapphire satin sheets on a bed the size of a lake, the duvet turned back and waiting. A champagne bucket and chocolate-covered strawberries sat on the bedside table. A fire flickered in the hearth and French doors opened onto a private patio complete with a steaming hot tub and a million-dollar view of the sunset over the Rockies waiting to be enjoyed.

Though Jax figured that by the time he got Claire into his bed, the only sunset he'd care to view was the one that glistened in her luscious auburn hair.

If pressed, he would admit to a little nervousness himself. It had been a long time for him. Years, in fact, since he'd made love with a woman who mattered to him as much as Claire.

If anyone had ever mattered as much to him as she did. Maybe Lara, although he didn't remember having feelings this strong for her in the beginning of their relationship.

Relationship.

The word stopped him as he dragged the towel across his body. Is that the point where he and Claire were now? If so, when had their mistletoe fling become more than a simple fling? Especially since they hadn't actually started flinging?

It worried him. He didn't know how they'd make a relationship work. She'd put down roots in town. He couldn't ask her to leave her shop, but he couldn't work in Eternity Springs forever. Not in the profession in which he'd been trained, anyway. How could he provide for Nicholas, give him what he needed, working as a handyman? That Boeing job offer weighed heavily on Jax's mind. There was an option for them in Seattle. A good one.

And they wouldn't be able to live with free rent forever. Their life at Mama Bear was really just a fairy tale. Living like a family—well, except for the separate-bedroom thing—who were they kidding, other than themselves?

"Stop it," he muttered to his reflection in the mirror. No

sense worrying about that now. Besides, he might be totally off base. He didn't know how Claire felt. The R-word might not be anywhere on her radar.

He was here for a fling, so a fling he'd have. With romance, mistletoe, and lots of sex. That's a fling.

Because if he thought about it in any other terms, it got downright scary.

He wrapped his towel around his waist and dug his razor from his shaving kit. He shaved, brushed his teeth, and combed his hair. Then he exited the bathroom and headed for the closet.

He stopped dead in his tracks. Lust hit him like a freight train.

Claire was in his bed.

Seeing him, she sat up. The blue satin sheet slid down her chest and pooled at her waist.

Claire was in his bed *naked*.

His gaze swept over her. Her glorious hair hung loose and long and fell like a sunset over her creamy shoulders. Taut rose-colored nipples crowned her full breasts. One shapely leg stretched out from beneath the covers. She wore scarlet polish on the toes she'd curled around and tucked beside her hip. She offered him a wobbly smile.

Claire was in his bed *completely naked*.

"Hi."

"Hi."

Jax's mouth went dry and his dick went hard as a submarine. Without conscious thought, he yanked off the towel wrapped around his waist. Fully aroused and drawn like a moth to a flame, he moved toward her.

He'd had all sorts of plans for their first time. All sorts of fantasies. After all, he'd been thinking about it since July. He'd intended to continue this seduction in the manner in which it began. Slow and steady and steamy. Dinner in their room, then dancing beneath the mistletoe to a playlist of songs from singers she'd told him she loved—Frank Sinatra, Michael Bublé, some Righteous Brothers. He'd hold her close and nuzzle her ear. Breathe in the scent of her. Kiss her temple, her throat, her lips. Jax loved kissing, and the past weeks had shown him that Claire did, too. Slow, sizzling seduction.

When they reached the point where, up until now, they broke it off and went upstairs to their separate bedrooms, he'd planned to take her by the hand and invite her to his bedroom. Slow, scorching seduction.

He'd fantasized undressing her. Piece by piece. Down to her glorious lingerie. He couldn't know which color she'd wear, but he expected it to be a jewel tone. He lived with her. He'd seen the lacy, front-clasp bras and tiny thongs she preferred in the laundry room once or twice. Slow, scorching seduction.

When he had her naked, he would breathe her name in a whisper, like a prayer, and press her down against the mattress. He'd take his sweet time exploring her luscious body. He'd lose himself in the scent of her, the taste of her, the wonder of her. He'd stroke her all over. He'd knead and massage and discover how she liked to be touched. He'd use his mouth on her. Tasting the hollow at the base of her throat. Suckling her full breasts. Licking his way down her flat stomach to . . . heaven.

Slow, scalding seduction.

He'd make her come. He'd make her scream. He'd make her sob his name before he slipped inside her tight, moist heat. He'd ride her then, going deep, going slow, making it last. Making her come again before he finally . . . finally . . . let go.

Claire was naked in his bed waiting for him.

Who needs plans?

Thank God she pressed a condom into his hand before he touched her. He managed . . . just barely . . . to put it on before he entered her. Hard and fast.

Too fast.

It was over in about a minute.

He collapsed against her, breathing hard. "I can do better than that. I can *so* do better than that."

He lifted his head and frowned down at her. "You ambushed me."

Her eyes sparkled and her mouth lifted in a self-satisfied smile. "I made you lose control."

"Well . . . yeah. It's been hanging by a thread since we moved into Mama Bear. To find you gorgeous and naked and waiting . . . damn, woman. Talk about a surprise. It's a wonder I didn't have a heart attack."

"I was nervous," she admitted a bit bashfully. "It's been a long time for me, and I wanted to get our first time over with."

"Well, you got it half right."

"What do you mean?"

"I had *my* first, but unless I'm misreading the signs, you're still waiting."

"Waiting?"

"I have plans for you, Claire Branham." Jax rose up on his knees. His gaze burned a path up and down her gorgeous nakedness. "Slow, steamy, sizzling, screaming plans."

Jax leaned over and licked the tip of her breast. And then proceeded to show her his plans. In detail.

Slowly.

Chapter Nineteen

Something positive? Men are positively idiots!
—CLAIRE

Claire lost track of how many times they made love. In bed and on the sofa, on the floor, in the shower, in the hot tub. They didn't leave their room until after lunch the following day, and by then she was sore enough to really need the massage he'd booked at the spa.

She'd enjoyed startling a laugh out of him when they arrived for their appointments and she innocently told the clerk that their reservation was under the name S. Sven.

"Stamina Sven," he murmured into her ear while they waited for their masseuses to lead them to their room. "I'm glad to know that I've redeemed myself."

"Any more 'redeeming' and I wouldn't have had the energy to walk to the spa."

Following the spa appointment, pampered and relaxed, they returned to their room for a decadent nap. She awoke three hours later to find Jax propped up on his elbow, his head resting in his hand as he watched her.

"What? Was I snoring?"

"No. I was just enjoying the scenery."

Her gaze stole to the wall of windows and she smiled. "It snowed while we were sleeping!"

"Yes. The forecast called for four inches. Looks closer to six to me."

"It's beautiful."

"Not as beautiful as you are, Claire. Flat-out, drop-dead beautiful. Inside and out."

The look in his eyes, the admiration in his tone, made her melt, and her response almost made them late for their dinner reservation.

The following morning, she awoke before he did, and leaving him a note, she went down to the pool for a swim. It was her favorite form of exercise and one of the things she missed most about living in Eternity Springs. Swimming freestyle. Maybe if she ever decided to spend the money that was accumulating and build a house in Eternity Springs, she could build a pool like this one. The indoor/outdoor aspect was pretty darn nice.

Maybe Jax could be her contractor. Nicholas would love to have a pool to swim in year round. Nicholas would love to live in Eternity Springs year round.

But what about Jax? He'd promised Nicholas that they'd stay until summer. He believed he had to move in order to financially provide for his son. What if . . .

Stop it, she scolded herself as she made a racing turn. That was dangerous thinking. Despite the sweet things he'd said and done, despite the fabulous sex, Jax Lancaster had given her no indication that he wanted anything beyond his mistletoe fling.

Of course, she hadn't given him any such indication either, had she?

What if . . .

She could so easily imagine a life with Jax, being a mother to Nicholas and maybe another baby or two. It wouldn't even have to be in Eternity Springs. She loved Eternity Springs and the life, the friendships she was building there, but she could leave it. There was no reason why she couldn't open a Christmas store somewhere else, if that's what she decided she wanted to do. Maybe she'd be happy being a stay-at-home mom.

Jax was building a life and friendships in Eternity Springs. Maybe if she told him about the health of her bank account, he'd decide to make a life in Eternity Springs, too.

Right, Branham. Nothing like having a man want you for your money, is there?

She was gun-shy. She wanted to be wanted for herself. But she also believed that Jax wasn't anything like Landon.

She heard a splash and lifted her head to see who had joined her. Jax.

They raced for two laps, and she thought she just might beat him until he pulled away with a quarter lap to go. Waiting when she reached the end of the pool, he grabbed her around the waist.

"To the victor go the spoils," he said, and then he kissed her.

When his hand began to wander underwater, she laughed and pushed away from him. "The swimming pool is public, Mr. Lancaster."

"Yeah, that's a shame. Maybe I'll win the lottery and buy Three Bears from Bob Hamilton and build one of these. Nicholas would love it. And on those nights when he's at a sleepover . . . how do you feel about skinny-dipping, Ms. Branham?"

The intensity of the yearning that filled her at the idea of living permanently with the Lancasters at Three Bears shocked her. The feeling stayed with her as they went horseback riding and while they showered together afterward, then packed to leave.

When her bags were ready, she stood at the window gazing out at the incredible view. She heard Jax exit the other bedroom and set his suitcase beside hers near the suite's doorway. Without turning around, she said, "This is a breathtaking spot. Thank you for bringing me here."

"My pleasure." He walked up behind her and wrapped his arms around her, holding her against him. They stood without speaking for a bit, then Jax said, "This weekend has been one of the best weekends of my life."

She smiled. "Same for me, Jax."

"So where do we go from here?"

Outwardly, she went still, but her pulse began to thunder. "What do you mean?"

"This no-strings fling of ours hasn't turned out quite like I'd imagined." He turned her around and stared down into her eyes. "I have feelings for you, Claire. Strong feelings. I know that wasn't our deal, and I should probably keep my mouth shut about it, but I want to be honest."

Honest. A lump formed in her throat, and she swallowed hard.

"You matter to me, Claire."

"You matter to me, too, Jax."

He exhaled a heavy breath. "Okay, then. That takes us back to my question. Where do we go from here? I'm teetering right at the edge of the deep end of the pool here. I can probably still take a step back if I need to do that. The fact is, we have a couple of obstacles that stand in the way of a relationship. We'd be stupid to ignore that."

Obstacles. "You're talking about Nicholas?"

"Actually, I don't see my son as a problem. A consideration, definitely. I think we need to be careful that we don't dangle a dream in front of him and then snatch it away."

"A dream?"

"A mother. We've been careful so far not to let him see that we're anything more than friends. Before we change that particular status quo, I need to know where we stand obstaclewise."

"And those obstacles are?"

"My career and your business. I can't be a handyman all my life. I still need to provide for my son, so I still need to leave Eternity Springs after school is out. Here's the million-dollar question. How settled are you in Eternity Springs, Claire?"

Million-dollar question? How about twenty million? She bit back a little hysterical giggle.

Nervous now, she pulled out of his arms and began to pace. What did she say to him? How much truth did she tell?

How much do you want a life with him?

A lot. She wanted a life with Jax and Nicholas as badly as she'd ever wanted anything.

You have to tell him. You can't keep your secret any longer. You have to trust him. He's not Landon.

He's not Landon.

She drew a deep, bracing breath. "Jax, I love Eternity Springs, but I don't have to stay there. For the right reason, I would be willing to leave."

"Am I the right reason?"

"You could be."

A fierce, bright look entered his eyes. He grinned and took a step toward her, but Claire held up her hand, signaling him to stop. "I have more to say."

"Okay."

"Like I said, I'd be willing to move, but you should know that if you and I worked out, it wouldn't be necessary."

"What do you mean?"

She took a deep, bracing breath, then said, "Jax, I'm wealthy."

His smile froze. "Wealthy."

"Yes."

He slipped his hands into his pockets, the light in his eyes dimmed. "Okay. Well. 'Wealthy' means different things to different people. Maybe you could define it a little better for me?"

She wasn't exactly sure why, but Claire felt insulted. "I could probably buy this resort. With cash."

"Holy shit." He literally took a step back, and when he finally spoke again, his entire demeanor had changed. He accused, "You never told me."

"I'm telling you now." Claire felt tears sting at the back of her eyes.

Jax took another step backward. He turned and looked out the window and remained pensively silent for an eternity. When he finally spoke, it was to spit a curse worthy of the sailor he'd once been.

That put Claire's back up. "Excuse me?"

"It puts a whole new spin on things," he said, his eyes blazing with sudden anger. "I've been down this road before and, frankly, I didn't like the view."

"What do you mean by that?"

"The imbalance in our individual financial situations is what doomed my marriage."

"So?"

"It's a bitch of a thing to deal with."

She wasn't Lara Hardcastle. She got that his wife was a spoiled brat, but Claire had never acted that way around him. Hadn't she proven herself? He was being irrational and a jerk for no reason.

"I wish you'd told me before this, Claire."

I wish you weren't such a jackass.

She folded her arms and pasted a fake smile onto her face. "It really wasn't any of your business before now, was it? We weren't in a relationship. We were having a fling. A no-strings, mistletoe fling."

He scowled and rubbed the back of his neck.

Claire continued, "Only when we started to discuss changing the parameters of our relationship did it become relevant. And now you know, and so do I. It's been fun, Jax, but me being wealthy . . . well, it's obvious that the obstacle is insurmountable. I'm glad we had this talk. So, shall I call for a bellman now?"

He ignored the question and said, "Wait a minute. Wait just a minute. That sounds like . . . what . . . are you ending this?"

"Our fling?" Claire was proud of her nonchalant shrug. "I can go either way on that. I enjoyed the sex. Now that we've cleared the air about any potential emotional entanglements, I don't see why we couldn't continue as we have been."

It was a lie, but she'd figure a way to get out of it if he called her bluff. "Of course, our chaperone will be back from Seattle, so opportunities will be limited. Since I'll be moving back to Baby Bear—"

"What?" he demanded.

"The work there is finished, isn't it?"

"Well, yes. It's been finished for two weeks."

"I was tied up with the Twelve Dogs of Christmas reception, but I have time to move now, a little gap between now and the start of the Christmas season."

A muscle worked in Jax's jaw. "You're just pissed because I'm pissed that you weren't honest with me. Now you're trying to rile me up even more by saying you're going to move out."

No. She was trying to hold her tears at bay. "Honestly, Jax, I'm looking out for Nicholas. Your comment about a mother struck home. I think we've been playing house a little too realistically, and it's better for all of us, Nicholas in particular, that we redefine our boundaries. Now, about the bellman?"

"I'll carry the damned bags down," he groused, marching toward the door. He wrenched it open, gathered up the bags, and banged his way out of the room.

With great gentleness, Claire shut the door behind him. Then she leaned her back against it and allowed the tears to fall.

Jax needed time to rein in his temper. The woman had totally blindsided him. He had known she wasn't destitute. She had a lot of green tied up in inventory at her shop. But lots of times small-business owners had all their assets wrapped up in their business. If Eternity Springs had been Aspen or Vail, he might have wondered. But it wasn't. It was tiny little almost-off-the-map Eternity Springs. And she'd never acted like a society princess. She'd never acted like someone who could buy him and sell him a dozen times over.

Wealthy. Claire Branham was wealthy with a capital *W*. He'd fallen for another wealthy woman.

Frustration rolled through him like a big black wave. Wouldn't it be easier to stick a knife in his heart now and get it over with?

Been there, done that. Lost the custody fight because of it.

Because he needed to blow off steam, a full half hour passed before he returned to their suite, ready to calmly discuss the situation. Claire was nowhere in sight. His name was on the outside of a note lying on the coffee table. He picked it up, read it, and about a million pounds of torque flooded into his jaw.

The damned woman had bailed on him.

Under the circumstances, she'd written, she thought that a four-hour drive would be uncomfortable for them both. She'd find her own way back home.

"Probably phoned in an order for a Rolls-Royce and is having it delivered," he muttered, quitting the suite.

He unloaded her bags from his truck and left them with the bellman. He'd kept a heavy foot on the gas pedal and made the four-hour trip to Eternity Springs in three hours and twenty-seven minutes.

He picked up Captain from the Cicero house, thanked them graciously for watching him, and drove home to Three Bears Valley, leaving Tinsel with the Raffertys for Claire to retrieve. Captain proved to be a good listener, but Jax's temper hadn't subsided much by the time he reached Mama Bear. So the first thing he did upon arriving was to take down every last piece of mistletoe and throw it in the garbage.

Then he packed up all her stuff and hauled it over to Baby Bear. "Just being helpful, after all," he murmured to Captain as he left the key to the cabin on the kitchen table. "Gotta define those boundaries."

Back home, he grabbed his toolbox and headed for Papa Bear. An hour of swinging a hammer helped, but after he showered and went scrounging in the empty refrigerator for something to eat, he muttered, "Screw it."

He drove back into town to grab a burger and a beer at Murphy's Pub and ended up playing pool with Brick Callahan until close.

A light was on at Baby Bear when he came home. He glanced around the clearing for a Rolls. Nothing. Not a Jag or a Maserati, either.

"A chauffeured limousine, then," he'd said to Captain. Or else she'd sent the Rolls back for a different color.

He found her key to Mama Bear on his kitchen table. He kicked the plastic trash can across the kitchen and went to bed. Alone. Lonely.

Damn woman.

After a fitful night's sleep, he awakened in a foul mood and spent the two-hour drive to the airport trying to talk himself out of it before Nicholas arrived. If he were being totally honest with himself, he would admit that he could understand her keeping quiet about her money. But the way she'd turned up her nose and used that snippy little tone when she calmly announced she was leaving him and moving back to Baby Bear rubbed in his craw. Then, to run off and hide rather than ride home with him—that really took the cake.

Jax was pissed, and underneath the anger, he was sad. Dammit, he'd been falling in love with her.

And she was rich.

Really rich.

Son of a bitch.

A part of Jax recognized that he'd overreacted to her news. But she'd darned sure overreacted to his reaction, too. If she hadn't decamped from their room while he'd been busy blowing off his first head of steam, then maybe they wouldn't have reached the key-trading stage.

The whine of a jet engine drew his notice, and he lifted his gaze to the sky to see the private Cessna that was ferrying his son home approaching from the west. "Let it go, Lancaster."

His boy was coming home. He was coming home and he deserved to have a father who wasn't as grouchy as the Grinch. He would have questions about Claire and Jax needed to be ready for them.

What answer would he give about why Claire wasn't here to meet him? Because Nicholas would expect that. Claire had been right about the whole playing-house thing.

He'd tell the truth. Claire had to work today. Except, did she ever really have to work? He wasn't sure why, but something about the way she'd snotty'd all up made him think that her money might put Lara's family's to shame.

If that's the case, then why did she work so hard at Forever Christmas? Retail wasn't for the faint of heart, and from everything he'd seen, Claire did work at it harder than most.

The plane landed and taxied to a stop. It took a good

ten minutes for the ground crew to get stairs in place and the hatch to open, but when it did, Nicholas was first off the plane.

Jax's heart swelled. He'd missed the squirt. The boy started talking long before Jax could hear him.

". . . took me to the market and watched 'em throw the fish. Then we went to the Space Needle. I'm taller than Trevor now. And Mimi made chocolate chip cookies. Pops took us to a Seahawks game! They won!"

"That's awesome," Jax said, giving his son a fierce hug. "I'm sorry you had such a terrible time."

"I didn't have a terrible . . . oh. You're teasing me."

"Yeah." Jax ruffled the boy's hair, then shook Brian Hardcastle's hand. The two men visited for a few moments and finalized their plans for the Hardcastles' visit for Thanksgiving. Then Nicholas hugged his grandfather good-bye and asked Jax if they could stay and watch the Cessna take off. Jax agreed and they grabbed a sandwich in the terminal and found a spot where they could watch the planes.

After Brian's plane was airborne, Jax and Nicholas headed for his truck. Nicholas asked the question that Jax had anticipated. "Where's Miss Claire? I thought she'd be here to meet me, too."

"She had to work, Nicholas."

Actually, that wasn't precisely true, was it? The woman *chose* to work.

He couldn't argue that she didn't dedicate herself to the activity, either. He wondered why. What would make her work so hard at her business when she didn't have to do it? He wondered if he'd ever have the opportunity to find out.

The boy continued to rattle on about his trip. His grandparents had certainly packed a lot into the visit. Nicholas finally wound down an hour into the trip home and fell asleep. Jax appreciated the peace and quiet, and yet, without his son's chatter he returned to his brooding.

He'd probably screwed up big-time. Claire was the best thing that had happened to him in years. She wasn't Lara. She wasn't anything like Lara. Why had he reacted to her news as if she were?

Because you're a too-proud SOB, that's why.

In the front passenger seat, Nicholas stirred and rubbed his eyes. Jax was glad for the distraction from his troublesome thoughts.

"Where are we?" the boy asked.

"About ten minutes out of town."

"Can we stop by and see Miss Claire? I want to tell her about my new Christmas book. I thought she had every Christmas book there is but Mimi gave me one Miss Claire doesn't have. I want her to read it to me tonight."

Well, crap. "About that, Nicholas. I'll be the one reading Christmas stories from now on. Miss Claire moved back to Baby Bear."

"What?" The boy's brows knitted. "Why?"

"It's her place, and I finished all the repairs."

"But . . . I like having her with us. Does that mean she won't fix me breakfast anymore? And dinner? And take me to school?"

"Probably not, Nicholas."

"That stinks. So, she's not your girlfriend anymore?"

Jax whipped his head around to stare at his son. "What makes you think she was my girlfriend?"

"I'm not stupid, Dad." Nicholas folded his arms. "I saw you kissing her."

Busted.

"I like her. A lot. I was hoping that . . . well . . ." He shrugged and added, "Miss Claire would be a really good mom. Did you make her mad?"

Just plunge the knife into my heart, why don't you?

Better nip this in the bud right now. "Nicholas, remember our deal when I agreed to bring you to Eternity Springs? It hasn't changed. We still have to move when school is out."

His son turned his head away from Jax and sat staring out the side window. They rode in silence for a few minutes, then Nicholas asked in a timid voice, "Couldn't she come with us?"

Jax sighed. "Nicholas, here's the deal. Just because grown-ups kiss doesn't mean that they're ready to get married and leave their friends and business and move across the country. I'll be honest with you. I may never want to get married again. The first time I did it, it didn't work out so great."

"Did you hate my mom?"

"Oh, buddy, no. I loved your mother. I truly did."

"So why did you break up with her?"

She dumped me for another man was his immediate response. But Jax couldn't say that to his son about his son's mother. Besides, honesty made him admit that it wasn't as straightforward as that, either. "That is a simple question with a complicated answer. I think your mother and I were too young and too selfish to love unconditionally, and that's what it takes to make a marriage work."

"And you don't love Miss Claire that way, either," Nicholas said in a mournful tone.

Apparently not.

The black mood that his son's return had dispelled returned. Nicholas remained quiet after that insightful remark, so Jax didn't have a distraction from his brooding. He hated this. Maybe he was too proud and stubborn and gun-shy to love Claire the way a man should love a woman, but dammit, he'd needed . . . they'd needed . . . more time. He'd no sooner begun to start thinking long-term when she went and threw a grenade into the works.

Hell, if she'd told him she had five ex-husbands it wouldn't have thrown him as bad as learning that he'd gotten tangled up with another wealthy woman.

Jax didn't realize he'd exhaled a heavy sigh until Nicholas reached across the seat and patted his knee. "It'll be okay, Dad. It's like what Miss Celeste says. You just have to think positive and believe that good things will happen, and they will."

Jax's mouth twisted in a crooked smile. Eternity Springs was definitely rubbing off on the kid.

Nicholas launched into a story about his friend Trevor that lasted until they approached the outskirts of Eternity Springs. At that point, the boy said, "Could we go by Forever Christmas before we go home, Dad?"

"Nicholas, did you hear anything I said about Miss Claire?"

"I'm still her friend, aren't I? Besides, I want to get Mimi a present and mail it right away. I want to get her something from Miss Claire's Angel Room. I have my allowance money. Pops and Mimi didn't let me pay for a thing."

Of course they hadn't.

Jax considered his son's request. The kid had just given him the perfect excuse to see Claire. He realized he wanted to see her. They had some unfinished business between them.

Not that they could finish said business in front of Nicholas, but a visit to her shop could be a good icebreaker. Besides, think of what a huge step his son had just taken! Nicholas nonchalantly asked to go to a Christmas store. How could Jax possibly say no?

"On one condition. Don't say anything to her about the girlfriend stuff. Let me work on fixing this in my own way, on my own time. Okay?"

"Okay."

Jax found a parking place right outside of Forever Christmas. The moment he switched off the engine, Nicholas grabbed up his backpack from the floorboard and scrambled out of the truck. He didn't hesitate a second, but ran right past the planters with their lighted Christmas trees, pushed open the door, and ran into the shop. Where . . . oh, hell . . . Claire had Christmas carols playing.

Jax bolted for Forever Christmas, fearful he'd find his son in the midst of a panic attack. But when he rushed inside, he heard his son's animated voice saying, ". . . Trevor's dad will bring him skiing over the Christmas holidays. And my Mimi and Pops want to come, too, but they don't want to intrude so we have to wait to see if Dad invites them after they come for Thanksgiving."

Well, what do you know. Jax breathed a sigh of relief. "What Child Is This" wasn't bothering him one bit.

Claire shifted her gaze away from Nicholas long enough to send him a look he couldn't interpret. He said, "Hello, Claire."

She might have nodded imperceptibly before turning her attention back to his son, but he couldn't be sure.

Nicholas unzipped his backpack and pulled a couple items from inside as he continued to talk. "I want to show you what my Mimi gave me to keep as a special treasure to remember my mom."

Jax's throat went tight. He recognized the music box that his son removed from his backpack. He'd given it to Lara, the first gift he'd ever given her.

Nicholas twisted the key, and the music box began to play "Lara's Theme" from *Doctor Zhivago*. Jax closed his eyes as the memory of his wife . . . a good memory, for a change . . . washed over him.

"The song has the same name as my mom. It was one of her favorite things. Mimi said my dad gave it to her as a present. So whenever I get missing her, I can play her song, and it's like she is with me."

"That's a lovely idea, Nicholas."

"I like it. So, I told Mimi about your sister and we got a present for you." He pulled a box from the backpack, one covered in Valentine's hearts like the one she'd given to Nicholas with his ornaments.

"Oh, Nicholas." Claire's expression went a little weepy.

"Open it."

She set the box on her checkout counter, but before she managed to remove the lid, the boy spilled the beans. "It's a music box, too, only it's a snow globe and the song it plays is called 'Michelle.' Mimi said you'd know it."

"By the Beatles. Yes. I do." Claire pulled back white tissue paper and lifted a snow globe from the box. Jax saw a model of the Eiffel Tower before she turned it over, wound the key, then set it on the counter. As the haunting notes of "Michelle" rose on the cinnamon-scented air, Claire traced the sphere of glass with her index finger.

"Do you like it?" Nicholas asked.

"Oh, Nicholas." Claire went down on her knees and took him into her arms. "I love it. I just love it. It's the nicest present anyone has ever given me. Thank you so much."

"I thought you'd like it. Now we have to find something for my Mimi. I need a present for her, Miss Claire. An angel present for the bedroom. It used to be my mom's room, but Mimi is redecorating, and she let me pick the paint color so I picked blue because heaven is blue. That's why I want to send her an angel present because my mom is an angel and when Mimi looks at it, she will think of Mommy. Will you help me find the perfect present, Miss Claire?"

"I'll be proud to help, Nicholas. Let's go see what we can find."

Neither Claire nor Nicholas paid any attention to Jax as they went into the Angel Room. He hung back, his gaze on the music box, memories of Lara drifting through his mind. They'd been happy for a time. Young and in love and blind to the differences that would prove too significant to overcome. Jax had been exactly right when he told Nicholas that they'd been selfish. They'd been selfish, both of them. Both unwilling to compromise.

But he'd loved her. Once upon a time, oh, how he'd loved her. He'd asked her to marry him during a romantic, after-dinner walk on the beach in Cabo. She'd worn a filmy white linen dress, carried her sandals in her hand, and she'd gazed up at him with such love in her eyes it made him feel ten feet tall. And the morning when he came home from his run to find her standing in their bathroom, her expression filled with surprise and awe and happiness, her hand holding the positive pregnancy test, he'd never known such joy.

Jax reached out and flipped open the music box. *Somewhere my love.*

When she'd left him, it had ripped his heart out.

That's what he couldn't forget or forgive. The soul-wrenching pain. The hollow sense of loss. The transformation of love into something dark and ugly that sucked the soul from a man.

Jax closed the music box and followed the sound of Claire's voice to the Angel Room. His gaze was drawn to the angel in his son's hands. The hand-painted face on a round wooden ball was simple and sweet, her dress made of something shimmery blue beneath a tan muslin overskirt. Her wings, six white feathers, three on either side.

Not the fanciest angel in the room, for certain. Not the angel he'd have chosen with Lara in mind.

As Nicholas handed his choice to Claire and she carefully wrapped it in white tissue paper and placed it in a gift box, Jax's throat closed on a lump of emotion and his eyes grew misty.

His son had come into Claire's carol-blaring Christmas shop today. He'd talked about his mother. In memory of her, he'd bought an angel to send to the grandmother who'd finally redecorated her late daughter's bedroom.

Nicholas had defeated his demons. His heart had healed.

Why hasn't mine?

Suddenly, Jax needed to be out of that shop, away from Claire, far away from her Angel Room. "Nicholas, I'll wait for you at the truck."

Taking two long strides, he reached Forever Christmas's front door, yanked it open, and barreled out onto the street. He shoved his hands into his pockets. He gritted his teeth. He was breathing hard, and he didn't know why.

He almost ran right over Celeste Blessing, who had her arms overfilled with bags from the Trading Post grocery store.

"Sorry," he said as she lurched out of the way and her bags went swinging. He dove for the bags, catching one of them just before it hit the ground. "So sorry, Celeste. I wasn't looking where I was going. Here, let me help you." He scooped the other three bags from her arms. "Are you heading home?"

"Thank you, Jax. I'm on my way to Lori's house to stock her refrigerator. Since you're keeping Captain, I'm sure you know that she and Chase are due back from their honeymoon late tonight? I'm afraid I bought more than I'd intended. I'm happy to have the help."

Lori's house was two blocks away. Jax smiled at Celeste and said, "After you."

She and Jax made small talk as they walked, and he was glad for the distraction from his thoughts. By the time he followed Celeste up onto the newlyweds' front porch, he'd begun to relax.

So he had absolutely no explanation for what he did next.

He set the grocery bags on Lori's kitchen counter then met his companion's gentle, blue-eyed gaze. The question came out of nowhere. "Celeste, how do people earn their wings?"

Her smile beamed right into that dark part of his mood. "You are referring to the official Angel's Rest blazon awarded to those who have embraced love's healing grace?"

"Yeah." He'd noticed a handful of people around town wearing them, and he'd asked what they were.

"The path is different for everyone, dear, but in order to walk it, you must find your way onto it to begin with. You can do that by listening to your inner angel."

Angels, again. He couldn't get away from them. They were everywhere he turned and, frankly, it was getting a little creepy.

"Unfortunately as we grow older, we often have trouble tuning in to them. Luckily for you, you have an angel hearing aid."

"Excuse me?"

"A child. Angels don't use an inside voice to speak to children, so they hear the message better. Learn from your Nicholas, Jax. Soak up his truth and you will find your path. Then . . ."—she reached up and patted his cheek—"walk it and be a raindrop."

"Be a raindrop?"

"Moisten the parched heart of someone around you with your love and watch her flower before you. Together you will walk in beauty, light, and love."

"Celeste, I suspect you just said something important, but I don't have a clue what it could be."

She laughed and reached into one of her bags and pulled out a box from Fresh bakery. She handed it to him saying,

"Here. This is a new product we're going to be selling in the gift shop at Angel's Rest. I want you to have the first box."

Jax read the label aloud. " 'Angel's Rest Fortune Cookies'?"

"Sarah's recipe, my fortunes." She slipped her arm through his and ushered him toward the door. "Now, thank you for the help, but you should run along back to your truck. You don't want to keep your son waiting. Thanks again for the help."

"No problem. Thanks, Celeste."

He was halfway down the street when he heard her call, "Oh, Jax?"

"Yes, ma'am."

"Be sure to listen closely. You'll hear your angel cheering you on."

As Jax approached his truck, Nicholas exited Forever Christmas carrying a box wrapped for mailing. "It's all ready, Dad. Miss Claire let me call Mimi and I got her address."

They stopped at the post office. Jax waited in the truck while his son mailed his package, and his gaze stole toward the box of fortune cookies. "What the heck."

He opened the box, took a cookie, and cracked it open. He removed the little white paper from inside and unrolled it. Aloud, he read, " 'Forgiveness is fresh air for the soul.' "

Forgiveness? Who was he supposed to forgive? For what?

Or maybe he was the one who needed to be forgiven.

"Huh."

Nicholas returned to the truck, and as they continued the drive to Three Bears Valley, Jax subtly questioned the boy about the time he'd spent with Claire. He listened very closely to Nicholas's answers.

The kid said a lot. He didn't shut up the whole way

home. Nevertheless, Jax didn't hear one damned thing he would label as a "truth."

Nicholas played with Captain while Jax worked at Papa Bear that afternoon. He fixed hamburgers for supper, and when bedtime rolled around, read more Percy Jackson to Nicholas along with his new Christmas book—*The Christmas Angel Waiting Room*.

When Jax went to bed that night, an oppressive silence seemed to hang over Mama Bear. He couldn't fall asleep and couldn't get comfortable, tossing and turning and punching his feather pillow into shape.

So far, his angel wasn't talking.

So much for help from Celeste and his "hearing aid."

Deciding a late-night snack was in order, Jax went downstairs to raid the pantry. Pickings were slim.

Then he remembered the cookies.

He chose three cookies, set them on a paper plate, and poured a glass of milk. He cracked open all three cookies and ate them without bothering to read the fortunes inside. The cookies were good. Full of flavor. Cinnamon and ginger and something else he couldn't quite place. Almond, perhaps?

He drank his milk. Stared at the fortunes. Listened for those cheers Celeste had promised. Sighing heavily, he unrolled the three papers and read them one after the other.

Don't give up. Let go.

Take a leap of faith and fly.

Believe.

Jax drained his glass of milk. He picked up the slips of paper and took them upstairs to his bedroom. There, he dug the fortune he'd opened earlier from the pocket of his jeans and added it to the stack.

He picked up his journal and a pen and wrote, "I think I might have heard my angel today."

When he closed the book, he traced the embossed word

upon the cover with his finger and thought of Claire. *Believe*.

Then he tucked the four angel-cookie fortunes in the journal and turned off his light. That night, Jax slept like a baby and dreamed of a red-haired angel atop a Christmas tree.

Chapter Twenty

You've done dumber things in your life.
It's just been a while.
—JAX

"Hand me the knife," Claire said, extending her palm like a surgeon in the operating room.

Brick Callahan's wary voice drawled, "You're not going to stab me with it, are you?"

Kneeling on the floor of an old silver-mine-turned-storage-facility on the grounds of Angel's Rest, she looked up sharply at her friend. "What?"

"I'm not exactly sure why, although I do have my suspicions, but I'm already bleeding from a thousand cuts from that tongue of yours. Are you ready to put me out of your misery?"

"I . . . oh." Awareness washed over her and she winced. "I'm sorry, Brick. I'm terrible."

"You're in a terrible mood." He handed her the box cutter. "Have been for a week or so."

Claire couldn't argue with the observation, so rather than respond, she busied herself by slicing through cardboard and packing tape with the blade and yanking the box open. Inside she spied the lighted green wreaths with red all-weather bows that would be mounted around the streetlights in town.

Under other circumstances, the sight would make Claire smile. Celeste had lobbied the chamber for this style because, she'd confessed to Claire, they reminded her of halos. Count on Celeste to get her angel on whenever possible.

Only, Claire didn't have any smiles inside her. She was not a happy woman.

"Want to tell Dr. Brick why you are such a grouch?" When she didn't immediately answer, he added, "I suspect it has something to do with a certain hammer-swinging sailor. He's been almost as pleasant to be around as you of late."

Her attention perked up at that, and the recognition of her reaction only served to stoke her temper. "Men are so stupid."

"Because . . . what . . . we forget to put the toilet seat down?"

"Because . . . just because." She handed him the box cutter and said, "Would you please open up the other boxes for me? I've learned the hard way how important it is to inspect each box. I'd hate to wait until next Friday to discover that something was shipped wrong or is damaged."

Brick chastised her with a look, but thankfully refrained from commenting.

Claire knew she was acting crabby, but honestly, she was tired of being nice. Tired of pasting a smile on her face and acting like holly-jolly Miss Christmas when she was feeling Halloween witchy. Black hats and black cats and a high-pitched cackle—that suited her much better than the Twelve Dogs of Christmas these days.

Men *were* stupid. But *she* was an idiot.

She'd let her guard down. Again. It had bit her in the broomstick. Again. One would think that after the debacle that was Landon the Lying Lizard Lawyer, she would have known better. But oh, no. The first low-slung tool belt who struts by makes her forget everything she'd learned. She'd let her glands do her thinking for her, and she'd let

Mr. Mistletoe into her heart. She'd fallen head over heels for his son, and she'd allowed herself to dream of love and marriage and family.

Again.

Stupid. Stupid. Stupid.

Her temper hadn't cooled in the two weeks since she'd returned from Silver Eden. If anything, the constant reminders of her foolishness served to stoke its fire. It didn't help that she couldn't seem to get away from the man. Every time she turned around, something was there to bring Jax Lancaster to mind.

Go to brush her teeth and there was the bathroom sink that leaked before Jax fixed it. A stop at the market to pick up produce and she automatically reached for bananas. She didn't eat bananas. Jax and Nicholas had one every morning with their breakfast. And then there was the blasted mistletoe. Every time she turned around someone was buying something mistletoe related. It didn't help that over the past six weeks she'd ordered a ridiculous amount of mistletoe-themed items. Nor was she happy that the Chamber of Commerce had elected to store their new Christmas decorations in the space Celeste had donated in Mistletoe Mine.

Maybe she should close the shop and go on a vacation. One that lasted until June.

"Okay, sugarplum," Brick said. "All the boxes are open. Are you sure Eternity Springs has enough public square to display all of this stuff?"

"Oh, yes. The committee was quite deliberate about what they ordered. Thanks for the help, Brick."

"I'm always ready to help a friend." Following a deliberate pause, he added, "That includes listening. Why don't you tell me what Lancaster did that has put a burr beneath your saddle?"

"I don't want to talk about him." She rose to her feet

and braced her hands on her hips. "Or his idiotic pride. Or his exceedingly stupid prejudice."

"Okay."

"I had a fling. No strings. No big deal. It happened. It's over."

"Sure it is."

Now she folded her arms and glared at him. "Wait a minute. What do you mean by that?"

"If it's over, then why the attitude? You should be happy as a pig in mud right now, checking in the fruits of your not insignificant labor." He waved his arm expansively toward the row of open boxes. "You worked hard to make this happen. You should be enjoying it."

"I am enjoying it," she snapped.

He rolled his tongue around his cheek. "Uh-huh."

"I am. I'm proud of my contribution to this project. I can't wait to decorate next Friday."

It was such a lie. The Christmas Comfort-and-Joy Season bore down upon her like a big black tornado. Which reminded her. All the lights and ornaments and, yes, the angel tree topper that she'd taken out of inventory and set aside for the tree she'd hoped to put up at Mama Bear next week needed to go back into stock. What Landon had begun, Jax had finished.

"I talked to him yesterday. He's no happier than your are."

Claire went still. She should tell Brick she didn't want to hear anything about Jax Lancaster.

"He said he's tried to talk to you, but that you refuse to let it happen."

"He has no business spreading my personal business around town."

"Wasn't exactly around town. He was finishing up the work on the dance hall at the North Forty, and he was swinging his hammer so hard I thought he might hit right through the wall. Not all that different from the way you handled that box cutter a few minutes ago. I asked him what the heck was wrong, and he said the two of you had a misunderstanding."

A misunderstanding? A misunderstanding! "Grrr . . ."

Brick looked at her and shook his head. "Honey, as someone with up-close-and-personal experience with living with a broken heart, I think—"

"He did not break my heart," she snapped. "I don't want to talk about Jax Lancaster, Brick."

He held up his hands in surrender. "Okay. Okay. I'll change the subject. What do you need me to do next here?"

She put him to work testing strings of lights, and by the time they completed their job and departed Mistletoe Mine, she had a short list of items that needed to be exchanged and a longer packing list of items she needed for the ski trip to Aspen she'd just decided to take. She would close the shop, load up Tinsel, and spend Thanksgiving on the slopes.

Happy with her plan, she returned to Forever Christmas and made reservations at a pet-friendly lodge in Aspen. Then she chose a piece of holiday-themed printer paper and wrote out a CLOSED notice for her front door that included the day of her return—Black Friday.

"Wait." She crumpled up the paper, tossed it into the trash, and got another sheet. "Just because your outlook has changed . . ."

She changed the return date on the second notice to "Deck the Halls Friday."

She'd have some disgruntled customers from now until then, but she didn't really care. People could delay their shopping until Deck the Halls Friday. She was the boss. She could close the shop whenever she wanted, and what's the use in being rich as Midas if she never spent anything? She wanted away from Eternity Springs. Away from Three Bears Valley.

Away from Jax Lancaster.

Maybe she'd go to Aspen and find a boy toy to use for the weekend. She could have another fling. An Aspen fling. Mistletoe didn't grow in aspen trees, did it?

She should have known better than to go down that mistletoe path from the start. After all, mistletoe was a parasite. She should have picked up on the message of that.

Except, Jax was the farthest thing from a parasite there was. Unlike Landon. Landon was . . . is . . . a parasite.

As she carried her notice and Scotch tape toward the front door, it opened and a whirlwind blew inside, calling, "Miss Claire! Miss Claire! Guess what?"

Nicholas came to a halt in front of her and pushed his black-framed glasses up on his nose. "You'll never guess what happened at school today!"

Excitement lit the boy up like the Christmas tree behind him, and Claire couldn't help but smile in the face of his joy. "Hmm . . . whatever happened is obviously very exciting. Did somebody throw up their lunch or break their arm at recess?"

"No! I got a part in our Christmas pageant. I get to be an angel and I get to say something. I was hoping I'd get to be a camel because they get to wear a hump, but it's okay that Galen got that part. I get to talk. Will you help me make my costume, Miss Claire? I need wings. And a halo."

Oh, Nicholas. You already have them.

"You will come watch me in the pageant, won't you?"

"Of course I'll be there. I'll go early and do my best to get a seat in the front row."

"And the costume? You'll help me with the costume? I think we are gonna have to sew something this time, and you know Dad."

Yes, she knew his dad. If only she could figure out a way to forget him.

As Nicholas continued to rattle on about his costume, Claire's attention remained divided between his actions and his words. Nicholas explored while he talked. He picked up snow globes and shook them. He pushed buttons and switched on switches. He flipped through the pages of books.

Claire's heart gave a little bittersweet twist. Look at him. He'd told her and Jax back before the Twelve Dogs of Christmas reception how badly he wanted to be like everyone else—a normal kid. As he turned and watched the miniature electric train chug through her Christmas village display, it was clear that Nicholas had defeated his demons.

She wished she knew his secret.

Jax loaded the last of the Thanksgiving dishes into the dishwasher, then filled the sink to tackle the pots and pans.

"Where are the dishtowels?" Brian Hardcastle asked.

"Underneath the coffeepot. Third drawer down."

Since Linda had prepared their Thanksgiving feast, she was taking a well-earned after-dinner nap. Nicholas was sitting in the living room perusing the pet finder Web site and dreaming of getting his heart's desire.

Jax gazed out the window toward dark and empty Baby Bear. *One of us might as well get our heart's desire.*

Standing beside him with a white flour-sack dishtowel in hand, Brian noted the path of Jax's gaze. "Nicholas expects her to come home sometime today."

"Yeah. She left a sign on the door to her shop saying she'd be open tomorrow."

"So what did you do to screw things up with her?"

Jax gave Brian a sidelong look. "Nicholas must have been saying a lot."

"No. I have keen powers of observation. Following our first visit to Eternity Springs, I predicted that you'd be engaged to marry her by the end of the year."

"Yeah, well, I'm going to have to dig myself out of a pretty deep hole to prove you right."

Brian went still for a minute, then he nodded. "So she is what you want. I thought so. It's difficult for me to think of another woman filling Lara's role of mother, but he needs someone. I liked her. She seems like a lovely young woman."

"She's wonderful." Jax realized that Brian Hardcastle had just given him his blessing. He also realized that receiving it meant more to him than he ever would have imagined. "I just hope I'll get the chance to make things right with her."

"I have faith in you. You're a hardheaded SOB, Lancaster. You'll get the job done."

Throughout the rest of the afternoon, Jax kept a close watch on Baby Bear. He had a lot he wanted to say to Claire Branham, and he didn't care what it took, she was going to listen to him.

Jax would be the first to admit that he'd acted like an ass when she'd shared her news at Silver Eden. Under the circumstances, he could understand why she hadn't wanted to make the return trip to Eternity Springs with him. Sometimes a person needed time to work off their mad. Heaven knows he'd needed time to process the information she'd thrown at him. A little time apart can be an effective tool to be used to repair a relationship.

But enough was enough. She'd dodged him long enough.

He needed to talk to Claire. He had apologies to make, explanations to share, and questions to ask. He had a game plan to put into motion.

If only he could get the woman to sit still long enough to listen.

Events of the past few weeks had proved one thing. Claire was definitely a runner. It shouldn't have come as a surprise. Hadn't she told him she'd been running away from home when she met Celeste at that little town in Texas? She'd run from him at Silver Eden. She'd run from him by leaving Mama Bear. She'd run on this mystery Thanksgiving trip.

Jax recognized that instincts were difficult to ignore, so his intention, his challenge, was to convince her to change direction, to run toward him, toward love, rather than away from it.

If he ever managed to pin her down long enough to talk to him again, that is. The woman was as slippery as an eel.

He watched for her arrival all afternoon and into the evening. When her car finally drove past Mama Bear shortly before ten P.M., he breathed a sigh of relief. *She's back.*

He briefly considered marching over there now, but better sense prevailed. Who knew how long she'd been traveling today? She might be exhausted. The confrontation could wait one more day.

Besides, it made sense strategically to wait until tomorrow to approach her. After all, Deck the Halls Friday was right up Miss Christmas's alley. She'd be in a good mood tomorrow, full of Christmas cheer. The timing was actually working out quite nice.

Jax went to bed with a lighter heart than he'd had in days.

Claire awoke to her cell phone sounding Jax's ring tone of "You're a Mean One, Mr. Grinch." She glared at her phone, then pulled the covers over her head and told herself to go back to sleep. This was not how she wanted to start her day.

She didn't want to talk to Jax. She didn't want to see him. She didn't want to think about him.

She lay in bed, hiding beneath the covers. He called

twice more during the next ten minutes. She didn't answer. When her phone rang for the fourth time that morning, it took her a moment to recognize the different ringtone— "I Hate Everything About You" by Three Days Grace. Her day went from bad to worse before it even started.

Not Jax this time. Landon.

She let that call go to voicemail, too. She *might* work up her courage to listen to it later, but probably not. She wasn't up to dealing with Landon today.

Today was Deck the Halls Friday. She had to put on her big-girl panties and go to town and be nice. Be happy. Be Miss Christmas.

"Bah, humbug."

She threw off her covers and rolled out of bed, groaning a little due to muscles sore from three days of skiing. She took a long, hot shower and decided to call the Angel's Rest spa and book a massage.

An hour later, wearing a red ski jacket, a green wool scarf, and a knit cap with antler ears to complete her ensemble, she pasted on a smile that apparently passed as real and accepted the townspeople's kudos for her efforts toward making their new decorations possible. As president of the Chamber of Commerce, Celeste heaped such praise upon Claire that under other circumstances, she'd have basked in the glory.

However, Jax's constant presence and steady stare had her anxious as Frosty on a summer afternoon.

She'd tangibly felt his gaze during the entire Deck the Halls kickoff gathering in Davenport Park. She'd tried her best to pretend he wasn't there, but the man was impossible to ignore. She felt as if she were under siege. When the mayor assigned volunteers into decorating teams of three, she'd closed her eyes and prayed she wouldn't be paired with him.

Fate had been kind to her. She ended up on Chase and

Lori Timberlake's team and got to hear about their travels in Tibet on their rafting-trip honeymoon. Claire had been so relieved to escape Jax Lancaster's undivided attention that she actually enjoyed herself while hanging lights and garlands and red all-weather bows along Cottonwood.

Her tension returned when Three Days Grace sounded from her cell phone again. What was so freaking important that Landon wouldn't leave her alone?

"If you'd listen to one of the twelve voice mails he's already left, you probably would discover the answer," she muttered as she slipped her key into the lock at Forever Christmas and opened the door for what she expected to be her biggest sales day ever.

She traded her jacket and cap for her usual Forever Christmas apron. In the twenty minutes she had to herself before opening the shop, she added mulling spices to apple cider in an electric beverage urn, which she switched on to heat. Soon the aromas of apples, cinnamon, and clove drifted through the shop.

She should probably restock her cider supply, she decided as she removed the day's cash from her bank envelope and added it to her register drawer. When Liz came in for her shift, Claire would send her over to the Trading Post for some. Liz Bernhardt was one of two part-time workers Claire had hired to help her from now until Christmas. Both of her new employees were high school seniors saving for college, and they'd impressed her with their enthusiasm. She hoped they'd be as dependable as their resumes led her to expect.

Claire restocked the ornaments on her depleted Doghouse tree and carried the empty boxes out to the trash dumpster in the alley behind the shop. She turned on the music and moved about the shop, switching on light fixtures, Christmas tree lights, and the Christmas village display. She added more peppermints to her giveaway bowl and decided everything was ready for the opening. Everything but her, that is.

She checked her watch. Ten minutes. She had ten minutes of freedom to scowl and be cranky and fight back tears. She wished she'd never come to Eternity Springs. She wished she'd never gone to the hot springs to soak her sore shoulder that night in July. She totally wished she hadn't moved to Three Bears Valley and fallen in love with the cabins, the man, and his son.

She had to talk to him. She realized that. Eternity Springs was too small to avoid him much longer. Besides, despite his ridiculous overreaction upon learning the news . . . she missed him.

Maybe she should listen to one of Jax's voice mails. Maybe just one. The last one?

Her finger shook just a little as she hit the voice-mail icon on her phone. "Hey, Claire. I miss you. Can we talk?"

Oh, Jax.

A rap on her front door interrupted her musings and demanded her attention. Liz had arrived for work. Claire worked up a smile and let her in. "Before you take your coat off, I need you to run to the Trading Post for me."

"Okay," the teenager said.

Claire gave her a list and money from petty cash. "When you return, come in the back door—it's open. Leave the groceries in the storeroom, and you'll see a couple aprons hanging on hooks. Wear one of them, and you can hang your jacket there."

"Yes, ma'am. I'll be right back." Liz beamed a smile and added, "I can't tell you how excited I am about having this job. It's like I get to have Christmas every day."

Claire smiled and sent Liz on her way. Alone in the shop once more, she repeated, "Bah, humbug."

When the Rudolph cuckoo clock sounded the hour, Claire flipped her sign from CLOSED to OPEN and prepared to get Christmasy. Three shoppers arrived immediately. She sold ornaments and lights, two Christmas village collectibles, and an angel tree topper in the first five minutes.

Claire had anticipated a busy day.

Catastrophic caught her by surprise.

She never expected Landon Perryman to slither into Forever Christmas with Jax Lancaster right behind him.

Chapter Twenty-one

You've done dumber things in your life.
It's just been a while.
—CLAIRE

Jax didn't want to confront Claire while she was at work.
If she'd answer his calls or one of his knocks, he wouldn't
have to do it. But she wouldn't, so he would. This nonsense
had gone on long enough.

He headed toward Forever Christmas armed with a sincere, ready-to-grovel apology and a heartfelt declaration
of love. While he hoped he'd arrive to find a lull between
customers, he was prepared to state his case in public. He
wouldn't risk her running again before he had a chance to
talk to her.

He sighed inwardly when he realized that the tourist in
front of him was headed for the shop, too. *Oh, well, an
audience it is.*

Bells jingled on the door as Jax followed the man into
the shop. He scanned the room for Claire, and immediately
realized something was terribly wrong.

She spared Jax barely a glance, her focus fixed on the
tourist. She'd gone as pale as the snow on the ground of
her Christmas village.

"Hello, Claire," said the stranger.

"What are you doing here?" she demanded. "I don't
want you here. Go away."

"If you'd answered my phone calls, this visit wouldn't have been necessary. You didn't, so it is."

"Landon, you need to leave right now."

Landon. The lawyer. The Lying Lizard guy. Quadruple L. Jax's gaze skimmed the store looking for other shoppers as he stepped forward to join Claire, setting his mouth into a grim line. Thankfully, Forever Christmas appeared to be empty of shoppers at the moment. Claire wouldn't want observers for this exchange.

"I'm not leaving until you hear me out, Claire. This is something you can't refuse or ignore. You've been invited to read at a White House holiday party! It's December nineteenth, and they need our answer by this afternoon."

"No."

"Claire, the party is for sick children. The invitation is from the First Lady herself! You can't say no to this!"

"Yes I can. I am."

"I already told them yes!"

Claire twisted her head to look at Jax. Her eyes had gone wild and round like a reindeer caught in the headlights. "Make him leave, Jax. Please?"

Jax stepped forward, planted his feet wide apart, and folded his arms. "The lady has asked you to go."

"And I will. As soon as she tells me she'll make the appearance." He reached into his jacket pocket and pulled out an airline ticket folder. "It's the White House, Claire. All the arrangements have been made. You fly out of Denver on the eighteenth and return on the twentieth."

"Okay," Claire snapped. "Okay. Just go. You have to go now."

The lawyer nodded once, then turned to go. He was halfway to the door when, her voice filled with despair, Claire asked, "Why?"

"Because Starlina is every little girl's fantasy and you are her creator."

As Landon exited the shop, a group of seven women entered. Jax recognized the members of the Eternity Springs Garden Club and knew them as the biggest gossips in town. Thank goodness they arrived after Landon's big announcement or the news would be all over town in minutes.

Jax stood at an angle that allowed him to see into the storeroom. As the garden club entered through the front door, he saw Liz step inside through the back. She set down a grocery sack and swapped her jacket for a Forever Christmas apron.

"Hello, Claire, dear." Janice Peterson, the grande dame of the gossips, swept forward. "I want to be one of the first to tell you how lovely all the decorations look. You are a treasure for our town. Just a treasure. I predict that merchants this year will double their usual sales. Walking around town has surely put me into the Christmas spirit like never before. I'm just . . ."—she clicked her fingers—"spending, spending, spending.

"Which brings me to the reason for my visit. My dear sweet granddaughter just had her visit with Santa Claus in Davenport Park. She asked Santa for that Christmas angel doll, Starlina, from *The Christmas Angel Waiting Room*. I heard on the news that it's going to be one of the year's hottest toys, so I thought we'd best get one while we still can. Will I find it in your Angel Room, dear, or somewhere else in the shop?"

Claire whipped her head around. Her eyes went round and wide and wild. In a high, shrill voice more befitting the Wicked Witch of the West than Miss Christmas, she said, "I don't carry that doll. I will never carry that doll. It's ugly. It's a bastardized commercialization. It's everything that's wrong with Christmas. You just said it, Mrs. Petersen!

You're spending, spending, spending! That's not what Christmas is supposed to be about! Who cares about gifts? It's supposed to be about love, family, and charity. But one look at that bug-eyed Starlina and everyone forgets that part. She is the worst of all. You know why? Because she's a fake. A lie! The message of that story is bullshit. I hate that doll! I hate that story! And I! Hate! Christmas!"

The women in the shop gasped as one.

"Well, I never!" Janice huffed. "Who do you think you are, talking to me like that?"

Claire burst into tears and ran into the storeroom. A moment later, the back door banged open and slammed shut.

Jax headed after her, pausing only long enough to instruct Liz. "Call the other worker in. Do the best you can. If it gets to be too much for you, close up shop."

"Okay. I will. What just happened, Mr. Lancaster?"

"I'm afraid Miss Christmas just got outted."

Claire fled Eternity Springs. She might not have stopped at Baby Bear had she not left Tinsel snuggled in her bed this morning. Claire might be willing to walk away from the responsibilities of her shop, but she couldn't abandon her dog.

She sniffed back tears all the way to the valley, but when Tinsel met her at the door of the little cabin, tail wagging and jumping happily, Claire broke. She sank onto the floor, cradled her dog against her, and sobbed. She cried for herself, for her sister, for her parents. She cried for all of the losses in her life. She cried for the self-destruction she'd just visited upon herself with her outburst in Forever Christmas.

Tinsel mewled and licked the salty tears from her cheeks. But then, like everyone else, she abandoned Claire, trotting away toward the kitchen where a moment later, lapping sounds arose from the water bowl.

Lonely. I'm so blasted lonely.

Lonely and alone.

Lost in misery, she wasn't aware of being lifted from the floor or carried to her bed. She didn't make a conscious decision to lay her head against the broad chest and sob, but that's what she did. Claire clung to the silent offer of compassion, the comforting stroke of a gentle hand, and cried until her tears ran dry.

Only then did Jax speak. "Want to tell me about it, sweetheart?"

No. It was a humiliating story. She didn't want him to know. She didn't want anyone to know. So why she opened her mouth and started babbling, she absolutely couldn't say.

"I volunteered at a local hospital. I held storytime. I read to the kids who were like me, the siblings who sat in hospital waiting rooms while their parents dealt with their sick child. I wrote the story for them, and when a few of them asked for a copy of it, I self-published it so I had copies to give away."

She closed her eyes and recalled the moment she'd first noticed the handsome man who had taken a seat near her story circle. "He was there one day. Landon. He listened and afterward told me how much he loved the story."

She'd been so flattered. So . . . easy. "He invited me to dinner and after that—it was a whirlwind romance. I slept with him. I fell in love with him. I believed him when he told me he loved me. We got engaged, but never quite managed to set a wedding date."

Jax murmured a soothing sound and pressed a kiss against her hair.

"He was so slick. I was so trusting, stupid, and naïve. I have terrible instincts. I signed the partnership agreement without getting independent advice."

She'd signed it without even reading it, that's how stupid she'd been.

"You're business partners with him?"

She nodded. "He's an entertainment lawyer. He got the movie deal, and I was so excited. I thought all my dreams had come true. I didn't like that they changed her name. She's Gardenia, not Starlina. He convinced me to listen to the marketing gurus. I resent that so much. He convinced me about everything. The only good piece of advice he gave me was to use a pseudonym. I used my sister's first name."

"M. C. Kelley," Jax murmured.

"We both went by our middle names. I'm Mary Claire. Stupid Mary Claire because I never suspected Landon. That's what is so hard to take. He told me he traveled a lot, and I took him at his word. I didn't suspect a thing—until I met his wife."

"Ouch," Jax said. "The men in your life have certainly let you down, haven't they?"

"I have terrible instincts. I'm stupid."

"What you are is stubborn. You have to let me apologize, Claire. I was an ass. I'm sorry. Money was a hot button in my marriage, and I let that experience color my relationship with you. Please forgive me."

She pulled out of his arms, a wave of despair washing over her. She couldn't do this. "It doesn't matter."

He reached for her hand and held it. "Yes it does. You deserved better than that from me. Hear me out. I was gun-shy. And I let my past and my pride get the best of what is usually my good sense. I shouldn't have reacted the way I did. I should have listened."

"Jax . . ."

"Hush, now. Listen. You were right. You don't owe me an explanation about your finances. Hell, you don't owe me one even now. It was stupid to make you think I was comparing you to Lara, because you're not remotely like her. And you know what? I'm not the guy I was back

then, either. I've changed, too. For the better. I don't care if
I'm a handyman for the rest of my life. Nicholas is happy
here. I'm happy here. We can stay here, but I can be happy
anywhere—as long as you are part of the picture. I want
you, Claire. I don't care if you're a billionaire. I want to be
with you. You make me happy. You make me believe."

"No. Truly. It doesn't matter." Agitation propelled her
from the bed. She stalked nervously around the room. "It
was a fling. We said it from the first. That's all it was. All
it can be."

Jax rose and faced her. "I want more than a fling, Claire.
I want you. I want a future with you. I am in love with
you."

Claire held up her hands, palms out. "Don't say that.
Don't you say that to me! Not today. Not ever!"

"Honey . . ." He took a step toward her. "It's going to
be okay."

"No! It's not going to be okay!" Hysteria added a shrill
note to her voice. "I just humiliated myself in front of all
of Whoville. News of my meltdown has probably made it
to Gunnison by now! There is no coming back from this.
I can't show my face around here anymore. So I won't. I'll
leave town. I'll close up Forever Christmas and just go."

"Claire, you can't do that."

"Yes, I can! This is America. I'm free and I'm the boss."

"Honey, it's time you stopped running away. Run to me.
To us. We need you."

"No. I can't stay in this town. I can't be Miss Christmas. I tried. I tried to take it back, but I can't do it. I failed.
I have to leave."

Jax slowly shook his head. "That first instinct of yours
is a killer to overcome. Okay, Claire, if you're determined
to go, then we will go with you."

"What?"

"Nicholas and I will go with you. We aren't anchored

to Eternity Springs. Where do you want to go? We will go with you."

"What? Why you say that? You can't say that."

He braced his hands on his hips. "Yes I can. I love you."

I love you. Oh, God. She was too raw. It was too risky. "You promised Nicholas you'd stay until school is out. You can't go back on your word. Nicholas is happy here. You can't uproot him."

"Okay, that's a problem. However, I'll bet on my son. I'll bet if given the choice, he'll choose you."

"No. You can't bring him into my crazy world. He found Christmas. You can't take it away from him."

"You're being irrational, Claire. No one has taken Christmas from you! You can get it back. Don't let that bastard ruin this for you. So you had a public meltdown. I'm sure it's not the first one that's happened here in Eternity Springs. And you don't have to go read your book at the White House. You're right. This is still America. You have the freedom of choice. I get it that it's a big deal and it's sick children, but if that lying loser is going to be there, too, then the hell with that. You don't have to go. None of that matters, anyway."

Her heart was breaking. Crumbling into pieces. It was too much. She couldn't think. "Please go, Jax. I need to be alone." *I'm always alone.* "Please, just leave me be."

"Irrational and overwrought," he murmured. "All right, honey. I'll give you time alone this afternoon—as long as you give me your word that you won't pick up and run on me. Promise me you won't disappear."

"I have to leave Eternity Springs, Jax."

"Not today. You don't have to go today. Promise me."

"Jax, I—"

"Your word, Miss Christmas."

She closed her eyes. "Okay. Okay. I won't leave today."

He walked toward Baby Bear's front door, pausing at

her side long enough to give her a kiss on the cheek. "I'll stop by the shop and check on things, make sure your girls are handling it okay."

Guilt fluttered in Claire's stomach. Poor Liz. What a horrible way to begin a new job. "Thank you. Please tell her I'm going to give her two weeks'—no, a month's—pay as a bonus."

"Will do." At the door, Jax paused and glanced over his shoulder. "You can trust me, Claire. I am a man of my word."

When the door shut behind him, she buried her face in her hands. She wanted to believe him. She wanted to believe *in* him. Would she never learn?

Claire spent the rest of the day huddled in Baby Bear, curled up with a historical romance novel. Nothing like a good old Viking love-story fantasy to make her forget all about the realities of her own existence. Her phone rang off and on all afternoon, but she didn't bother to check the numbers. When a knock sounded at her door just before dark, she tried to pretend that she didn't hear it.

Tinsel put the kibosh on that by perking her ears and thumping her tail. *"Woof. Woof. Woof."*

That particular three-bark hello invariably announced that Nicholas had come to call. No matter how badly Claire wanted to ignore the knock, she couldn't refuse to respond to Nicholas. She opened the door.

The boy beamed up at her. "Hi, Miss Claire."

"Hello, Nicholas."

"Can I come in?" Without waiting for her to respond, he strode inside. "Dad told me your secret! He said you wrote *The Christmas Angel Waiting Room*, and that you have the original version, that it's different from the one Mimi read to me. Daddy said it's about Gardenia from your Angel Room instead of Starlina, and that he saw the book when he saved it from the fire. I want to see it, Miss Claire. That's the coolest thing ever! Will you show it to me? Will you read it to me?"

"Oh, Nicholas." The maelstrom of emotion that she'd quieted with Viking tales came roaring back. "Nicholas."

"Were you maybe saving it for sometime special? Today is a pretty special day. It's Deck the Halls Friday, and I helped decorate the town just like any other kid."

"Nicholas." *You're breaking my heart.*

"Please, Miss Claire? Read to me about Gardenia. Read to me about how she learned to have faith. To believe."

Believe.

Claire closed her eyes and surrendered to the power of a child.

Jax stood in front of his bedroom window staring down at Baby Bear's front door. It had just about killed him to send his son alone into battle, but strategically, he believed it the best approach. He didn't think Claire had it in her to refuse Nicholas's request. Based on the fact that seventeen minutes had passed since the boy disappeared into her cabin, Jax had guessed right.

Thirty-seven minutes after he'd knocked on Claire's front door, Nicholas stepped outside and headed toward Mama Bear. The boy's furrowed brow and worried frown gave his father pause. That didn't look good.

Jax hurried downstairs and met his son at the door. "Well?"

"She showed me the book. I couldn't get her to read it to me, though. She tried, but she would read a couple of sentences and then she'd get choked up, and finally, I took it and read it for her. I don't think it worked, though, Dad. She told me she has to leave town."

Jax swallowed a curse.

"She said that tomorrow she was going to close down Forever Christmas and leave Eternity Springs." Lip quivering, he added, "She told me good-bye, Dad."

"Damn," Jax said, unable to hold that one back. "Was that before or after you read her book?" The book whose theme about believing was so wonderful and strong that it had struck a chord in the hearts of millions.

"After."

"Stubborn, stubborn woman." He rubbed the back of his neck.

"She's just scared like me, Daddy."

From the mouths of babes, Jax thought. "Okay, well. Did you bring up the Christmas pageant? Remind her of her promise?"

"Yes. She promised she'd come back for it."

"Good. If she said she would, then she will."

"So you'll give her the present?"

"Yeah."

"Okay." Nicholas nodded decisively. "That's good. I think the present will work. I'm going to believe it."

Jax slung his arm around his son's shoulder. "Me, too, son. Me, too. We just have to believe."

The Lancaster males worked late into the night on the next phase of their battle plan. A labor of love, it turned out better than Jax had imagined. As he wrapped it in plain brown paper and tied it with a bow made of twine, he sent up a little prayer that their message would get through the hard head of the woman he loved.

She'd promised not to leave today, but he didn't trust her not to run at first light, so before he went to bed that night, he carried the package over to Baby Bear and leaned it against the door.

In the morning when he looked, the package was gone. So was she.

Chapter Twenty-two

My faith is bigger than my fear.
—JAX

Claire almost didn't pick the package up because she expected it would be something that would tug her heartstrings. However, she didn't have the strength to resist it. People didn't give her presents very often. She didn't have the heart to leave it behind. He'd used duct tape and a cut-up paper grocery sack to wrap it. She found that so endearing.

Yet, she feared if she opened it, whatever was inside might sap the strength she'd gathered to leave. She couldn't afford that. Staying required even more, and her bank of strength was overdrawn.

She compromised by taking the package with her, but placing it in the backseat of her car.

She drove into town and before even the early birds stirred, she slipped into her shop, wrote checks to her two employees, paying them full-time wages for the weeks that she'd committed to employing them, and finally drew a FOR SALE sign by hand. She taped the sign to her front window, locked the door, and returned to her car where she tried to tell herself that the wetness in her eyes and on her cheeks was the result of the cold winter air, that's all.

She didn't have a destination in mind when she left Eternity Springs. She had a couple weeks to kill before the Christmas pageant. Then another week until the White

House event. She guessed she would go to it. It seemed easier to attend than to beg off. And she would sleep better knowing she hadn't let the White House down.

Where would she go after that?

What would she do with herself after that?

"What do you think, Tinsel? Shall we shoot for something totally different? Somewhere warm? South Beach? The South Pacific?"

Tinsel rested her snout on Claire's leg and went to sleep. Claire drove mindlessly, lost in thought and trying not to think. She didn't consciously make the decision to drive to Silver Eden, but when she found herself at the entrance to the resort shortly after snow began to fall, she was glad to be there.

Luckily they had a room for her and were willing to accommodate Tinsel. After hours in the car, Claire and Tinsel both needed exercise, so they played in the snow for a while before going up to their room. She took a long, hot shower, ordered room service for dinner, then sat cross-legged in the middle of the plush bed, staring at Jax's box.

Why her heart thundered, she couldn't say. Why fresh tears threatened was more obvious. His words echoed through her mind. *I want you. I want a future with you. I am in love with you.*

I love you.

It scared her so badly.

She pulled the box toward her and tugged on the bow of twine. She tore off the paper, licked her suddenly dry lips, and slowly removed the lid from the box.

Two handwritten notes lay atop the tissue paper. She picked up Nicholas's carefully printed page and read:

Dear Miss Claire,
    I love you.

It's okay to be scared. Remember what Gardenia says. The trick to learning to fly is to wear a helmet.

Thank you for being my friend. Please come home. Daddy and I miss you. We want you to be our family.

Love,
Nicholas

Claire closed her eyes and clutched the letter to her heart. That sweet, courageous, darling boy. If only she could be as brave as he.

The thought fluttered through her mind like an angel's whisper. *Maybe you can.*

Claire sucked in a shuddering breath and picked up Jax's note.

Dear Claire,

I love you.

I love you for a million different reasons, but for the moment, allow me to focus on one of those reasons in particular.

The night we met, you changed my life. You taught me to Believe.

Let me return the favor.

When I was growing up, one of my favorite family traditions of the Christmas season was opening the door on the Advent calendar. Using that as a framework, I invite you to . . .

Believe.

Find your faith, Claire. In me, in us, in what we can become. Change directions. Run to us. Run to me.

I love you,
Jax

Claire's hands trembled as she pulled back the tissue paper and revealed the contents of the box. Surprise washed through her. It was a journal like the one she'd given him.

She picked it up, traced the word "Believe" with her fingertip, and noted the worn corners. She flipped through the pages and caught her breath. She recognized the handwriting. Pages and pages of it. Six months' worth of it.

This *was* the journal she'd given Jax. He'd been using it.

And now he had given it to her? Why?

For the answer to her question, she looked at the other item in the package. It was a box made of wood, a rectangle about twelve inches wide and twenty-four inches long. A script *B* had been burned into the wood, its lines broken intermittently by little square doors. Upon each door was a number.

Claire opened the door marked "1" and saw a date beneath it. October 12.

She couldn't recall anything special about the date. What did he want her to . . . "Oh."

She picked up the journal, flipped to the entry marked October 12 and began to read Jax's bold handwriting.

"Today, Claire proved once again that she is a force of positive energy and light in my life."

The entry went on for a page and a half. Claire read it through the blur of tears.

Jax strode into Forever Christmas on Saturday, December 12, with his arms full of boxes. Meeting the gaze of the clerk behind the counter, he said, "I think those angels you've been waiting on came in."

"Excellent!" Celeste beamed a smile his way. "When Liz arrives for her shift, I'll ask her to call our customers on the wait list."

Jax carried the boxes to the storeroom and set about unpacking them and marking them into inventory. Luckily, Claire ran a straightforward system, and he'd been able to easily pick up on what needed doing in order to keep the business open. He'd made the decision to do that the morning Claire left town.

It was a case of putting his money where his mouth was, so to speak. He had to have faith in Claire. He had to believe that she would be back to stay. Keeping the shop open expressed that viewpoint loud and clear to the people of Eternity Springs, to Nicholas, and to himself.

When he'd put out a call for help, the response had been gratifying. In addition to Celeste, his temporary workers included members of the Eternity Springs Garden Club, led by none other than Janice Petersen. Miss Christmas was in for quite a surprise when she came home.

Jax was elbow deep in Styrofoam packing peanuts when Nicholas ran into the store calling his name. "The show starts in an hour and a half. Daddy, has anyone seen Miss Claire? Is she back?"

"No, son. We haven't had a Miss Christmas sighting yet."

"Oh." Nicholas's two front teeth bit his lower lip. "You're not worried, though. Right? She promised she'd come."

"She promised and I'm not worried." Much, anyway.

"What if she goes to Baby Bear before coming to town? What if our surprise gets ruined?"

"She doesn't have the new key yet. And I pulled the window curtains closed. The only way into Baby Bear is down the chimney, and she's Miss Christmas, not Santa Claus."

Nicholas laughed. "She's way too skinny to be Santa. I can't wait to see her, Dad. I hope she likes everything we've done. I've said so many prayers that our plan works and she says yes to marrying us."

"That's good, Nicholas. I believe in the power of prayer. And, I believe in Claire. We've got to keep thinking positive." Jax held out his fist. "We've got this. "

Nicholas fist-bumped his dad and repeated, "We've got this."

Jax continued to tell himself that as the afternoon waned and the clock ticked toward the start of the Christmas pageant. As usual, it was the hottest ticket in town, and the school auditorium was packed to the rafters.

Rather than sit in the front row with Brian and Linda, who'd come to town for Nicholas's big performance, Jax stood at the base of the stage in the spot that allowed the best view of the entrances.

A chime sounded from the school's loudspeaker, and then the principal asked visitors to take their seats. "Our pageant begins in five minutes."

Jax's stomach made an uneasy roll. Softly, he whispered, "Where are you, Miss Christmas?"

Claire skulked in the science lab among the taxidermy collection of small animals native to the Colorado Rockies, muttering to the glassy-eyed beaver. "I don't think I'll be this nervous when I meet the president."

The beaver offered neither comfort nor advice.

She had arrived in Eternity Springs half an hour earlier, having timed her departure from Silver Eden carefully. Her plan was to slip into the back of the auditorium just as the curtain rose. With any luck, she could watch the pageant and escape at its finish without having to speak to a soul.

"There you are, Claire," came a cheery voice from the door at the back of the room. "I've been watching for you, but I almost didn't recognize you in that puff coat, knit cap, and sunglasses. It's a good thing I recognized your walk. Come along, now. Nicholas said you promised to sit in the front row, so I've saved you a seat beside me."

Claire dropped her chin onto her chest. She should have anticipated Celeste.

"Chop-chop, dear." Celeste snapped her fingers.

Claire surrendered, cast her friend the beaver a rueful look, and joined Celeste. At least there wouldn't be time for more than a few seconds of chitchat before the lights went down.

They entered at the auditorium's side door and Celeste led Claire toward one of three empty seats in the first row, center. As the lights began to dim, Celeste rose from her seat and walked up onto the stage as someone took the seat beside Claire. Jax leaned over and gave her a quick kiss on the mouth. "Merry Christmas, Claire."

A floodlight illuminated Celeste, who sparkled in a floor-length gown of cream-colored silk trimmed in dazzling gold. When the applause died, she smiled widely and said, "Good evening, everyone. Merry Christmas."

"Merry Christmas," the audience responded.

"I know we are all excited to see tonight's show, but before we get started, I have a special presentation to make. Nicholas Lancaster, would you join me, please?"

The audience applauded. Jax sat up a little straighter as Nicholas walked out onto the stage. Claire's heart melted at the sight of the boy dressed in jeans, a white shirt, a black bow tie, and wearing the feathered angel wings Claire had helped him make. "What's this?" she asked. "And where are his glasses?"

"He got contacts last week. I don't know what Celeste is up to."

Celeste's voice rang out over the auditorium like church bells. "Dear friends. As you know, we live in a special place that has a unique energy. Eternity Springs is where broken hearts come to heal. Because I believe that such accomplishments should be recognized, a few years ago I commissioned the design of the official Angel's Rest blazon that I award to those who have found love's healing grace. Tonight, I want to award our young angel here a pair

of wings that are a little easier to wear than the feathers
he has on right now."

Laughter rose from the audience. Celeste motioned
Nicholas to come closer, and she slipped a silver necklace
and angel wing pendant over his head. "Nicholas, you are
an inspiration to us all."

"Thank you, Mrs. Blessing."

The crowd erupted in cheers. Jax and Claire and everyone else rose to give Nicholas a standing ovation. The boy
shot Jax a bashful grin, but when he noticed Claire standing beside his father, a smile as bright as the spotlight burst
across his face.

When the cheering finally died down, Celeste motioned
the boy backstage. "I don't know about you all, but I'm
ready to see the show."

Gracefully, she seemed to float off the stage and return
to her seat. Jax met her, kissed her cheek, and said, "Thank
you, Celeste. I know Nicholas will treasure his wings forever."

The houselights dimmed once again and the crowd quieted. A trumpet fanfare sounded out and the curtain
slowly rose. Once the set was revealed, the smile that had
graced Claire's face since Celeste's presentation froze. Her
mouth went dry.

Nicholas stood to one side of the stage at a microphone.
He thumped it with his finger, then said, "Welcome to the
sixteenth annual Eternity Springs Christmas pageant. I am
the master of ceremonies, Nicholas Lancaster. This year,
in honor of our very own beloved Miss Christmas, we
present to you our production of *The Christmas Angel
Waiting Room*. Ladies and gentlemen, we hope you are
ready to Believe. Please welcome our narrator tonight, the
one and only . . . Gardenia!"

Claire clapped her hands over her mouth. "Not Starlina," she murmured.

"Of course not," Jax responded. "This is Christmas in Eternity Springs. We don't do the commercial version here."

On the stage, twelve-year-old Holly Montgomery spoke the opening words now made famous in storybook, song, movie, video games, and more. " 'When nighttime falls in the tiny Christmas shop, the angels come out to play.' "

And so began the most magical hour of Claire Branham's life.

Jax had attended dress rehearsal earlier in the day, so rather than watch the play, he seldom took his gaze off Claire. She cried through the whole thing, but he *thought* they were the good kind of tears. He hoped so, anyway.

When the pageant ended and the children on stage took their bows, Jax and Claire rose with the rest of the crowd to give them a standing ovation. Then when the pageant director released the kiddos, they dispersed to find their parents. Nicholas shrugged out of his wings and ran toward Jax and Claire.

"Miss Claire! Miss Claire! You came. Dad and I knew you would. We believed, just like Gardenia and the other angels in your book do. Did you like our play?"

"I loved it," Claire said. "It was wonderful. You did a fabulous job."

"My wings kept drooping. But at least they didn't fall off." Nicholas focused his attention on his father. "Has Miss Claire been to Baby Bear?"

"I don't know." Jax gave Claire a sidelong look. "I haven't had the chance to ask her."

When Nicholas turned his questioning gaze her way, Claire shook her head. "No, I was late getting back into town, and I didn't want to miss any of the pageant, so I didn't get out to the valley."

"Okay. Good. Dad said you are Miss Christmas and not

Santa Claus, but I was worried. Let's go home, Miss Claire." He tugged her hand toward the door. "We have a surprise for you. Dad and I worked really hard on it."

"I . . . um . . ."

Further conversation was interrupted by a swarm of people surrounding them. Nic Callahan told Claire how much she loved her story. Sage Rafferty complimented her on keeping the facts about her fame quiet. Hope Romano thanked Claire for the positive message her book passed along to grade-schoolers, and Janice Petersen patted Claire's hand and said, "Don't you worry about that little meltdown you had at the shop, dear. Jax explained where you were coming from. Perfectly understandable. Why, if I were in your shoes, I'd have totally blown a gasket."

"I . . . um . . ."

Janice continued, "Now that you're back, I want to get my dibs in first. I had such fun working at Forever Christmas. You know, Christmas has been a challenge for me ever since my Harry died and with the children living so far away. Working in your shop has allowed me to find my joy in the holiday once again. If you find that you need a pair of helping hands, I hope you'll consider me. I work very cheap."

Claire's eyes had gone round with shock. Jax figured he'd best step in before she committed herself to anything involving the shop. "You've been a lifesaver, Janice," he said. "I'll be sure to put in a good word for you with the boss. But now, if you all will excuse us, Nicholas and I are anxious to get Miss Christmas alone."

Even as he spoke, Jax began easing Claire toward the side door. He managed to get her into his truck without resistance, and then Nicholas filled all the empty spaces with chatter and questions. "I knew you'd keep your promise. I wasn't really worried. Well, maybe a little worried. Did you like our pageant, Miss Claire? I'll bet you were surprised."

The boy twisted around in his seat, trying to see out the back window. "Are Mimi and Pops behind us? Think they can find their way to Papa Bear in the dark?"

"Yes, son."

"Good. They're staying at Papa Bear tonight. It's done but for the punch list." He let out a giggle and added, "That's not when you hit somebody, don't worry. It's a funny name. It means the last things you do before the project is completely finished."

When Nicholas finally paused to take a breath, Claire spoke to Jax directly for the first time since her return. "What just happened? Why is everyone being so nice?"

"Honey, why would you expect anything different? This is Christmas in Eternity Springs."

She fell silent then and stared straight ahead. Nicholas was off and running again, catching Claire up on events in Eternity Springs over the past three weeks. Jax let him ramble. He was busy trying to project a calm and collected attitude, when inside he was a bundle of nerves.

What if his Believe calendar hadn't done the trick? What if she'd missed the point of the kids' pageant production? What if the surprise they had waiting at Baby Bear missed its mark?

You'll keep trying, that's what. You'll keep believing in Claire, believing in yourself, believing in you as a couple. You'll keep trying until you convince her to believe, too.

"Okay, then," he murmured beneath his breath. She'd taught him to think positive. From here on out, he'd be the most positive-thinking man in Colorado.

They arrived at the turnoff to Three Bears Valley, and when they rounded a curve, light from the full moon reflected off the light of six inches of new-fallen snow and illuminated the three cabins, lights glowing golden and warm and welcoming within. "It's so beautiful," Claire said.

"It's home," he said simply.

Despite all his positive thinking, nervousness continued to rumble in Jax's gut as he drove the truck toward Baby Bear. Even Nicholas seemed to feel it, because his chatter had subsided. When Jax shifted the truck into park and twisted the ignition key to kill the engine, a pregnant silence settled over the occupants.

Jax cleared his throat. "Claire, if you'll give us a couple minutes' head start, Nicholas and I need to add a few final touches inside. Okay?"

"Okay."

Jax glanced over his shoulder. "Nicholas? You have the package?"

"Yep."

The boy opened the back door of the extended-cab pickup and jumped down into the snow. Immediately, he reached for Claire's door, opened it, and stepped up onto the running board. He held a box the size for a bracelet and wrapped in red foil in his hand. "This is for you, Miss Claire. I love you."

He threw his arms around her neck and hugged her hard. Then he scrambled down from the truck and darted around toward Baby Bear's back door.

Jax opened his door and followed his son, pausing only long enough to meet Claire's gaze. "Believe, Claire."

Claire's hands trembled as she tore the paper off the box. She didn't know what to expect from the Lancaster men. She didn't know what to think of anything that had happened tonight.

She drew a deep, bracing breath, then lifted the lid from the gift box. Against a layer of white cotton lay an old-fashioned, ornate gold key. String attached a tag the size of a business card to the loop at the top of the key. The tag read "The Christmas Key."

"Okay," she murmured. She glanced up toward Baby Bear. The light visible between the cracks in the window curtains appeared brighter. She had the sense that something spectacular waited inside for her.

If she only dared to believe.

The porch light flashed on and she took that as her signal. Heart pounding, she exited the truck and approached Baby Bear's front door. That's when she spied the new lock on the door.

A simple latch had been added at shoulder height to Claire. The lock that secured it was shaped like a heart. Her lips fluttered up in a little smile when she slipped the Christmas Key into the lock and turned it. *Snick.* The lock released.

She took a deep breath, then opened the door.

To . . . Valentine's Day.

Jax and Nicholas each held a large, heart-shaped box and stood on either side of a Christmas tree that stretched to the rafters. White lights and red lights trimmed the tree along with ornaments shaped like hearts and garlands made of hearts. Hearts adorned the ribbon that encircled the tree. Hearts, hearts, and more hearts. Hearts were everywhere.

Claire blinked back sudden tears that threatened. She tore her gaze away from the tree and spied other additions they'd made to the room. Three red and white stockings at the chimney. More hearts. Heart-shaped throw pillows on the sofa. A heart-shaped rug in front of the hearth.

Even a plate of heart-shaped sugar cookies on the coffee table.

She cleared her throat and asked, "Am I having a Rip
Van Winkle moment? Did I sleep through December and
January and it's now February 14?"

"I know the Rip Van Winkle story," Nicholas said.
"That's not it, Miss Claire. You know what this is. You are
the one who told me. Remember when I was afraid, and
you brought the Twelve Dogs of Christmas to me? You told
me Valentine's is your favorite. Then you told me what the
key to Christmas is."

"Love," she murmured.

Nicholas nodded. "Yep. You don't have to be scared,
Miss Claire. You have the key."

He crossed the room to her and solemnly offered the
candy box. "This is for you from me, Miss Claire. I hope
you like it. We took the candy out, but don't worry.
We saved it. We got the idea from the Angel's Rest fortune
cookies."

Claire opened the box. Inside were dozens of scraps of
paper, all marked with Nicholas's carefully printed handwriting. She picked up one and read aloud. "I love that you
make pancakes in different shapes."

A second paper read: "I love that you love dogs as much
as I do."

A third: "I love how you make my daddy smile again."

"Oh, Nicholas. I don't know what to say. This is wonderful. Just wonderful. You put a lot of work into this."

"There's a hundred of them. I was kinda running out
of things to say at the end, so some of them aren't real
good."

Claire dropped down onto her knees and wrapped the
boy in her embrace. "I will treasure every single one of
them. Thank you so much. This is one of the most special
gifts I've ever received."

"I love you, Miss Claire. Please say yes to Daddy."

Claire lifted her gaze to Jax. He smiled tenderly, and said, "Nicholas, I heard your grandparents drive up a few minutes ago. I imagine by now they have the video they took of the pageant loaded up and ready to watch on the TV."

"Cool. Okay. I gotta go, Miss Claire. I'll see you in the morning. Right?"

"Right." She could give him no other answer.

Seconds later, the door slammed behind him and Claire and Jax were alone. Still on her knees, she went to rise and accepted the hand he offered to help her.

He didn't let go. "So did you read my journal?"

"I read the days you marked with your calendar."

"One each day?"

"Yes. The Advent calendar was a tradition in my family, too. I had forgotten how much I enjoyed it."

"What else did you learn from my gift?"

"I learned . . ." Her voice trailed off when he raised her hand to his mouth and kissed it.

"I missed you, Claire. Have you forgiven me yet?"

She closed her eyes. "For what?"

"For being an ass. For being stupid. For being prideful."

"Have you forgiven me for being rich?"

"Again, let me be clear. That was totally stupid of me." He cupped her cheek in the palm of his hand. "Thank God you are such a forgiving, understanding woman."

Her lips quirked. "I don't know that I understand anything, Jax. I wasn't truthful with my friends and the people of Eternity Springs. I expected to come back to scorn and ridicule. Instead, Janice Petersen has been playing sales-clerk and wants a job?"

"You should hire her. The woman is a selling fool."

"Why did you do that, Jax? Why did you keep the store open?"

"Because one warm summer night, a redheaded water sprite challenged me to believe, and it changed my life. You see, I believe in the magic of Eternity Springs, in the goodness of its people, and the capacity of their hearts. I believe in the power of positive thinking."

He set down the candy box he held and grabbed her free hand. His stare never left her face as he brought both her hands up to his mouth and kissed them. Sincerity and something else, something warm and wonderful, gleamed in his eyes as he said, "Most of all, Miss Christmas, I believe in you. I believe in us. I believe in the family that we can create with Nicholas and, God willing, a brother or sister or two for him. I believe that you love me as much as I love you."

"I do love you. I'm just afraid."

"I know, baby. We are all afraid. You need to forget all the reasons why it won't work, and believe in the one reason why it will. Love. I love you. You can trust me. You can believe in me. Believe in me, Claire."

Yearning filled her. She wanted to say yes. She wanted to believe. It was so close. He was here. He loved her.

Yet her lips couldn't form the word her heart was screaming.

Jax sighed. "Okay, then. Guess I'll have to bring on the big guns."

He released her hands and picked up the heart-shaped candy box. His look chastising, he handed it to her.

"More fortunes?" she asked.

"Open it."

She lifted the lid. Nestled inside among Valentine's-red tissue paper was Gardenia. Claire lifted her gently from the box. Tears stung her eyes. "You fixed her wing."

"Believing fixed her wing, Miss Christmas. Here's the problem. You neglected to turn the page. There's an epilogue."

"There is?"

"Absolutely. In the epilogue, Gardenia meets a new, woefully tarnished angel with a broken heart and his little boy who had not one but two broken wings. Gardenia befriends them. She challenges them to believe. As so often happens in nature, the boy learns quicker than his dad and, lo and behold, the boy's broken wings are made whole again. He learns to fly."

"Lo and behold," Claire repeated, not lifting her gaze from the angel.

"But the tarnished old guy isn't so dull that he completely blows the lesson. It's close, but he pulls it out. Gardenia has taught him that the way to mend a broken heart is to give it again. Once that tarnished angel's heart is mended, he's ready to fly again. There's just one problem."

"What's that?"

Jax put his finger beneath her chin and tilted her head up toward him. He stared down into her eyes. "He doesn't want to fly alone. He has to convince Gardenia to stop running and fly beside him, instead. He has to convince Gardenia that her broken wing has mended, too."

Claire swallowed hard. She darted a glance toward Gardenia with the mended wing, then returned her gaze to Jax's. "How does he do it?"

"Love, of course. Love is the glue that can mend everything. You just have to believe, Claire. Will you believe? In me? In us? Will you fly with me, beside me, wherever life takes us? I give you my word, my solemn promise, that I will never let you fall."

Tears welled in her eyes. She lifted her hand and cupped his cheek. "I believe you. Oh, Jax. I love you. I believe you. I believe."

He sealed the promise with a long, heartfelt kiss that wordlessly conveyed his devotion, his commitment, his love. When the kiss finally ended, he continued to hold her, staring down at her with such tenderness that it brought new tears to Claire's eyes.

In an effort to lighten the mood, she quipped, "So, that's the epilogue, hmm? I guess that means that this is the end?"

"Oh, no, Miss Christmas. Not at all." With a roguish grin and wicked twinkle in his eyes, he added, "This is just the beginning."

Epilogue

Don't be afraid to turn the next page.
—JAX AND CLAIRE

WASHINGTON, D.C.

"That's a big Christmas tree, Daddy."

"Yep, Nicholas, it sure is."

"It's not as good as ours, though. They don't have any bubble lights or tinsel or dog ornaments. What good is a Christmas tree without the Twelve Dogs of Christmas hanging on it?"

"Shush, now, son. Here comes Claire."

Claire, along with the First Family of the United States, entered the room to an enthusiastic round of applause.

"Look, Daddy. There are the president's dogs. I've seen pictures of them. They're pretty cute. Maybe Santa Claus will bring me a puppy like those dogs."

"Maybe, but I think Santa leans more toward mutts."

"I love mutts, too."

The First Lady stepped up to a podium and welcomed the visitors to the People's House. She gave a quick summary of the scheduled events for the afternoon, spoke of her love of reading, then introduced M. C. Kelley.

Wild applause erupted. Claire smiled her thanks, returned the little wave of a girl in a wheelchair, and when the room finally went silent, she opened a copy of *The Christmas Angel Waiting Room*.

" 'When nighttime falls in the tiny Christmas shop, the angels come out to play. With pretty porcelain faces and brilliant wings unfurled, they shimmer and sail and sing "Glory . . . Glory . . . Gloria"!

" 'One wears a gown of glittering gold and turns cartwheels through the air. Another floats, serene in green, with her hands folded in prayer.' "

Jax watched the rapt faces of children and adults alike as Claire brought her characters to life. It was a gift, he thought. Her gift.

She'd certainly brought life back to the Lancasters.

Life. Love. Believing.

If they were ever blessed with a daughter, they'd decided to name her Faith.

As Claire turned to the last page of her book, she lifted her head and their gazes met and held. She recited the last line by memory.

" 'And Starlina said, "We all will live happily ever after." ' "

Don't miss these other heartwarming novels
in the Eternity Springs series by
New York Times bestselling author

EMILY MARCH

Reunion Pass
Heartsong Cottage

Available from St. Martin's Paperbacks

And look for the next Eternity Springs novel

A Stardance Summer

Coming Summer 2017